DISAPPEARING ACTS

Tony Harrison

Copyright © 2023 Tony Harrison

All rights reserved

The characters and events portrayed in this book are fictitious. Any similarity to real persons, living or dead, is coincidental and not intended by the author.

No part of this book may be reproduced, or stored in a retrieval system, or transmitted in any form or by any means, electronic, mechanical, photocopying, recording, or otherwise, without express written permission of the publisher.

ISBN 9798391452041

Cover design by: Art Painter
Library of Congress Control Number: 2018675309
Printed in the United States of America

FOR LORRAINE

When the student is ready the teacher will appear.
When the student is really ready the teacher will disappear

TAO TE CHING

CONTENTS

Title Page
Copyright
Dedication
Epigraph
Disappearing Acts
November 11th 2018 — 1
December 1997 — 6
Chapter One — 7
Chapter Two — 23
Chapter Three — 39
Chapter Four — 56
Chapter Five — 74
Chapter Six — 82
Chapter Seven — 105
Chapter Eight — 114
Chapter Nine — 127

Chapter Ten	151
Chapter Eleven	158
Chapter Twelve	172
Chapter Thirteen	185
Chapter Fourteen	205
Chapter Fifteen	213
Chapter Sixteen	226
Chapter Seventeen	234
Chapter Eighteen	244
Chapter Nineteen	269
Chapter Twenty	276
Chapter Twenty-One	285
Chapter Twenty-Two	296
Chapter Twenty-Three	311
Chapter Twenty-Four	322
Full Fathom Five	327
November 11th 2018	329
Acknowledgements	349
About The Author	351

DISAPPEARING ACTS

NOVEMBER 11TH 2018

The old man knelt down at the foot of the memorial and nestled the last wreath at its base. He was still agile enough, even at ninety, to raise himself unassisted from the floor, and although his legs were shaking from the cold and the damp and all the emotion of the occasion, he was still firm enough on his feet to make his way back to his son and his great grandchildren waiting for him in the rain with the rest of the congregation.

'Well done, dad,' his son said to him.

'Did you fight in the war, grampa?' the younger boy asked. The old man ruffled the lad's hair and quietly shushed him as the Last Post commenced its melancholy refrain. As the bugle sounded in the grey morning air, the old man looked around him and registered the silent approval captured in the glances of those in the crowd who knew him. He was honoured by the parish, as the last surviving offspring of a soldier who had fought in the Great War, to place the final wreath at the memorial that morning. Were there others in the congregation, like his great grandson, who actually believed it was he and not his father who fought in the trenches? If that were true, he would have to be one hundred and ten, some twenty years older than he already was. He smiled to himself but then had a more serious thought. This possible misunderstanding, and the fact that he was actually too young at the time to have even seen combat in World War Two, made him feel a bit of a fraud. But such doubts were overcome by his sense of pride at being able to represent those men who had died in the four years before the guns had finally gone silent, exactly one hundred years ago. His own father had survived that terrible conflict, but had never spoken of those who didn't return, or those who were wounded or damaged beyond repair. It seemed that now people were speaking about those men, long dead, much more than anyone ever did at the time. And yet, despite all the contemporary concern and the sympathy for the fallen, when the old man helped out at the church food bank each week, he noticed with sadness the two veterans of Iraq and Afghanistan who came there for assistance. Just like his father, these men, with their haunted expressions and forced banter, never spoke of what they had witnessed in Helmand or Basra, or what had brought them to seeking handouts from charity. Maybe next time he would speak to them. It might be a way of making up for never talking to his father about all this. It was never too late to make amends or to build bridges.

The old man suddenly realised the bugle notes had faded, the two minutes' silence had passed and his son was speaking to him. 'Dad, did you hear me, I said, we're going now. Got to get these two home to their mum and dad.' The old man looked down at the two boys who were obviously bored, shuffling their feet and pummelling each other beneath their rain hoods, a couple of miniature sparring partners.

'You go ahead, he said. 'I think I'll stay a while.' He wanted to enjoy the occasion for a little longer, wanted to soak up just a little more of the tender spirit he saw in people's eyes when he lay down the wreath.

'You sure?' his son said. 'How you getting back? Have you got your mobile?'

The old man took the Smartphone out of his pocket

and winked at Jonathan, the older of the two boys, who had spent the previous weekend setting it up for him with the croaking frog ringtone that he really wished he could now get rid of but didn't know how.

'Someone will give me a lift. I'm fine. If I'm stuck, I'll call a taxi,' he said, hugging his great grandchildren and then shaking his son's hand.

And to a great extent he was fine. He could walk without a frame or even a stick and his eyesight and hearing were better than some in the congregation twenty years younger. There had been a minor heart scare back when he was eighty-five but medication seemed to help with that and, the occasional breathlessness and dizziness apart, he did not give it too much thought

But faces were a bit of an issue sometimes. His memory was generally good, and people with whom he was in regular contact were not a problem. But there were times, more and more frequently, when he knew he should recognise the person standing before him but found himself desperately searching to put a name to a face. Now, as he sat in the church hall drinking his coffee, this infirmity seemed all the more pronounced, exacerbated by the number of people who wanted to shake his hand, pat him on the shoulder, or in the case of ex-military types, exchange in some brief army camaraderie which he couldn't really reciprocate. He realised staying behind was probably a mistake after all and he should have gone home with his family. The occasion was beginning to take its toll and, even though it was not that warm in the hall, he began to feel rather hot, rather unwell.

He reached for his phone and was scrolling down the numbers in his contacts for the local taxi firm he used, when he became aware of someone standing very close by. When he looked up, he could tell from the stranger's expression that this was yet another person who had the advantage over him of a familiarity he was unable to share.

TONY HARRISON

'I hope you don't mind. I saw you lay the wreath,' said the stranger, smiling and offering both hands in welcome. The old man rose wearily hoping this latest encounter would soon be over. He felt the floor reel away from him as he got to his feet and amidst the sudden light-headed dizziness, he reluctantly took the stranger's hands in his. But when he looked into the other's eyes, his memory no longer failed him. In a flash of sudden recall with a time long gone, he knew exactly who this person was. He opened his mouth to utter a name, but no sound came out. He had no breath to speak and instead he held on to the other's arms tightly to stop himself from falling. The last thing he saw was the expression on the face before him shifting in a second, from friendly concern to fear, as the old man fought for breath and his legs buckled under him. And then everything went black.

DISAPPEARING ACTS

DECEMBER 1997

CHAPTER ONE

'Go on, say it. You think your poor mum's losing her mind.'

Michael looked at his mother. What could he say? Yes – he *did* think she was going crazy? No – he *too* believed the house was haunted? She stood there with the hoover in her hand ready to vacuum the lounge carpet into oblivion. And all he wanted to do was escape.

'So, it's just in my room you hear them,' he said.

'I've told you, it's behind the walls. You must have heard it, the amount of time you spend up there.'

'No – but let me check, now that you've alerted me,' he said with thinly disguised sarcasm. Thus, he made good his escape, anticipating with well-practised masochism the gloominess of his room at this time of day, when the sun would be dipping and the last of its rays would be flicking across the ceiling.

Flopping onto the bed, he strained his ears for strange, ghost-like noises that might confirm his mother's sanity. But there was only silence from behind the jaded, pin-punctured 'Thunderbirds' wallpaper. His gaze wandered as usual to the single bookshelf above his bed. The tired old covers of *Treasure Island*, *Beau Geste*, *Coral Island*, as worn as the values of empire they once represented, all mocking him with their battered remnants of boyhood fantasy. And lurking amidst these volumes, his teenage journal, unopened for many years but a constant reminder of what could have been. He shrunk from contemplating what his younger self would have thought of him now, forty-three years old and waiting in this same room for sounds only his mother could hear, and, once again blinking such considerations away, he reached instead for the photograph he kept readily to hand, face down on the shelf.

Maddie. Looking sideways on at the camera, smiling, happy, her long black hair floating across her face in the breeze, her strange grey eyes hidden from view. It took him back each time to that summer picnic in the woods, a scene from another life, just a few months but a world away in Barton. What was she doing now, this minute? Who was she with? Probably the Head of PE, Rick Campbell? Or if not him then someone else who could give her what, apparently, he couldn't. Someone able to devote himself fully to her and her six-year-old son, Tommy. A role model, maybe a father, for the boy. Someone who didn't have a mother who needed his help every other weekend. A mother who was depressed, alone, vulnerable.

He sighed as the wailing vacuum cleaner climbed the stairs. What was there left for him now back in Barton? No more summers with Maddie, that was for sure, and possibly no job either. Although the school had only suspended him until after Christmas, could he really see himself teaching there again after what happened? There would certainly be little respect from the students or colleagues and how could he endure encountering Maddie every day, her impersonal formality in the staff room and on the corridors reminding him daily of what he had lost? He feared that return to Barton in January, to his empty house where she had once stayed at weekends, in a town that now no longer wanted him. He told himself he'd returned here, after his suspension, to his hometown of St Vincent's on Sea, to look after his mother. But in his most honest moments, such as right now, he also knew he'd come back to his mother's house to hide away. To flee from failure both in his career and personal life. Only Maddie's photo now remained as a memento of his lost love, which he just had time to replace between the covers of the boyhood journal, when the hoover stopped and his mother poked her head around the door.

'Did you hear it?' she said, switching off the machine.

'Hard to hear anything above that racket. Do you have to do this every day, mum?'

'I like to keep busy. Unlike some people.'

'You've been at it like you're possessed.'

His words were drowned by the vacuum cleaner as it howled and advanced into the room.

'The toilet isn't flushing properly. I need you to take a look at it,' she shouted above the din.

'Later,' he shouted back. 'I'm going out now'.

'Don't forget to take your shoes off when you come back in. Everything's clean.'

He ran downstairs and threw on his coat. If it wasn't for these nightly trips to Blockbusters, the sanity under scrutiny would be his.

Michael's mother was reading a newspaper when he returned home, but she tucked it quickly beneath the cushion of her armchair as soon as she noticed him come in. 'Who's in the film then?' she asked, trying to push the paper further out of view.

'You won't be interested.' In the video store, Michael had, as usual, bypassed the indie and arthouse sections, for times like these required a daily dose of violent escapism: Van Damme, Schwarzenegger, Willis. Today it was the indestructible Steven Seagal and *Executive Decision* – enough mayhem and machismo there to get him through another evening.

'If I'm going to watch it, I want to know who it is,' she insisted.

'You're going to watch it? Why?'

'Take my mind off things.'

'It's Steven Seagal. You won't have heard of him.'

Grace's hearing could be patchy. 'George Segal? Course I've heard of him. He's one of my favourite actors.'

There was little point in correcting her as he started up the film. She'd soon fall asleep, or so Michael hoped. Instead, however, she launched into a running commentary: 'George Segal's put on a lot of weight... Why has George Segal grown a ponytail?... I always thought George Segal could act...but this is dreadful,' and then, just as *Steven* Seagal crossed from the stealth aircraft to board the Jumbo Jet with its lethal cargo of nerve gas and terrorists, 'He'll never squeeze his huge backside through that hatch....' When the unbelievable happened, when the connection between the two aircraft came adrift catapulting Seagal into oblivion, it was difficult not to blame his mother as though she had laid a curse.

Eventually, Grace muttered, 'Not a patch on *The Quiller Memorandum*,' and left for the bathroom where there was 'much more interesting entertainment to be had.' Sometimes, as far as his mother was concerned, he wondered who was kidding who.

But right now, Michael was actually in a state of mild shock. He fast forwarded, expecting to see Seagal, the indestructible hero of *Hard to Kill* and *Under Siege*, hang on to the tail wing of the jet, climb back on board and kill all the terrorists before flying the plane to safety. But, unbelievably, it seemed that Seagal, normally immune to bullets, swords, dynamite and gravity, had been despatched halfway through the film. Hard to kill? Apparently not. He should demand a refund. He rewound, pressed 'Play' and

Seagal once more cartwheeled away off screen, Michael's eyes following the doomed hero in imagined flight across the living room.

That was when he noticed the newspaper, poking out from beneath the cushion of his mother's chair, and remembered how hastily she had buried it there on his return. Curious, he retrieved it, the previous evening's *St Vincent's Herald,* folded around the middle page. The headline struck an immediate chord with his own recent crisis in the classroom. And once he started reading, he could not stop.

Mystery Disappearance of Teacher

Police are investigating the disappearance of local schoolteacher Gilbert Soames, 49, who has not been seen for several days. Soames, an English teacher at Pennington Grammar School in St Vincent's on Sea, went missing after a performance last Friday of the Christmas school production of *The Tempest.* Soames joined the school in 1970 after graduating from Cambridge. In recent years he has been troubled by bouts of illness but has continued teaching at Pennington and has maintained a popular following with members of staff and students. Head of Geography, Steve Lawton....

'What're you doing reading that?' his mother said, swiping the paper from his grasp. He hadn't heard her come back into the room, so suddenly immersed had he been in the article. Gilbert Soames, his beloved teacher from Pennington twenty-six years ago. Not a day went by when Michael didn't think about that man.

'It *is* him, isn't it?' she said, as he stood up and reached out in vain to grab back the paper.

'You mean Mr Soames.'

'That man, yes him.'

'He's disappeared, mum. It's sad.'

'I've no sympathy. None in the slightest.' She shook her head and briskly ushering him out of the room, said, 'Right now I need you to look at the toilet. It's still not flushing.'

Not only was she wilfully changing the subject, but also raising another opportunity for him to feel so useless. He was no handyman and all he wanted to do was finish reading the article.

'What good can I do in the toilet? I'm not a plumber.'

'I know. Just try and do something. It's broken already so even you can't make it any worse.'

He sighed and made his weary way up the stairs, his mind on Mr Soames, wondering what had happened to him. Were there parallels between his former teacher and himself – the overlapping mid-life failure and self-sabotage? Had Soames' life, like his own stalled and then stuttered to a halt? Was Soames as desperate as he had been when he abandoned his class at Barton Secondary that day? Had Soames joined him in walking away from toxic teenagers, exhausting low-level disruption, blood-pressure-soaring confrontation…?

'Have you had a look at it?' His mother shouting from the bottom of the stairs interrupted his thoughts.

'Just getting the coat-hanger,' he said, recalling, with some sadness, a quick fix for the toilet that might just work.

'Yes OK, but you can tidy your wardrobe later. The bathroom's the priority.'

He opened his wardrobe and tried twisting the hanger. It was Maddie who'd shown him how to do it. She had laughed at his attempt to fix his own broken cistern that left a pair of shoelaces floating in the tank like a pair of dead tapeworms. 'You bend the coat hanger out of shape and use it as a wire to connect everything in the tank together.' He remembered her words as clearly as if they were poetry. Hanging on the racks before him were sad remnants of their affair, one of the three fashionable suits she picked in her attempt to rescue him from his 'schoolmaster shabbiness'. Staring now at the garment and the bright multi-coloured tie that she also bought to go with the mood of that vibrant spring, Maddie's coat-hanger solution only made him feel even more bereft. Too forlorn to re-enact the repair, he took the tie off the rack – he would never be wearing this again.

'Don't make a mess in there. I've been cleaning up all day,' Grace, still at the bottom of the stairs, called to him as he went into the bathroom and began removing the cistern lid. Sinking his hands into the cold water, he looped the tie several times around the handle rod and the ballcock. The end of the tie reached out from the lid like the limp hand of a corpse. But, to his surprise, when he pulled the handle a torrent of water filled the bowl and then stopped at the correct level. He repeated this process several times in celebration.

'What are you doing? Not flooding the place, I hope,' his mother said as he returned to the living room.

'Far from it. I'm flushed with success.'

'What? Don't tell me you've managed it.' She sounded almost disappointed that he hadn't lived up to his usual incompetence around the house.

'Yes, my own custom-made solution.'

'Something involving a bucket with a hole in it, no doubt.'

'The tie.'

'What're you talking about?'

'The tie. The tie that binds.'

'A total eyesore, I bet.'

'A tie-sore you mean.' Sometimes these exchanges reminded him of a desperate comic duo. 'But it works. It'll do until we get a plumber out.'

'I hope that's not one of your dad's old ties.'

'It's one Maddie bought for me.'

'Oh, one of those horrible garish things.'

'Yes, and it's in the toilet now – along with my relationship.' The ghost of a smile passed across her face. What was it that amused her? The fact that he was single, alone with no prospects, bored out of his skull most days doing odd jobs he was hopelessly ill equipped to carry out? Some desperate comedy there somewhere if he felt like laughing. Which he didn't.

'Anyway, I've run the full quota of maintenance checks.'

'I was just getting off to sleep when you flushing woke me up.' She stared straight ahead at the TV screen, where *Executive Decision* lumbered onwards towards its noisy violent finale.

'And that dreadful film's still on. I don't know how to switch it off.'

'I think I can manage that as well,' he said hitting the remote. 'See? No end to my talents.' An awkward dead air silence descended on the room.

'Can I have that article back now?' he said finally.

'What article?'

'You know what I mean. Mr Soames' disappearance. Why were you hiding it?'

'I wasn't...'

'Where is it then?'

She shrugged and shuffled in her chair. 'It's gone.'

'No it isn't. I can see it right there under your seat.'

He was about to make a lunge for it when she pulled her feet beneath the chair to block his move.

'That man. He always was a law unto himself. No use to anyone. Even back then.'

'Mum, it was a long time ago.'

'Exactly, so why are you still interested in him? The disgusting old fool. No sense of responsibility. I always knew he'd come to no good.'

This was troubling and depressing to witness – her bitterness and anger even after all these years.

'Come on, mum. Let me read it, will you.'

'If you must know, he's walked out of school. Typical of him.'

She knew nothing of Michael's own similar desertion of his teaching duties. His cover story that he was back here on sabbatical seemed to satisfy her for now. However, even though she was oblivious to his own suspension from Barton, her condemnation of Soames still felt like a personal rebuke.

'He must have his reasons,' he said.

'He always had his reasons. Reasons for completely ruining your studies. Reasons for destroying this family.'

'A lot of things were going on back then, mum. It wasn't just him.'

'Everything was fine until you went to that school.'

'Is this what's been upsetting you today? You knew about Mr Soames and it's why you've been so…'

'I'm not upset.'

'Crotchety. Cleaning everything.'

'I'm not crotchety. What about you? Storming off just before tea.'

'And then hiding the article from me. Look, I want to read it.' She shook her head and adjusted her position in the chair and the newspaper poked out beneath her cushion, once more inviting him to wrench it from beneath her.

'I don't want you to,' she said, folding her arms. Short of dragging it out from under her he would have to wait until she got up.

'Why?'

'It might upset *you*?'

'I just feel sorry for the guy. I hope he's OK.'

She guffawed and waved her arms at him.

'Don't waste your sympathy on him. All those things he did to you, to us. To dad.'

This was the first time for years she'd mentioned anything about those days. But for him, since he'd come back to live with her after his debacle at Barton, those teenage years had seemed so much closer. And now this article had appeared out of the blue, bringing the spectre of Gilbert Soames directly back into their home.

'I know. It's a long time ago. But he meant a lot to me, Mr Soames. Back then.'

'I don't want to hear any more about him. I hope he's dead in a ditch somewhere.

'That's awful. What if he *is* dead? Actually dead?'

'If you had any sense, you wouldn't care tuppence about him.'

But the truth was, he *did* care. He was shaken by just how much this news about Soames affected him. His own recent failure as a teacher was one reason, but there was also what Soames had meant to him, still meant to him, after all these years. The life that man once offered him, the life he might have had.

He pointed the remote at the TV. 'If you don't hand me the paper now, I promise I'll put that film back on. And unless you tear it up right now before my very eyes, I'm only going to read it later.' These last words sounded melodramatic and ridiculous, charged with a sudden unfamiliar flood of emotion. The first signs of real life he'd felt since leaving Barton.

She reached beneath the cushion and flung the paper at him petulantly.

'Go on then. Read it. Mess yourself up again like you did back then.'

This reference to his 'mess', a weakness, an inherent character flaw ready to re-emerge like a disease, was something she held over him from time to time. Nevertheless, he unfolded the paper eagerly while his mother stormed out of the room muttering, 'I don't care anymore.' And then, as a parting shot as she entered the kitchen, 'Just as long as he never comes back here again.'

Although he wanted to read the article right away, he was even more concerned by what she had just said. Had he heard her correctly? She'd tossed the comment into the room like a hand grenade. Soames had once come here? To this house? He followed her into the kitchen where he found her flustered and out of breath, heaving pots and pans around, in readiness for a mammoth baking session. It was very warm in there, the oven already going full blast, and his spectacles steamed up at the edges. His mother was a flurry of activity in the heat and he worried about her blood pressure, as he worried about most things about her, but he still needed to know.

'Did I hear you right? Did you just say Soames came *here*?'

She pulled a large bag of flour out of the cupboard. 'Don't get under my feet. I've got to make the mince pies for Christmas.'

'You never make them until Christmas Eve.' It was still a week away and she was strict about this, made it a ritual. Heralded the start of Christmas when he was a child.

'Well, there's a first time for everything.'

'You just told me, listen to me,' he said as she smeared the tins with grease and seemed intent on blocking any dialogue with a clatter of crashing pans and pots. He had to shout which made him sound angrier than he wanted to. 'You just said, Soames came around here. When? Last week? Last year? When?'

'Did I just say that?' she shook her head, now cracking eggs into a bowl like they were her worst enemy. 'Silly old me. You're right, I must be going daft in my old age.'

'Stop pretending, mum. I want to know.'

She half turned her back on him, beating the eggs furiously. 'Look, Michael, go away and read your article will you. I'm busy.'

'No,' he said. 'No, no, I want to talk. This, this visit that I've just found out about.'

She shook her head. 'Forget I said anything. It was years ago.'

'Why didn't you tell me he'd been here? Where was I?'

'I don't remember.'

'Don't give me that. There's nothing wrong with your memory.'

'I don't know where you were. Look, for what it's worth, I sent him away with a flea in his ear. He'd done enough damage for one lifetime.'

'What did he want?'

She still had her back to him rattling away at the pastry mixture. 'It was a horrible time, Michael. Please don't let's dig any of this up again.'

'Just tell me what was going on? Why he came here?'

'All that happened back then, you know it made you ill. It won't do you any good raking it up.'

'It must have been important if he came here.'

'Just wanted to do more harm more like. If you must know, some nonsense about wanting to speak to you. I wasn't going to let that happen, was I?'

'But why not?'

She turned to him and shook her head, the air filled with her inaudible, short-tempered grievances and the pounding of the spatula in the bowl. There was perspiration on her upper lip and a vein stood out on her forehead.

'What was important was that he stayed away,' words she spat out clearly. 'From us. From you. He wanted to talk to you. It was back when you were ill, when you were seventeen. Your dad would never have let him through the gate, would he, so I wasn't going to.'

'Mum, can't you understand how wrong this is? Mr Soames came here to see *me*?'

'Really? I mean, what right ever had that man to say anything about your father? He wasn't fit to lick your dad's boots.'

This was even more upsetting for a whole load of reasons Michael was unable to process there and then. All he could muster through this gathering mist of shock, surprise, and anger was, 'Dad? What did he have to say about dad?'

'He didn't get chance to tell me. I sent him packing as soon as he mentioned your father's name.'

Soames, for whatever reason, had made the effort, had come here to tell him something about his father. What could it have been? Whatever it was couldn't have made Michael feel any worse than he did at the time about what happened. It might even have helped.

'If I'd known I would've gone to see him, found out what he wanted to say,' he pleaded with her.

'And what good would that've achieved? The real damage was already done by then.'

He recalled those awful days, the wreckage of his dreams, his ruined life, his broken mind. His mother was right. It was horrible. All the more reason why, right now even years later, he just couldn't let this go.

'What gave you the right? Not to tell me. What bloody right?'

She sighed and smiled sadly. Was she, perhaps, somewhere in the midst of her righteous indignation, actually enjoying this?

'Look at you, the state of you now. Maybe, that's why I've kept it quiet. Anyway, it was years ago.'

'If it was so long ago like you say, then why hide the article from me.'

She slammed down the bowl and reached in the oven for more pie tins. 'I think I'll make the Christmas cake tonight as well.' Her voice sounded muffled from the recesses of the stove.

'It might have helped me, you know, talking to him.'

She sighed and separated the tins. 'You'd left the school, by then. He had no more hold on you, thank god.'

'But Soames, wanting to say something about dad, why didn't you listen to what he had to say?'

'Michael, please, stop all this. We all know what

happened. That was all there was to know. And it still is exactly that – all there is to know! There's nothing more!' she cried.

She put the tins down on the work surface and then suddenly began to weep uncontrollably, covering her face with her apron. This stopped him in his tracks, as it always did. He had to back off. He'd taken it too far, pushed too hard. Despite his anger he couldn't bear to see her cry.

'Sorry, sorry, mum,' he said. 'I didn't mean to upset you.'

She lowered the cloth, her features streaked with tears and lined with anguish. 'Well, you have. You *have* upset me.' she wailed. 'I can't stand any more of it.'

He went to hold her and she pushed him away. 'I need to get on,' she said.

He backed away into the lounge and overwhelmed by remorse and confusion couldn't read the article now unless he was far away from her in another part of the house. Had he nearly made her ill? He worried all the time about her health and frailty. Perhaps he should, for her sake, forget the whole thing. But the hold his old teacher had on him all those years ago, and this new information that Soames had actually visited the house looking for him, made the article too strong to resist. He ripped it from the paper and hurried to his room to read it in secret.

There wasn't that much more to it than what he'd already learned. According to the report, Steve Lawton, Head of Geography was the last person to see Soames last Friday evening before he disappeared after the final performance of the Christmas school play. Was it *that* Steve Lawton, a fellow student back then from Michael's old class, still at the school but now a current member of staff? A fading photograph from the early seventies accompanied the newspaper report, grainy black and white, the teachers, all male, regaled in dark gowns like actors from a post-war

Ealing comedy, peering out from the distant monochrome past. Soames' eyes burning with energy and promise, summoning him through a portal in time, reproaching him for his failure, taunting him with the memory of what could have been. He instinctively took his teenage journal down from the shelf above, and Maddie's photograph dropped onto the bed. He ignored her smiling face for once and weighed the leather-bound volume in his hand. Should he open the journal and begin reading about a world long gone but which had suddenly re-emerged with this article? Those days with his father, his mother, and Soames, and, also, of course, Laura, always Laura – the first love of his life, a life he may have had, a different world, a different path he might have taken. Where was she now? No doubt far, far away from Pennington School, the town of St Vincent's on Sea, and any thoughts of Soames.

Yet, to him, those days, although years away, always still seemed so close, that time with Laura, those brief magical moments when he was seventeen, alive again now in the article he read, in the journal he held in his hands, in the astonishing news that Soames had once been here at this house to see him. He sat looking at the cover of his teenage diary, lost in time, the unopened volume in his hands feeling heavier and heavier. He then inserted the newspaper article and Maddie's photo inside – another lost love, more recent and yet somehow connected, as all things were, to that first heartbreak. He returned the journal, for now, to its safe place on the shelf. He lay on the bed hoping to hear the noises his mother had heard so he could repair their row with some reassurance that she wasn't imagining things. He would go down there soon to the kitchen to check that she was alright. But whether or not the house was really haunted by some restless spirit in the walls, he knew other ghosts waited for him in that journal when he could find the courage to face them. His mother was right, of course, it was so long ago, but it didn't feel that way. It never had.

CHAPTER TWO

The house resounded with his mother's radio alarm, loud enough to be heard across the landing to his room. Waking up to Wogan and 'Perfect Day', the Children in Need celebrity single. But Grace was already up and about the house as the music blasted out. There was no point in trying to sleep through this and when he met his mother halfway along the landing to the bathroom, she greeted him with, 'Michael, get up, we need to get the plumber out.'

'And good morning to you,' he replied, 'on this perfect day.' She tutted, either at his sarcasm, or with the aftertaste of last night's argument still poisoning her mood, and made her way downstairs. In the bathroom he was pleased to see his toilet repair still worked and would have been happy to carry on with that makeshift solution for a few more days. But on returning to his room, he found a copy of the Yellow Pages waiting for him open on the bed at the double page spread of plumbing firms. He sighed at the long list of ads with their self-mocking, jokey, irritating cartoon characters holding oversized rubber plungers, or tradenames sporting depressing, whimsical puns. He attempted to amuse himself by eliminating them one by one: 'Round the Bend' – too disturbing; 'The Drain Brain' – reminiscent of Ed Wood 1950s B-movies; 'Pipe Dreams' – sounded too much like a porno flick; and the most dispiriting of all, a whole lifetime of predestined blocked drains and fractured dreams condensed in the tragi-comic 'Born to Plumb'. He scanned the advertisements with an increasingly heavy heart until Shakespeare made the decision for him and he booked an appointment with 'To the Spanner Born' for later that morning.

He hadn't slept much, the revelations about Soames, his visit to the house, his recent disappearance, had haunted him throughout the night. He took down his teenage journal once more from the shelf. Did that world ever really exist, a world away from plumbing firms, broken toilets, failed careers and heartbreak? The newspaper article poking from the journal's leather cover evoked more memories – Soames reciting the whole of *The Love Song of J Alfred Prufrock* by heart, Laura hanging on the teacher's every word, Michael watching Laura, her auburn hair, long and flowing, the green eyes, the large mouth always half-smudged with the beginnings of a smile or an aside, the ever-present trench coat with its scent of roses, the welcoming 'V' of her throat.....

'Have you phoned anyone yet?' his mother called from downstairs. 'Yes,' he cried. How he needed to get out of the house again, away from his mother's incessant demands and housework. Where could he go? What could he do? He looked at the article again and the staff photo and Soames at the centre. He felt sadness and bewilderment, familiar enough emotions, now layered with these latest revelations, but also something else, a sudden yearning to forge a connection with this lost world. He went downstairs shaken by this restlessness, and was duly alarmed by another version of yesteryear, the Christmas tree from his childhood, emerging from the garden shed and walking across the back patio to the house. He rushed out to meet this ghost from Christmas Past, and to take the tree from his mother's arms before she had a heart attack. Without another word she went back to the shed to retrieve the box of decorations, the tarnished silver baubles and the fairy with her yellow stained dress just visible beneath the lid. The claustrophobia of the impending season here, in this house, accelerated the desire to escape out into the street, somewhere, anywhere. But he couldn't leave her to struggle with the box, the tree, the lights, although he really just wanted to throw the whole lot into the bin. Christmas was the last thing he wanted right now.

'Do we have to do this today?' he said, a few moments later, once they'd assembled the decorations in the lounge. The effort to prevent the tree from falling over on its rickety stand had exhausted the remnants of his patience. His exasperation was also aggravated by her refusal to acknowledge anything they had discussed the previous evening. It was as if it had never happened.

'Of course. I'm already really late with it. We need to put the tree up and everything else today.'

Anger, bewilderment, shame, the heady cocktail of emotions which for most of the time he kept buried, welled up again, as they had last night, and ever since he'd read the article and knew that Soames had visited this house. He tried one last time.

'I know you don't want to talk about it, but...'

'Remember this?' she said, and his chest tightened as she rattled the tiny red and white plastic Santa on his sleigh. 'I bought this for your first Christmas.'

'I know, mum.'

'You used to go crazy every year whenever I first put it out on the tree,' she said, stepping back to admire the decoration in its usual place, second branch down from the top, beneath the crooked fairy.

'You mean like last year,' he said, flippantly, hoping to stem the flow of seasonal mawkishness.

'When you were three, four, five, six, silly. Should we try the lights?'

Nostalgia seeped through his veins like a toxin as the bells and stars bloomed and transformed the room with their multi-coloured array. His mother smiled and clapped her hands twice. 'There!' She looked younger, transformed in the glow of the lights.

'I'm sorry if I upset you about Mr Soames,' he said, trying to sound as reasonable as he could muster. 'But it was a shock to find out he'd been here to see me.'

'These are always a pain,' she said, as the lights flickered on and then off and didn't come back on again.

'Mum, please, I know it's hard but I do want you to tell me why he came here.'

She unplugged the lights angrily. 'Look, I don't know why, and I never want you to mention that man again! Understand? Never ever again.'

'Are you sure he didn't say at least something to you?'

She threw the assembly of wires at him. 'Fix the damned lights will you. Rather than mithering me about this, do something useful!' she yelled, storming back into the kitchen.

He plucked listlessly at the bewildering spaghetti of wires as he wrestled with fight or flight. Flight won. It usually did.

'I have to take the video back,' he called to her.

She re-emerged, looking flustered and angry. 'Right now? What about the plumber?'

'I'll be home again before he arrives.'

If he stayed there any longer, he would either rip the light socket from the wall, and the fairy's head from her shoulders, crunch the god-forsaken plastic Father Christmas under foot, or take his mother in his arms and tell her, yes, he was sorry, sorry about upsetting her again about Soames, and yes, he did remember the white-bearded Santa dangling from the tree and how happy those childhood Christmases were. He couldn't bear doing either and the only option was to get away.

She looked at him and frowned. 'Before you rush off, did you hear it last night?' she said, burying the unused baubles, shepherds and angels back in the box for another year of darkness.

'Hear what?' he said, anxiously reaching for his coat and the Seagal video.

'Them, it, again. Whatever it is. Them, *it,* behind the walls.'

'There's nothing there, mum. It's not a ghost.'

'I didn't sleep a wink. And then the noises started again.'

'What? You slept like a baby. I could hear your snoring across the landing.'

'I wasn't,' she said. 'I was awake with that scratching sound. I don't know how you can't hear it.'

'It's probably a bird's nest, or something.'

'Or something….? You mean…rats or something?'

'No.'

'Oh my god. How could you say that? Suggest that we have vermin.'

'I didn't say it.'

'Do you have to go right now? It's not as if the video shop is going to disappear in the next few hours.'

'The quicker I get there, the quicker I will be back,' he called out from the front door, Wogan's annual rendition of 'The Floral Dance' ringing in his ears as he hurried off.

It was a grey December morning, barely light, and yet he welcomed the breeze, the open spaces of the street. Mother was getting harder to deal with – he was unable even to go to Blockbusters without her making him feel guilty. And she was obviously as shaken as him by the return of Soames' name into their lives, increasing her obvious nervous anxiety and obsession with unexplained sounds. Noises apart, he knew he had lied. There were, indeed, ghosts within those walls, one unacknowledged phantom in particular that could never be talked about. Last night was the nearest he and his mother had ever come to discussing him. He quickly stashed the Seagal video in the bin at Blockbusters and then stood marooned on the corner of the street.

Going straight back home and a morning of fixing the tree lights and making small talk with the plumber filled him with dread. He set off wandering in the opposite direction. How had his life come to such a standstill? This time last year he was looking forward to Christmas. Both he and Maddie so excited, planning their time together, Christmas Day with friends for dinner at her home. Her son Tommy opening presents. It was truly magical being around a kid at Christmas time, witnessing the enchantment, the wonder of it all through the little boy's eyes. But, in the end, his mother couldn't join them, because she was unwell and he had to leave Maddie on Boxing Day and catch the train back to St Vincent's to make sure she was alright. Tommy, of course, was disappointed that Michael didn't have time to play with the Scalextric he'd bought him and had spent all Christmas Day setting up. Perhaps the seeds of failure were planted way back then, although he didn't realise it at the time. But in the end, looking back, the tension between Maddie's needs and his mother's, could never have been reconciled. And finally in September, just before the start of the new term at Barton, Maddie had resolved his dilemma for him by ending the affair.

Now all he had were days of monotonous time-filling chores, moping in his room over Maddie's photo, until the evening when he could lose himself in the daily fix of macho movie nonsense, the pure escapism that took him away from the mostly unbearable present. As he walked aimlessly along the tree lined streets of St Vincent's, he couldn't shake off the agitation and restlessness caused by that newspaper article and the knowledge that Soames had tried to pay him a visit all those years ago.

What would Mr Soames think of him now? What would he make of his most devoted student these days, washed up with no future, still in the same town at forty-three, watching such trash as *Executive Decision*? Soames, who had first introduced him to the miracle of cinema, the wonders of Wilder and Welles, the magic of Kazan and Kubrick. Gilbert Soames, himself a wayward maverick, his imposing frame, distinguished voice, large pronounced forehead, creased smile, eyebrows arched in ironic amusement. He was always the Orson Welles of St Vincent's in Michael's memory. He recalled the first time he had watched *Citizen Kane* at one of Soames' magical Sunday evening screenings he held at the school. How that film and Soames' commentary had transformed movies from entertainment into an art form, a way of seeing things that went beyond cinema into seeing life itself as a great adventure, life as a canvass onto which a man could project his own glittering, multi-faceted perspective. Welles' first and greatest film with its contradictory, shapeshifting retelling of Charles Foster Kane's rise and fall as newspaper magnate and failed political campaigner, recounted through the eyes of those who knew him or thought they knew him, had mesmerised Michael. And lit by just the spotlight from the film projector and casting a giant shadow across the school hall that Sunday evening, Mr Soames' pre-film commentary was just as compelling. How Soames had alerted them all to the tiny moments, how no detail on the screen is wasted. He remembered Soames' exact words, to this very day.

'Be aware,' he had said, 'of the mystery at the heart of the film and how you may, if you're not careful, or because you're half asleep, or too lazy to notice, miss the most important moment, my dear students, in cinema history.

Who or what is Rosebud? If you pay attention, you may solve the riddle very early on. Because it's there staring you in the face. But no one notices it. And that's why the end is so haunting, so devastating when the secret is finally revealed.'

At the end of the film Soames asked, 'Well did anyone get it? Did anyone know what Rosebud really was before the final reel?'

And, of course, no one did.

'Just like little boy, Charles,' he said, 'unaware that his life was about to change, you all missed it. Everybody does. That's the magic. In the little moments, the details.'

Why had Michael always remembered *that* night so vividly? And why had he tried, so many times and failed, to recapture the magic Soames instilled in him with his own classes at Barton whenever he screened those cinema classics? What was he hoping for? To bring the same wonder to young people he had felt when Soames opened up that world to him? How foolish, how presumptuous to imagine he could carry it off with just a fraction of the charisma that Soames possessed.

The world had also changed. Something had shifted in young people's perceptions and expectations, a frightening dramatic decline in the universal attention span, maybe some shift in brain chemistry that made such movies inaccessible to teenagers today. Never mind close attention to details, his classes couldn't focus for more than five minutes on anything without special effects or gross-out comedy. The reactions he got to these classic films ranged from bewilderment and boredom to outright hostility, but nothing compared to the last time, recently, the most disastrous attempt of all, his final day at Barton when he'd shown *Citizen Kane* to that awful Year Eleven group. He wasn't sure why he'd acted in the way he had, but the riotous, loutish upheaval in the room that morning felt like a desecration of something he held sacred. Was that why he'd physically attacked its instigator, a thuggish bully who deserved a lot more than the moderate punishment Michael had meted out? Moderate or not, you couldn't lay hands on a pupil these days without severe repercussions. Technically speaking, he hadn't actually touched the boy as the cardboard box Michael had stuffed on top of Carl Bridgford's head was the only contact he'd made with him. But perhaps the most culpable act had been the one that followed – flight again – his walking out of the class and the school and not returning until he was summoned for disciplinary action. He'd just run away and, if he was honest, he knew he was running still.

But now he'd run into a complete dead end. He dreaded the prospect of going back to Barton after Christmas, working every day alongside Maddie, facing the boy he had assaulted, the class he'd walked out on. His suspension until after Christmas was the least to expect, although he had secretly hoped they might dismiss him completely. Despite his agreement with the Head to return to Barton on terms of probation in January, he hadn't yet fully agreed it with himself. But how much longer could he stand this half-life here in St Vincent's on Sea, living with the ghosts his mother heard behind the walls? His world was closing down and there was nowhere left for him to go. And so, he walked along, not knowing where he was heading, through streets that weaved through the town in a direction away from his mother's but which were still vaguely familiar. As the morning sun struggled to free itself of the horizon, and with nothing but memories drawing him on, he followed his restless instincts through the fallen leaves littering the pavement, along the way that led eventually to the shore and beyond, where a blue rim of daylight nestled. Although it was many years since he'd walked this path, he knew the road so well, the one that led back to Pennington School.

He'd never been back there since his schooldays,

always afraid of what terrible memories he might encounter. But what would be the harm in just having a look at the old place? Wallow for a few moments in the remnants of a past that still shone so bright, so vivid, so frightening, in his memory. That uneasy stirring still gnawing at him, he strode ahead in anticipation of something. Maybe Soames might already have returned and be back at the school this morning – all laughter and long strides along the corridor to welcome him, shaking Michael's hand, patting him on the back, putting his life back on track. The bare trees waved in the wind either to welcome him, or to throw up their arms in recognition and dismay, as he found the familiar pedestrian crossing and the old railway bridge, now converted to a two-way road with a narrow pavement. He pushed forward breathing a large buoyant lungful of sea air until across from the school entrance he stopped in his tracks at the sight before him.

He knew, first-hand, what had been the effects of eighteen years of Tory cutbacks on school buildings, but still could not have been prepared for this extent of dereliction and decay. The school was on the point of collapse in places. What had been the Science Block was falling apart, one side of the building open to the elements. The school playing fields, once a vast green space, now choked beneath rampant wild grasses where diggers clawed at the earth. It was only the fading sign at the rusting entrance gates and a few electric lights shining behind dirt-stained windows that indicated the school was still open. The drab building slumped before him, an old man too tired for visitors, saying, go home, leave it be. But that was just it, he couldn't leave it. Now he was here, after all these years, the memory of Soames, Laura, his seventeen-year-old self, were all still trapped within those walls. He knew somehow part of him had never left, had never moved on from the boy who walked those corridors.

Maybe he could have a quick word with Steve Lawton who was actually still there as Head of Geography, and the last person to see Soames before he disappeared. Perhaps a chat with Lawton would help to put some of these ghosts to rest. What was the alternative? Turn around. Go home to his mother and her depression and silence. More than likely it would all be over in a few minutes anyway, that neither Lawton, nor anybody else would know or care who he was. He might not even get past the front door, schools these days so suspicious of strangers after the Dunblane shooting a year earlier. He faltered but then imagined Soames bursting out of the dark winter morning, shouting from the blazing fenders of a DeLorean – 'Mikey, I have something to tell you. Get in the car – we can save your life. I'll explain on the way back to 1971!' And the prospect of his old teacher somewhere within those corridors, even as an absence that silently awaited his return, gave him confidence to pull open the doors to the main entrance. And no one stopped him.

He was hit by a wave of claustrophobic heat and his glasses briefly misted over. The lenses cleared to reveal a deserted front office and an interior just as shabby as the outside of the school. Broken and missing floor tiles patterned the corridor leading up to the common room. Dark stretches of damp mapped the ceilings and walls with unknown lands, or stared down at him with gruesome faces. He saw his grim pale reflection in the grimy entrance windows, a vagrant intruder in an abandoned building. Then there was an ear-splitting explosion as the bell rang right above his head and students and staff suddenly appeared from everywhere. How quickly he had forgotten the hectic rhythms of the working school life as small boys carrying huge bags twice their size bumped him along the corridor and older students weaved in and out and past him without a word.

Three boys, aged about twelve or thirteen, ran past him, muttering 'Penfold, Penfold.' The boys sniggered and whispered, sneaking looks at him, obviously entranced by this intruder, who apparently suggested to them a sudden hilarious materialization of that cartoon character on the corridors of Pennington. He considered for a moment freaking all three of them out completely by blurting out Penfold's catchphrase, 'Crumbs, DM!'? Instead, he stared at them sternly over his black-rimmed spectacles which amused them further.

The boys' laughter dried up when someone yelled, 'Davies and co! Stay there! Face the window. I'll deal with you three in a minute.' They stood to attention while the tall, imposing figure approached, his ivory shirt, encased in an immaculate blue and black pinstripe suit, topped off with a matching silk tie. The face above it was crimson-red, the hairstyle military, close-cropped and steel grey.

'Bob Dillon, Headmaster. How can I help you?' Michael, much more comfortable with the boys and their sneaky ridicule, stood his ground to face this intimidating figure of all-commanding authority. 'How can I help you?' the Head asked again, and then, without waiting for an answer, 'Is there a problem here?' The boys turned from facing the window, intrigued to see an adult being humiliated. Michael thought briefly of beating a hasty retreat straight back out of the door, but instead stood his ground. Sometimes, even Ernest Penfold could display moral fibre under pressure.

'I'm Michael Freeman. I used to be a pupil here. I was wondering if I could see Steve Lawton.'

'Why?'

'Steve Lawton. He was one of my classmates. I think he's Head of Geography.'

'Yes, that's right. Mr Lawton is heading that department,' Dillon, replied, before adding, rather ominously, 'at the moment.'

'I was a pupil here. The school took me on in the Sixth Form after I failed the Eleven Plus.'

'That must've been many years ago,' Dillon said, before looking at his watch. 'The school destroys most records before 1980.'

'Yes, it was 1970 I joined.'

'No recording of those times. We had another proper clear-out recently.' Dillon took hold of Michael's arm, gently but firmly. 'Er, the staff, Mr....'

'Freeman, Michael.'

'The staff, I'm afraid haven't really got time to be chatting away with friends during school hours. Maybe you could arrange to see him after school has closed.'

Dillon ushered him silently down the corridor like some beggar off the street. They cut through a back exit, a narrow door, and with a brief word of farewell, he dispatched Michael outside. And that was it. His grand return to the old school. He needed to get away from here quickly now, to avoid any further humiliation. But though he tried to make his way back along the outside of the school to the main entrance, after stumbling around for a few minutes in a wasteland of shattered glass and ruin, he found himself at the rear of the old Science block with even more portakabins and several skips filled to the top with soil and rubble. The potholed yard where there was once a grass verge that circled back to the main entrance now led to a muddy expanse of tyre tracks and felled trees. A regular parade of wagons rolled back and forth churning up the ground, and beyond, some large diggers carved up the earth and carried away great buckets of brown soil and debris. And where the playing fields once rolled on forever, seagulls now swooped on a moonscape of noise, chaos and dirt. Eventually he retraced his steps to the narrow entrance where Dillon had left him and he had no choice but to go back inside and head for the main exit.

He was about to open the narrow door when he heard 'Penfold' from one of the portakabins. He turned and was quite relieved to see the three boys, Davies and co, in the doorway smiling at him. Maybe they could give him directions so he could leave without encountering Dillon again. Inside the kabin there was an almighty commotion, signalling a classroom riot, or an absent teacher whose lesson was not covered.

Davies, came down the steps and smiled at Michael. 'You're him that was talking to Dildo.'

'Aren't you meant to be in class?'

'This is our class.' A gathering of boys and girls at the windows formed their hands into rounded spectacles and chanted louder and louder, 'Penfold! Penfold!'

'Who's meant to be with you now?' he asked.

'A teacher. But he's not been in for days.'

'Which teacher?'

'He's disappeared,' said Davies, 'so, we have a sub, whoever that is, and whenever they turn up.' Michael waved at the crowd clustered now at the kabin doorway and the chanting grew louder.

'Is Mr Soames, your normal teacher?' asked Michael.

'Yes. Soames. Do you know him?'

'He used to teach me.'

'We knew he was old, but not that old.'

'He was a great teacher in my day.'

'My dad thinks Soames's killed himself,' said the boy sadly, before looking beyond to the school corridor window where Bob Dillon was standing watching them.

'If you want to find old Lawton, you're better off looking down at the café,' Davies said, climbing back up to the portakabin. 'At the café, at the beach.' He mimed smoking and then put his hands behind his back as Dillon approached. The kabin was now silent, all faces at the window and doorway gone. There was just Davies rooted to the spot on the steps.

'Mr Foreman,' said Dillon. 'I see you're still with us.'

'Freeman. Sorry, I got lost and couldn't find my way out.'

'I thought you said you were a pupil here.'

'Yes, but things have changed a bit since then.'

'What were you talking to the boys about?'

'I was just asking them about Mr Soames.'

Dillon's face bloomed into a deeper and darker red. 'Davies!'

'Sir.'

'What've you been saying to this man?'

'About what, sir?'

'About Mr Soames.'

'Nothing, sir.'

Dillon moved in very close to Davies and grabbed him by the ear and twisted it. The boy's cries blended with those of a seagull scratching on the kabin roof. 'Don't lie to me, sunshine.'

Michael, still troubled by his own assault on Carl Bridgford was in no position to take the high moral ground here, but the boy was in pain and Dillon didn't care.

'Hey, leave him alone. You can't do that,' he said.

Dillon held on to the boy's ear and turned on Michael. 'If you know what's good for you, you'll get off the site now. Schools have to be very careful about strangers coming on to the premises. Children could be at risk.'

'Just let the boy go, will you? He was trying to help with directions back to the entrance. I got lost.'

The Headmaster released the boy who stole sly glances back at the kabin window while rubbing his ear. Dillon snarled at Michael. 'I thought it was Lawton you were here to see.'

'Yes, but Mr Soames used to teach me.'

'Well, Soames isn't in school. And I doubt he'll be coming back. Not that it's any business of yours, or yours either, Davies.'

'Yes, sir,' Davies said, hurrying back inside the kabin, accompanied by a wave of noise.

Dillon yelled, 'Keep it quiet in there! Any more and you'll all be starting your holidays this afternoon an hour or two later' He loomed over Michael from the tops of the steps. 'I have to take this class. You, sir, you need to go right now and don't come back. That's your way to the main gates. If I see you here again, I'll call the police.'

CHAPTER THREE

He edged his way along the fenced areas, heaps of debris and broken slabs of concrete obstructing his way, preoccupied with what he'd just witnessed. Why was Dillon so keen to keep Davies quiet? Was he trying to hide something? And why was he so sure Soames wouldn't be coming back? After squeezing past a further row of skips and a mountain of black refuse bags, he finally reached the gates. The fact he'd not been allowed to speak to Lawton coupled with Dillon's obnoxious manner, made him more determined to find his old school colleague and have a chat with him. According to Davies, Lawton could be found in the café on the promenade, but perhaps he wouldn't be there just yet until after school. He also now realised he'd been gone much longer than he intended and his mother would be waiting for him. He hurried along and when he got back the white van parked outside sporting the logo 'To the Spanner Born' was already there.

In the hallway he took off his shoes and could hear a man's voice from the bathroom and an unfamiliar sound – his mother's laughter.

'I sometimes think my son's other name is Heath Robinson.'

'Well, you did say he was a teacher.' Their voices interspersed with the hollow metallic tapping of tools and pipes.

'Yes, he's a clever boy, but I sometimes wish he'd taken up a trade, taken after his father. But he can't do a thing with his hands.'

'Well, you know what they say.'

'No, what do they say?' His mother's voice sounded younger, playful, perhaps flirtatious.

'How many teachers does it take to change a lightbulb?'

'Go on. How many?'

'Just the one who goes to find the caretaker.'

More laughter from her. It sounded like an instrument slightly out of tune, but still just about in working order.

She emerged on the stairs smiling and shaking her head, muttering, 'Oh dear, I don't know,' to herself. 'Oh, you're back, finally,' she said to Michael, standing below in the hallway. 'Joe's up there. Apparently, he knows me from church,' she said, going into the lounge, before whispering conspiratorially, 'His wife died six months ago. He's started going there to get himself out and about. Poor man.' She glanced above with an unusual warmth, before pointing to an envelope resting on the fireplace. 'Post arrived while you were out.'

The envelope with its Barton postmark and familiar handwriting tugged at his heart.

'Who's it from?' she asked.

'It'll be about my research project,' he said.

'Research? Haven't seen much research going on.'

'Probably new instructions,' he said, waving the letter and hurrying up the stairs.

'By the way, I fixed the Christmas lights myself,' she cried to him as he reached the landing.

On his way he stopped off at the bathroom where the plumber was packing up his equipment.

'It's all done there now,' Joe said. 'Toilet up and running fine.' He looked up from his tool bag and smiled, a man in his late sixties, healthy-looking with creased handsome features and a full head of grey hair.

'Thank you, for coming out this morning,' said Michael.

'Spoke to my son, didn't you? I'm supposed to have retired but I'm always around if there's a job to do.'

'Well, my solution was probably on borrowed time.'

Joe laughed. 'That was an original. You know you can use a coat-hanger.'

'Thought I'd try a new approach.'

'Your mum says you're a teacher.'

'Yes.'

'That's a great job.'

He examined the plumber's expression for any hint of irony, but could detect none. 'Yes. It's very rewarding,' he said. It wasn't worth saying anything else.

'What do you teach, if you don't mind me asking?'

Although entirely good natured and well meant, all this was making Michael feel uncomfortable. 'Er, English.'

'That was always my favourite subject.'

Michael really didn't care. 'I can change lightbulbs as well.'

Joe looked confused for a moment and then he slightly reddened. Michael smiled back, regretting this last remark. He didn't really want to come the smartarse with this elderly guy who'd come out, done the repair at such short notice.

'Sorry, you heard that,' Joe said, smiling back. 'Just a joke.'

'No, you're right. I am practically useless. My mother will give you chapter and verse.'

And here she was, as if on cue, emerging from the stairs with a cup of coffee. 'What? What's he been telling you, Joe?'

'Nothing, Mrs Freeman. We've been having a bit of a laugh at each other's expense.'

'I've brought you another drink, Joe.' she said.

'Oh, I'm sorry, I've just finished.'

'Oh. Haven't you time for another brew?'

'Well, I'm not doing any more jobs today though, so...'

'Come downstairs, in the lounge and have it there,' she said. 'You can let me know how much I owe you.'

'Thank you, Mrs Freeman.'

'Grace,' she said. They both sidled by Michael and onto the landing, Joe smiling shyly as he passed. On the cistern, twisted and bedraggled, drained of all colour lay his tie. He carried it dangling and dripping across the landing.

From his room Michael heard more laughter downstairs, as he opened the letter. His heart leapt at Maddie's handwriting stretching in neat rows across the thin notepaper. But then he hesitated. What good could come of this letter after all these weeks? Why not tear it up before hearing what she had to say? Forget all that Maddie and Barton stood for in his life. Forget about ever going back there after Christmas. But while thinking this he had unfolded the letter and was already reading.

Tel Barton 376345   28 Windmill Road

Barton

Monday 15th December

Dear Michael,

The main reason for writing is sad news, I'm afraid. Derek Fletcher is once more extremely ill and back in hospital. I thought it best you know. The cancer has spread beyond any possible further treatment and the outlook is bleak. It's so heart-breaking, although he remains, as ever, cheerful and brave. I'm writing so you know and maybe you can find the time to go and visit before it's too late, if you understand what I'm saying. He would be delighted to see you and it would make his day.

This sadness over Derek has brought me down. He is such a kind friend, such a source of comfort through the difficult time I had when my marriage broke up. He is so loved by everyone in the Common Room and by the students. But, apart from that deep sadness, I am basically OK, looking forward to a break from work. There have been big changes in my life recently. Tommy and I have rented a new house that has more space and in the New Year I intend to look for somewhere to buy. I can afford it fully now as Ben Carter announced his retirement at half term and I have been appointed Head of Department in January.

I know you have been through a difficult time. Maybe you don't want to hear all this again, maybe you are moving on somehow with your life, I don't know. Whether or not this is the case, I want you to know these last weeks since we parted have been difficult for me too. Sometimes we have to make heart-breaking, hurtful choices and that is what I felt I had to do for everyone's sake. As we agreed, I had to consider Tommy and his future and how the person I was with would always have to be there for him and for me. Neither you nor I could guarantee that, and I couldn't carry on with a part-time relationship, sharing you with your mum and her needs. This is all old ground, but nevertheless worth saying again as we both move on into the next term and I hope our working together once more. This time as good friends. I hope we can do that. Remain friends. You always were my closest friend, Michael, long before we became lovers.

Speaking of school, I am really sorry about what happened to you with Carl Bridgford. That boy is a menace, but what you did was so uncharacteristic. I did my best for you with the Head and I am relieved he's invited you back in January. I don't understand what was going on with you at that time. But then you, Michael, for all your good qualities and kindness, will always remain something of a mystery to me. I hope time away from Barton has given you the space you need and that you are feeling happy about coming back. We value you as a colleague and respect your dedication, humour and professionalism.

On this basis, I was wondering if you wanted to give me a call to talk things through about your classes and the syllabus ahead of the new term. I think it might be useful to break the ice and ease us into working together in a professional manner and help avoid any further awkwardness. You are still a highly regarded member of our department here and we are all eager to see you again. Moving forward I hope we can once more be happy and productive colleagues despite what happened.

Maybe I will hear from you before the beginning of next term. Please find some time to see Derek if you can before it's too late.

In the meantime, I hope you are keeping well. Take care of yourself, Michael.

All best wishes for Christmas and a Happy New Year

Love,

Maddie

PS Tommy's doing well at school and is getting excited about Christmas with all the things he is expecting from Santa. Buzz Lightyear's high on his list this year.

Why hadn't he followed his instincts and torn the letter up in the envelope unread? He crumpled and un-crumpled the pages and they curled in his hands like an unfolding of autumn leaves. Smoothing out the creases he tried to reconcile the formality, the detached business-like tone, with the warm loving person with whom he'd shared an intimate relationship. From lover and best friend just a few weeks ago he was now relegated to valued member of her department. This was in many ways more devastating than her silence. Furthermore, suddenly, he seemed such a so called 'mystery' to her. But what was so mysterious about caring for your mother? Had Maddie ever really granted him the space to deal with his mother's illness? Why couldn't Maddie have accepted that time is the only healer of depression, and that it was *his* time that Grace had needed? Could Maddie never understand how her increasing expectations of him as partner and role model to her little boy had torn him in two? Tommy was a great kid and he was very fond of him, but he wasn't *his* kid. Whereas Michael's mother was his mother, and always would be.

And what did she mean by these so called 'big changes'? Obviously, the Head of Department was significant, but that had been on the cards for a long time. Were there things she wasn't telling him? Maybe to do with her and Rick Campbell? Campbell, the new young Head of PE who had all female members of staff in a spin. Ten years younger, persistent in his attentions to Maddie from the day he started in September, Michael was familiar with his serial philandering type, his square jaw permanently shadowed with dark stubble, his too-tight shirts, his self-regarding film star smile. He recalled how, in those awful weeks at the beginning of this last term, Maddie's laughter at the younger man's feeble jokes and asides rang out around the Common Room. Even so, he still squirmed at his own poor behaviour on his last day at Barton, when he told her and Campbell that he 'hoped they would be very happy together'. Were they now enmeshed in what she considered to be the secure and happy relationship she desired? Was Campbell the kind of man whom Maddie believed would provide the commitment and reliability she so wanted for her son? If she thought that, then she was a fool. Campbell was a fraud, a beefcake with a smooth tongue who would abandon her the minute another pretty face came along. None of this was his business now, but he still wanted to know how deep she was involved with this charlatan. He also hated himself for needing to know so badly.

Granted, she did seem to have a passing sympathy regarding his assault on the Bridgford boy. But what she didn't understand was the real reason for his uncharacteristic behaviour, the fact his short fuse with his classes all stemmed from her decision to end their relationship right at the beginning of the September term. Going into work every day, greeting and working with Maddie in the same department, trying to act normal while watching Campbell making his moves, had driven him to despair. And so he was expected to go back there and work with her again, well actually work *for* her, now she was Head of Department. Probably with Campbell as her new lover. He couldn't see how this would be possible.

All these feelings overrode the purpose of the beginning of the letter, conveying the sad news that Derek Fletcher, his friend, was fading. Yes, this was very upsetting, but he felt such a strange distance from all that. Derek, only in his late fifties, wise counsellor and colleague, should be looking forward to a long and well-earned retirement. Of course, he should have gone to see him, should go and visit him soon. And Maddie was right with her unspoken condemnation. What kind of a person abandons a friend in his dire need? Maddie's implication stung and he'd no leg to stand on. He didn't drive, had never wanted to drive, but there was a regular train service that would have taken him to Barton in over an hour. But he'd wanted to leave behind so many things about the school and Barton and moving back with his mother was a way of cutting off all ties with that world. Besides, a trip to Derek's house or Barton Hospital might have entailed a distressing, heart-rending encounter with Maddie. Could he ever really go back to that town, to that school, after this letter, after not going to see Derek, after humiliating himself in front of his class, after Maddie ended their relationship and now insisted on such a professional distancing between them? Perhaps the sooner he managed to sell his house over there in Barton and sever all connections with the place the better.

In the lounge below, the muffled rhythms of his mum's conversation and laughter was a new development. Maybe she was, despite the setback associated with Soames' newspaper article, getting better after all. She might hear things in the night, be convinced that the house was haunted, but eventually that would pass. If only Maddie had given him the time he needed to see all this through. He held the letter in one hand alongside Maddie's photograph which he took from inside his journal. A welter of feelings fought side by side. Despite his efforts to forget, despite his anger over her letter, he had to admit he was still hopelessly in love with her. Distance, if anything had only intensified his feelings. He closed his hand around the thin paper. At his feet the yellow tie Maddie had bought him in the early spring leaked a small patch of damp into the carpet. He folded the letter into the pages of his journal alongside her photograph and placed them all back on the shelf. He then picked up the tie and lowered it like a dying creature to the bottom of the bin where it lay limp and unrecognisable.

Downstairs the conversation between Grace and Joe

continued, the loud confident sounds of a man's voice, so unusual, so unsettling. He needed to be away from Joe, from his mother, from Maddie's letter. What was there here in this house for him but recriminations and sadness? Anything was better than lying here mulling over the past with Maddie, listening to his mother chortling away downstairs in the lounge while he spent another afternoon pretending to do research.

At the front door, the smell of more baking from the kitchen drew him back into the house. And there was Joe, alone on the sofa, working his way through a plate of mince pies.

'Your mum's just making me another coffee,' he said. 'I'll be needing to use that toilet I've just fixed in a minute.'

Michael stooped and helped himself to the biggest juiciest pie, before Joe could get his hands on it.

'Yes, help yourself,' Joe said, a trail of fragile crumbs scattering down his front, as he also took another from the plate. His mother always had this strict rule about no mince pies before Christmas Eve. Why present an early batch before this stranger?

'Mum makes them all herself. None of your pre-packaged stuff for her.'

Grace re-entered carrying a tray of bone china and a coffee-maker – another first.

'You're spoiling me. I could get used to this,' Joe said, taking another bite of pie in one hand and the freshly brewed cup of coffee in the other.

'Joe says he can do us a walk-in shower,' his mother said.

'What about a walk-in future?' Michael mumbled under his breath.

'What was that?' said Grace and she turned to Joe.

'What did he say?' Joe shrugged and she shook her head. 'Michael, I wish you wouldn't mutter.'

'I said, that's something to look forward to in the future.'

'Sufficient unto the day is the evil thereof,' Joe said, smiling at Michael.

'Joe is a member at our church, Michael,' his mother said.

'Yes, you've already told me.'

'You two talking about me behind my back?' said Joe.

'Were your ears burning?' said Grace.

'Michael, please have another mince pie, or else I'm going to have to eat them all,' said Joe, leaning forward to pick yet another off the plate.

Grace looked at Michael. 'Sit down or something, will you, you're making the place untidy.'

'I'm going out.'

'Again? Where to now?'

'Library. More research.'

'He's on sabbatical,' she said to Joe.

'Sounds interesting,' said Joe. '

'Well research can be interesting,' Michael replied. How much longer could he keep up this charade?

'What you researching?' asked Joe.

'Whatever it is I can't see what good any of it is to the school,' his mother interrupted, unaware she was coming to his rescue. But then followed it with an even more embarrassing topic of conversation. 'But then what do I know. All he does, as far as I can see, is sit up there in his room looking at the photo of a girl.'

'She's not a girl, mum.'

'No, woman, then. A woman who's just left her marriage with a little boy in tow.'

'Her husband left *her*, mum. Three years ago.'

'And now she's gone and left you.'

'Yes, mum, she's left me so I can look after you. Wasn't that kind of her?'

His mother looked at Joe and smiled. 'Well, at least he has his uses, my Michael.'

'It's good that a lad looks after his mum. Not many do these days,' Joe said, smiling at Michael, a raisin lodged between his top front teeth.

'I need to go,' Michael said, 'before the library closes.'

He took another mince pie, one less for Joe to have, mumbled a brief goodbye through a mouthful of pastry and headed out of the door. He'd seen more than enough of Joe, there on the sofa as if by right as alpha male fixer of the toilet, his mother attuned to his lame banter. He'd also had enough of her sudden levity, her baring of his private life, the dismissive tone towards him she usually only reserved for their time alone together, now shared with an outsider. After just a morning with Joe there she was – laughing, joking, running around after the guy with coffee and pastries. Making mince pies for god's sake. Before Christmas Eve. She'd never even done that for dad. But one thing, at least he could now leave for once without feeling guilty while she was occupied with this new exciting visitor. He was out again, and this time it wasn't just to go to the video store.

When he reached the promenade, the front was dormant with empty shops and boarded-up stalls. But the pier was open, with its kiosk offering a rack of fading postcards.

Maddie's letter probably required a reply, something, anything, to let her know *he* was OK too, was managing well, his life carrying on regardless of their break up. Maybe pretending would not only save face but help to convince himself, just a little. Perhaps not, but he chose a card anyway that looked suitably upbeat with summer crowds and sunshine, along with a cheap biro and a stamp. But what could he really say to her that had any meaning? That it was impossible for him to return to Barton and work with her? That it would be too painful? Even if he couldn't bring himself to explain all in the card, he would have to make his mind up one way or another very soon. Perhaps he didn't need to tell her, the Head, or anyone. Just not turn up in January. What could they do to him now anyway that they hadn't done already? If he informed them about going back or not, either way there would be no more salary after the end of December. What if, like Soames, he too could just disappear without a word of explanation?

Right now, he badly needed something to take his mind off it all. And so, he wandered along in search of the café that Steve Lawton frequented, that the boy at Pennington had mentioned before he had his ear wrenched off by that sadist of a headmaster. Steve, the man Headmaster Dillon didn't want Michael to meet, the last man to see Gilbert Soames before he disappeared. On the horizon the sun hovered above the distant line of sea, way out where gulls wheeled and dropped like black confetti against the light. The first star of evening swam above a green and red fire and he breathed the air deeply. The tide was so far out it may never return. Could he walk all the way from here to some distant land? Would that solve everything – if he just set off now to a new country, one that existed perhaps beyond the green and blue horizon, underneath the star whose brightness grew and beckoned by the minute? Had Soames, too, arrived at this point and kept on going out there until the waters surrounded him and cut off his final journey?

The young boy Davies's father thought Soames had committed suicide but there had been no pile of clothes abandoned on the ribbed sands, no body reported washed up in the rounded humps to the east where night settled in the wilderness of dunes and grass. If Soames had stood here summoned by the mud and marshland that awaited those who ventured too far, then he had left no trace. As the last rose diamond of sunlight sank beneath the sea, Michael scoured the horizon looking for a figure silhouetted against the deepening blue. The shoreline that stretched before him in the fading light had changed so much. The sea had clawed back the dunes, hollowing out a wide bay of sand that reached back in places almost to the road and the tideline was now a jagged graph of flotsam and jetsam dumped and piled in heaps across the beach. Bulldozers were parked everywhere, and mountains of sand awaited removal. Someone was plundering this beautiful landscape, transporting it for sale. The coastline was literally up for grabs.

To the south where lurked the darkened mounds of the dunes, his eyes reached into the twilight for the hunkered monument of the pillbox. The place that haunted him every day of his life. He shuddered as he recalled its cold, damp, salty-dark interior. Once it rested neatly out of reach of the tide but now stood isolated in the flatbed of the receding shore. It fell back into the shadows along with the memories it carried. Where was Soames? Could he lead Michael back to those days before the terrors of that pillbox took something from him? There were no answers here. Only the boarded-up buildings that slept along the silent shore and a cardboard box that scraped across the ground in the wind like a wounded dog.

Deepening darkness reigned on both sides of the promenade, out to sea and all along the shopfronts across the road. No signs of life, except one disparate gentle lantern glow about fifty yards to his left. He crossed to where a flickering yellow sign beckoned above a steamed-up window. 'Vics Vinyls' Café and Music' flashed its faulty apostrophe on and off. Was this Steve Lawton's café, the place where he came to hide away from his pupils? Maybe Soames would be hiding away in here too, and a grand welcome would await him. Joni Mitchell's seasonal 'River' and the smell of frying bacon and cigarette smoke greeted him as he entered. His glasses misted up in the warm interior and when they cleared, he saw the place was empty apart from another man in the corner opposite who glanced across before returning to his newspaper and his fry-up. A fibre-optic Christmas tree glowed by the man's table, casting fluorescent shades across his face. The man looked up again and nodded a friendly enough greeting. Michael nodded back but realised, with only a fleeting glance, there was no way this bearded giant could be the stick-thin Steve Lawton of 1971.

He took a seat by the window as another man emerged from the back of the café wearing a Santa outfit and a stained reindeer-decorated apron. He carried a second plate, this time of pancakes, to the man in the corner, before wandering over to the racks of LPs stacked along all one wall, where a range of movie posters from the sixties and seventies were displayed: *If; Blow Up; A Clockwork Orange; Straw Dogs; Midnight Cowboy.* The man in the Father Christmas suit, now towering over the racks and rifling through the records beneath a poster of *The French Connection,* actually resembled Gene Hackman in his Santa disguise at the beginning of that film. At any moment, he might burst out of the café and pursue some phantom drug dealer along the deserted promenade of St Vincent's on Sea.

Joni Mitchell's 'River' faded into 'A Case of You' and Michael took the postcard from his pocket and stared at it. The blank space reproached him, but how could he respond to Maddie's letter, now in softer perspective than the one inciting his initial anger? Perhaps it was his own wishful thinking, inspired by Joni Mitchell's plaintive heartbreak drifting from the jukebox, but the letter's kinder intimations, along with the memories which he tried his best to avoid, suddenly overwhelmed him.

Maddie's reference to Tommy wishing for Buzz Lightyear from Santa recalled that wonderful time just a few months ago, in Porthcawl. The afternoon at the cinema to see *Toy Story* and Tommy being Buzz Lightyear and Michael Mr Potato Head for the rest of the week. Racing with the boy on the go karts – 'no wonder you never took your test,' Maddie jibed as he blundered around the track, outwitted by Tommy's speed on the bends. Fishing in the rock pools, Tommy inspecting each small crab before placing it back in the rising waters. The twisting funfair ride that rattled and rolled its way around the amusement park like a giant trainset. The kite bursting inside out in the gale and diving earthward, Tommy in pursuit as it flapped across the sand.

He looked down at the waiting empty card in his hands. What did all this still mean? Was he, during that week of family seaside happiness, the kind of man Maddie wanted him to be? But what would be the point of recalling any of it now even if he could find the right phrases? The time for those words were back then in Porthcawl, or the weeks after when she wanted to hear them. Time had called on a summer affair in these final dark days of the year. But, despite his desire to indicate otherwise, he'd not moved on. Compelled to say at least something, in the end he wrote merely scraps of feeling that said hardly anything at all.

> Dear Maddie,
>
> Thank you for the letter. I'm glad to hear you are keeping well. Congratulations on your appointment as Head of Department.
>
> I'm so very sorry to hear about Derek. Please give him my love and keep me informed as to how he is, if you so wish.

PS. Hope Buzz Lightyear makes it home to Tommy this Christmas

Love,

Michael.

He was about to append, 'Alias Mr Potato Head', but then thought better of it.

When he looked up again, the man in the corner had finished his meal and was looking straight at him.

CHAPTER FOUR

'Any requests, Caz?' The Popeye Doyle look-a-like in the Santa suit asked the man in the corner still staring at Michael.

'Don't know, Vic, surprise me.'

'Well, in that case,' Vic replied, picking *Blonde on Blonde* from the rack and waving Bob Dylan's face on the album cover at Caz.

'Very funny, Vic. Thanks for the wind-up.'

'You averse to a little Mr Zimmerman in the late afternoon?'

'No, I'm averse to that cunt at Pennington with the same name.'

The trombone intro to 'Rainy Day Women' kicked in and Vic walked back to the kitchen, squeezing Caz's shoulder for a moment, muttering audibly in his ear, 'Take it easy, bud.'

'Yeah, sure,' said Caz, looking angry.

Despite Caz's and Vic's oblique references to Headmaster Dillon and Pennington it was impossible to square this haystack of a man sitting in the corner with the slender Steve Lawton that Michael remembered. Schoolboy Steve of firm chin always lightly adorned in a stubble as advanced as school regulations allowed, never shaved too often or too close as his acne would bleed. But the man mountain in the corner, beneath his full-length beard probably had so many chins and was so large there was no room on his side of the table for anyone else. Besides Student Steve never answered to the name of Caz. Having demolished this plate of pancakes, 'Caz' now pushed his plate away to roll himself a cigarette on the plastic tablecloth. Vic re-emerged from the back to bring Michael his coffee and turn the 'Open' sign around to 'Closed'.

'You're OK. No rush,' the man said to Michael. 'I just like to put the shutters up early this time of year, especially if my friend over there starts on the weed.' Caz blew a cloud of smoke into the air and waved.

Michael smiled as the aroma of cannabis drifted across the room from the corner.

'School's out now. Are you ready for the road tomorrow, man?' the owner asked Caz, walking back to the big man's table.

'Yeah, I suppose. Remind me, where's the first gig again?'

'Darkest Morecambe.'

'Followed by? Don't tell me, Carnegie Hall?'

'Even darker Barrow on Furness.'

'Hardly the Worldwide Tour is it? Can't see Scorsese filming it.'

'You never know – White Rhino – the Cumbrian Coastal Tour – could go down in legend. *NME, Rolling Stone,* queuing up for exclusives.'

'Yeah, I can hear the interview now: You played the West Coast. That's so cool. Monterey? Carmel? No, Morecambe and Carlisle.'

'We're a local band, Caz.'

'And that's what we'll always be. We need some decent PR.'

'Yeah, the latest buzzword.'

'It's not one word, Vic, it's two. Public Relations.'

'Says the master of marketing. Naming us after an endangered species.'

'Captures our essence, don't you think,' said Caz, smiling over at Michael. And the more he spoke the more Michael began to see the Lawton of schooldays emerging.

'Yes, White Rhino, big, ugly, and slow-moving,' said Vic.

'Full of tragic unbowed dignity.'

'And pancakes.'

Caz looked off into space for a moment and then over at Michael and called, 'What do you think, man?'

'About what, sorry?'

'The name of our band, White Rhino'?

Michael paused, about to say, 'Better than White Elephant,' but thought that might come across as a sly reference to Caz's bulk. Instead, he just gave a thumbs up.

'Sorry, man, but do I know you from somewhere?' said Caz, and as he smiled the beard faded and the extra weight fell away to reveal the hidden younger version Michael knew.

'I think you might,' he said. 'Is it Steve, by any chance?'

Caz and Vic both looked at each other. Vic replied with both hands stretched out in a ceremony of display, 'This is the very man. Steve 'Caz' Lawton – lead singer with White Rhino.'

Michael headed towards the corner of the café and sat

down and offered his hand.

'Hi, Steve, I'm Michael Freeman. We used to be at school together.'

'Fuck me, I knew it.'

'Listen guys, I'm done with food for the day. Just coffee now if you want it,' said Vic, taking off the apron and the hat. Only the red, grease-stained trousers remained of Popeye Doyle as he headed back to the kitchen area where he began clearing up.

'Michael Freeman, the man who disappeared,' Lawton smiled reaching out his hand to Michael.'

'Hi, Steve.'

'It's Caz. As in Fidel, as in Castro,' he said, laughing, stroking his beard, staring in wonder at Michael.

'Oh, OK, Caz.'

'Freeman. Far out.' Lawton shook his head in disbelief.

'This is a great place. The music, the posters,' said Michael, trying to deflect from this much warmer welcome than he anticipated. Maybe it was the cannabis but Lawton seemed quite emotional.

'I helped Vic set it up – wrote the sign out there as well. Apostrophe all over the place, apparently. You can tell I teach Geography can't you.' He shook his head and smiled. 'Michael Freeman. Wow. You were my fucking hero back then,' he said, sitting back in his chair to reveal the full expanse of midriff. 'Went out East, didn't you? Kabul? Or was it a beach in Goa?'

Michael had no idea what Lawton was talking about. The sickly-sweet smell of cannabis hung in the air, an unwelcome memory of those days. A memory that did include a beach, but not in Goa. A beach much nearer home.

'Oh, yes. Out East,' he said, considering it better to play along for the moment.

'So radical what you did, man. Just dropping out like that. What you up to these days?'

'Oh, this and that, doing research.'

'Wow, eternal student. What you researching?'

'Er, the research? It's not very interesting.' He could see Vic through the hatch moving around in the kitchen, and said the first thing that came into his head. 'The movies of Gene Hackman.'

'Gene Hackman? Lex Luthor, wasn't he?' said Lawton.

'Among other things.'

'What's the one where the girl has her head taken totally clean off by a seaplane?'

'*Night Moves.* Ends with the dead girl in the water and Hackman with a busted arm steering a boat around in circles.'

'Awesome,' Lawton said, looking suddenly lost, his eyes glazing over as if trying to focus on some distant, forlorn space. 'Steering in circles, going nowhere. Just like life, eh.'

Vic appeared briefly to top up the coffee from a pot, before parting again with, 'Don't let Caz bum you out about his shitty job. You'll be slashing your wrists listening to him.'

'I've been to Pennington. Just this morning,' Michael said.

Lawton nodded and smiled. 'It was you then.'

'Me?'

'Yes, you, the one who showed up there asking for me.'

'How do you know?'

'My inside man. Young Davies. He came to see me at Final Assembly.'

'That poor kid got clobbered by the Head.'

'You've met the Dildo?'

'Bob Dillon? Yes. He nearly pulled that lad's ear off just for talking to me.'

Lawton shook his head as his eyes narrowed and lips tightened in anger. 'What a bastard. Davies tipped you off about this place?' he said.

'Yes, never expected to find you though.'

'I thought it was you when you walked in. Those glasses. They haven't changed in nearly thirty years. Joe 90.'

'The kids at Pennington thought I was Penfold.'

Caz laughed. 'What the fuck were you doing at Pennington anyway?'

'I don't know – I just thought I'd pop back and take a look. It's the first time since way back... It's not the same.'

Lawton drew deeply on the last of the joint, sucking the air into his lungs and holding it there until his face began to change colour. But the weed didn't mellow his mood.

'Independent now, mate. Three years since that happened. Turned it from a struggling comp with a soul into a fucking business. Ripped the heart out of the place along with most of the buildings.'

'It looked like one big construction site. I got lost in it all.'

'Final nail in the coffin was when they sold off the playing fields to the same fucker who's digging up the beach.'

'I noticed that – bulldozers all over the sands.'

'Yeah, and you'll never guess who's behind it.'

'Who?'

'The prick who used to pontificate in class. Used to get up your nose with all the Marxist bullshit.'

'You don't mean...? Not...March?'

'The very same.'

'Dave March?'

'Mao Tse Tung March. Don't think you and him saw eye to eye back then, if I remember.'

Lawton nodded. David March. Michael recalled David March alright. His radical rants, his ultra-cool demeanour, his rebel chic with Laura looking on, entranced and adoring. Yes, he remembered March. His politics, his maturity, his command of language, his theft of Laura's heart. But most of all he remembered the despair and chaos he caused in Michael's life.

'King of the fucking capitalists now,' Lawton continued. 'Lives down South but he's back here at St Vincent's as well. He's got a weird, creepy place amongst the sand dunes. Can't live in a normal house like everyone else. Gives him great views of the shoreline he's carving up.'

'Why is he interested in this god forsaken place? Big shot like him, thought he'd be long gone by now.' He realised too late this sounded like a judgement on Lawton who was far from long gone from Pennington School and St Vincent's on Sea.

But, more intent on airing his grievances, Caz didn't seem to notice. 'He's a hand here in everything. The council, the Pennington School Board of Governors. Got some scheme buying up public land for private development. Selling sand to Saudi Arabia for fuck's sake.'

'Why the hell do Saudis need more sand?' Michael could feel his own ancient animosity for March returning.

'God knows. Glass-making, foundries, all manner of shit they don't want to waste their own stuff on.'

'And the playing fields at Pennington? They're all churned up as well. Such a horrible mess.'

'New leisure development. Cabins, leisure-park, log flume.'

'Don't tell me March's behind that too?'

'Yeah, he even turns up at school, comes into classes, snoops around looking through the kids' books. He came to one of the Rhino gigs the other week, dressed like one of the students, with some Bosnian girlfriend half his age in tow. Told me not to give up the day job just yet. Overbearing twat.'

'But, how can that be the same Dave March? He was…'

'Well, yeah, I know – Che Guevara. Now he's carving up the home town for profit.'

Vic returned with a plate of chocolate brownies. 'Here guys,' he said, 'on the house.'

'Are these what your sister made?' Lawton said.

'No, they're brownie through and through.'

'Hey, Vic, you wouldn't believe who this guy here is. Michael Freeman. Dropped out of school way back when and went to India somewhere. Total legend. The Kwai Chang Caine of Pennington.'

'Awesome, man. Caz here could use some spiritual guidance,' Vic replied, before disappearing once more into the kitchen.

Meanwhile, Michael struggled to make sense of all this. There was David March who once wanted to blow up the world for the revolution now returned as free market privateer, asset stripping his home town. And then what was all this from Lawton about Michael taking it to the limit, way out there in Goa and Afghanistan stuff? The furthest East Michael had been back then was Scarborough. Lawton looked suddenly spent with his outburst over March. His mind seemed to be drifting as his attention turned to rolling another joint.

'Kwai Chang Caine actually went west,' Michael said, to break the silence. 'Or maybe he did go east, because he travelled from China to the American West, which would, technically, have been east.' He realised he was rambling.

'Yes but while I was watching the TV series you were living the life.'

It didn't seem a right time to point out to Lawton that none of this was remotely true. Besides Michael was actually quite enjoying this undeserved hero worship. He'd almost forgotten why he was there – to find out about Soames.

'Am I going to fail a dope test if I have one of these?' he said reaching across for the tray of brownies.

'No, they're kosher,' Lawton winked at him, and they silently munched away on the cakes. The conversation seemed to be running dry again, given Michael's inability to offer any details of his non-existent teenage adventures on the hippy trail, when Caz presented an opportunity he'd been waiting for.

'Glad you dropped in on us at Pennington, man,' said Lawton. 'Sorry I wasn't around and you got third degreed by the Dildo. Just how did you know I was teaching there?'

'Newspaper article. About Gilbert Soames.'

Lawton shook his head. 'Soames. Sad, sad business. You've heard...'

'I don't know any more than was in the paper.'

'Poor guy. It's not him to blame, it's the illness. And the bastards who have driven him insane.'

'Mr Soames is ill?'

'Manic depression. It's got worse recently. Struggled for years. For a long time, no one knew, apart from his wife. By the time I landed my job there, he was already beginning to melt down or burn out.'

'He was always so...' Michael struggled for words...'together.' It was hard to imagine Soames melting or burning.

'Wait a minute,' Lawton said, examining the brownie in his hand. 'The Afghan Black darkens the chocolate. Fuck, that's the really good stuff you're eating.'

'You said they were...'

'Oops,' said Lawton. 'Got you there, man.' Lawton burst out laughing. Michael looked at the brownie, shrugged, and stuffed the rest into his mouth.

'You were saying...' Michael said. Doctored brownie or not he wanted to keep Lawton focused, get him back on track. 'About Soames...'

'Oh, yeah. Such a shame. It doesn't help that Dave March hates him.'

'How do you mean?'

'You remember, surely, back when we were students there, how March got expelled? Blamed Soames.'

'Expelled?'

'Oh, yeah of course, you weren't there were you? You were lost somewhere out in Samarkand.'

'Yeah... but why was March expelled?'

'It was something to do with that chick you were with. And old man Soames.'

'Laura?' It felt strange, speaking her name out loud, for the first time in many years. The last time he was with her he was really stoned then. More than stoned – deliriously trapped in a waking nightmare of paranoia and dread.

As if summoned by Laura's name and memory, Dylan's ghostly, surreal 'Visions of Johanna' kicked in on the jukebox. The fibre optic tree in Lawton's corner began to glow and take on a vibrant life of its own, blooming and reaching across the table with pinpoints and tentacles of light. Flashbacks of a malevolent cheese plant that overwhelmed him in Laura's lounge on that awful long distant October afternoon, threatened his concentration.

'Yeah, her,' Lawton continued. 'She was the one who told us you'd gone away, a long, long way away. Said you were in some blissed-out commune out on the hippy trail. You left a real shitstorm behind. Some rumours went around that you'd taken an overdose. What the fuck *did* happen to you out there, man?'

The brownies were dragging his thinking out of kilter. And Lawton kept pulling the conversation around to this. Despite the fact he badly wanted to get back to the topic of Soames, Laura and March, he realised Lawton wouldn't be satisfied until he made something up, no matter how ridiculous. He vaguely remembered a distant James Ivory movie he'd seen back in the seventies in a deserted cinema on the St Vincent seafront. *The Guru*, about a failed pop star in search of a Zen master.

'Er, I landed in Benares – nothing but me and my guitar. Found a hippy commune there run by a maharishi.'

'I never knew you played. Wow man, what a dark horse.'

'Er, just strummed a few chords. Nothing in your league.' This was obviously a mistake and he needed to change the subject fast. 'But you say there was a major scandal after I left?'

'A maharishi? Like him the Beatles fell out with?'

'Don't remember. I was out of it most of the time. It's all a blur...' He couldn't remember any more of that wretched film now, nor did he want to. 'Anyway...as you were saying... back then at Pennington?'

Lawton, disappointed at Michael's reticence needed further prompting.

'I'm really interested in this, Caz. I missed out on all of this stuff way back then. Soames meant a lot to me. He still does.'

Lawton seemed mournful, but his anger was returning. 'He means a lot to me too. I love that guy.'

'So, can you tell me what happened after I left? I know it's a long time ago. But you're the only one who can tell me all the things I missed back then. It's kind of important to me.'

'Patience, amigo,' he said, licking the papers to finish rolling the joint. 'It all kind of fits in with what's just happened.'

'How do you mean?'

'March's grudge against Gilbert. Why he's driven the poor guy over the edge.' He took the joint, even bigger and fatter than the last and lit it, inhaling deeply, before continuing. 'Back then, while you were on Nirvana Beach with the maharishi, there was a great big crackdown at Pennington. Laura and March suspected of all kinds of stuff.'

'Like what?'

'All hush-hush. Some bad karma going down and March was kicked out. I saw him one time and he vowed he'd get even with Soames one day.'

'Why?'

'I don't know exactly. But there was also something to do with Laura and the girl that Soames finished up marrying.'

'Which girl? Who was that?'

'You remember Joan?'

'Joan in our class? Joan Turner?'

'Yeah, she's devoted to him. If it wasn't for her, Soames would've gone under years ago. They married soon after she graduated.'

'Soames married Joan?'

'No biggy in their case. They kept in touch after she left Pennington to go to university. After they wed, she came back and taught at the school for a while. Eventually she left and kind of dedicated herself to Gilbert. Kept him from going under.'

Joan Turner, kind, decent Joan, Michael's friend back then, always doted on Soames. Michael couldn't imagine her ever getting involved with March. She thoroughly despised him. The December dark outside, the soft light interior of the café, the pungent aroma of weed curling through the air and mingling with fibre-optics pluming through the spectrum, all worked their spell as he leaned further in across the table towards Lawton. Past and present blended into each other like the colours passing across the plastic tablecloth onto the whitewashed walls behind Lawton's chair.

'Steve, Caz, you say March had it in for Soames back then – something to do with Joan and Laura?'

'No, no one ever really knew. Soames just mentioned to me once that something happened back then to one of the girls.'

'He told you while you were there as a student?'

'No, later, when I was staff.'

'To one of the girls? Which girl?'

'Not sure.'

'Did he say what it was?'

Lawton shrugged. 'Again, don't know. Soames wouldn't tell me.'

He felt on the verge of discovering something, then losing it again amidst the haze of cannabis and shifting timelines.

'So, why was March expelled from Pennington?'

'The Head found a stash of drugs in March's locker. Kicked him out of the school straight away. March ranted on about how it was all Soames' fault. None of it made any sense.'

'And what happened to Laura?'

'You never knew? She came through it all with flying colours, got her place at Cambridge and, I suppose, just made one great fucking success of her life.'

There it was, suddenly, the shock of that lost world, that life that Soames had laid out for him. This might've been Michael's life with Laura. One glorious step into the future after another, Cambridge together, a brilliant career, marriage and family, instead of the path he took, or was taken for him – the dead-end jobs, the teaching disaster at Barton, on the scrapheap at forty-three.

Lawton looked back at the kitchen. Vic had finished clearing up and was switching off the lights in the back. There wasn't much time left to find out more.

'Last week, the night Soames disappeared, the paper...said you were the last person to see him before....'

Michael hesitated and Lawton was silent for a few moments, a deep sadness haunting his features. Finally he continued, 'That's right. I gave him a lift home. I didn't watch him go into the house, which I should've. Really should've.'

'You weren't to know he'd disappear.'

'I don't know. I knew he was close to breakdown. It was the last night of the show. I'd been working backstage and he'd been getting weirder as the week went on.'

'How do you mean?'

'More and more hyper. We were doing *The Tempest* and the guy playing Prospero went off sick. So Gilbert stepped in and took on the part. I think the stress tipped him over the edge. He got a little too much into character.'

'He always did enjoy centre stage.'

'Yeah, man, but he was on a real power trip. Impossible to deal with and it was touch and go whether the cast and crew would stick with it.'

'But you did?'

'Yeah, we weren't going to let those bastards get the better of Gilbert,' Lawton said, his mouth tightening with tension.'

'You mean the cast? The crew? Which bastards?'

Lawton shook his head. 'We all knew Dillon and March wanted Gilbert to crash and burn. A reason to get rid of him, especially if it happened in public. So, we hung in there to stop that happening. Soames just about managed to keep it together. But when it came to the last night curtain call March stands up and makes a speech about how the production's just another stunning achievement by him and Dillon to turn the school around. No mention of Soames or the weeks he spent rehearsing the kids, painting the set, taking the main part. Meanwhile Gilbert's seething backstage and I'm trying to calm him down. He was in a bad way'

'Did he mention going away or anything?'

'No, but he was talking weird – saying he had something on March and it was about time the world knew.'

'What was it?'

'He wouldn't tell me, said it would involve me in heavy shit – best if I didn't know, for now. It stresses me out just to think about it all.'

'Did you believe him? About March?'

'I don't know. He was totally manic, wasn't making that much sense. I don't think he'd been taking his meds. On the way home he wanted to get out at the end of the street. Feel so bad about not seeing him to the door, man.'

'Where do you think he is?'

'Fuck knows. I'm really worried about him. I hope he hasn't done anything stupid.' Lawton settled back, slumping in his chair, and took another cake before handing the tray to Michael.

'Better not,' Michael said. 'These days two brownies my limit. Can I ask you one more thing? It's a long shot?'

'Sure. To be honest, it's good to talk to someone about this. Someone who, you know, is from back then, who understands.'

'It's just another question about Soames. I've just found out he came to see me years ago to tell me something, but I never found out what it was. Did he ever say anything to you about me?'

'About you? Er, no, sorry, man. You'd disappeared off the face of the earth. Who knows though with Gilbert? He came to see you? Where?'

'At my mother's. After I left. My mum never told me he'd been to see me until now. And with him disappearing and everything I've been wondering what it was he wanted to say.'

'Sorry can't help you there. Look, man, if you want to find out more why don't you look up Joan?'

'Joan?'

'Yeah Joan, his wife.'

'Do you really think she'd want to see someone like me? I mean she's probably got enough on her plate at the moment.'

'Joan always liked you. I keep in touch with her. But I'm away on the road next few days and she needs some company at the moment. She'd be cool if you showed.'

'I'm not sure she'd even remember me.'

'You…? Course she would. You're Michael Freeman.'

'Do you know the address?'

'They both still live in that house Soames rented all those years ago.'

'That big old place. I used to go there for extra seminars.'

'Oh, yeah, I remember, you were one of the Oxbridge golden boys.'

Vic emerged from the kitchen again. 'Sorry, closing time now guys,' he said.

'Freeman's looking up old connections,' Lawton replied. 'Putting the pieces together. Aren't you, buddy? Like Gene Hackman in *Night Moves*.'

'Just trying to understand what's happened to our friend.'

Vic just handed Michael a card. 'Hey, man. If you don't re-connect with your guy you could do worse than come to our gig.' Michael looked at the card: White Rhino Saturday 20th Dec, The Nag's Head, Morecambe. 'And even if you don't make it there then maybe Barrow-on Furness on Sunday.'

'Yeah,' said Lawton, raising his colossal frame and half pushing the table over in the process. 'You could bring your guitar.'

'Guitar?'

'The one you took to Benares?'

'Oh, I lost that on the road. Haven't played in years.'

Well, we could always plug you back in, man.'

Michael nodded uneasily and then shook hands with Vic as Caz sidled around to Michael and embraced him.

'Great to see you, man. Keep the faith. It's taken a load off just sharing. I'll let Joan know I've seen you and that you're heading over some time. She needs all the help she can get at the moment,' Lawton said, before collapsing back into his seat, exhausted but looking relieved at unburdening his story to someone who would listen at last.

CHAPTER FIVE

When he left, the evening breeze along the promenade was icy cold but welcoming after the cannabis and smoke-tainted atmosphere of the café. The stars scattered over the dark canopy above the sands and the clear skies promised a hard frost for the night ahead. At a postbox he took out the card to Maddie and, after a moment's hesitation, dispatched it and stood still a moment, listening to the sound of it fluttering like the last leaf of summer in the empty chamber.

As he made his way home, the effects of the cannabis wore off along with the brief excitement he felt hearing more of Soames' story. After posting the card the hopelessness of the situation with Maddie merged with other gloomy reflections on how everyone's life had moved on while his had remained stuck. David March's enterprise, achievements, and vast wealth were hard to bear. And Soames' defiance and rebellion against the establishment at Pennington made Michael's own pathetic walkout at Barton, followed by a return home to his mother, feeble by comparison. Soames had found someone to love and support him through all this – kind, sweet, thoughtful Joan who stood by him through thick and thin. Even Lawton had kept the fire burning with his rock star dream. Things had turned out alright for Laura too. Another path he'd missed along the way – Cambridge and a world of success, a world that could have been his. Instead of this world, a failed teacher with no prospects, his future washed up in a dead end seaside town in winter.

He thought of the fascinating person he'd pretended to be in front of Lawton – the romantic dropout who went East. He had lied to his mother, and he'd lied back in the café about his research and with all that nonsense about the hippy trail, the guitar and Benares. But it was surprisingly easy to lie once you got going. And with these retreats into fantasy, he felt himself drifting further and further away from a sense of who he really was. But then, who was he really? Maddie's son, Tommy, called him Mr Potato Head – a child's innocent comment that revealed a truth of what he probably had always been – a character of composites, a bits and pieces person, fragments of a self, cobbled together from movies and books.

These sad reflections, however, dissolved when he rounded the corner to his mother's house and was taken aback by what confronted him – Joe's van still parked outside. Why had the plumber not gone home by now? But his irritation soon gave way to more sinister thoughts as he reached the garden path where the vehicle's abandoned nature, parked crookedly across the drive, and the van's logo with a man holding a large spanner took on disturbing implications. His mother never entertained any man and he'd been gone hours and left her at the mercy of a complete stranger. The curtains were drawn, behind them the lights were on in the lounge, the Christmas tree flickered, but there was no sound of TV or conversation. He turned his key in the front door quietly and entered, taking off his shoes as a matter of habit, but retaining one in his hand as a weapon. Everything seemed normal enough in the hallway, nicely warmed by the central heating, the corridor illuminated by the standard lamp in the corner. However, the silence was unsettling, and, up above, the landing and bathroom were in darkness.

'Hello,' he called out from the bottom of the stairs, but there was no answer. 'Hello, mum,' he called again, a little louder this time. He opened the door to the lounge and peered in. She was lying slumped in the chair with her head arched back at an unnatural angle, mouth wide open and face deathly white. He dropped the shoe and rushed to her side, taking her by the shoulders and shaking her. She jolted into life with screams, choking coughs and gasps, then flailing her arms while at the same time lunging forward, struggling for breath. Eventually she sat back slumped in the chair, very red in the face, tears streaming from her eyes as she heaved great gulps of air.

'Mum, it's alright, it's only me.'

Unable to speak, she pushed him away and he rushed to get a glass of water. On the kitchen draining board there were two glasses, both unwashed with the ruby liquid remnants lining the bottom, and on the table was the annual Christmas sherry bottle three quarters empty. When he got back, she looked a little more normal.

'What on earth are you doing? Trying to kill me?' she said, still breathing heavily while snatching the water from him.

'I'm sorry, I thought you were....'

'What? Having a nap? Could've had a heart attack with you jiggling me around like that.'

'Where is he?'

'Where is who, for god's sake?'

'You know, *him*, the plumber.'

'You mean Joe? He left hours ago.'

'But his van's still here.'

She paused, looking sheepishly at her watch. 'We had a few drinks. And he had to leave it. He says he'll pick it up in the morning.'

It was Michael's turn to feel indignant, the bitterness

he felt about his life on his walk home spilling over into irritation.

'What's going on? He came here to fix the toilet and you finish up have a drinking session with him. He could be anybody.'

'Don't be ridiculous.'

'I'm not being ridiculous. You've opened the Christmas sherry, fed the mince pies, to a total stranger.'

'There are mince pies left if you want one.'

'That's not the point. You never make them until Christmas Eve and serve them up then. It's been that way for years. And now this stranger comes along, laughs at my repair job, parks himself on the sofa and you run around after him like he's some long lost relative.'

'Aren't I allowed to have a little fun? You weren't here were you, so fat lot of good *you* would have been if he *had* been Jack the Ripper.'

Relieved that she was looking better, he sat down. But he was still annoyed about Joe.

'Well, where were you while this time? she said.

'I met an old school friend.'

She looked at him warily. 'Oh yes, who might that be?'

'Steve Lawton. He was in my class that last year at Pennington.'

'I know. I remember. What were you up to meeting with him?'

'I didn't meet with him, well, actually I went looking for him, after I went back to the school this morning.'

She looked concerned. 'Oh no, what did you want to go back there for after all these years? I hope you're not stirring anything up. We don't want any more of that, do we?'

77

'I wanted to see Lawton. I was curious.'

'Curious? That's exactly what I mean – raking things up. First the newspaper article, then heading back to that school.'

'I just wonder what's happened to Soames.'

'It's none of your business. All that happened a long time ago.'

'No, it didn't, mum, he only went missing last week.'

'That's not what I mean, and you know it.'

'Lawton thinks Dave March has something to do with it.'

'David March? That awful boy who was the drug dealer?'

'Yes, but he's not...never mind. He's back in town now. Very rich and Chairman of the Board of Governors. Lawton thinks he's driven Soames away, or worse.'

'I don't want to know. And neither should you.'

'Lawton's a good guy. He's Soames' friend.'

She began to look flustered again and he realised he should've just told her the afternoon was spent on his research. But in the mood for an argument, he'd wanted to annoy her.

'I've told you, no good will come of this, Michael,' she said. 'You getting involved with these people. You have your own life, your own job and career now. The past is the past and there's nothing there for you.' She got up to leave.

He wanted to call after her – What life? What career? What future? This was it – here in this room bickering with her. Chewing the fat with Lawton, reliving the past, and even his visit to the old school, amounted to the most exciting experience he'd had in weeks.

'Do you want some tea?' his mother asked, now

standing by the kitchen door. 'And maybe a mince pie?' she added sarcastically.

'Yes, please,' he said, before adding, 'Sorry I was late.'

'By the way, he wasn't.'

'Wasn't what?'

'He wasn't Jack the Ripper.'

'Who?'

'Joe. He was nice.'

'Sorry for being an idiot,' he said. 'You're right. He seems a decent enough guy.'

That evening, as Michael lay in his room, he pondered on why he'd reacted so badly, so mean-spiritedly to Joe's presence. No, worse than that, he'd been suspicious, paranoid even. Armed himself with a shoe for a weapon just because his mother had entertained someone, another man, for an afternoon. Maybe he shouldn't have eaten the brownies. But he knew the cannabis wasn't to blame. Was this what he was becoming? St Vincent's answer to Norman Bates, possessively jealous of his mother's company? And weren't he and his mother both as bad as each other – she reacting with equal hostility to his interest in Soames and Lawton? Were they driving each other mad? The strange noises, the fear of outsiders, the terror of the past, the secrecy. Both locked indoors, a couple of obsessives closing down on life until they lived in fear of their own four walls. He needed to get away. But where? Back to Barton after Christmas and the classroom, watching Maddie every day with Rick Campbell or someone else? Teaching those awful kids once more after he'd made such a fool of himself? That seemed a prospect even worse than going mad with mother.

The afternoon with Lawton had offered an escape from all this, a distraction beyond these four walls, a world of intrigue at Pennington. He'd enjoyed his old school colleague's warm welcome, although it did seem to be based on a totally mythical version of who he was. But even that had been exciting – to pretend to be someone else for a short while. Someone who evoked mystery and excitement and was still remembered by Pennington and the people there. His pulse quickened at the thought of Laura, and of her friend Joan, as he tried to assemble some picture of what had happened there in the past and in the recent days leading up to Soames' vanishing act.

It was clear that Soames remained highly regarded by some of the staff and his students – Lawton, the Davies boy, those who'd supported him through the production of *The Tempest*. But equally there was a strong element amongst management who wanted him out. March evidently had his own reasons, dating back to his time as Soames' student – details of which were unclear but involved a long-standing vendetta between the two of them. Soames' claim to have damning evidence on March and his possible threat of disclosure may have provided March with another reason for wishing to see the back of him. Pressure of work, his persecution by management at school, his mental instability, had probably all contributed to his disappearance. But did this also connect in one way or another to something in the past regarding Laura and Joan and what March had done to one of the girls back then? All this brought back memories Michael could never bury despite years of trying – his own last disastrous days at Pennington caught up in his love for Laura, her hypnotic influence on his life that he still felt. What part had she played in what had happened back then? Was she March's purported victim or was it Joan? Furthermore, why had she concocted that ridiculous story about Michael leaving for the hippy trail and beyond? There were many unanswered riddles from that time, about March, Soames, Laura, Joan, and underlying it all, his own secrets and betrayals. Did any of this ultimately have something to do with what Soames came to tell Michael all those years ago?

He looked up at the shelf above his bed to the teenage journal. Maybe within those pages were some answers to be found from that time long gone and yet now so dramatically brought near at hand. For many years he'd been afraid to read of those days, afraid of the memories, afraid to confront the young man whose dreams blossomed for a brief moment and then so disastrously died. But his meeting with Lawton, his confrontation with Dillon, the news Soames had once been to this house to see him, all these released something locked away for years. There had been too much hidden, too much avoided and buried. He took the leather-bound volume from the shelf, and as the letter from Maddie and then her photograph fell out of the journal into his hands, for once, he put these to one side. Instead, he turned the pages back to a time when a different path lay before him and a teacher showed him the way.

CHAPTER SIX

Monday 21st June 1971

Dear Mr Soames,

'Write,' you said. 'You have to, Michael, because that's who you are. You have talent. Why wait for someone to give you permission to use it?'

It was like a lightbulb going on in my head. But I couldn't speak. I just stood there and nodded. I had told you I wanted to write, but I never thought you or anyone else would take me seriously. Until now.

I was silent today when you said those magical words. These letters, Mr Soames, are my answer. I know you'll never read them. But maybe you *will* see them one day, the day I'm famous that is, and you'll discover you were the only one who believed in me. The only one who really knew what I wanted to be.

My life as a writer.

And where to start, but here. Make it happen, you said. Make your dream happen.

Maybe the reason I'm always dreaming of writing is because, away from the dream, real life is so confusing. Here I am, torn between two futures, struggling to make friends, longing for Laura. But in these pages, I can make sense of it all.

But where then to begin?

Maybe with yesterday and you, Mr Soames, and your insistence that I apply for Cambridge. When I arrive home to tell mum and dad I'm an Oxbridge candidate.

Dad immediately insists I apply to read Law. I'm not sure this is right for me. So, I take to my room and write this in secret and here, alone, as I've said, try to make sense of things.

Because more and more at home and at school, apart from my time with you, your lessons and our talks, I feel I don't belong anywhere.

Take today for instance. We're waiting for you to arrive to take the class and David March and Laura are talking about a pop concert down south over the weekend. They're holding hands across the desk, Laura gazing at him in adoration. To take my mind off this, I ask Roland Beacon what he's doing over the summer and he's going to help his father in the parish. He wants to bring the Holy Spirit to the community.

So, while David and Laura are talking about sex and drugs at a rock concert, I'm listening to Beacon's godly mission and he goes on and on, until David says, 'You joining the Jesus freaks then, Michael?' Laura's laugh hurts far more than David's sarcastic remark.

I can't think of a reply and Joan Turner says, 'It's more interesting than listening to you going on about Hawkwind.'

Poor Beacon blushes as usual and goes quiet. But I envy him though, in a way. At least he looks like a complete outsider, like a middle-aged man in a school tie.

I'm an outsider but I don't look or feel like anything.

Even here at home.

I need to talk to you about the Cambridge application

and dad's wishes.

Sunday 27th June 1971

Dear Mr Soames,

Walk home thinking of Hank Quinlan floating away on a tide of sewage and Marlene Dietrich's final words about him. I want to stay behind and discuss the film with you.

But you're talking to Laura and David March.

Are you avoiding me because I told you I have to apply to do Law at Cambridge?

I can't talk to my father. As far as he's concerned it's already decided. No discussion needed.

I wish I could explain it to you, why I can't talk to dad. But I don't really know why myself. Is it because I am just a coward? Meanwhile dad is telling his friends all about his son at Cambridge studying to be a barrister. And in a strange way I am happy that I make him so proud of me.

I'm late for the Sunday night screening at school because I've been washing dishes to help mum.

Dad says, 'Michael will make someone a lovely wife,' and he laughs but later I hear him telling mum she shouldn't let me do woman's work.

I'm worried about being late because it's your last Sunday night film for this term, and you told us not to miss this one – Orson Welles' film noir masterpiece *Touch of Evil*

So I'm just about there on time but the room's already dark with the projector counting the black and white numbers down from 10 to 1, on 3 by the time I find a seat at the end of one of the rows. But Steve Lawton stops me and says the seat's taken. But on the chair are just the two LPs he's had tucked under his arm all this last week – *The Court of the Crimson King* and *The Five Bridges Suite.* These albums are more important to Lawton than people.

At the end of the film, you talk about Welles' tracking shot that opens the picture which I missed as I was still busy tracking down a seat. It takes me a good while to concentrate on any of the film at all because I finally find a place right behind Laura and David. She has her head on his shoulder which gives me a clear view of the screen, once I stop watching them.

As you know David talks constantly of revolution, daily arguments with teachers about his hair, his shoes, his non-existent tie, Laura backing him up, always on his side. She looks at me these days with a kind of sympathy, like a loyal pet dog. I could say to her – hey I'm part of the revolution too – a real women's libber doing my mum's dishes. She might laugh but then she might think I'm being serious. Which I suppose I am, because it's true.

When the film ends Laura turns and sees me on the row behind and looks for a moment as if she hardly knows me. It's always a shock to see her out of uniform. Red hair flowing down around her shoulders, cheesecloth blouse, her breasts beneath, possibly no bra. Will she go back and have sex with David somewhere after this?

That's why walking home it's easier to think about the end of the film and Quinlan's body floating in the water than Laura's head on David's shoulder, why she no longer wants to be my friend, why all three of you laughed at what David said when I came up to speak to you.

Does it matter what people say when you can't hear it? Is it worse because you can imagine what it was?

Thursday July 1st 1971

Dear Mr Soames,

In class today you don't want to discuss my point that Hamlet is trying to be a different kind of man from his father. Have I really upset you? I don't know what to do to put it right.

You seem bored. A man of your genius and calibre must get tired of contact with lesser minds. You ask us what we thought of *Touch of Evil*. Lawton just talks of how the soundtrack needed some Pink Floyd. It's pointless telling him the film was made ten years before Floyd existed. He thinks history began when Dylan went electric.

But this gets David going about the Floyd soundtrack to *Zabriskie Point*. How, after seeing the movie he wanted to drive out into the desert. Blow things up. Fuck the system and then some woman.

'Do you mean fuck metaphorically or literally?' you ask him.

David says he means it both ways.

'Isn't having sex while buildings are being blown to pieces mindlessly nihilistic,' you say.

And David says, that is the *whole* point.

Laura then says, 'You can't have sex without something being destroyed.' I don't know whether she means it personally for David or it's a general comment.

Then there's that special smile you save for her. 'What a pity you think that way,' you say and she blushes.

'Laura's just pissed off because I didn't take her to see the film,' David says.

'Does someone have the soundtrack?' says Lawton,

'If someone brings it in, I'll hire the record player,' you say.

David says he can get hold of a copy and the room buzzes with Lawton, David and you discussing *Atom Heart*

Mother and whether Sid Barrett will ever return. I have nothing to say. My thoughts on Hamlet long forgotten.

When I tell dad about this later, he says that you're too familiar with us all. That you're trying too hard to be liked. That you're typical of the arty-farty teaching types these days filling young people's heads with nonsense.

Friday July 2nd 1971

Dear Mr Soames,

Today you stop me in the corridor and hand me a copy of *Bleak House*.

'Some summer reading for you to prepare yourself for the entrance paper. Read it to see what the Law does to people,' you say.

I look up and you shift to the side as the light from the windows behind throws your frame into relief. I'm at ground level looking up at a silhouette.

'Can you give me one good reason for this intention of yours to read Law rather than literature at university?' You sound annoyed.

I say what dad says, 'The law's good for career prospects. A secure profession.'

'No doubt, but life isn't a distant planet, Michael, a future that may or may not happen. Life is here and now, and who you are in that moment. And *you*, my friend, are a writer.'

Then you smile, and put your arm around me: 'Remember, Polonius. I know he's a bit of an old windbag, but his advice to his son is sound: To thine own self be true.'

But the problem is, Mr Soames, and I've been thinking more about this, thinking about it a lot. What is this self to which I should be true?

I think of dad and his idea of who I am. And it's not who *you* think I am.

But *who* am I? Who do *I* think I am?

Tuesday July 6th 1971

Dear Mr Soames,

Dad catches me reading your copy of *A Farewell to Arms*. He takes the novel from my hands and flicks through the pages.

'Are you enjoying this?' he says.

'Yes,' I say. 'I've just read the chapter where he's wounded.'

'And you enjoyed that did you? Why would anyone want to read about that? Why would anyone want to write about that?'

He rarely talks about the war, but I think he's going to say something then about his time in Burma. But instead he hands the book back to me.

'Hemingway blew his brains out, didn't he?' he says. 'Might have been different if he'd had to get up every morning of his life and do an honest day's work.'

Thursday July 8th 1971

Dear Mr Soames,

You're always late and stuff happens while we're waiting.

'I was just trying to cheer you up,' Lawton says.

'He's dead. Please don't try and fucking cheer me up,' David replies.

Lawton's been playing 'LA Woman' on an imaginary keyboard on the desk. Jim Morrison died two days ago and he and David are both depressed.

Lawton then nudges David and says, 'Wait I can hear Beacon coming.' Roland Beacon wears these shiny black shoes with leather soles that clomp along the hard corridors and can be heard for miles in advance. With his immaculate grey suit and even shorter back and sides than usual he's like someone straight out of The Forsyte Saga.

David asks him if he's upset about Jim Morrison.

'Jim who?' says Beacon.

David pauses, looks at Laura and says, 'You know, Jim – it's Soames' dog. He died last night.'

'Oh dear,' says Beacon, 'I wonder if that's why he's not here.'

Laura and Lawton are giggling into their hands and Joan just rolls her eyes at me.

Lawton re-starts his imaginary desk organ, his lips pursed as he makes the sound of the synthesiser through his teeth. David groans and Lawton says, 'David, it's OK, it's not Doors. It's Nice – "America".'

Beacon says, 'You're right. It is nice. From *West Side Story*.'

David looks around the room in disgust and says, 'Jesus Christ, let me out of this fucking madhouse.'

He walks out and misses the lesson.

Afterwards in the library Lawton tells David how hilarious it was when Beacon asked Soames about his poor dog, Jim. David's been to the pub and he's been smoking grass as well, so he's falling about laughing. Laura's feeling left out because he's been out of school doing stuff without her. Then she starts trying to get his attention by telling him about what happened in class.

'So funny,' she says. 'You should've been there.'

But what happened isn't funny.

Beacon asks you about his dog, and you want to know what he's talking about. Beacon gets flustered and you think he's trying to make a fool of you. Joan says it's not Beacon's fault, that David's tricked him. But then, sir, you call Beacon 'a brylcreemed idiot', under your breath, but so we all can hear it and Laura laughs. Beacon goes beetroot red and remains that colour all the lesson. Afterwards I try to talk to him but he just shrugs and leaves the room without speaking.

I'm not sure why you said that to him. Maybe you were really angry at David and just took it out on poor Beacon.

Friday July 9th 1971

Dear Mr Soames,

I still don't know how I feel about what happened this evening at your house. I waited so long outside for an answer that never came. And now, with the long summer ahead, I'll have to wait until September to find out. But even then, maybe I'll never know.

The end of term seminar at your home for your Oxbridge group, David, Laura and me. David and Laura not speaking. Rumour goes around that when he cut school yesterday, he met another girl at the pub who was home from university for the summer.

I could've walked there but dad insists on giving me a lift, says he's curious where Soames lives. Dad's angry when he drops me off, shaking his head at the grand house. He can't believe how a teacher can live in such a neighbourhood. This is where lawyers and doctors live, not teachers. He says that this is the kind of place he wants for me, the kind of house I will own when I've qualified as a barrister.

You serve up tea and cakes in your study and David's disappointed, half joking, half serious, that the cakes are home-baked, but cannabis-free. You open up discussion with a question on the Cambridge general paper: 'Music cannot evoke emotion, only the memory of emotion.' I'm still thinking about dad's comments and feel his anger following me into the room.

David, as usual, has plenty to say. The statement, he says, only applies to capitalist music, the music of death, classical and popular music, and they can't evoke anything other than dead emotions. Usual David rant and nonsense. He harks back to the Hawkwind concert and the feeling he had there. How he felt totally alive while totally connected to Vietnamese farmers being napalmed into oblivion.

Laura says, half under breath, 'Yes, but you were completely stoned out of your head at the time.'

'I know what you mean, David,' you interrupt, with a gleam in your eye. 'Once I listened to 'Frosty the Snowman' while smoking some weed and I felt such sympathy for all such creatures of ice and snow out there in the cold with no home, shelter or food except the odd carrot.'

Laura and I both look at each other and burst out laughing while David glares at her and mutters, 'It wasn't the drugs that made me feel that way.'

I can't stop staring at Laura. No make-up apart from eye-liner, her pale skin beautiful in the rosy evening light filtering through the bay window.

'I was trying to make a serious point,' David says.

'Talking of serious points,' you say, 'David, why weren't you in class yesterday?'

David looks at you. 'You *are* kidding aren't you?'

'No. Regular attendance is crucial. You were in school. I saw you both before and after the class.'

'I can't believe you're saying this, man.'

'Maybe you thought I wasn't in school, after what had happened to my dog.'

David gets up, knocking the tray of cakes off the small coffee table. 'You're all taking the piss,' he says, and with that he's gone. Walking out seems to be his latest form of protest.

For a moment I think Laura might follow him.

'Obviously not partial to my landlady's Victoria sponge,' you say.

'He's been upset the last few days, about Jim Morrison,' she says.

Then you and Laura pick up discussing the essay question again but I can't concentrate because I'm thinking ahead to the walk home, her trench coat unbuttoned in the evening warmth, maybe her arm nestled in mine. In the setting sun her hair is shining and free around her shoulders. We walk into the twilight together. I can ask her if she wants to see *Zabriskie Point*.

But then you suddenly say

'You seem distracted this evening, Michael. Maybe you should head off. I want to discuss Laura's summer reading list with her. You've already got yours. Have a good summer and don't get too lost in Chancery.'

And that's it. I'm dismissed for the summer.

I wait outside for an hour but she doesn't come out.

It's past midnight now and as I lie here in my room, I wonder is Laura still there with you?

Monday July 19th 1971

Dear Mr Soames,

I finish *Bleak House* over the weekend. I wonder if, like Richard Carstone, I'm destined to drift forever from one profession to the next – never content or settled. Is this what you meant by being lost in Chancery? Or did you mean being lost forever in a life that isn't my own?

I go to see *Zabriskie Point* on Saturday afternoon. I can see why David identifies with the main character – he's good-looking, angry, arrogant. Flies a stolen plane backwards and forwards across the sands until he meets a girl searching for the meaning of life. They have interminable sex in the desert which looks very uncomfortable rolling around amongst all the rocks and sand.

The film goes on forever – *The Flight of the Phoenix* it isn't.

Friday July 23rd

Dear Mr Soames,

Three times this week I've walked by your house. Not sure why. Hoping to see you? To see Laura coming to see you? Are you and Laura spending time together this summer? Since school ended two weeks ago, I haven't been able to forget that night waiting for her to come out of your house. It's such a long time until term starts, until I can see Laura again, until I can see you again. A long summer stretches out ahead. If I catch you both together how would that make me feel? I don't know.

Tuesday August 4th 1971

Dear Mr Soames,

Dad takes *The Bell Jar* from my hands and looks at the blurb on the back. 'How can you read this? It's so depressing?' he says. 'Another suicide case. These writers, they're all neurotic.'

I find my mother's old school dictionary in a drawer and look up 'neurotic'. I skim over the definition uneasily – something about agitation of the nervous system and a derangement of feeling. Do you have to be mentally unsound to be a writer? Am I mentally unsound because I want to be a writer? Would it be safer to be a lawyer? To bury these thoughts with something secure, something solid. Is this why dad wants me to forget these novels, these writers who speak to me and make me feel alive but afraid. Afraid of their darkness, their freedom?

You also gave me *Slaughterhouse Five*. Vonnegut explains how the horror of Dresden was impossible to write about. His sad and frightening account of the bombing took him over twenty years. But it's also very funny. Dad never speaks of his own service in Burma. And especially hates anything that makes jokes like Vonnegut does about war.

But I'm not saying dad has no sense of humour. He loves The Goons, Round the Horne, Hancock's Half Hour. He often says I need to have a break from all the gloom I'm reading.

So tonight he comes up to my room and I hide another novel under the pillow in time.

'Come on,' he says, 'let's have a beer.' And we watch Laurel and Hardy – the one where Stan mistakes Ollie's foot for the murderer's hand at the bottom of the bed.

Stan blows Ollie's foot off with a shotgun. I think dad's going to have a heart attack he's laughing so much.

We have a new pedal bin in the kitchen and I'm dropping the empty beer cans in when I notice my copy of

The Bell Jar at the bottom. I fish it out and take it upstairs, put it under my bed, along with Vonnegut's novel and my journal.

'Who's the funniest? Laurel and Hardy or the Marx Brothers?' I ask dad as we both crack open another can.

'These guys take some beating,' he replies. Another Stan and Ollie film has started. They are chimney sweeps and Ollie keeps getting poked in the eye by Stan's brushes. 'But, if I had to choose, I'd say none of them. Because Hancock is now the best.'

'Didn't Tony Hancock commit suicide?' I say. He looks at me. He's had a few by this time and I'm a bit tipsy too. I'm taking a risk with this if he thinks I'm being smart, making comparisons with writers who've killed themselves. Which I suppose I am.

But he seems oblivious. 'Yes, poor sod. He should never have left Ray Galton. Galton and Simpson, they were the writers, they were real talent.'

This is it, my chance to say, 'Dad, I'm a writer, too.' But I don't. Now wouldn't be the time anyway, because dad has gone quiet. I can tell he's mulling over what I said about Tony Hancock's suicide. Making the connections. A mood grows in the uneasy silence

Then he relaxes, smiles at me and winks.

And all is well with the world. I am his best pal again. His Laurel and Hardy buddy.

Thursday August 6th 1971

Dear Mr Soames,

Dad's got me a job for the summer – 'to stop me moping about the house.' He would have me down at the factory with him but for the trouble with the workers, threatening strike action. Instead, he's had a word with his golfing pal Brian who manages the bakery and he's got me a job on the ovens.

Part of my 'moping around' involves more reading. You recommended *The Love Song of J Alfred Prufrock*. A man who can't make up his mind. And does nothing. Trapped in indecision. Like me. I could break free by telling dad I am not going to Cambridge to read Law. Why does that feel like it would destroy his world and mine?

Instead it's just sunny day after sunny day here in St Vincent's on Sea. Isn't summer supposed to be happy when you're seventeen? Dare I destroy that sunny world? That question is all I think about. That and Laura, of course.

Mum catches me writing this today. I didn't know she was there and I can't hide the journal in time.

'What are you doing?' she says.

'Just writing my diary,' I reply.

'Are you OK, Michael?'

'I'm fine, mum.'

'It's just that you've not been yourself recently.'

Something about the kindness in her voice encourages me to say more.

'Mr Soames says I could be a writer.'

'What would your dad say?'

'He throws the books I'm reading in the bin.'

'You know your dad. He doesn't mean anything by it. He has his own views about things. The way things should be.'

'I have to read those books to prepare for the Cambridge exam.'

'Dad knows that. He's just worried the school is filling

your head with ideas, and that you're drifting away from him, from us.'

'I will have to go away, though, won't I, properly? Next year. If I'm going to do the Law degree.'

'Just between you and me,' she says, 'you really don't have to, do you?'

'Don't have to do what?'

'Go away to college. If you don't want.'

'Yes, of course, I do.'

'You could stay at home and do all that writing here.'

'But what would dad make of that? He wouldn't put up with it.'

'No, I don't suppose he would,' she says. 'But maybe it can be our little secret, for now.'

It's the nearest I've got to anything like a discussion about this. And I'm not sure it helps. My mum and I now have a secret. But even that feels like a betrayal.

I wonder about that definition of neurosis in the dictionary. 'Derangement' it said and I wonder if writing is a kind of madness, a sickness of the mind? Sometimes it seems like that. Like I am going mad.

Saturday August 15th 1971

Dear Mr Soames,

I completed my first week on the bakery night shift. Twelve hours at the oven face in sweltering heat. We have three long breaks when I just drink water and listen to the men – desperate characters whose lives are spent doing this every night. It's horrible hot work, like being at the doors of hell. I have burns from handling the pans and the scorching loaves as they come out of the furnace.

'Now you know that's what happens when you don't have an education. When you don't have a profession. It's a tough old world out there,' dad says.

But then there's a guy on the shift, Ray, has a Chemistry degree and he's been at the bakery for the last couple of years. He has a hip flask which lasts him through the night. He says going to university is a waste of time. He reads a lot and passes stuff on to me. So I'm ploughing through Herman Hesse's *Steppenwolf,* about a man who has a split nature. Another man in torment. I can't stop reading it.

Wednesday August 19th 1971

Dear Mr Soames,

Today I'm in town when Laura comes out of the record shop followed by David. I hang back in a doorway so they don't see me. She slips her arm into his as they walk off laughing. They're back together. Does that mean you and Laura aren't together? That would be a relief. But it means she's obviously made it up with David which is worse somehow.

When I see her all those old feelings come rushing back. Will she ever see or understand the person who really loves her?

Because, you see, Mr Soames, what you and David don't know is just how far Laura and I go back, way back before either of you came on the scene. We were at Tindall Secondary together – both of us devastated when we failed our Eleven Plus. We vowed we'd get to the grammar school someday. We were friends, but we were always far more than that.

She's the only one left from that time at Tindall. All my old friends have gone. Barry is a joiner, going steady, talking of getting married. Pete has joined the Merchant

Navy. Sam is working shifts as a printer. I've drifted away from them all. And them from me.

All except for Laura. The only connection to that world. But as she walks away with David by her side, I wonder if she still thinks of me and those days back at Tindall and where we came from. Like that one day I remember above all – that summer six years ago. It seems like another life now, years away and yet, for me, still so real.

It was another long endless summer holiday. I was worrying about starting at the secondary school in September, whether I would fit in there, still upset about failing the Eleven Plus, dad still disappointed in me.

Then one afternoon while dad was at work, mum suggested we go to the cinema to cheer us both up, a *Mary Poppins* matinee at The Rialto. When we get there, just by chance, Laura is outside with her mum. It's a bit embarrassing for us both bumping into each other with our mothers but I'm so pleased to see her – it's been weeks since school and I've missed her. It's a warm day so she is without a coat and is dressed in a tartan plaid skirt and pink cardigan with a matching headband. She has her hair cut shorter than now, in a bob which she flicks away with her hand and smiles shyly at me. She giggles as my mum recalls my new school uniform she bought last week, with the blazer three sizes too big. My mum and her mum confide in each other about the unfairness of the Eleven Plus. Laura and I shake our heads in exasperation. We've both heard this so many times. It doesn't change anything.

The grown-ups decide we should all sit together in the cinema and soon we're laughing along at the chimney sweeps all dancing and Uncle Albert on screen floating through the air. And then when it comes to the bit where Mary sings 'Feed the Birds', Laura places her hand in mine. It nestles there like a sparrow, and it's as if she's saying it will all be alright, we'll make it out of there, out of Tindall together. And five years later, after our O Levels we do just that.

But rather than bringing us closer together it seems to have driven us apart.

Afterwards Laura never mentions that afternoon, I never mention it. And nothing like it happens again. But, you see, Mr Soames, despite our distance recently, I dream she still thinks of that day. How can she not when it still means so much to me? And these last weeks, this long lonely summer long, I remember each moment as if it was yesterday.

Monday August 24th 1971

Dear Mr Soames

Early Saturday evening I meet up with Ray from the bakery. We head off to The Eagle and Child and he orders a couple of pints of lager. Ray is twenty-seven but he looks so much older. Since graduating he's had a lot of different jobs but can't, doesn't, want to settle down. When it's my round the landlord won't serve me. This is embarrassing but Ray says don't worry, we'll go somewhere else.

He heads to the nearest off licence and comes out with a carrier full of cans and we finish up in a shelter on the promenade. It's a warm evening and we watch the sun going down over the sea, drinking Carlsberg Special Brew which is really strong and goes straight to my head. Ray starts into his favourite topic – how education is a waste of time – how the only university worth attending is the University of Life. He wants to travel, to live freely without the burden of regular job, wife, kids. To do what he wants.

He asks me if I've seen *Five Easy Pieces*. Says the film will change my life. And if I want to write, really write, I should forget about Cambridge, that's just a trap. Go travelling, different jobs, living – that's the key to great writing. 'Go on the road. Follow Kerouac and Cassady,' he says, finishing another can of lager

This is great for a while. I am drunk, really drunk and I start to tell him about you and Laura, that night at your house. I am sorry, Mr Soames, and I feel really bad about this. Ray thinks this is just typical of teachers – 'They're all hypocrites,' he says. And when the cans have gone, he starts rolling a joint. I say I have to get back home – mum and dad think I'm out at the cinema – and then he starts telling me he knows dad. He's worked for him as a technician at the factory.

He lights the joint and hands it to me and when I inhale I feel very light headed, but then I quickly fall asleep. I don't know how long I'm out but when I come round, Ray has gone. I eventually make it out of the shelter and decide I will take a walk out on the beach to clear my head while there's still some light.

The sands are deserted, stretching for miles with the tide-line somewhere out of reach beyond the horizon. Nothing out there but the dunes stretching to the south. The lonely pillbox hiding away in the mounds of sand. I walk out to sea scattering clouds of birds that circle and regroup behind me but never land. I take detours around streams and gullies that increase in force and flow but I'm not really paying attention. I feel like I'm disappearing out there in all that space and sky. And suddenly and strangely I come right upon the sea, or it comes to me in frightening surging waves. I am partly surrounded by water and so far out I can't see my way back through the rivers around me. The tide is moving quickly and I have to walk through gullies and wade through a channel several feet wide in order to get safely back to land. My shoes and trousers are soaked through and the dry sand clings to my clothes as I make it to the sea wall. The tide follows me in. As the brown waves suck and circle in the steps and stones below, larger waves come crashing forward spraying me with leaping curls of grey foam. I head away with the roar of the sea and the footfalls of surf on the promenade behind me.

It's dark when I arrive back and mum is in the hallway waiting. She takes one look at my wet sand-covered clothes and puts her hand to her mouth.

'Where on earth have you been?' she asks.

'I just went for a walk.'

'Where?'

I try to push past her up the stairs to get to my room, when dad appears in the hallway as well.

'Look at the state he's in,' she says.

'Where've you been, Michael?' he asks.

'On the beach. It's OK.'

'It doesn't look OK,' dad says.

'No really, dad, it is. I just went for a walk.'

'It's dark, lad. You're wet through.'

I stand in front of him, waiting for the anger to build. But instead, he takes me in his arms holds me close and says slowly and quietly, 'You've been drinking.'

I look at him and he just shakes his head.

'You know, Michael, lad,' he says, 'if you don't buck your ideas up, you're going to be a very mixed-up person.'

Mixed up person? Neurotic? Derangement of the senses? I wonder if mum's been telling him stuff about me wanting to be a writer. She says it's our little secret but dad can be very persuasive at getting her to admit things.

Later, after I've had a bath, I get into my pyjamas and lie on the bed thinking of where Laura and David will be tonight. Another concert maybe, or just out somewhere taking drugs, having sex, planning their trip around the world together next year.

Tuesday August 25th 1971

Dear Mr Soames,

My days at the bakery are at an end. Dad won't let me go back now he knows Ray Mason works there. He sacked him from the factory last year for smoking cannabis on his break and for being a dead-leg who thinks the world owes him a living. If he'd known Mason worked at the bakery, he'd never have let me anywhere near the place. Dad asks if I've done any drugs with him. He doesn't seem to mind too much about the alcohol. Obviously, I don't tell him about the spliff. I don't tell him about the Kerouac either that I've borrowed from the library to get me through the last week before I can see you and Laura again.

'Haircut for you, young man, before you go back to school,' dad says.

My heart sinks. My hair was just getting a bit longer over the summer, just a little like everyone else's, and now I will look more like Roland Beacon again when we go back.

I can't say I'm sorry to be away from the bakery, though. The burns on my hands and arms are healing but mum caught sight of them the other day and asked me if I was deliberately hurting myself. I told her how I'd got the scars and she wanted to go down to the bakery to complain. I told her it was my fault for handling the trays and pans so clumsily. Management provide gloves but I didn't bother with them.

So, I say to her, 'Yes, I suppose I was deliberately hurting myself, after all.'

She doesn't understand I was joking. She asks me if I'm happy and when I just shrug she then says, 'When your dad says you're mixed-up, he doesn't really understand. He doesn't know what depression is.'

'Depression?'

'It's a mental illness,' she says.

'An illness? A mental illness?'

'I know, believe me. It runs in the family on my side.'

I don't know what to say. Does this mean I can't do anything about it? A family curse? Is mum depressed? Mentally ill? Am I the same?

'But don't worry,' she says. 'You have some of your dad in you.'

Mum might have meant well but this doesn't help. My mother and me. Struggling alone keeping this secret, this illness, from dad who doesn't understand.

Thank god this endless summer is nearly over and I will be back to Pennington, to your classes, Mr Soames. Your glamorous and exciting world. Literature and film and culture. Anything is possible there. Away from this secrecy and fear of depression and illness.

But for how long can I avoid the big questions that have haunted me all summer?

What should I do with my life? What does Laura see when she looks at me? What do I see when I look in the mirror?

CHAPTER SEVEN

He put the journal down and closed his eyes. But it wasn't Soames or Laura or even his mother he now recalled the most vividly. It was his father, Bill, sitting in his chair, laughing at Laurel and Hardy. Bill winking at him as they shared a beer that summer evening. How he lived back then for that wink and nod of approval. Sometimes he would catch his father's eye just to see it, a moment of recognition that would make an ordinary day so special. That would make him feel chosen. He sighed now as his heart went out to the boy who'd written these pages. How his seventeen-year-old-self had struggled with that interminable summer. How the days had dragged on endlessly with the backdrop of his mother's talk of depression and family illness. Maybe she thought she was helping him to feel less alone in sharing her experience. But it had only made him feel more isolated, more confused and uncertain as to who he really was. But was he any better now, after all these years, at understanding any of this? Was this still her same illness, her same malaise that explained these noises behind walls? Some remnants of the damage of those days lingering in the air, in the fabric of the building, in the paralysis of time itself. But now the only sounds he heard were the radiators cooling and the ticking of the clock.

He slept fitfully, waking every half hour through the night, until he awoke suddenly to his mother screaming in the bedroom next door. She was shouting out in her sleep something about a man at her bed. He rushed into the room and turned on her reading light. She was awake now and looked terrified at the sight of him standing there.

'Oh, my god. I thought it was your father for a second,' she said. She was white as a sheet and breathing heavily.

'Mum, you were having a bad dream. You were calling out in your sleep.'

'Your dad came into the room. He was so very angry with me.'

'Just a dream, mum.'

She sat up staring straight ahead of her. 'I'm not so sure,' she said into the blank space beyond the bed. 'Tonight I heard them again. In the wall. I know you think I'm barmy. But it was there, a scraping, like someone trying to get out.'

'I don't think you're barmy, mum.'

'And I was thinking about what you said – about me spending afternoon with that man I hardly know. What was I thinking?'

'Oh, mum, I'm sorry. Take no notice of me. I was being daft.'

'What would Bill say about me gallivanting around like that? There's never been anyone else but him you know.'

'I know.'

'And then I was asleep, but not really asleep, and it felt like he was here, Bill, here, in the room.'

'It's just me, mum. Try and rest for a bit. Breakfast in bed sound OK?'

'Yes, but leave the light on, will you.'

Daylight crept wearily into the house as he drew back the curtains. Joe's van was still on the drive and he hoped he would come and pick it up soon or his mother would be worrying what the neighbours might be thinking. Curtains drawn back, toast in the toaster, the kettle on, concern over his mother's contagious fear and anxiety displaced, for the moment, by menial tasks. A tired grey dawn leaked in beneath the kitchen blind. It was as if the newspaper article, the arrival of Joe, and then opening the journal had all conspired to summon noises and dreams from the past. While reading his journal, he had felt strongly his father's presence, felt that old tightness in his chest, that secrecy and concealment, and the deadly betrayal lurking in the pages that followed. His mother believed in something waiting behind the walls, but Michael knew his father's ghost did not have to hide away. He was always somewhere in that room, in all the rooms of this house.

Then his heart stopped as a sudden, terrifying, banshee-like scream filled the kitchen, a fearful, screeching cry that grew to a piercing unbearable pitch. His first thought was his mother but she was still upstairs. It couldn't be the kettle because that was electric. The sound completely filled the room. He looked up at the ceiling but there was nothing there and the sound was now more centred on the work surfaces. He peered inside the toaster, and stepped back in horror at the enlarged head of a trapped mouse pinned between the grills, writhing in agony. He cried out and ran into the lounge. Then, as he stumbled towards the kitchen door, he began to smell burning fur, or worse, and the screaming stopped and was followed by an even more awful silence.

He crept back to the kitchen. Smoke was rising out of the toaster which he quickly unplugged. He managed to look inside again. The mouse was still there, its head reduced to normal tiny proportions, its eyes and mouth open, its one visible paw poking through the metal in a final entreaty. He touched the creature with the handle of a teaspoon, praying that its suffering was over. Its scorched lower body disappeared beneath the slice of blackened bread which he pinched between his fingers and dropped in the bin. The mouse's body sunk to the base of the toaster, the charred twisted tail settling amongst crumbs like a worm shrivelled in the sun.

Without any warning his face crumpled, tears flowing down his cheeks and onto the kitchen worktop. He turned away from the dead creature but when he closed his eyes all he could see was that bloated head pleading for help. And once he started crying, he couldn't stop. Something broke from his chest and was now flooding the weak morning light, his sobbing heart swollen and exploding with grief for the poor wretched thing now dead in the kitchen. But it wasn't just the mouse – there was so much sorrow, so many sad memories. His lost relationship with Maddie, Derek Fletcher, good, decent Derek, living in the shadow of imminent death, Soames disappeared, maybe dead, his mother frightened of what lay behind the walls of her own house, his father laughing along to Laurel and Hardy, a little boy and a girl holding hands in the cinema all those years ago. He leaned for support on the wall, without a clue what to do with the charred limp body lying at the base of the toaster, when the front doorbell rang. Drying his eyes with the tea towel, he went to answer. Anything was better than going back to that tiny lifeless creature.

'Hello, Michael,' Joe's smiling face in the doorway greeted him. 'I've come to pick up my van and saw the curtains drawn back and thought I'd just see if everything's still alright with the toilet.'

'Everything's fine with it, thanks.'

'Is your mum OK?'

It was freezing outside, Joe's breath pluming in the morning air. The elderly man's cheerful demeanour, slightly irksome the previous day, was now a welcome distraction.

'Would you like to come in?' Michael said. 'Mum's still in bed, but I can let her know you're here.'

'Oh, no, don't put her to any trouble.'

'It's no trouble. Do you want a cup of tea?'

'Only if you're making one.'

'Yes, just making one for mum. I'd make you a slice of toast as well, but we've had a bit of an accident this morning.'

'Oh, don't worry, a brew will be fine. One sugar if you don't mind. What's that smell?' he asked.

Michael, still shaken by the experience, was only too happy to reach out for help. He ushered Joe into the kitchen and pointed to the toaster. 'Have a look for yourself.'

'Poor little chap,' Joe said, picking the mouse up by its tail.

'I don't know quite what to do with him.'

Joe stepped over to the waste bin and opened the lid.

'Wait,' said Michael. 'Don't'

The shrivelled remains, a few minutes ago alive and seeking crumbs in the toaster, now about to be dumped with last night's potato peelings, dangled reproachfully from Joe's pinched fingers.

'I don't know. Maybe bury him?'

Joe laughed. 'Bury him?'

'Outside in the garden?'

The older man raised his eyebrows and then shook his head and smiled kindly. 'Blimey, come on then. I suppose so. Must be going soft in my old age.'

They ventured out into the cold morning sunlight, the plumber still holding the mouse by the tail, as Michael went to fetch a garden trowel from the shed. They found a patch of earth that wasn't too hard from the overnight frost at the back of the border behind the winter-stricken fuchsia.

Joe held out his hand for the trowel. 'Yes, well, let's put this little fella away then.' He laid the remains in the scooped-out hole and covered it with soil softened with the first rays of sun. 'Goodnight, sweet Prince, and flights of angels sing thee to thy rest,' he said, half ironically, but with a tinge of genuine sadness. As he bent over the earth, Michael remembered something his mother had said about Joe recently losing his wife.

'You know *Hamlet*?' Michael said, a few minutes later, as they sat down at the kitchen table over a cup of tea.

'Oh yes, never forget. I had a great teacher. Mr Grimes. Made us memorise Shakespeare. It's stayed with me all these years.'

'To the Spanner Born.'

'Yes, but most folk think of that TV series with Penelope Keith rather than Hamlet. Sally never liked the fancy name. Thought it was pretentious. Said it would put off the customers.'

'Sally, your wife?'

'Yes, Sally,' he paused. 'She passed away last March. That's when I started going to church. Get me out of the house.'

'I'm sorry, Joe.'

There was another moment of silence before Joe replied. 'Sally never really took to Shakespeare much.'

Michael nodded. 'That name was actually the reason I rang you in the first place, strangely enough.'

'It attracts some folk then, doesn't it?'

'Your teacher, the one who had you memorise *Hamlet*. He must've made an impression.'

'You never forget them do you? Teachers like Mr Grimes. He always wore a bow tie.'

'My old teacher, Mr Soames, he's gone missing.'

'I know. Sad business. My grandson started at Pennington in September. He's really upset. He has Mr Soames for English. He was in the middle of reciting *A Christmas Carol* to them by heart.'

'That sounds like Mr Soames, alright.'

'He's a right old character. The kids love him.'

'Nobody seems to have a clue where he might be.'

Joe sighed. 'Maybe he doesn't want anyone to find him. Who knows? Maybe he wants to disappear for a bit.'

'How do you mean?'

The plumber sipped his drink, his white hair coppered by the winter sunlight streaming through the window, his bright blue eyes fixed on the distance.

'I think we all feel like that sometimes. When it all gets too much. When Sally died, I wanted to just go away. Anywhere.'

Both men contemplated their mugs of tea until Joe broke the silence again. 'You married, Michael?'

'No, but I was with someone until recently. It didn't work out though. My mum was talking about her when you were here yesterday. She has a boy, Tommy. Nice kid.'

'Sally and me, forty-five years together, had three kids. Hard times but good times. Mortgage to pay. Trying to get the business started. We had our ups and downs. But I'd have her back in a heartbeat, if I could.'

Joe looked up at the ceiling. Grace could be heard moving around upstairs. The plumber carefully pushed a lock of his grey hair that had strayed across his forehead. He suddenly looked uneasy.

'Maybe I shouldn't be here,' he said.

'It's fine. Mum will be glad to see you. It's good to have some company.'

Joe gestured to the garden. 'You know something will dig that little fella up don't you. Have him for its supper tonight,' he said.

'Well, we'll see. Thanks for helping anyway. I was a bit freaked out to tell the truth.'

'Thought you looked a bit shaken up.'

'If you'd heard the screams. You wouldn't think something that small could make...'

In the silence that fell between them again, Grace's movements upstairs became more pronounced. Joe tapped the glass top table with his wedding ring and said, 'What's she called? If you don't mind me asking?'

'Who?'

'This girl. The one that's making you look so down in the dumps.'

'Sorry, not sure what you mean.'

'The one your mum mentioned yesterday. Don't mind me.' Joe paused, before continuing, 'It's not my business. But you're still a young fella. Plenty more fish in the sea.'

Just what had his mother been saying about him to this stranger over their afternoon sherry? A kind, open and friendly presence, but a stranger, no less. And yet, there was something about Joe that made him think he could confide in him, in a way he couldn't with anyone apart from...

'Maddie. That's her name.'

He would probably have said more but Grace suddenly appeared in the doorway. Without her makeup in the rose-coloured light of morning, and blushing slightly at the surprise of seeing Joe there at her kitchen table, she looked younger than her seventy five years.

'What are you two up to?' she said.

'Morning,' Joe said, standing up. 'Sorry to bother you. I popped by to see if the toilet is working.' He immediately looked awkward and shy, hastily picking up the toaster. 'I'm afraid you're going to need a new one of these, you know.'

'And, mum,' Michael said, 'I think we've discovered what's been making those noises behind the wall.'

CHAPTER EIGHT

It took both Joe and Michael some time to placate Grace when she discovered she was harbouring mice. She would face a horde of demons from hell rather than the Pest and Vermin Control Van parked outside her door. Joe, ever keen to invoke the legacy of Mr Grimes, launched into 'there are more things in Heaven and earth than are found in your philosophy, Horatio,' when she told him she had thought the house was haunted. But she laughed when she offered to make Joe some toast for breakfast and realised this was no longer possible. He asked if he could have another mince pie instead. 'As long as that's alright with Michael,' she teased and soon she was recalling mornings from long ago when she would toast bread on a long fork at an open fire. While Joe and Grace reminisced, Michael gratefully seized the opportunity to make his exit.

The emotion he had felt over the mouse and subsequent chat with Joe, had somehow lifted the tension he was feeling and, with anticipation stirring, he pulled the collar of his coat together to protect him against the sudden fierce chill that came off the sea. After about half an hour walking, the character of the district began to change. The bare trees lined along the streets and avenues of St. Vincent's affluent district stood out in the clear early sunlight. Crisp morning air filled his lungs and lifted his heart as he headed for Soames' residence and a possible meeting with his wife Joan. Solving the riddle of his mother's haunted walls now gave way to this much deeper, far more compelling mystery – what had happened to his own beloved teacher.

Lawton had told him that Soames and Joan still lived in the same house Michael visited for the Oxbridge seminars. As he approached the road with its large Edwardian properties, he recalled his father's resentment of Soames not long out of university, living in a district such as this. What would his dad think of him now, heading down the same street some twenty-six years later, hoping to make contact or find some information about this man? You are a fool chasing after ghosts, Michael, he would say. Why does this mean so much to you? But he couldn't find the words to defy his father's mockery. He wasn't even sure what he was going to say to Joan, but it was a better way of filling his time than pretending to do research or fixing toilets and tree lights.

Michael felt the presence of both Soames and his father, and of Laura too, as he approached the gate where he had waited for her that summer evening all those years ago. And then suddenly, there it was, the large detached property standing before him – its long sweeping path through the trees leading to the enclosed porch, the leaded windows, the ornate redbrick and timbered grandeur. For a moment he was transported back to that seventeen-year-old boy with his life all ahead of him.

He had his hand on the gate, transfixed by memories and the strangeness of his return, when the figure of a woman appeared in the front window. She was staring at him with her hands at first raised and then cupped around her chin, as if in surprise or shock. Heart racing he headed down the driveway, not daring to look again at the window until he rang the bell and waited. It seemed to take forever and then a shadow appeared in the stained-glass porch. The door opened and the same woman stood before him, wearing a green housecoat pulled in at the waist with a thin belt, and a pair of jeans. Her hair was short and the light from the morning sun was at her back flooding through the side porch window and blinding him so that he couldn't clearly see her features.

'I'm sorry to bother you, but I was just passing by and...I wasn't sure I had the right house.'

'Michael, is it, Michael?' the figure said, caught in the shadow from the streaming light.

'Yes, I think so,' he said in a feeble attempt at humour.

'My goodness, yes, Michael...'

'As I said, I was just passing, and then I saw you at the window, and so I thought I'd just say hello. I hope you don't mind.' He already felt foolish standing at this woman's front door, a strange interloper from the past.

But she didn't seem threatened or even surprised. 'Steve Lawton said he'd met you yesterday and that you might drop by. You're more than welcome, Michael.'

As the figure emerged from the porch into the doorway, the woman's features arranged themselves into something from recognisable memory. She took his hand and held it in hers before backing into the porch. He reached down to remove his shoes.

'There's no need for that,' Joan said.

'Sorry, old habits.'

'Come on through.' Then she led him into the entrance hall, lined, as it had been back then, with two large bookcases. On the staircase wall were Hollywood movie posters in stylish narrow black frames. Film noir from the nineteen forties – *Out of the Past, Double Indemnity, The Maltese Falcon.* As he followed her into the house, the door to the room on the left of the hallway, where Soames had held his seminars, was closed. He imagined Soames and Laura still in there, discussing her reading list, or whatever else it was they were doing that summer evening all those years ago. But the house was so different now – no longer the dark carpeted interiors and low melancholy shadows. The light from the stained-glass staircase window cast rainbow hues onto the white-painted walls, and the polished laminated floor stretched out and beyond into a bright sitting room with a conservatory extending onto a spacious paved garden and leading to a summer house.

'Sit down, Michael. Can I get you something to drink: tea, coffee?'

'Yes, tea please.'

He seated himself in the middle of a large leather settee piled on either side of him with elaborately patterned cushions. More prints abounded on the walls of this room – Michael recognised Rothko and Klee. On the mantelpiece was a framed photograph of Soames in middle age, dressed in heavy Crombie coat and hat, standing in a doorway with the light shining on him from an upstairs window – an obvious homage to the famous Harry Lime scene from *The Third Man.* Soames had not aged particularly well and he no longer looked anything like the young Orson Welles that Michael remembered. While Joan was in the kitchen making tea, he questioned once more whether this was a good idea, intruding into a woman's home and privacy, a woman he hadn't seen for twenty-six years, at a time when she was vulnerable and distressed. Maybe his mother was right – he should leave all this well alone, forget the newspaper article, forget Pennington School, leave Joan be. But Lawton had said Joan would welcome the company and she did seem genuinely pleased to see him. Then she re-entered carrying a tray with a teapot, china mugs and a plate of delicious-looking biscuits. He hadn't eaten breakfast and he was hungry.

'Michael, it's good to see you,' she said sitting down in the armchair across from the sofa. The morning light showed up the wrinkles on her face, but, despite this, time had been kinder to her than it had been to her husband.

Joan's skin was clear, not a trace of makeup or even lipstick.

'It seems strange being here, in this house, after all these years,' he said.

'Of course, you used to come for Gilbert's seminars, didn't you? The Oxbridge group.'

'Yes, me, David March and Laura.'

'I was never clever enough for that,' Joan said.

'You were brighter than any of us.'

'No, I don't think so. I just worked hard. What are *you* doing with yourself these days?'

'Er, research,' he said quickly. 'The films of Orson Welles...These are great, by the way,' he said, munching through one biscuit and taking up another from the tray, while trying not to choke on more of his lies. Joan just smiled sadly and looked at the photograph of her husband on the mantelpiece.

'Home made. Chocolate chip,' she said and then stared into the paved area beyond the conservatory where birds were feeding on the crumbs and seeds scattered there. On closer inspection a careworn and melancholy weariness settled around her eyes. She was also very thin, he now noticed, a pared down version of her younger self.

'We've thought about you often over the years,' she said. 'Are you OK?'

'I was OK, until I tried to make some toast this morning.' He still had no clue how to go about this conversation.

She looked at him curiously, as if she wasn't sure if he was joking or not.

'I killed a mouse, you see. Rather gruesome. It got stuck inside the toaster and, well, you can imagine. Not knowing it was there, and next thing there's this awful screaming.'

'Oh God, that does sound awful.'

'Then I had to get the mouse out of the toaster. Well, I didn't do that bit. The plumber did that.'

'The plumber?'

'Yes. And then we buried him in the garden.'

'You buried the plumber?'

'No, the....' At that point he stopped and they both laughed, only to lapse once more into silence. He crunched another biscuit, while trying to say something that wasn't idiotic.

'What are *you* doing these days, Joan?'

'I was teaching at Pennington for fifteen years. When I left university, I wanted to come back to St Vincent's and then...You know Gilbert and I are married don't you?'

'Yes, Steve told me.'

'We've lived here ever since. We rented at first. Then bought the place after we were married.' His father's bitterness about his son's teacher living in this house was always based on a mistake. Soames didn't own the property back then. He was just a young man renting from the landlady who made the Victoria sponge and scones for the seminars. He became lost again in memories until Joan brought him back to the present and his purpose.

'We had so many plans,' she said.

'Did he ever form his own theatre company. I remember back then you and he....'

She shook her head. 'You say you're doing research on Welles. That's interesting.'

'Yes, it is.' This pretence and the persistent hedging around the absence of Soames made Michael feel even more uncomfortable.

'If Gilbert were here, he'd be enthralled,' she said pointing to the photograph of Gilbert impersonating Harry Lime. 'But, unfortunately, he's not.'

He took a deep breath and said it: 'I've read the newspaper, Joan. I'm sorry.'

'Nobody knows where he is,' she said blankly into space.

'Steve told me a little bit about it. He's very worried.'

'Yes, he said you were concerned too. It's kind of you to come. Not that many people seem to care about Gilbert these days.'

'That's not true. Our plumber, Joe - he has a grandson in Year Seven at Pennington. He's very upset about it. Gilbert means a lot to people. The kids still love him. All those students and staff like Steve who supported him through that final school production.' He immediately regretted the use of the word 'final', but Joan didn't seem to notice.

'That's very kind of you to say. It means a lot.'

She looked like she wanted to say more and it encouraged him to go further.

'Steve says he was the last person to see Gilbert.'

'Yes, poor Steve. He blames himself, but absolutely none of this is his fault.' She paused, took a sip of tea before continuing. 'It was last Friday evening. Gilbert left to go to the school. He wasn't just producing the play, he was performing as well.' She shook her head. 'I tried to stop him going. I should've stopped him. He wasn't well. We argued about it…But you don't want to hear all this.'

'No, really, it's OK. Have the police no news?'

'To be honest, they're not really interested. They think Gilbert's having an affair, just another frustrated middle-aged man making a break for freedom.'

Michael suspected these explanations unlikely, but didn't say so, because the alternative was worse – that Soames had joined the countless lost souls unmoored from their lives, drifting into mental breakdown, psychosis, suicide.

'That's why I was at the window...I can't stop looking out for him. It's so silly but what else is there to do?' She looked like she was about to cry and then took one of her biscuits off the tray instead. 'We were going to buy a boat and tour the rivers and canals. The old dream, presenting Shakespeare. Bard on the Barge we wanted to call it.'

'Maybe that's what Soames is doing. Setting all that up.' But even as Michael said it, he knew how desperately fanciful it sounded.

'Wherever Gilbert is, he definitely isn't buying a boat and sorting out a business deal.' She paused as if considering whether or not to carry on. 'He's been working so hard at the school. But things have been horrible at Pennington. I'm afraid, it's not the place it was.'

'He carried on with the play, although he wasn't well, you say?'

'He put his heart and soul into those productions.'

'I remember them. They were brilliant.'

'I know. But it's no longer appreciated.'

'That's awful. They should be grateful they have someone so gifted.'

She looked at him and then muttered, as if to herself more than anything. 'Far from being appreciated, Michael, there are people there out to get him.'

'I just can't understand that.'

'No, you wouldn't, but that's because you're a normal, decent person.' She looked at him and smiled sadly. 'It won't do any good me sounding off.'

Michael suspected, however, she really wanted to carry on now she had started.

'No, I'm interested. This is very upsetting. Mr Soames was a great teacher. He shouldn't be treated badly by anyone.'

'It's the Head. Bob Dillon, awful man. And David March. You remember David March?'

'Yes, I remember Dave March.'

'He's had it in for Gilbert for a long time.'

'Steve said something about March having a grudge against Gilbert.'

She paused again. 'It all goes back years when David was his student.'

'I remember March was always causing trouble in class.'

'Well, yes. You could say that... causing trouble. Still causing trouble.' Her voice trailed off. She went quiet again and the silence grew between them. A robin dropped down on to the patio outside and began feeding on the seeds.

She took a sip of her tea. 'And then Gilbert hasn't been a well man over the years. It's no secret, everybody knows it. And these men have taken advantage,' she said, eventually. She nibbled listlessly at the biscuit and then placed it back on the tray. Michael reached for another and waited for her to continue, but she was silent once more.

'I remember his lessons so well,' he finally managed to say. 'They were good times.'

She looked at him oddly, as if she couldn't really believe what he'd said, before replying, 'Yes, good times, some of the time. Some, not so good.' She walked over to the window and looked at the sky, the blue light streaming through the trees. 'Do you ever have any contact with people from back then? With Laura?' she asked.

'No,' he said. She was once more in silhouette against the bright sunlight. 'Not since those days at Pennington. Do you ever see her?'

She turned again to the glass, her posture now pained and stiff, stooping slightly. 'We were sort of in touch for a time during and after university. But we drifted apart.' Just mentioning Laura's name cast a spell upon the room which Joan dismissed with a swift movement of her hand. 'Oh, but she was always going to get on. Another one who had her eyes on the prize. Sorry, I must sound very bitter.'

'No, not at all. Not all of us got the prizes, Joan.'

She smiled but the rumour Lawton divulged, that something happened back then to one of the girls, hung in the air and Joan suddenly looked so bereft, so abandoned by everyone. He wanted to do something, or just say something that would make her feel a little less lost and alone.

'Maybe David March knows something. About Mr Soames – where he is.'

She looked at him with concern. 'David's made my husband's life hell.'

'Maybe, I don't know, if someone spoke to March they might be able to find something out.'

Joan looked at him with concern. 'Something? Someone?'

'Someone not involved with the school anymore. Maybe someone like me who could just have a word with him. Discover something people have missed.'

'Why?'

'Why? What if he's got some idea where Gilbert might have gone, or why he's gone wherever he's gone?'

'He may have driven Gilbert to distraction but I doubt he knows more than anyone else where my husband is. If he knew anything he'd have told the police.'

'Lawton says he has that house on the beach.'

'House? Folly more like. Built in the middle of the dunes with a private road. Don't think of going anywhere near there, Michael. Really, you'd only make things worse.'

'What do you mean?'

'It doesn't matter.'

She looked like she was about to say something else and then stopped, and instead tears were rolling down her cheeks.

'I'm sorry,' she said.

Michael put the tray of biscuits to one side and, sitting on the side of the chair, wanted to put his arm around her.

'It's such a mess,' she said, her head bowed and her shoulders trembling.

'It's OK,' he said, awkwardly, helplessly in the face of this despair.

'It's not, it's hopeless.'

'It's OK,' he said again, clasping his hand around hers.

She shook her head and suddenly broke away and, glancing at him briefly, stood up, wiping the tears away with the back of her hand. Then she cleared the tea tray and the plate from the sofa and disappeared into the kitchen. He gathered his coat and made his way into the entrance hall where he waited until she re-appeared, her face and eyes now clear of the streaks of tears.

'I think I'd better be going now,' he said. 'I'm really sorry, Joan. I've upset you coming here.'

'Don't worry, Michael,' she said, grabbing his hand again. 'I'm the one who should be sorry, burdening you with my problems. It's been lovely to see you. Perhaps we can meet again, sometime. Under happier circumstances, maybe.'

'Are you sure you'll be OK. I'll stay a while if you want me to.'

She gave him a brief hug and then smiled. 'Don't worry, I'll be fine,' she said. 'Really, Michael. I'm OK. Thank you for listening to me.' It was clear she wanted to be rid of him so she could maybe cry in peace.

He waved one last goodbye from the gate as she stared at him through the window, her face forlorn and pale. He felt bad about upsetting her, didn't want to disturb her any more, but worried about leaving her and reluctantly headed home trying to make sense of what he'd just heard. What had been the point of his visit if it meant abandoning her in such a state? Joan was obviously in a wretched place, desperate to open her heart to someone who might listen to her grief, but he'd only succeeded in stirring up her emotions to breaking point. Confronted by her despair, he'd had no chance to ask her if she knew why Gilbert had come around to his house, why he'd visited only to be turned away by his mother. He'd been too preoccupied with her sadness to ask anything else. He'd always been fond of Joan when they were at school, and he felt compelled now to do something to help, something to unlock the mystery deepening around her husband's disappearance.

And, as he headed reluctantly homeward, despite the awkwardness of the situation with Joan, despite her grief and his regret that he had left her in an emotionally vulnerable state, despite the fact that their conversation had unearthed nothing new or revelatory about her husband's disappearance, he still felt buoyed up by the encounter. He was, he realised, along with an accompanying sense of guilt for feeling this way, enjoying this investigation, his own antidote to the miserable mundanity of life with mother, her newly hatched rodent-induced paranoia, her insistence that this case of the vanishing Mr Soames, for which he now felt an instinct developing, was doing him no good, when it was the most exciting thing that had happened to him since those heady, dream-like and now distant weeks with Maddie. And this instinct now told him that, although perhaps attributable to grief, nevertheless Joan was definitely holding something back, unwilling to reveal all she knew about what happened to her and Laura all those years ago. And, despite Joan's warning to stay away from David, he felt more and more it was his old adversary who held the key to that particular mystery. David March who had obviously caused Joan and her husband so much suffering, so much pain in the face of which they felt powerless and oppressed. He suspected that March was at the back of all this. Joan's tears, Soames' suffering and the apparent huge success March had made of his life reignited Michael's long standing antipathy towards the man. After all, if there was one person to blame for the failure Michael had become, one person responsible for depriving him of the life he might have had, it was David March. For so long there were many things he had wanted to say to him, questions he wanted to ask relating to that afternoon in October twenty six years ago that changed Michael's life. If he was to just turn up at March's house he might find something out. Michael had no influence, no job or reputation to lose. Being a local nobody with no agenda, would be a perfect cover. Surely it was all too late for settling old scores, but the more he thought about it, the more curious, the more excited, he became at the idea of meeting with this spectre from the past. Exorcising that ghost, maybe. Or at least doing a bit of haunting of his own. And in the process he might help Joan find some more answers to her husband's disappearance.

So first, without further ado, when he arrived home, he went straight to his room to seek a more immediate encounter with those phantoms from the past, waiting, as they had waited for years, within the pages of his teenage journal.

CHAPTER NINE

Tuesday September 7th 1971

Dear Mr Soames,

First day back Laura is pinning up a poster of Jim Morrison on the inside of her locker door. It's wonderful to be in the same room with her again. I want to ask her about that night we broke for the summer, what she was doing there at your house. But that was the summer and the summer has gone.

Then David sweeps into the room, hair even longer, dressed in duffel coat and boots. Gives Laura a kiss, and then hugs Joan as well who just stands there stiffly. Joan says she's been working with you setting up a local theatre company. David raises his eyebrows at Laura, forms a hole between his thumb and forefinger and pushes the index finger of his other hand through the hole. Laura bursts out laughing. Thankfully Joan sees nothing of this.

David's been working on a farm, saving up for his round-the-world trip next year after A Levels. Laura's been in the States with her father, which David waves away with, 'America, the cess pit of capitalism. You need to go East not West.' Beacon's been working in the parish and Lawton has been at his dad's undertaker's. He's formed a band – Cosmic Creation. David calls it Comic Cremation and Laura laughs out loud again. She's obviously hanging on his every hilarious word.

I wait until Joan's on her own and I mention the job at the bakery. And then I ask her about her working with you at the theatre company. She tells me how wonderful it is working there. She really likes you, sir, but I haven't to tell anyone. That you are a genius and have great plans to form a group of travelling players. And one day she hopes to take this company on a tour of the country with you. She says you're only twenty three and she won't be your student forever.

I can't believe you're only five or six years older than me. You seem so sure of yourself and the world, while I flounder around feeling about twelve years old most of the time.

For some reason Joan tells me things that she wouldn't tell anyone else. It would be good for you too, sir, one day, to be with Joan. She is such a kind and thoughtful person. You're not that much older and you wouldn't have to wait too long for each other. I wonder again about you and Laura. Maybe I was imagining things, but it didn't feel like that at the time. But now she's obviously besotted with David once more. That doesn't make me feel any better. In fact, in some ways, it's worse than if she was with you.

But then I remember dad saying how you're too familiar with us all. How you want too much to be our friend. Is there more than just friendship between you and Joan and Laura? If there is it can't, surely, be right? Part of me doesn't know what to make of it. Part of me doesn't want to know.

Wednesday 8th September 1971

Dear Mr Soames,

The moment I have been dreading today – the moment when I have to face you and discuss my choices – Law or Literature for Cambridge. You can see I haven't decided and you say, 'So, do you still desire to be a Ward of Chancery?' You see the look of uncertainty on my face because you point a finger in the air. 'I sense a wind from the East, Michael. Make your own mind up – follow your dream or your duty.' You produce a copy of *The Catcher in the Rye.* 'Here, take this. Read it. Let Holden Caulfield show you how to write your own story.'

Thurs Sept 9th

Dear Mr Soames,

Do you think I'm like Holden? He has failed all his exams, has been expelled and doesn't seem to care all that much. He is so negative and going nowhere. But I want to keep reading about him. Because there's a part of me that actually feels very much like him. Unable to fit in at school, afraid to tell his parents what he's really thinking.

Even though Salinger was a war hero, survived the D-Day landings, I'm keeping Salinger's novel a secret from dad. Holden Caulfield is everything my father despises.

Friday 10th September 1971

Dear Mr Soames,

Dad's under a lot of pressure. He comes home and the moment he walks through the door he complains his tea isn't ready. He says, it's all mum's had to do all day so why isn't it there waiting for him on the table? She's made him fish stew, which he likes, but I don't, I don't even like the fishy smell, the way it lingers in the house for days afterwards. So, mum serves up leftover cottage pie for me. Dad then starts on how he's the one bringing the food to the table and what he eats everybody else eats. But he doesn't end up eating anything at all, because right there he throws the whole plate across the room and it hits the wall and slides down like someone's brain slipping to the floor.

Mum's crying saying she doesn't know how much more of this she can take. I help her clear up the mess and then make her a cup of tea. We don't mention depression – we haven't mentioned it since that day in the summer holidays, but she doesn't look well. Large rings around her eyes and lines on her forehead. She looks so much older.

I study harder that evening with the Cambridge entrance exam coming up. I want to show dad I won't be the one to let him down. But part of me hates what he's doing to mum. I think of ways in which I might hurt him back, like not applying for Law, writing here in my journal about what a frightening bastard he can be sometimes.

He comes home after closing time and mum's waiting up for him. I'm here reading *The Catcher in the Rye*, ready to hide it in case he comes into the room. The house soon fills with the smell of frying steak and later I can hear mum speaking softly in the room next door and then dad snoring loudly.

It's well after midnight now and she gets up and she's in the kitchen washing pans. I go down and she tells me she's so worried about dad. There's this trouble at the factory with the union working to rule. Dad can't afford to keep shutting the machinery down and starting it up again, so he's been there on his own keeping the equipment running.

Then she's crying. Dad's had an accident in his car driving home from the pub. She says, it's nothing serious, nothing to worry about, but that we have to do our best to help him. I tell her I will work hard to get into Cambridge, for dad.

Then she stares at me long and says, 'Are you OK?'

'I'm fine, mum.'

'Have you ever thought of working in, say, a bank, or

something like that?

'No. Why?'

'You look tired, my love. All this studying. Instead of going to university you could get a good job here.'

'I have to go, everyone's going. That's what everyone does.'

'I know that's what you're supposed to do, and what your dad's set his heart on. But I wonder, though, if it's all too much for you, all this work, this pressure, the thought of leaving home. I worry about you.'

'I'm OK.'

'You weren't OK over the summer, though. Are you still, you know, depressed?'

I repeat, 'I'm fine, mum.'

Then she tells me to go back to bed and not to worry.

But she's right, I do worry. About what I really want to do. About dad driving home drunk, not wearing a seatbelt, having an accident. How we all need to make him happy.

Then I also start to think something else. What if dad wasn't around? What if it was just me and mum and I really didn't have to go to university after all. Am I just doing it all for dad? Or for you, Mr Soames. What do *I* want? And the answer is, I *don't* know.

I don't even know who I really am. So how can I know what I want?

But if dad wasn't around, would that make my life so much simpler? And the answer that comes back is awful, because, in a way it would.

Even as I think and write this, I feel terrible. No one can ever know this, Mr Soames. How can you unthink a thought? Do I really want something bad to happen to dad?

What sort of a person am I?

Saturday September 11th 1971

Dear Mr Soames,

Dad has a hangover so I watch what I'm doing when I'm around him. He announces there's a great film on this afternoon – I'm supposed to be film fan, he says – so I should watch it too. I don't want to annoy him, and, to be honest, I don't really feel like staying up in my room reading up for the exam. The film is *Shane,* Jack Palance, the hired killer, gunning Elisha Cook down outside the saloon, his body left lying in the mud as thunder rolls over the valley. Dad says this is his favourite Western, a film about a real hero who faces the bad guys. This is how the good guys handle things like he has to handle with the union at the factory who threaten his livelihood, our future. If he doesn't face them down now and beat them then he will never be free of their demands.

At the end of the film the little boy runs after the wounded Shane, calling him back but Shane just rides on because he's in love with the boy's mother. Something strange happens to dad. His eyes are watery and he suddenly gets up and leaves the room saying he has to put some coal on, but there is no need, the fire is fine. I hear him blowing his nose next door as the little boy in the film still calls out for Shane. Dad returns, his eyes are red and he is quiet for a long time. 'That kid,' he says, finally. 'That kid always gets to me.' Then he looks at me for a long time and looks sad. As if he knows some of the thoughts I've been having.

Then he gets up and smiles. 'I was talking to my solicitor, Jennings, yesterday,' he says. 'About the legal situation, you know, at the factory, with the workers taking strike action.'

He's standing over me, looking out of the window, but

very close by. 'That man, Jennings. He's a fool. Hasn't got half your brains. If he can make a fortune out of the law, god knows what you can achieve. You'll be able to retire at fifty. None of this worry and hard graft your old man has to put up with.'

Then he ruffles my hair. 'You're a good lad. Keep your nose to the grindstone for the next few years and you'll have it made.'

Monday Sept 13th

Dear Mr Soames,

Dad gives me a lift into school on his way to the factory. The car's a bit of a mess after his crash on Friday night but it's mainly the bodywork. 'El Condor Pasa' comes on the radio and he says this is the one song that he likes of my music. I've been playing that album to death up in my room these last months, thinking of Laura.

I look across at dad driving, heading to another lonely struggle at the factory. I want to say, 'Pay them, dad, pay them the money they want,' but I know he'd think this cowardly. Not the words of a man, a man like dad, a man like Shane, a real hero.

Laura and David went to see a band called The Groundhogs on Saturday. They're telling Lawton about how they smoked cannabis while the band played. Lawton wants to know about the music, did they play all four parts of 'Split' at once, or something like that, and all David wants to do is brag on about the great Moroccan he smoked all night.

Beacon looks across at him and asks, 'How can you smoke a Moroccan? Did he mind?' This cracks all three of them up.

Joan tells them that the guy who wrote that Groundhogs song based it on a panic attack after taking

LSD. David says he can't wait to drop acid again and Beacon claims LSD is like demonic possession and that people who take it are risking their souls.

David says, 'Yes and thank you from the Archbishop of Canterbury.'

'What was Pete Cruikshank's bass like?' Lawton says.

I think of 'El Condor Pasa' and dad at the factory alone with the machines and the polythene in the vats, working so hard for me, for my future, and here I am stuck with these people with their pointless talk about music and drugs. And worse than that, why does Laura find it all so fascinating, find March's every word so compelling?

So, I say, 'Why go and pay money to see people who deliberately make the worst noise possible?' The others look at me like I'm about fifty years old.

David half turns away and says wearily, 'And why would an artist ever deliberately make the worst noise possible?'

I should leave it there but I don't. I am suddenly my father, arguing with these young people with their drugs, their long hair, their awful music. And I can't think of anything more to say, but cannot walk away from this either. Shane wouldn't. Dad wouldn't. I remember dad's comment whenever he's watching Top of the Pops.

'Music will come back some day,' I say

'And what music would that be then, Michael? Andy Williams, Neil Diamond?' David replies and Lawton and Laura laugh along with him.

'Simon and Garfunkel,' I say.

Lawton groans, but David waves away Lawton's fake vomiting and says, 'No, Simon and Garfunkel are OK, actually.'

I smile at him. He just might, possibly, be a decent guy

after all. Maybe we can talk some more about other music I like – James Taylor, Carole King – but then –

'Yeah, Simon and Garfunkel *are* OK,' he pauses and then continues, 'if you happen to like diarrhoea.'

And they all laugh, even Beacon thinks this is funny.

And with that they all turn away from me. But I don't want to be on the outside, I don't want Laura to think I'm like Beacon, or worse and so I say, 'Well who do you like then?'

And I sit and listen to the one-word names they fire at me – Who, Tull, Cream, Taste, Nice, Doors, Love, Zappa,' and then March says, 'That's Frank Zappa, not Sinatra.' And they all start laughing again.

On the way home I make a detour for the record shop in the town centre and I buy Jethro Tull's 'Aqualung'. I go to my room and play it as soon as I am home before dad gets in. I have to work my way into the sound but I soon relax and I imagine Laura right here, maybe smoking some grass and this soft fluting melody taking us away to dreams of rivers and woodland.

Saturday 2nd October 1971

Dear Mr Soames,

I'm in the kitchen, breakfast being well and truly over, I think the coast is clear and safe to be reading something outside my room. When suddenly mum and dad come in arguing. She's not had a night out in months and he says what do you want to go out for? The same reason that you go out five nights a week, she says. He says, yes, but it's so different for me, I need to go out to take the pressure off. If I didn't have a pint or two every night, I'd go mad.

The strike at the factory has got worse. Dad has hired temporary labourers, who aren't very good but better than nothing. The regulars are picketing the entrance each morning. It's me or them, dad keeps on saying.

I'm under pressure too, mum says, and he just laughs. And she reels off her daily unremitting routine – washing, ironing, cooking, cleaning, going to see his mother.

Dad just says, 'Call that work?'

I'm trying to concentrate on Orwell's *Essays* when dad starts in on wider targets. The bums on the dole, the idle layabouts at university, commie unions and their members like sheep, women who don't know their place anymore, lefty teachers filling their students' heads full of nonsense. Then he demands to know what I'm doing reading Orwell – socialist claptrap, he says. His face, even the whites of his eyes look to be blood-filled and veins pulse at his temples. He goes on about how people like you, Mr Soames, are a menace trying to indoctrinate me with left wing ideas, how one day he's going into that school to teach you a lesson of his own that you won't forget.

'This is a war,' he says. 'This country's at war. We didn't fight for freedom, men didn't give their lives to throw it away to the Communists in the unions and schools, brainwashing our kids. Look at those long-haired bums at university with their so-called revolution. They want to destroy this country. Do you really want to turn out like them?'

The strange thing, Mr Soames, is that it's frightening but I don't want him to stop. His world is truly a simpler place. All I have to do is stay there in that world, without thinking or worrying and do what he wants me to do. Get my hair cut again on Monday. Study Law. Become a solicitor. Live a decent and safe life. Make a lot of money like he says.

But in my room, I look at my secret store of records I borrowed from Lawton after the argument the other day with March. Laura asked me afterwards why I had to be so square. The records are there with Salinger and Orwell, hidden under the bed. *Aqualung, Blind Faith, Thank Christ for the Bomb* and I know I'll be unable to play any of them while dad's around. I'm carrying a lump of concrete in my chest, a weight that's dragging me down.

Better to give Lawton all his music back. It's more trouble than it's worth.

Friday October 8th 1971

Dear Mr Soames,

I feel my life beginning to change

Just before afternoon registration Joan tells me she's seriously worried about Laura. It's drugs. All kinds of stuff and now acid. Then, after school, there she is, Laura, in the library, all alone, staring out of the window. She turns to me with tears streaming down her face.

'It's over,' she says. David's finished with her.

'He's such an idiot,' I say and she looks at me as if I'm the stupid one.

'No, he's not, he's just doing his own thing. He's free,' she says.

'He's selfish,' I say.

'It's this Tina. At the Groundhogs gig he was talking to her all the time. She's at university. At the end of the night, I know he went off to a club with her and her friends.'

We go for a walk but all she talks about is David the bad, David the good, David the brilliant, David the bastard, until we've walked all the way around the playing fields and we're back at the school.

I don't mention the drugs, and neither does she, but outside the gates she tells me something else. Her parents are splitting up. Things have been bad between them for a long time and her dad has moved to the States for good. She's about to start crying again and it's beginning to rain and we go back inside.

In the corridor we bump into you and Laura asks if she can have a word with you in private. You go inside the room and shut the door and I stand outside and try to listen in, but I can't hear anything except the sound of crashing mops and buckets in the corridor and nearby toilets.

I wait for a long time at the door but nobody comes out and I head off home. It reminds me of that summer night waiting outside your house. Is she still seeing you in secret? If she's finished with David does that mean she'll go back to you now? Are you having an affair with a student? I have no proof, only what I've witnessed and I just don't know.

I come home to an empty house and play Gordon Lightfoot's 'If You Could Read My Mind, Love', over and over again until I can hear every word, every chord in my sleep.

Saturday October 9th 1971

Dear Mr Soames,

Saturday morning dad says he was in the pub Friday and Tom Montgomery comes up to him and says the men all want their jobs back and they'll go back to work on Monday. Dad agrees on condition they resign from the union as well. And that's the strike over. Dad cock-a-hoop all Saturday. Parades in front of me and mum with his arms in the air like his hero, Rocky Marciano. He lifts mum up and tells her she can choose wherever she wants to go Saturday night. They're going to celebrate.

After they've gone out a miracle happens. The telephone rings. It's Laura. I just can't believe it. I can't breathe all that well. She tells me she's going to see *Straw Dogs*. Do I want to go with her, meet up in the pub outside the cinema?

I leave mum and dad a note and on the bus there I keep telling myself that Laura is just a friend, has been a friend for so many years at our other school, long before she met David. But none of this helps much with my nerves. When I get to the pub, she isn't there. Has she changed her mind, or has David phoned and she's back with him? I order a Coke as I don't want to risk not getting served. Waiting makes me even more nervous, my Coke going flat in the glass. I'm worrying about the film. It's an '18'. Will they let me in?

I don't recognise her at first. Taller in stacked boots and red hair cut shorter and shaped around her neck and shoulders. Still wearing the trench coat and tartan mini-dress with black tights. More make-up than usual. She sees me and smiles and looks amazing, and could pass for someone in her early twenties. I ask her what she wants to drink and my heart sinks when she says Bacardi and Coke.

But somehow, I get served OK and I ask about her hair and she says she's tired of looking like a hippy. She tells me that she's told you, Mr Soames, about David. And that you've told her I would be good to talk to and will listen and help.

'You're a good friend,' she says again, making me feel special. The James Taylor song plays on in my head as she speaks of her heartbreak and anger.

I don't mention my fears about getting in the film, although I do ask her if she really wants to see it, hoping she will say no or something. I warn her about how violent it's meant to be and suggest we go and see a movie I've had my eye on – *The Last Run* with George C. Scott. He is one of dad's favourite actors. The film billed as being in the tradition of Hemingway and Bogart.

'George C. Scott's an old fart,' she says and besides she has to see *Straw Dogs* because she's heard so much about it from David who's already seen it. He's told her about a rape scene that turned him on and she wants to see what all the fuss is about. She thinks he's probably seen it with 'that tart, Tina'.

As we get to the kiosk it's as if Laura knows what I'm thinking and she links arms with me and asks for two tickets and the woman behind the glass doesn't bat an eyelid about our age. Laura's arm stays in mine and she puts her head briefly on my shoulder as we go through into the darkness and my heart's beating so fast, I'm sure she can hear it through my coat and hers.

When the picture starts, she whispers that Dustin Hoffman looks like me. I can feel her hand in mine like a small bird, just like last time all those years ago watching *Mary Poppins*.

Should I try to kiss her? Does she want me to kiss her? Will she be angry or bored with me if I don't? The film moves slowly on and then there's a bit where Susan George stands naked in the window so that the builders can see her, and somehow, I can't try to kiss Laura after that. She starts sighing when the first builder attacks the woman and when she starts to kiss the rapist back Laura moves around in her seat and pulls her hand away from mine. Then the second man forces the first rapist at shotgun to hold Susan George down and she starts to scream and at that point Laura gets up and walks out. I follow her outside.

She's furious. 'Well, what did you think?' she says.

'About what?'

'That fucking rape. The woman enjoying it.'

'I don't know. I wanted it to stop.'

'Well, it didn't, did it?' she says. 'It just went on and on and it was awful.' She's so angry like it's somehow my fault even though I warned her about the film.

We head back to The Kings Arms and this time I get a pint of Double Diamond for me and another Bacardi and

Coke for Laura. She's says it shows what a sick bastard David really is being turned on by that shit. I try to think of James Taylor again. Then at the end of the evening she puts her hand on mine and says it's great to have someone she can talk to who isn't like everyone else – only interested in one thing.

And that means I don't have to worry about whether or not I should kiss her goodnight, because that would make me like everyone else.

When I get home mum and dad aren't back yet and I really wish I hadn't returned all Lawton's music. I look through mum's cabinet of LPs, pick the soundtrack from *Camelot* and play 'How to Handle a Woman' over and over. I think of Laura alone at home now, her father gone to America, her hand in mine at the cinema.

Sunday October 10th 1971

Dear Mr Soames

This morning dad asks me what film I went to see, and I realise I forgot to tear up the note I left them.

'*The Last Run,*' I say, 'George C. Scott. He was like Bogart.' I leave out any mention of Hemingway.

'George C. Scott's a great actor,' he says. 'I wish I'd the time to go to the cinema.'

That afternoon I tell mum that I am going for a walk, and she lectures me about staying away from the beach and the shore. I just tell her I am off to the park to clear my head after the reading I've been doing. I sneak back to the Rialto and an afternoon showing of *Straw Dogs*. There is hardly anyone in the cinema and when the lights go down there are blue solitary curls of smoke with feet perched like single rabbits on the seats in front scattered around the cinema. It feels lonely and sad watching the same film without

Laura. In the rape scene one of the rabbits' ears across from me starts making gasping noises in the dark and I can feel Laura's presence judging all this. Am I 'turned on', like David? Not really – the rape is boring and monotonous and goes on for a long time. And ultimately just depressing.

What is exciting is what follows when Dustin Hoffman takes his revenge and defends his home with boiling oil, a shotgun and a bear-trap that he wraps around a man's head. This is what a man has to do to protect and keep what is his, to defend his woman against the rapists and the beasts. What he must do against the likes of David March, who thinks rape is a turn on, who treats Laura like dirt.

Laura my Guinevere.

Wednesday October 13th 1971

Dear Mr Soames,

Laura and I meet at The Kings Arms. She complains that David's ignoring her in school and she's noticed he's now wearing a bracelet that Tina's bought him. He's also forgotten about the Kabul hippy trail next year and is hell bent on Goa where Tina has some friends living on the beach there.

After a couple of pints, I finally get fed up of just listening about David and tell her of the decision I have to make soon about Law or English.

She is trying to light a cigarette and doesn't seem to be paying attention. But finally, she says, 'Well? What do *you* want? After all, it *is* your life,' as if it's just nothing, this thing I've been worrying over for months, as if I'm agonising over whether or not to order crisps or peanuts at the bar. Just like that, so simple. In many ways, she sounds just like you, sir.

But I shrug and say I don't know what to do.

And then she says, suddenly alive and interested,

'Why don't we go to Cambridge together?' I look at her and she says, 'Why not, Michael? We've been together forever. Failed our eleven plus together, came here to Pennington together. We were meant to be together. You and me.'

She laughs and there it is. The rest of the evening we talk of nothing else. The present and the future all reconciled. With Laura by my side, I can do anything. Running away now with her forever into the blue, out of sight. As we are leaving, she starts talking about David again. But I'm not really listening anymore, for all I can hear is those words over and over again, 'We were meant to be together,' as in a beautiful dream that has no end.

In fact, the dream is only just beginning. But it's real – this thing that is suddenly happening to me.

Saturday October 16th 1971

Dear Mr Soames,

We're waiting in class for you to arrive and David's telling Lawton about Goa and how cheap the drugs are and how you can live for free in the beach community. How everyone supports everybody there.

Joan's trying to talk to Laura about an essay that's due on *Persuasion*, but Laura's chewing on her lip, staring at the silver bracelet on David's wrist. I can see the letters T and A from where I am sitting. Tina. With her friends on Goa Beach. David babbles on about everyone making their own music out there and there's no capitalist scene to fuck with the free sharing of sounds.

And that's when I say, 'It's just another beach, for god's sake.'

Laura looks at me as if I've just set off a grenade.

David takes a breath and replies, 'OK...enlighten me,

Michael. How do intend to expand your horizons? In your dad's plastics factory, maybe?'

I go blank, and all that comes out is, 'Why, is your dad so clever he's doesn't have to work?'

David just smiles and says, 'How would I know, I never speak to him.' He follows this with, 'Hey, Laura, when's Michael going to show you his polystyrene balls?'

'Fuck off, David, just fuck off!' Laura shouts. And that's when you enter the room.

'What's the matter here then?' you say. You smile, but you know something bad has happened to this group, the tension like a poison in the air. You try to lift the mood and bring us all back together by asking us what we're reading at the moment. When Beacon says *The Pilgrim's Progress* David snorts with laughter. Lawton's reading *Tarantula* but hasn't got a clue what Dylan's on about, Joan's on *Mansfield Park*, and Laura's just finished *Play It as It Lays*, a Californian novel she picked up while in the States over the summer, about a woman who has an abortion.

'That sounds a barrel of laughs,' David says, again to Lawton, as if he's not really part of the group anymore.

You ignore David and turn to me. I recently watched *The Third Man* again on TV and when I say I'm reading Greene's novel David makes sucking up noises.

I can see you're losing patience, but you ask him what he's reading. 'Henry Miller *Tropic of Cancer*,' he says. 'Miller's so cool. He writes about sex in a way that's real,' and Laura tuts and sighs, but David carries on. 'He's a revolutionary, he's changed the way we think about the world.'

I've not read any Miller but I remember Orwell's essay I've just read, so I can say, 'Orwell claims Miller's not really a revolutionary. He says he's like Jonah – a man swallowed by a whale and living in its belly, without any hope.'

'What would *you* know about Henry Miller? What

fucking whale?' David says.

'Michael's raised an interesting idea here,' you say. There's an angry edge to your voice which I haven't heard before.

So, I go on, treading a bit carefully. 'It's Orwell's essay "Inside the Whale". He's not criticising Miller. He says Miller speaks for the ordinary man. How to be happy when things are hopeless.'

'The ordinary man doesn't drop out of society and go and live in Paris with artists and write. The ordinary man doesn't experience life like Miller, doesn't have sex the way Miller has sex, doesn't write about sex the way Miller writes,' David says.

'Why does it always have to be about sex with you?' Laura says.

'Because it's real, because it makes you feel alive.'

'Yeah, like rape makes the woman feel alive,' she says.

'Well,' he says, waving his copy of *Persuasion* in her face, 'I mean, let's face it, it's what this here Anne Elliot needs most of all – a good fuck.' And he throws the book across the room.

'Typical,' says Laura.

Joan says, 'Well that certainly helps with my next essay. You know, for a clever person, David, you're such a moron.'

'Fuck off, Joan,' David says. 'Why don't you and Beacon get it together some time, turn each other on? The Old Maid and the Archbishop. Ken Russell could make a film of it.'

Then suddenly you stand and I realise just how tall, how big, you are looming over David's desk. 'I think, young man, you'd better leave the room for a while. Take a break.'

David remains sitting, his lip curling into half a smile. When he doesn't move you say, 'Leave the room, or I will have to escort you personally. And, believe me, you wouldn't want that.'

David stands, and although he's tall, he's still half a head shorter than you. Neither of you move for a moment, head-to-head, six inches apart, almost nose to nose.

David's the first to break eye contact and with a half-muttered, 'God, man, you're such a hypocrite,' he's on his way, slamming the door behind him.

You sit down again and smile at the group and say, 'Now what about this for an essay title? Would more sex improve Anne Elliot's judgement?' And that sort of breaks the tension.

But I feel like it's my fight with David. I started it and should finish it. I can't let you, sir, fight my battle for me. Afterwards at the school gates I see Laura and tell her I'm waiting for David. I need to face him, like Shane, gun him down in the saloon and then ride off into the mountains. Beat him to death with a fire poker, hang a bear trap round his head.

'Would you really blow off his foot with a shotgun?' Laura laughs and then says, 'Don't be silly. Come on, Little Big Man, lighten up. He's just not worth it. Do you want to come back to my house? Listen to some sounds?'

We go back there and Captain Beefheart's on Laura's turntable in her bedroom. I try hard to get into it but I hate this music. But it's not important. What is incredible is that I'm actually here watching her crumble the cannabis into the flaky tobacco. I can't believe this is the room where she falls asleep beneath her poster of Robert Plant, where she dreams of who knows what, as the lava lamp dances and glows.

She touches the skins of the Rizla papers with the

tip of her tongue. Her mother is always out, her father is on the other side of the world and she's invited me up to her bedroom. She tears and folds the corner of the cigarette packet into a small funnel shape and packs it into the base of the joint, twists the other end two or three times. I could watch her do this forever.

Before she lights the joint, she scrapes her newly cut hair back off her face and ties it back into a short ponytail. Her face is softened by the glow from the lamp and the candles she's lit on the bedside cabinet. She opens a window and with the last light of day fading, Beefheart drifts off into the street below.

'The only downer,' she says, 'about finishing with David is that I'll have to find another supply from somewhere. I have a stash but it won't last forever.' She lights the twisted top of the joint which she takes to her lips and then draws down a deep lungful of the smoke and holds it there. She breathes it all out slowly somewhere in the direction of the open window.

'You and me and Cambridge,' she says smiling, extending the joint to me.

Without worrying about the last and only time I smoked a joint – with Ray from the bakery – I take a deep draw. My head and lungs explode at the same time. When I finish coughing the room's spinning and I see Laura swimming in my tears and she is laughing. The room slowly settles down, and I get my breath, and I reach again for the spliff. After two or three more tokes I feel happier than I have felt for a long, long time.

'Yes, Cambridge, two punts on the river,' I say, and for some reason she thinks that's very funny.

The Beefheart album comes to an end. She asks me if I have any requests and raises her eyebrows. Does she mean sex? I don't think so. It's cold in the room with the window open and she still has her school blazer on. What she needs

147

now, more than anything is a true friend. Not someone like David only interested in one thing.

'Have you any Andy Williams?' I ask, and she starts laughing again.

Sunday October 17th 1971

Dear Mr Soames,

We're smoking down by the lake in a shelter amongst the trees. It's one of Laura's secret places where it's quiet and no one bothers you. Across the water is the golf course and it seems very far away. Four figures with golf bags walk up the hill into the wind. I tell her it's probably my dad out there, my dad who wants me to go to Cambridge to study Law. She says all Dads can go to hell as far she's concerned. They only care about themselves and their scene. Her father is now back in the States and she is missing him but she hates him for going, for abandoning her with her mother who is some hotshot accountant who is never around and is always working.

Then she says, 'David's father's a lawyer, and he's a creep. But then, hey, like father, like son.'

She looks sad for a moment but then says, 'If you do Law you'll be surrounded by these straights, squares and bread-heads. You'd go mad with those people.'

Laura doesn't think I'd fit in with the straights. She doesn't think I'm a square anymore. We smoke another joint as the twilight comes down upon the lake.

Friday October 22nd 1971

Dear Mr Soames,

A spliff in Laura's room tonight to give me courage for

what I have to do. She passes me the gear and tells me it's about time I had a go at rolling one myself.

My first effort I can't get the papers to fold or roll well. When I've finished it's three times the size it should be and most of that is air.

She says, 'Hindenburg,' as it blazes away like the airship that came crashing down all those years ago.

'What a blimp,' I say and we fall about laughing amidst the papered ash floating in the draught from the open window.

She pretends to be my dad while I tell her I've applied to read English not Law and she goes into a mock rage cutting off my inheritance and sending me packing with a shoebox of belongings. We smoke another joint which she rolls this time. 'When you get down to it with him,' she says, 'just imagine it's me you're speaking to.'

On the way home, I get the full-blown shakes and I'm sick down an alley. It feels like a past self I'm vomiting on the cold tarmac, leaving me drained and vacant. When I see him I feel so wasted and exhausted I don't really care anymore and the words come out and it feels like someone else is saying them.

'Dad, I've applied to do English at Cambridge.'

Dad's not exhausted at all. He doesn't disinherit me or kick me out onto the street. It might have been better if he had. Instead, he sends me to my bedroom but follows me up there to deliver a never-ending torrent. First of all the Eleven Plus. Even after all these years he still holds that against me. Tells me I'm setting myself up for failure again as a student bum and why should he work his fingers to the bone to support another layabout. Then, I've gone behind his back, broken all trust, been disloyal. He rarely talks about the war but he brings that up now – how when he was about my age, he was in a trench in Burma standing up to his waist in water. And there you had to rely on the men around you and that was loyalty. The enemy would kill you if you let your friends down. You knew you were only as good as the man next to you, and you'd give up everything for him. And that was what being a man was. A man is someone you can trust, no matter what.

And on and on about how I was obviously not that kind of man. How he fought for his country only to see it go backwards and be taken over by communists and scroungers. And this brings him on to you, Mr Soames. You are the enemy and I've chosen to side with you. He says he no longer knows me. He includes me with all the hippy dropouts that his taxes go to supporting while all we want to do is smash the things up that many good men died for. But this isn't going to happen under his roof. I need a dose of what it means to do some proper work and on Monday I'll be down at the factory and working there over the half-term. I need a taste of the real world and I've been pampered and mollycoddled for far too long.

And through it all I say nothing. In fact, I agree with him. Dad's right. He's always right. I *am* a traitor. I *have* let him down. I *have* been influenced by you. But what I don't tell him is – that's *exactly* what I want. I *want* to be like you. I want to read great works of literature, and write my own. I want to be with Laura. I want to be with her in her room, in her secret places with her dope, her music, her future, my future at Cambridge. With her. If suffering this rage is what it takes to live that life, then so be it.

CHAPTER TEN

He lay the journal down, his feelings as mixed as the dust stirring through the air in those last rays of sunlight shafting through the curtains. His rebellion against his father that evening didn't last of course. The debacle that followed a few days later put paid to that. His defiance could not withstand the overwhelming recrimination and remorse in the wake of that disaster. And amidst the waves of punishing guilt that swept over him in the ensuing days, weeks and years, his father's account of the war that night, the only time he'd ever spoken of the suffering and sacrifice involved, served as added retribution to haunt and condemn him. As a boy, Michael tried to ask his grandmother what her son had been like when he came back from Burma in the late months of 1945, and she was just as tight-lipped as his father about the experience. All she would say was that he was 'yellow and weighed seven stone.' Michael thought many times how he would have fared had he been drafted into action, and each time he came to the same conclusion. No way would he have coped in Burma, wading through the muddy, leech and reptile infested Irrawaddy, exhausted, diseased, under fire from land and air. So he understood why his father saw him in that way, an affront to the men who died, typical of an arrogant post war generation with no respect for the debt that was paid to keep them free.

And yet reading that passage now rekindled that brief burst of pride when he withstood his father's onslaught, when he knew there was something that called to him like nothing had done before or since, not just in the form of Laura and Soames and Cambridge, but beyond, in a world of endless possibilities awaiting him on the other side of his defiance. The years just peeled away to that moment of silent courage in the face of his father's rage. That was what love had done all those years ago, the love for a girl and the belief that a teacher had in him. The future he dreamed of with Laura had given him that strength. Sometimes he thought that was the last time in his life he'd felt totally whole. The first and last time he felt equal to his father's will and strength of character. He looked down at the journal, knowing the sadness in the entries ahead that followed, compelled now to read on, to face those days again. But as he turned the page, he became aware of voices downstairs and his heart sank as he heard his mother and Joe heading up to the landing.

'We need to come in,' she said, hovering in the doorway. 'Joe's setting traps around the house for the mice. He wants to put one in here.'

'Not in here, he's not,' Michael said.

'Oh, Michael, you're not reading that now, are you?' she cried out.

He put the journal down. 'Just flicking through it.'

'Once and for all I wish you would forget about those days.'

She shook her head and turned to Joe. 'Here's where I was hearing noises. We need at least one in this room, maybe under the bed.'

'The mouse is dead, mum.'

'And there may be others.'

'Then get the council out, or pest removal.'

'I'm not having vans outside the house.'

'And I'm not having a trap in here. It's inhumane.'

'This is silly. Stop being squeamish. Joe, tell Adrian Mole here to get out of the way so you can sort it out, will you.' She marched down the landing as Joe, still stranded in the threshold, let her pass by. He looked at Michael and shrugged his shoulders, before knocking on the open door gently like a man tapping a pipe to see if it was frozen.

'Your mum got a new toaster,' he said.

'Oh, thanks.'

'I don't want to disturb you reading.'

'It's OK. It's just a journal I kept, a long time ago. About my schooldays and that teacher. You know, the one who's disappeared. Mr Soames.'

'My grandson had a card and a present ready for him for Christmas. It's strange that no one has any idea where he's gone.'

'I went to see his wife this morning. She's devastated. And she has as much idea as anyone as to where he might be.'

'It's a strange business.'

'I saw a colleague of his as well. The last person to see him before he went missing. He says the management at the school have been giving Soames a really difficult time. That they've driven him half mad.'

'That's awful. My grandson will be very upset if anything's happened to him.'

'He sounds like a nice kid.'

'He is. Ben. He's a grand lad.' Joe glowed with pride. 'He's one boy who won't be going into the plumbing business. He's doing so well at that school. And he loves English. A teacher like that can make such a difference to a kid's life.'

'You had your Mr Grimes.'

'Yes, I loved school. Best days of your life. I'd have liked to stay on, but my dad had other ideas.' Joe paused before continuing. 'Those were different times then, though.' He lingered in the doorway, seemingly unsure at whether he should leave or insist on setting the trap.

'Was your dad tough to be with?' Michael asked, the violence of that last journal extract still with him.

Joe looked puzzled.

'You know, making you go to work when you wanted to stay on at school?'

'No. He was a good father to us. Worked hard for us all. Kept food on the table. Fought in the War.'

'The War?'

'Yes. He was at the Somme.'

'Good god.'

'Yeah, can you imagine? I can't fathom how anyone came back from that.'

'I know. My dad was in Burma, World War Two.'

'Those poor sods. Both wars. They went through hell. And those that stayed behind. The women. What they went through as well. People these days. They don't know they're born. I sometimes think we've all gone soft.'

'Like worrying over a dead mouse in a toaster, you mean.'

'I don't know. Maybe it's not so good to bottle stuff up, either.'

Michael looked at the plumber. Did Joe know Michael had been crying in the kitchen that morning just before he arrived? If he did there was no hint of sarcasm or judgement in his voice.

'You see,' Joe continued, 'my old man never spoke about the war. Best forgotten, he said. But he *couldn't* forget it. Had nightmares all his life.'

'My dad only ever spoke about it once.'

'They just didn't. Or maybe they couldn't.'

'Or no one would listen if they did.'

'I don't think people would ever have understood anyway. I've a brother-in-law in Australia. He was a bomber pilot over Dresden. He's now an alcoholic.'

'He dropped those firebombs?'

'It's over fifty years ago but my sister says it's like it's still only yesterday for him.'

'Were you in the war, Joe?'

'Too young. Did National Service. Didn't take to it much myself. Supposed to have made a man of you. Though I'm not so sure.'

'And then you became a plumber?'

'I was already a plumber. As I said, with dad on the building site at fifteen.'

'Your son works with you, doesn't he?'

'John, he's taken over the business. Grand lad. Married to a lovely lass. Got two kids of his own now. There's Ben and Charlie. Charlie's seven.' Joe rummaged in his coat pocket for his wallet, and brought out a photograph. 'Here, look, there they are.'

Michael got up from the bed and looked over Joe's shoulder at the picture of two boys, the elder with his arm around his brother.

'Charlie's a right tearaway. They keep you young though. They miss their grandma but kids get over things better than we do.'

'They're lovely kids.'

'They are. I'm a lucky fella. I had a good wife, a wonderful woman, best friend for life. And now I've got my son, his wife, grandkids.' He put the photograph away, his attention drawn to another photo, that of Maddie, which had fallen out of the journal and was now lying face up on the bed.

'Is that her? Your sweetheart?'

'That's Maddie,' Michael said, picking the photograph up quickly. But then he didn't know what to do with it. They both stood staring at Maddie's face.

'She's pretty,' said Joe.

'Like I said, we split up. After the summer.'

'But you've still got her picture.'

Michael shrugged. What could he say? He couldn't bear not to have her picture.

Grace shouted from the kitchen. She needed Joe back down there.

'Anyway, I need to go,' Joe said. 'That's a nice girl,' he said pointing at Maddie. 'She won't come alive by just staring at her photo, though.'

'It's over, Joe.'

'It's never over till it's over, when our time's up. Believe me, life's short. You've still got her picture, so it's not over.' He set off down the landing before turning around. 'Oh, don't worry,' he said, 'I'm not putting a trap in there if you don't want.'

'Thanks Joe.'

'How's the little fella we buried outside?'

'Nothing's dug him up yet.'

'If more turn up in the house we can rig up some extra

toasters.'

Michael laughed as the plumber disappeared down the stairs leaving him alone with the journal and Maddie's photo. No, as Joe said, her picture wouldn't come alive, but what could he do? What Joe said was all well and good, but she had a kid, Tommy, and she'd made it clear she could never carry on with their situation as it was. Perhaps it was better that way, that Maddie had made the decision for them. She needed something he couldn't give. He missed her every day and, yes, still loved her, probably even more now that she was no longer in his life. But at least there were the good memories, the good days, the week in Porthcawl, the afternoon of the photograph by the river. And it had ended before the stress, the arguments, the struggle that he had witnessed in his own upbringing. Reading the journal had brought back how that household shuddered under his father's rule, how he himself brought so much disappointment, sadness and then tragedy into his parents' lives. Perhaps it was always better for the affair to end before it all went badly wrong. He picked up Maddie's picture and placed it at the back of the journal. Then he carried on reading.

CHAPTER ELEVEN

Monday 3rd November 1971

Dear Mr Soames,

So much has happened since my last entry and all that happened before now belongs to another life.

I've always known you would never read these entries, but after what happened that day at Laura's house, I wouldn't want you to. Nothing was as it seemed to be. I'm not even sure *you* are the person I thought you were. I'm not sure why I am still writing to you or why I am writing at all.

But you are the only person who ever believed in me. And that still matters. Even though *I'm* not really that person anymore, either.

Everything's changed. I mean everything.

Mum visits the hospital again today and I ask her when dad will be coming to see me. She looks annoyed and just shakes her head and then says she has something for me and she produces my journal from her bag.

'I told Dr Carter about your writing,' she says, 'and he says it would be good for you if you could write about what happened. It might help you to come to terms with things. So, I found this under your bed. But don't tell your dad. It can be our little secret.'

Another little secret with mum. Not sure she realises

DISAPPEARING ACTS

that the person who wanted to write no longer exists. In the mirror I look like the same person, same skin, same hands, same face. But, like I said, everything's changed.

I take my three yellow and two white tablets three times a day.

Mum says I'm looking better as she hands me the journal. But who is this person who wrote those entries? The person I was before I came here to this hospital. Before that day in the pillbox.

Since that day, that day in the pillbox, at the factory, at Laura's house, nothing seems real. How can I write about that?

I will try but I'm not sure it will help.

Maybe tomorrow.

Tuesday 4th November 1971

Dear Mr Soames,

I have the journal in my hands and about to open it when I see the scar on my finger where I cut myself in the factory. The scar's healing but other wounds are still open. The doctor says writing this, writing about that day, all that will help me heal. I'm not so sure. Well, I *am* sure actually. It is hopeless. But I've nothing else to do in here except wait for the next round of medication.

So I will give it a try. Just to fill the time.

Writing myself back to that day, that morning…the first morning of half term, my first and my last day at the factory…the clear crisp autumn air….it seems so long ago, like a dream. The red and yellow leaves swirling and falling around and ahead of the car as dad and I drive along in silence.

The sky washed blue that day, forever stretching

ahead with me and Laura into the future. I remember the thrill of escape, just a week at the factory, a few more weeks before the end of term then the year's half over, and a few months after that I will be away to Cambridge, with Laura, away from dad. That's what I'm thinking in the car that morning – these all now seem another person's thoughts. That person sitting alongside my father in silence now a stranger to me.

At the factory I'm assigned the cutting detail at the front end where the plastic goes into the system.

Dad hands me the knife and speaks to me for the first time that morning, the first time for days. 'Start slicing those plastic sheets into strips and be quick about it. Once we've powered up the machines, we need to be ready to go.' And then he walks away and gives the signal for the great iron vat that looms above me to be fired up.

They call it The Creamer. It churns and heats the polythene and water into liquid paste maintained at high temperature. When The Creamer is full the stuff that comes out goes through another set of machines and containers until you get the end product – polystyrene. The Creamer can never be empty, its appetite must be satisfied from the beginning to the end of each day without a break. It roars and screams for more water, more plastic, more fuel.

The concrete floor is freezing and wet, my hands cold and numb as I slice through the sheets. I don't feel anything but there are suddenly streaks and lines of blood mixing with the strips of plastic and my finger's bleeding badly into the polythene. Jack, one of the new labourers, is emptying buckets of water into the howling grinding machine. I hold my hand up to stop the blood, but Jack doesn't notice as he gathers up the plastic and loads it in without looking. I wrap my handkerchief around my finger so I can keep on cutting and Jack can keep on feeding. My hand stops bleeding after a bit but the plastic sheeting is smeared in red all around me.

After about an hour another man, George, takes over from Jack but I'm left on the floor without a break, cutting sheet after sheet. Dad's with Monty, inspecting the first batch being bagged into sacks.

Monty says, 'Christ, look at this lot, Bill. Didn't know we were doing a special coloured batch for Christmas this year.'

'They're pink,' dad says.

'How the fuck's that happened? There's no contamination in the system.'

'Then it must've gone in like that,' dad says, and the knife drops from my hands.

'Have you cut yourself?' he asks, looking at my hand wrapped in the bloodstained handkerchief.

Dad stares at the sheets. There's no more blood on the ground but he knows what's happened and I realise what I've done. He rails on me telling me I've contaminated a whole morning's batch. That means late shipment, failure to meet deadlines, pissed off customers, lost orders, ruining the business's reputation. There's no end to the disaster I've caused. I'm on my knees at the centre of this circle of men I've let down. Dad points out each of them to me, how I've put their wages, their bonus at risk.

'Why didn't you tell someone you'd cut yourself?' he asks.

'I didn't want to stop the machine.'

'So, for the sake of two minutes while we got someone else on the cutting, you waste a whole morning's work.'

'You told me the machine had to keep going.' My hand starts bleeding again as if to give him further ammunition.

'Always the same with you, my lad,' he snarls. 'A fucking coward who never opens his mouth to let people know what's really going on. A little sneak who goes behind your back. And it all comes out in the wash doesn't it, in the end. The secrets. The lies.'

He throws the handful of screwed up polystyrene which falls all around me in a shower of small grey-pink crumbs.

'Get up,' he says. 'You're useless. Get out of my factory. Get out of my sight.'

Wednesday 5th November 1971

Dear Mr Soames,

I've thought about it a lot since – where I should have gone that day. Not home – I didn't want to involve mum. To your place? Maybe – at least I might've found out the truth about you if I had. But instead I went to the only place I really wanted to be.

When I get to Laura's house, she's just got out of bed, no makeup, looking tiny wrapped in her large dressing gown in the doorway. She makes coffee and buttered toast. You know, I've remembered that toast a lot over the past two weeks. Maybe it's the last good thing before the disaster that was coming. That and the way she listens to me as she washes my wounded finger, her hands soft and nimble with the dressing of cotton wool and a thick plaster which she cuts from a large roll.

When I get to the part about the pink polystyrene she starts laughing, and soon I'm laughing too. And everything is suddenly fine. She wants today to be a day to remember. 'Independence Day,' she says. 'You're free of the factory. Soon be free of your crazy father.' And it all sounds so wonderful, so simple.

We head out that afternoon to the beach to the old pillbox. Another one of her secret places.

'It's an old guard post from the war,' she says, as we

enter the dark claustrophobic interior. 'Set up to defend us from the sea.'

Inside there is a small bench and enough light from the lookout windows to read some of the graffiti on the walls

God Drops Acid and Dreams the World

'David wrote that one,' Laura says. 'We'd come here to do LSD.'

Then she tells me the strangest thing. The pillbox, she says, that's where she brought you, sir, in the summer.

'A mistake', she says, sadly. She tells me how kind you were, how you listened about her dad splitting up the family. How you went for a walk with her on the beach and ended up there, in the pillbox. How it was David who dared her to take you there – to see if you'd smoke some grass – find out how hip you really were.

I am confused again about you and her. All those unanswered questions I had about last summer.

'What happened that night?' I say to her.

'What do you mean?'

'That night when we broke up for summer. At Mr Soames' house. When I left and you stayed behind. I waited for you outside for ages and you never came out.'

'Oh, then. We stayed talking forever. About Cambridge, books, films, theatre, he's a genius, knows everything.'

'Nothing else happened then? Just talking?'

'Michael, are you serious?'

I say, 'I just don't think it's right to be seeing a teacher out of school, at his house, taking him here to this place to smoke pot.'

'Oh, we didn't smoke anything,' she says sadly. 'It

freaked him out when I started mentioning drugs. Gave me a lecture and told me he couldn't see me again outside of school.'

'So, you haven't seen him since?'

'Of course I have – seen him every day at school.'

'You know what I mean, Laura.'

'No, stop being silly.'

Convincing, she is. So convincing. But I can't get it out of my head there and then that you, sir, have been in this strange place with her.

'Remember that afternoon,' she says.

'When?'

'When we went to see *Mary Poppins*.'

This is the first time she's ever mentioned that day.

'You held my hand,' she says. 'You were so sweet.'

I don't quite know what to say. First she tells me about bringing Soames down here to this damp, cold place with David's graffiti on the walls. And now she is remembering that afternoon so long ago but so special. It feels wrong to speak of it down here in the darkness with the smell of sewers and rotten fish and the menacing tide roaring nearby.

'Of course I remember,' is all I can think of to say.

Then she says she has actually brought *me* here to do some acid.

'You can't do it on your own and you can't do it with just anyone. You have to totally trust the person you're with.'

I am wary. We all know the stories about LSD, about people jumping off buildings believing they can fly, staring at the sun until they go blind. And, yet I want to prove to her that I'm that person – the one she can totally trust.

She unfolds a small rolled up ball of tinfoil and at the centre there's a purple dot that looks like one of those hundreds and thousands that you'd put on a child's birthday cake.

'It's the last of the batch David gave me,' she says. I must have looked worried because she says, 'I've been saving it for a special day. Come on, we're celebrating.'

'Celebrating?'

'Your freedom. Our lives together.'

I'm really not sure how I feel about acid. About taking anything that David has given her, but those unbelievable, wonderful, magical words 'our lives together', are still hanging in the air.

'I'm not taking a whole tab on my own,' she says. 'Come on, Little Big Man. It will loosen you up.'

She produces a small penknife to cut the dot in half, but she makes a mess of it.

'Oh shit,' she says. 'David usually takes the larger share if he fucks it up. Are you ready for that?'

Even now I don't know why I take the bigger half of the dot, place it on my tongue and swallow, all done quickly before I can think about it too much.

Laura smiles in admiration. 'Wow, that is fucking impressive, Michael. Straight into the big league for you,' and she then takes the other half.

'Let's just be quiet for a while,' she says, and she sits beside me and holds my hand, just like we did all those years ago watching *Mary Poppins*. And I can hear the sea outside and it sounds so close. She recites some poetry about mermaids, oceans and drowning. And then I think of her and you, Mr Soames, here in this cold dark place, maybe holding hands, reading poetry. And I think of my dad and how I've overturned his world.

I look at my watch and only ten minutes have passed although it seems like time is stretching. And then I start thinking we aren't alone in the shelter. There's someone or something else in here with us. The sound of the sea approaching grows louder and I'm about to say it would be a good idea to get outside.

But Laura moves closer to me and she suddenly has her arms around me and then her tongue is in my mouth, strange, dry and rough, like it's covered in sand. And, her face suddenly close up now, isn't really Laura. It's Laura's hair and Laura's clothes, but this is not her. This is a much older, uglier person, someone, or something pretending to be Laura.

'What's wrong?' she says, hurt. 'Do I smell or something?' as I pull away.

'I think I need to get out of here for a while. Need to walk.'

'Are you freaking out?'

I can't tell her how I feel – she'll think I can't handle the acid. That I'm not cool. But something dreadful will happen unless we get out of that pillbox. If I look at her for more than a few seconds her nose and chin begin to stretch again into the witch's mask.

Outside she says, 'Let's walk into the sun.'

But the sun is a red boil of raging fire.

'I can't go that way,' I tell her.

'Are you OK? You're not OK, are you?'

'I'm sorry. Having a bit of a bad time.'

'Come on let's go,' she says, and she leads me back with my eyes half-closed, afraid to look at the beach and the sky. Already I'm praying for this to be over, but time has stopped.

I manage to reach her house. Things are no better there. Something awful has followed us. Someone or something dreadful watching me. Here in Laura's living room. A cheese-plant sways and waves in a storm of light and sound. Laura's witch-like features emerge every time I look at her. We sit both miles apart, not speaking. What happened to me before this eternal afternoon locked in this nightmare – Eleven Plus, Tindall School, *Mary Poppins*, Pennington, Cambridge, all happened to another person, not me. Whoever, or whatever I am, I have always been and always will be here in this room. Trapped in a world without time. Then Laura comes and sits beside me – once I dreamed of such moments but now I shrink from the horror of anyone close, but especially her. Something awful has happened to her. And then, she takes my hand in hers. It feels scaled, old, something inhuman.

'Cambridge,' she says.

Somehow it's the worst thing she can say, the last thing I want to hear with her changed face breathing close to mine.

'Come on, my buddy. Cheer up. Look at me.' I cannot look at her. All I can do is close my eyes but then I start seeing visions on my eyelids – waves of plastic sheeting covered in blood, shapes of faces, distorted, dad crying by the fire, you, Mr Soames entwined with Laura in the pillbox.

'There's someone in the house,' Laura says, suddenly. 'Fuck, there really is someone here, now.' Her voice comes from a place that's deep and lost.

She lets go of my hand and leaves me and I open my eyes. In the hallway I hear the man's voice recognisable and then Laura saying, 'I have missed you so much,' and I hear her crying. I hear the man say, 'I'm here now, and will always be here.' And I know that voice so well. And I know then what I knew from the start, knew from that night the previous summer as I stood outside your house waiting for her to come out. That you and Laura are lovers, and have been all along. You even have a key to her house, and you are both together now, here, in the room next door.

I run outside, not looking back, although I can feel both you and Laura watching from the window. I hear Laura's voice, calling me from her house, 'Bad comes back! Bad comes back!' I keep running afraid to look behind me. The road's a nightmare of shifting, melting light, trees with gaping sneering mouths, folding pavements that barely take the weight of my feet.

My mind races frantically from the blackness that is coming and cannot be stopped.

There's only one hope for me, to get back to the world I once knew. Before I threw it all away.

Back to dad's world.

Back to the factory.

'Michael! Joe's gone! Tea's ready! Are you staying up there the rest of the day?'

His mother's voice startled him out of the nightmare. She sounded distant, from another dimension. He looked around him and absorbed the familiar surroundings, comforting in their timeless presence – the childhood wallpaper, the soft single bed where he had slept a thousand nights, the battered boyhood novels of heroism and empire, the late afternoon sunlight casting shadows across the ceiling. He welcomed his mother's call to normal life, away from the horrors of that afternoon, back to the everyday certainties of tea-time and TV.

He knew he'd never fully recovered from that day in the pillbox. All his life he'd suffered peculiar sensory glitches, a sudden unexplained movement in the corner of his eye, or a person's features, for an instant, reshaping into something unrecognisably grotesque. The world of appearances, the trees, houses, clouds, on bad days, appeared as nothing more than a mere safety curtain concealing a blank terrifying void beyond – an eternal, naturally lethal state of things. Thankfully the worst flashback moments soon passed, ordinary life took over again, the real world was insistent and persuasive enough to keep him more or less sane, and, at times like this, he was grateful for the simple everyday ordinariness that most people took for granted. The scar on his finger had long since disappeared, but the wounds of that day remained.

He'd wondered over and over what would have happened had he just stopped cutting the strips, owned up to the blood on the plastic and asked for help? If he'd gone to Soames' house instead of Laura's? If he'd refused the acid? If he'd walked away from her as soon as she told him she and Soames had been in the pillbox together? Gone home, said sorry to his father, re-submitted his application to Cambridge? What would that have felt like – never to have been there in the pillbox that afternoon, never to have lived through that terror, never to have known Laura and Soames were lovers, never to have let his father down like he did? Never to have carried that and the disaster that followed around with him for the rest of his life.

But these unanswerable questions – all a torment of make-believe, always led him back to other memories too. That week with Laura, before the pillbox, still the most magical of his life. Everything that came after those days reduced to a minor feature in faded black and white. All hopelessly entwined with the way it had ended so disastrously, fleeing from her house and her treachery, her curse, calling after him – 'Bad comes back, bad comes back.' The haunting dread that stalked him through that afternoon with Laura had never really left. Was this why he couldn't ever really commit to anything or anybody, even someone he loved like Maddie and her little boy? Because there was forever something broken in him that couldn't be fixed, something he lost that afternoon, something he sought forever in his memories of those days at Pennington.

His evaluation of Soames should also have changed after that afternoon, after he knew, finally that he and Laura, his student, were seeing each other, that he was having an affair with a schoolgirl. As a teacher himself Michael would have joined in the common censure of any colleague at Barton being involved with one of his students. Soames' transgression should have helped him dismiss and forget Gilbert, give up on his memory in the years that followed. But somehow, he had never applied the normal ethical boundaries to his old teacher. The shock and realisation that afternoon of Laura and Soames' affair had only made him more obsessed with the man as the years had gone on. The traumatic circumstances in which he'd unravelled the truth of their relationship had, if anything, only added to the man's mystique. He never really fathomed this moral blind spot or questioned it too much. What had happened to him at Pennington indelibly scarred and shaped his memories, and the more he tried to forget, the more he was drawn back to that school, those classes, the afternoons with Laura. Maddie had helped him escape, but since she'd been gone he'd returned to those days, and despite everything bad that happened there, it was where he more and more wanted to be, with Soames, as always, calling to him across the years.

That night he fell into an uneasy sleep punctuated by strange dreams of a monstrous cheese-plant on an ocean bed haunted by the pillbox where his father, ill and unforgiving, greeted him, and then the dream that finally woke him – Soames, at the front door, dripping wet and carrying the drowned body of Laura in his arms. Wide awake, he replayed incessantly the memory of the terrifying acid trip and the retreat to his father's factory. He then lay there thinking of the person who'd provided the drugs and the visit he now intended to make to his house. Lawton had told him David March's was the only dwelling nestling amongst the dunes on the private road leading off from the main coastal highway. In the dark small hours, his thoughts moved on to fantasies of confrontation with the teenage drug dealer, now business tycoon, whose LSD caused so much ruin. Finally, in an effort to soothe his mind in turmoil with regret and revenge, he tuned in to the World Service.

He chanced upon a festive episode of 'Hancock's Half Hour' – 'Bill and Father Christmas'. Hancock dressing up as Santa because Bill, one of his housemates, still believes in him, even though he is thirty-four years old. At the height of their affair Michael had admitted to Maddie that writing radio comedy was something he might have a go at and she had bought him a Teach Yourself Scriptwriting manual and a CD box set of Hancock's recordings. Then through the summer he'd worked on a couple of short pieces but, since the break-up, had abandoned them. As Hancock and friends faced Bill's delusions about Santa Claus, Michael recalled Maddie's blind faith in his writing. But, without her, his purpose foundered and the sketches became another casualty of the break-up. He turned off the radio and lay miserably awake, his thoughts returning to the despair of those journal entries, the sadness of Soames' wife, Joan, and the shadowy figure of David March lurking behind it all.

CHAPTER TWELVE

Late morning and the frost was still on the ground and lingering in ghostly patches along the rooftops. All week it had been cold at night with temperatures below freezing, but there was now a biting sea breeze as well. As he struck out along the promenade, he watched the low, feeble sun engulfed by an ominous gathering bank of blue-grey cloud amassing from the west. Soon he was on the coast road, once more looking out at the vast beach infested with the bulldozers and wagons still busily carrying the sand away. He could see the mountainous heaps and the great trenches where the seawater ran through in canal-sized tributaries carved out of the shoreline. The smooth, uninterrupted plain which once stretched out for miles across the bay was now transformed into an alien landscape dominated by giant, roaring machinery.

The coastal route branched into a private track and his first glimpse of David March's house took him completely by surprise. It settled like a giant shell creature deep in the sand-hills ready to crawl slowly towards him. The roof sported a fake mast in the form of a giant cross supported with ropes and rigging straining against the wind. He wondered how March had obtained the planning permission to build this folly lurking in the gathering December dark amidst the sands and tide. The house disappeared as he ventured down the lane that twisted and turned through the dunes, until the way straightened and the residence now loomed ahead at the end, seemingly hunkered down in the sea bed.

He slowed down despite the freezing gale and the first twisting flakes of snow. The building was mostly grey reflected glass, like frozen water, perfect for observing intruders as they approached. He wondered if this was such a good idea after all. Now so influential in the community, March would also always remain that confident, commanding figure from schooldays. Back then Michael could never match his wit, his poise, his scathing rancour. Now waves of disquiet swept in from the house along the hostile shore. With the fierce snow-filled wind driving into his face, he did not hear the Mercedes approaching from behind until it pulled up alongside. The electric window wound partially down to reveal a steel-grey, close-cropped head of hair.

'Can I help?' said the voice beneath the window. The tone reminded him of Headmaster Dillon, perhaps here again to expel him from the premises. 'You realise this is a private right of way.'

'I was hoping to call on David March,' he said into the biting wind.

'That's his house at the end there. But you know you're trespassing?'

The wind was whipping the snow up around the Mercedes and the car window, which wound up further until there was just a small gap at the top.

'I'm sorry,' said Michael, about to turn around and leave, but the wind was blowing hard that way against him and he hesitated. 'I'd like to speak to David, if I can.' But he doubted the driver could hear him through the howling gale.

However, the man spoke through the gap at the top of the window. 'And who might you be then?'

'I'm Michael Freeman. I went to school with David. He might remember me....'

At that point the window closed up completely and the Mercedes accelerated towards the house. He was left stranded in the gathering gloom. If he set off home now, he could be back before the storm really set in. But still he stood, isolated and in limbo in the blizzard, when a sudden sharp whistle rang out and, just discernible in the darkness, he saw the driver standing by his car waving at him to come on forward. He bowed his head into the blinding snow, harsh as grit as it mingled with the sand whipping from off the dunes.

Nearer now, he could see the man stamping his feet in the cold and smiling. He was tall, slim, athletic-looking, well over six feet, dressed in a dark well-made suit, with an open-necked white shirt that emphasised his healthily-tanned face. Even at a distance, Michael knew by the commanding manner of his stance, legs astride defying the storm, that this was his old adversary. As he got closer, he saw that time had hardened March physically into a spare androidal reboot of the teenage David. Whereas Steve Lawton had expanded beyond recognition, this man had evolved into the lean utilitarian essence of himself.

'Hello, Michael,' he shouted amidst the gale and the sound of the wind in the rigging, reminiscent of a mouse in a toaster, screaming from the ropes and weathervanes straining at the mast above. 'Let's get inside,' March said, grey phantoms of wind and snow chasing them into the building. 'It's good to see you,' he continued, his welcoming grip a little too firm, held a little too long.

Michael's mind went blank in the face of March's welter of generous, patronising overtures. 'It's good to see you', again, a number of times, 'what a genuine surprise', more than once, all delivered while taking Michael's snow-encrusted coat and ushering him into the downstairs of the house, one huge room the length of a cricket pitch.

The warehouse-sized space resembled the galley of a cruiser with a banked console of lights along one wall at its centre. There was a modest open plan recessed kitchen area off the main room furnished with a shell-shaped island and a nest of surrounding high-legged stools. In the main room, apart from a large leather sofa and chair with a glass coffee table in the middle, there was little furniture. Beyond that a twisting metal staircase disappeared into the upper deck, boarded with peep slots and portholes, with miniature lifeboats and paddles suspended from the sides of the landing area. The building looked out on all sides through the grey tinted glass – one view directed at the road, the other three turned to the vastness of the sea and the darkening sky.

'Today's the winter solstice,' said March, shutting the door behind them as the suicide of flakes wheeled, danced and hurled themselves at the windows. Michael already wished he was back outside again, heading away from this house and the ridiculous mission he'd set himself.

'To think that the sun is somehow at this moment just setting precisely there,' March said, pointing to somewhere on the dark horizon in the right-hand corner of the near window. He then set off walking to the far end of the room and shouted across, 'And in six months' time that same sun will be setting here.' In semi darkness, pacing back towards Michael, he maintained his running commentary. 'From this room I can track its progress through the year. Too often there's cloud at sunset, but there are also some incredible storms. I love to watch them come in over the sea.'

March motioned Michael to sit down in a dark armchair, as soft and all enveloping as a giant sea anemone ingesting its lunch. Partly the design of the building, partly its owner's unsettling self-assurance, put him in mind of the modernist glass and limestone Vandamm House perched on Mount Rushmore in *North by Northwest*. With his back to Michael, darkly silhouetted against the metallic glass and the snow-filled sky beyond, David looked out imperiously into the storm. The house shook in the violent gusts from the sea and the weather was closing in for the night. Soon the darkness would seal them in here together.

'Nice place,' Michael said, to conceal his growing anxiety. As with the visit to Joan, he hadn't thought this through at all, hadn't really expected to gain access to March so easily, hadn't anticipated the instant effect David would still have on him, that he would be reduced to the same tongue-tied teenage paralysis he had so often felt around his old rival – now an even more impressive and unpredictable figure of maturity, status and power.

'It will be when it's finished. I'm digging out the basement and it seems we've hit a pipe that runs through to the sea,' David said.

There was, no doubt, a strong smell of sewers as the chair-cum-sea-creature absorbed Michael deeper into its belly and the shadows deepened.

'I like to enjoy natural light as long as possible. Even on this, the shortest day of the year,' March said, producing from inside his suit a device that looked, amidst the gloom, like a small pistol which he pointed straight at Michael and fired. The building immediately flooded with electric light.

'Lux in tenebrae,' David said, smiling, holding the remote. 'But of course, you didn't take the Latin A Level, did you?'

'No. I....'

'Total waste of time, to be honest, once the Cambridge option was no longer on the cards.' March's smile faded as he sat down opposite Michael.

'So, Michael. Why are you here? You said you wanted to speak to me.'

Michael, wrong-footed by March's immediate

reference to the Cambridge exam of years ago, attempted a casual reply. 'I've been looking up some old friends from Pennington. I visited the school yesterday.'

'Ah, the alma mater. Somehow pulls you back, doesn't it?'

'I was just passing. I saw Bob Dillon.'

March smiled. 'Bob Dillon,' he said, shaking his head. 'You wouldn't believe it, I mean, whoever heard of a headmaster named *Bob Dillon*?'

'Er, well, let's just say, free-wheeling, he isn't.' Michael recalled the look of pain on the boy's face as his ear twisted between Dillon's fingers.

'Good man, Bob. I prefer to think of him as that other Dillon, Matt Dillon in *Gunsmoke*,' March said, his smile hardening. Michael nodded, remembering the character from the Western TV series of early childhood.

'You recall?' March continued. 'Well, Bob's my new sheriff in town clearing out all the dead wood at Pennington. Say, would you like a drink?'

Without waiting for an answer, March retrieved a bottle of wine from one of the racks against the wall. Feeling hopelessly out of his depth, the last thing Michael wanted was any alcoholic fog clouding his brain. He considered making a run for it, but it would be difficult to get up quickly from the depths of the chair that had taken such a fond proprietorial hold on him. The snow was banking up against the windows in the darkness outside, enveloping the building in a velvet shroud, and March, having opened the wine with a flourish, was already filling and handing over a large crystal goblet.

'Margaux 1972,' he said, swirling the ruby liquid and circling his nose around the rim of the glass. 'What a coincidence, seeing we were – the Class of '72.' He smiled to himself. 'But some of us didn't make it to the end, did we?' he said, glancing across, eyebrow raised. 'Neither of *us*, in fact. Tell me, Michael. What happened to you... in '72?' The pause in delivering this rhyming couplet endowing the question with a knowing, ironic twist.

Michael briefly considered confronting him there and then about the drugs, the bad acid, the breakdown it caused, but he couldn't say it, couldn't make the words come out right. He knew it would just sound mad. After all, here he was, incredibly enough, suddenly in March's house, taking refuge from the storm, about to drink his high class wine. He would appear deranged, challenging him straight off the bat about something that happened over twenty years ago. March was already looking at him askance, as if eyeing a vagrant outcast. Instead, Michael decided the wandering hippy persona, the one that Lawton insisted on believing, would serve as an alternative history, provide him with the refuge, once more, of being someone else, someone far more interesting and far removed from the depressing reality of the last few months.

'Er, '72? I dropped out. The whole A Level scene was a drag.'

'That doesn't sound like the Michael Freeman I knew back then. That sort of rebellion wasn't really you, was it?'

'Er, going out East changed things for me.'

'East? How far East?'

He was immediately struggling with this. March's relentless, amused gaze seemed to pierce right through his pretence.

'Yes, that's right. Far East.'

'Yes, but where?'

Under pressure, his shaky memory of that distant film *The Guru* was again all he had to fall back on.

'Er, Benares.'

'Did you venerate the god there?'

What 'god'? What was March on about? He felt himself beginning to blush. He took several more nervous gulps of this awful-tasting wine which was quickly going to his head.

'Er, not sure about a ...god.'

'You know, the Hindu god, they all go to Benares to worship. Shiva!' March exclaimed. 'The Destroyer,' and he winked at Michael. 'Apparently if you die in Benares, it means your soul is saved.'

'Just like Benidorm, then,' Michael said, in a nonsensical effort to shift the topic as far away as possible now from Shiva or the East. But his host was enjoying himself and wasn't about to let him off the hook.

'What've you been doing with yourself all these years since…Benares.'

There was no point in pursuing the fake hippy trail, or other lies any further. Better to be as vague as possible and hope March quickly became bored with Michael and his life.

'Oh, this and that. A bit of teaching.'

'Teaching? Good god,' David shuddered. 'You, poor sod. Kids are such bastards. When I think back to what we were like. But back then, the teachers were even bigger bastards, weren't they?'

'Not all the teachers back then were bad…. that's why I went back to Pennington…' This was a good opportunity to mention Soames, but March interrupted him.

'In my business I employ young people fresh out of university and, as far as I can see we've educated a generation of pampered idiots. They couldn't wipe their own arse without instructions.'

Michael wanted to steer David back to his missing

teacher, but decided, for the moment, it was safer to shift the conversation to March's own career. Mainly to avoid any further investigation into his own disastrous history.

'You run your own business these days?'

'Not so much a business as a multinational. Finance, share dealing, stock trading, that sort of thing.'

'I wouldn't have thought you'd have gone in for that. At school you were...'

'Times long gone, Michael.' He finished off his wine and reached for the bottle. 'Want a top-up?' he asked, and without waiting for a reply he filled Michael's half empty glass to the brim, before sitting down and forward in his seat, his drink balanced in his hands.

'What made you change your mind about things?' Michael asked. March eased slightly forward in his seat with all the assurance and anticipation of a well seasoned raconteur.

'Oh, you're right, I started out with all those plans to change the world. Notions of being England's Hunter S. Thompson. Then Thatcher came to power and I began to wonder what I was doing with my life.'

Michael recalled the David of Pennington, railing against the evils of capitalism and free enterprise. 'I'd have thought you'd have hated Thatcher,' he said.

'Right again, I did. Until July 1984. Orgreave. Remember that? I was there when the horses and dogs hunted down the miners. Wiped the socialist republic of Scargill off the map. The wholesale destruction of a way of life, of people and their communities. A war between Thatcher and the far left, and there was me – stuck on the losing side.'

He paused here for effect, the corners of his mouth turning down as he shook his head to emphasise the gravity of what he was about to say, then shuffled to the edge of his seat, perching upright like a celebrity on Parkinson relishing the public platform from which to launch his life story.

'You see, Michael, it had taken nearly twenty years to finally destroy it, but that was the last gasp of the sixties and that fantasy of a better world,' he explained, his tone now grave and portentous, as if reciting his long awaited memoir. 'Yes, one neat horrible one-sided slaughter. After that the country could be carved up and fed to the wolves – no more obstacles in the way. The Left was finally dead and buried'

Time rewound and Michael was back in the Sixth Form at Pennington. David may have radically changed his politics but it hadn't changed how much he loved an audience, any audience, even just a random old school colleague wandering in out of the storm.

Michael, just about managing to get a word in, said, 'It's tragic what's happened to those communities.'

March paused for yet more dramatic significance before embarking on the next chapter. 'Yes, maybe, but their demise was *my* wake-up call. I realised I wanted to get my own snout in the trough. I mean, one day I took a good look at Michael Foot. If anyone embodied the walking corpse of the Left it was him. It was a zombie movement and I chose not to be a member of the living dead.' He drained his glass in celebration. 'You see, the counterculture was just a fairy-tale we told ourselves back then. This country's always been carved up by the butchers in the establishment. You've just got to know how to become one of them. Like Blair managed to do with New Labour.'

'Blair's got Labour and the Left back in charge of the country. Massive majority. That's good, surely.'

March sneered. 'You think Tony Blair's going to fight for the Left?' He laughed and then paused for more effect. 'Tony's really just another Tory. I've met him.'

'You've met Blair?'

'Yes, a conference for Cool Britannia Business. He told me I was doing great work revitalising my local community. He loved my plan to coordinate local development with trade to the Middle East and my little idea of selling the sand out here to the Saudis. They want to buy it so I'll sell it to them. Whatever's good for business. And he agreed with me.'

Lawton had warned him about March's political conversion to free market capitalism. But whatever his politics it was still the same self-serving David, who, at seventeen, preached anarchy and the gospel of free love to draw attention to himself and impress women. Back then Michael had hated but also envied him, and he realised he still did. What was it? The success, the confidence he exuded, the secure, self-gratifying delight he enjoyed in just being David March?

'Yes, I noticed the diggers out on the beach,' Michael said. 'The shoreline's changed so much. It's hardly recognisable in places.'

'You sound disapproving. You're not one of the beard-and-sandals-brigade, are you?'

'No. It just seems odd to be digging up the beach to sell sand to a country that is, well, mainly sand.'

Michael soon wished he'd kept his mouth shut because it promptly initiated an interminable justification of David's coastline project, citing profit margins, amounting to hundreds of thousands per annum to kick-start the failing regional economy, boosted by council regeneration and trickle-down but gradual floodgate bonuses for the community. Like a development brochure on steroids, March expounded forever on a whole new 'March Islands Theme-park', a recreation of a Pacific Paradise including adventure lagoons, a Captain Nemo Ocean-world with shark sanctuary, a Deepwater dive-ride, a simulated surf-beach. All this was already in the pipeline, financed by Saudi money from the sand contract.

His tidal wave of self-aggrandisement then swept relentlessly on, changing course as he now expounded plans for Pennington, detailing how his property consortium would transform the school, convert it to a private establishment which would re-emerge as a teaching powerhouse. Michael remembered the distant trucks digging up the earth in the bleak extended chaos of what David euphemistically described as the 'contraction and rationalisation' at Pennington. The whole insufferable performance, part sermon, part tirade, finally came to a sententious conclusion with, 'Nothing is more powerful than the market first and last. It is not clouded by morality or virtue. Only the money matters.'

Overwhelmed, exhausted, all Michael could bring himself to say was, 'It still seems strange you know, after all you were always so....'

'Yes, I know but even back then, in all my naivety, I wanted to change the world, and now I am ridiculously rich and the rich can do anything. There's a continuum here, Michael. It's the same David March. There are so many changes I want to make. And now I have the wealth to make them all happen.'

Michael, still reeling from the verbal onslaught, for some reason at that moment thought of his father and how this dynamic, wealthy, capitalist would have ticked all his boxes as the ideal son.

'Well, let me get you another drink,' March said.

'Er, I'm not sure.'

'Come on, where's your festive spirit?'

What, with the alcohol, the lack of sleep from the night before, the soft seductive chair folding itself around him and David's exhausting self-regard, he suddenly felt very tired. What was he doing here? Listening to this rant from a man he'd always hated? He'd made absolutely no progress in his quest to find some more information about Soames. But now, he struggled to keep his eyes open. But he did not welcome the sleep that beckoned. There were many reasons why he didn't trust March, and the diatribe he'd just witnessed only reinforced his already jaundiced view of the man. As his eyelids drooped he wondered if he'd actually been drugged like some hapless private eye in a movie stumbling unwittingly into a trap? He fought to stay awake fearing he would come round from his slumber tied up in a grim cellar with a spotlight shining in his eyes. It was a losing battle though, even more so when his host returned with another bottle of rare vintage and a further mind-numbing instalment from his illustrious life history.

'So, it was time to forget the gonzo journalism, start a new game,' he heard March intone, but sounding further and further away. He must have drifted off for a few minutes, or longer, because the next words seemed to belong to another volume in March's heroic narrative... 'I'd made a few contacts in the City, and with some insider influence and know-how got myself set up as a trader. Late eighties and I felt like some corporate scalp-hunter raiding and plundering through the market, up to my elbows in money and dead men who couldn't take the pace or the competition. Made a fucking fortune.'

But this was the last thing Michael heard before he succumbed and fell into a troubled sleep and a dream where he and Maddie were escaping from the Vandamm mansion, clinging to each other halfway up Mount Rushmore. He was about to lose his grip on her hand when he opened his eyes to see, far from being chained to a radiator with his hands tied, that he was still rooted deep in his all-encompassing chair. And standing before him was a stern, but very attractive young woman in a dressing gown, holding a tray with a bowl of soup and scrambled egg sandwiches.

CHAPTER THIRTEEN

'David says to make you something to eat, Mister Sleepy Head,' the young woman spoke with an eastern European accent, putting the tray of food down on a makeshift table wheeled in front of him. He blinked away the sleep from his eyes as she ascended briskly the spiral staircase and disappeared into the upper deck without another word, leaving him disorientated but very hungry. His watch said it was now 8.15. How had he managed to sleep for so long? He needed to be on his way as soon as he'd eaten. His mother would be worrying, and the appearance of the woman meant he was probably intruding and should make himself scarce. He hadn't found anything more out about Soames, but it was obvious all March wanted to talk about was his own tiresome success. He was just finishing his sandwiches when David, also in a dressing gown, silken and of higher quality than the woman's, appeared on the upper level, holding a drink in one hand and a cigar in the other.

'You nodded off back there,' he said, descending the stairs.

'Yes, I think I need to be getting on my way.'

'Nonsense. One for the road, at least,' March said, and before Michael could protest his host had placed a crystal tumbler filled with amber liquid in his hand. He still felt very tired, even though he must have slept for a couple of hours. He was also uncomfortable and stiff after sitting for such a long period and he badly needed the toilet.

'Benbecula, Single Malt,' March declared, holding up the flask shaped bottle. 'The first scotch to be awarded a royal warrant by George III back in 1793. I have a special case shipped over every Christmas. The only one of its kind in England.'

The contents of the glass tasted of disinfectant mixed with charcoal and the fumes took his breath away. But at least it woke him up.

March relaxed back on the sofa once more. 'You don't happen to have a crisp twenty-pound note on you, do you?'

'Sorry?'

'Just for a minute. I'll give it you back, old chap. I'm a little indisposed at the moment,' he said, patting at the empty pockets on his gown. 'It'll take a nanosecond, that's all.'

Still rather dazed, he automatically rummaged in his pocket, found a solitary ten pound note and handed it to David who produced a playing card, the Ace of Diamonds, and two small transparent plastic pouches of white powder from his dressing gown pocket. Kneeling before the coffee table he emptied the contents on the glass surface. He cut the powder with the card into two short lines, rolled the banknote into a tight cylindrical shape and inserted it into his nostril. Eyes watering, nostrils dilating, he pointed to the other line.

'Want a bump?'

'No, thank you, I *do* need to be on my way, if you don't mind.'

March hoovered up the second line of cocaine and settled back into his chair, shaking his head vigorously.

'Wife waiting for you at home?'

'No.'

'You'r best off out of it. What was it Larkin said about

the horror of family life? The morons who inflict their useless parenting skills on the world.'

Resisting David's contempt for all things family with his obvious reference to the opening lines from 'This Be the Verse', Michael replied, 'Maybe Larkin was recognising how difficult it is to bring up children, given how messed up most people are.'

March laughed and shook his head. 'Ah, yes, I always think Larkin deep down is really just another victim of the dreaded English disease of sentimentality. All it takes is for him to run over a hedgehog, and he's exhorting universal kindness.' Michael thought briefly of the mouse crying out in the toaster, his own helpless inexplicable tears. He also realised, too late, he was about to witness another David diatribe.

'The English are such hypocrites about most things, but animals and kids in particular,' March continued, while pinching one nostril and then the other. 'For some reason parents think they're entitled to add to the six billion of us already infesting the planet. Look at what the sixties achieved with its free love and harmony bullshit. Family breakdown on a massive scale, kids passed around like parcels at Christmas.'

Michael recalled Tommy, chasing a kite across the Porthcawl sands. 'Kids can also be fun, though,' he said, sadly. His head felt full of cotton wool and he wondered again if he'd been drugged. Or was it just March's soulless appraisal of the human condition, a bleak, mercenary scramble for wealth and status that sapped the joy out of living. But David, energised by pessimism, newly showered, hair gelled, robe open to the waist to reveal muscular power, glowed with life.

'Seriously, would you want to bring a kid up today,' he said. 'You see them hanging out in gangs in the park, sniffing glue, smoking weed, feeling each other up. What a fucking world.'

'I don't know. Aren't things better than when we were growing up? The Cold War's ended. Blair's Britain seems not that bad a place to be.'

'You've met Katya, haven't you?'

'Yes, briefly. Thank her for the food, by the way.'

'She likes to cook. She's from Dubrovnik. She's an asylum seeker. Shipped over here when old Milosevic started murdering and raping his way across what used to be Yugoslavia. Ask her about the way the world is.'

Michael sipped the whisky tentatively. It was as dreadful tasting as March's supposedly vintage wine. 'But this country has helped her. You've helped her,' he said.

March laughed 'Helped her? I suppose so. She was working in a dodgy bar down in Soho when I found her. A woman like that in a desperate spot shows her gratitude. But then again, she has to be. You know...grateful.' March shouted up the stairs, 'Don't you, dear,' but there was no answer. 'She's a feisty one, though,' he said. 'Plenty of spirit. Probably pass her on to one of my associates soon for safe keeping. Do you fancy taking her on? Home comforts provided.'

Michael shook his head, 'It's OK, thanks all the same.'

March raised his eyebrows. 'Suit yourself. Don't mention the cocaine to her, though. She doesn't approve. Milosevic junior's international drug deals help finance his dad's genocide. You sure you don't want some?'

'Er, no. Cocaine and genocide – think I'll pass, thanks.'

'You'll give abstinence a bad name, Michael. Some blow then. I have some great Caribbean pot from St Kitts?'

'No, I don't....'

'Is it because of what happened? The drugs that were

to blame?'

'What do you mean?'

'Back then, when you left Pennington? There was so much bad shit going around.'

What could he say? Was it really possible March could have known the tab of LSD he supplied was somehow wrong? But maybe March just didn't know. Maybe he was oblivious to the nightmare he had unleashed in Michael's life. After all, Michael might have had a nightmare trip anyway given his state of mind after the debacle at the factory and the row with his father. And he *had* taken the acid voluntarily. It suddenly seemed, after all March had told him of his life and adventures in the intervening two and a half decades, rather ridiculous, small-minded, pathetic even, to still be harbouring these doubts and accusations against what was a boy of seventeen, all these years later.

'I took LSD once. It didn't agree with me,' he said and tried to read March's reaction.

'Anyone who had a nightmare on acid should never probably have taken it in the first place,' David said, with a half-hidden smile into his whisky. Did this imply guilt or gloating, it was difficult to tell? And Michael, deadened by booze, felt all confidence draining away in March's commanding presence. There was no reckoning, or sympathy or retribution to be had here. It was all so long ago and Michael was very tired. He put the half-finished whisky glass down on the table.

'Even so, I wouldn't have thought you were the tripping type. You were always Soames' blue-eyed boy,' David said.

To combat the overwhelming slouching listlessness, Michael forced himself wide awake. He'd wasted enough time and had not managed to get any information on

Soames out of David. Now, at last was perhaps an opportunity to talk about Gilbert, to discover what March might know about the disappearance.

'You know about Soames. How he has gone missing?' he said.

David's mood darkened immediately, his brow furrowed and a vessel began to pulse at his temple. 'Of course, I know. I'm governor of the school that has the misfortune to employ the lunatic.'

'He's not well. He's a….'

'Yes, a total disgrace to his school and his profession. He shouldn't be allowed among young people.'

'I bumped into his wife Joan the other day. She's very upset, very worried.'

For the first time David looked genuinely disturbed, his cool demeanour shaken. 'You don't want to believe everything *she* says. She's married to that head-case, so it's going to be difficult for her to know what's true and what's nonsense.'

'She seemed genuine. And genuinely frightened for her husband.'

March's face, already red after snorting the coke flushed further in anger, his disposition clouding with an oncoming storm of feeling.

'Is that why you're here? Did she send you here? Has she been speaking to the Press again?'

'I don't know. No, she doesn't know I'm here. Why should she?'

'I know you've been poking around the school, Michael.'

He was taken aback. Was this why March was so ready to invite him in, so reluctant to let him leave? To find out how much he already knew about Soames?

'I haven't been poking around anywhere. What do you mean?'

'Bob Dillon told me you came to the school. Looking for Steve Lawton. You're not from the Herald are you?'

'No, I've told you. I'm a teacher.'

'Joan's a troublemaker. Like her husband. And Lawton's a drug-addled loser. He's another one needs booting out. Lots of dead wood there that needs clearing.'

'He's a friend of Soames. *He's* also very concerned about him.'

'OK, but why are *you* so interested in all this?'

'I don't know, it's just that it's sad to hear what's happened to him.'

March snarled at Michael. 'You know, it makes me sick – folks feeling sorry for someone who's only himself to blame for the shit he's in.' March stood up slowly. 'Let me get you another drink while I tell you the truth about Gilbert Soames.'

Finally, he felt he was getting somewhere. Despite the need to urinate and vague fears the whisky might be doctored, he drank the malt down and handed over the tumbler for a refill while David lit up another fat cigar which he puffed furiously into life.

'Don't suppose you want one of these?' David said, waving dense smoke in Michael's direction. Michael shook his head as the sound of the wind outside intensified, penetrating the double glazing, rocking the foundations. The house, trembling in the storm, seemed to lose its moorings, then settled once more. He took a few sips of his refreshed glass and settled back in his chair to relieve the pain on his bladder.

'Here,' said March, begrudgingly, 'thanks for this,' and

he pushed the tightly rolled ten pound note impatiently across the table. Michael left the money untouched as it unfolded slowly on the glass surface.

'So, Gilbert Soames,' March began, his eyes aflame. 'The man's a fraud. A fraud and a basket case. Do you remember all that Orson Welles horseshit? The raised Harry Lime eyebrows, the maverick genius act, that self-satisfied smirk,' he said, his voice wavering with emotion.

'I remember you and him not exactly seeing eye to eye.'

'That's an understatement.'

'He kicked you out of his class a couple of times.'

'No, Michael,' David was suddenly shouting now and waving the cigar around like a weapon. 'That bastard had me kicked out of the school. He planted drugs in my locker.'

'Soames planted drugs?'

'Yes, cannabis. Some home-grown shit I wouldn't have been caught dead smoking. There was a stash there when the Head dragged me round to my locker. I'm not even sure it was genuine grass – it could've been dandelion leaves for all I know.'

'I don't understand. You're saying Soames put it there? How do you know?'

March paused. 'Oh, I know alright.' He stood up, unable to contain his anger while sitting down.

Trapped and engulfed in the chair, Michael peered up at March looming furiously above him, lost in the past. 'Sorry to destroy your illusions. You sure you want to hear any more?' March sneered.

Michael nodded. 'You know he did this to you? But how?'

'You remember *Touch of Evil*?'

'Of course, the Welles film,' Michael said, immediately recalling the entry in the journal he had recently read. The night he sat behind David and Laura trying hard to concentrate on the film while they embraced and she rested her head on March's shoulder.

'The film where a very fat Orson Welles plays Hank Quinlan, the corrupt cop planting evidence on suspects to get his convictions,' March continued.

'Soames showed us that movie one Sunday night at the school hall.'

'Well, that's how I know.'

'I don't quite follow. What's that film got to do with Soames planting drugs in your locker? Someone else might have put the drugs there.'

March began pacing the room, consumed and galvanized by an injustice that hadn't died away with the years. 'The way Soames went after me, it was pathological. I knew for definite it was him who framed me.'

'You can't know that for definite, surely?'

'Yes, I can.'

'Just because of some film.'

'Yes, because of some film and because *he* told me. When I was collecting my shit from my locker to clear out, Soames came up behind, put his hand on my shoulder, and said, "Sorry it's turned out like this, old boy. Remember, Hank Quinlan *always* gets his man."' March held out both hands as if finally pleading his case before the jury.

'Might've been a casual remark. He might have just been winding you up. Not very funny, I admit, but he could have a weird sense of humour sometimes.'

'Yes, ha-ha, so very fucking funny. It had to be Soames. He wanted me to know it was him who'd set me up. Just like one of Quinlan's victims stitched up by the bent cop in the movie.' March stopped pacing and sat down again. He sighed and gazed into the past still seeking some retribution and justice there.

'Don't you see what he did to me? My life was down the toilet – it was just weeks before my A Levels. He ruined my chances of Oxbridge. After I got kicked out, I struggled to find somewhere where I could take the exams. I just managed to scrape into Keele through clearing in the end.'

It was difficult to respond to all this, difficult to comprehend that Soames would have done such a thing.

'I know what you're thinking,' David continued. 'Why didn't I protest my innocence? Well, of course, I did, protested until I was blue in the face, but it only made matters worse. The Head and Deputy insisted I was just trying to lie my way out of trouble with some far-fetched story and they threatened to bring the police in if I didn't stop making a scene. My only option was to pack my things that day and leave the school.'

David's outrage and sense of injustice were so unexpected, so heartfelt. Michael attempted a feeble consolatory response.

'Keele? Isn't that a good university though?'

March hissed back his reply. 'It wasn't Oxford. It wasn't Cambridge. That man ruined my life.'

David's story was ludicrous, but perhaps too outlandish to be fabricated. And it resonated somehow with Soames' talent for the theatrical. There was also Joan's testimony of how appalling her husband had been treated, how he had been driven to despair by this man. Was this March's way of exacting revenge? Michael opted once more for a non-committal reply to this bewildering news.

'Well, you've done that. You've certainly showed him. You've totally bounced back.'

'Yeah, but think what I *could* have done! Anything.

Maybe made Prime Minister by now if I'd gone to Cambridge, made all those connections.' David paused and stared into space, contemplating what might have been, before glaring at Michael and saying, 'But we all know what happened to Hank Quinlan in the end, don't we? At the end of the film. Dead – face down in sewage and shit. That's exactly where Gilbert Soames belongs.'

This image hung in the air between them and as the silence grew March looked more and more lost, his cigar forgotten and burning away in the ashtray like the angry grievances of yesteryear still smouldering. He pointed a finger straight at Michael. 'It was after *you* left things went so wrong. It was then Soames really had it in for me.'

'I'm sorry,' Michael said and regretted it immediately. Why on earth was he apologising to this man? But it was ever thus with David – despite all his strong intentions Michael could never quite find the right words, the right stance to take against him. All he could think to say, amidst this bewildering and upsetting array of accusations against his old teacher, was the question that had brought him here in the first place, the question that had disturbed him ever since he read the Herald article.

'But do you have any idea why Soames has disappeared?'

David exploded. 'What's with you and him? No, I don't have a clue, and I couldn't care less. As long as he doesn't come around here to this place again.'

'Soames came round here?'

'Yes, a week before he disappeared. He was raving then, obviously off his head. Spouting Shakespeare or some such shit I could make little sense of.'

'What did he want?'

'Who knows? Least of all him. He was deranged. Calling me Caliban and how he taught me to curse him, some nonsense in his head from that play he was putting on. When I saw you on the drive earlier, I feared the worst. I thought it was him again. You never know what he might do.'

Suddenly the house began to shake as if a subway train was passing beneath the floor, followed by the prolonged thunder of a vast latrine flushing in the depths of the earth. It lasted for about half a minute and all the time March's facial expression, already clouded with anger, became even more pained.

'Pipe trouble', he said. 'The main outlet runs more or less alongside the foundations of this place.'

'Trouble with water. It reminds me of *Chinatown*.' Michael was tired, thinking out loud, and had uttered something nonsensical to anyone but himself.

'What?' March looked thunderous.

'Er, sorry, nothing.'

'No! It's not nothing. What do you mean? Trouble with water?'

'Er…it's like the film *Chinatown*.'

'What?'

'That noise – it reminded me. You know, after all that about Soames and the Welles movie and corruption. For some reason it just popped into my head. *Chinatown*. The Polanski film?....The California Water Wars? ...Sorry, just a silly random remark….forget I said it.'

Random remark or not, March now seemed to be losing control, gesticulating fiercely. 'I'm not dealing with water down there. I'm dealing with shit! Shit here in the basement, and all manner of shit from Soames and other deadbeat staff at that school.'

It was late and he'd outstayed his welcome and it was definitely now time for him to go. 'I think I need to ring a cab,' Michael said. 'Could I use your phone, please?'

But March hadn't finished. He held up his hand to stop Michael getting out of his seat. 'Soames always hated me. Even before he planted those drugs in my locker, he was trying to turn people against me. Take Laura for instance.'

Despite his best efforts, Michael's face gave something away that immediately lightened David's mood.

'Ah!' he said. 'That's struck a chord with Michael Freeman, hasn't it? The mere mention of the old flame.'

'I'm sorry, I don't know what you mean.'

'You and Laura.'

'Laura was…'

March laughed and raised his eyebrows. 'Your darling sweetheart.'

'I need a taxi, David.'

'You were crazy about her.'

'It's a long time ago.'

'Exactly. But it's still like yesterday, don't you think?'

Michael recalled that last entry in the journal and Soames' arrival at Laura's house. Then there was also that summer night waiting outside Soames' gate for Laura to appear. Should he tell March what he really knew about Soames and Laura back then? No doubt March would pounce on such a revelation, exposing and condemning Gilbert. Yes, he could reveal all, but then how would Soames, if he ever reappeared alive, but now broken and ill, be able to recover from accusations of an affair with a student almost three decades ago. Similarly, was it fair to burden Joan, after all she'd already been through, with such knowledge and ensuing scandal? It took him only a few seconds to decide that rightly or wrongly, Michael couldn't bring himself to divulge what he knew.

Suddenly a voice cried from the balcony above: 'Are you going to be down there all night smoking the cocaine and whisky?' Katya stood there, hands on hips, shaking her head.

'One minute, my love,' March replied, now suddenly much calmer. His mood seemed to fluctuate like the wind battering the house one moment and subsiding the next.

'You promised you would bring me the Ovaltine half an hour ago,' Katya cried.

David looked irritated and rose and while his host was momentarily distracted, Michael made his way quickly to the circular wooden front door, but as soon as he pulled it open a wild swarm of snowflakes invaded the room. The black gaping hole of night outside was framed with ice and the pathway beyond impassable with a wall of snow two to three feet high. There was no way he could find his way back along the track to the road in this.

He closed the door again and faced David who was now smiling. 'Good luck calling a cab in this weather,' he said.

'Can I just use your loo?' Michael asked.

March was once more amused and knowing. 'Of course. Up the stairs, last on the left. Kick Katya out of there if she's still in the bathroom fixing her face.'

As Michael relieved himself in the small cramped toilet chamber, he considered David's allegations against Soames. What Michael had learned left him exhausted and with more questions he was too tired to formulate at this time of night in this claustrophobic sealed space. When he flushed the cistern, the house began to shake once more from its foundations and the pervading smell of sewage intensified. He thought again of the movie *Chinatown* and private eye Jack Nicholson broken by his efforts to uncover corruption and evil. Maybe his mother was right after all, and he too should leave all this be. It was all a long time ago and March might have his own valid reasons for hating Soames. Better to go home now, despite the storm, get away from David, the dangerous mood swings, the anger and bitterness of it all.

But then, at the bottom of the stairs, his host greeted him with, 'Why don't you stay? There's the spare room.'

'Er, thank you but better not, David. I don't want to put you to any trouble.'

He put his arm around Michael's shoulder. 'I'm sorry, Michael if I lost my temper. Nothing personal against you, old chap. It's absolutely no trouble. Have a nightcap before you turn in,' he said, preparing yet another drink.

'Can I just use your phone please?'

'Here.' March handed him one of the latest mobile gadgets. Michael looked at the hefty brick in his hands as if he didn't quite know what to do.

'It's state of the art,' David said, before placing another large tumbler of whisky for Michael on the table. 'Just punch the number in as you would with any phone. You need to get used to those things. They're the future.'

Michael rang the numbers of a couple of taxi firms he could remember, but they were engaged. He then tried again to persuade March to let him walk home through the storm, but his host would hear none of it, and another look outside convinced him it would be hopeless trying to make his way back in that blizzard.

He next rang his mother who picked up instantaneously. 'Where are you? I've been worried sick,' she said, her voice edgy with anger and anxiety.

'I'm OK. Are *you* OK?'

'What an evening we've had. I've had to go Casualty with Joe.'

'Oh no. What's happened?'

'He stayed here for tea and he forgot he'd put that mousetrap under the table. He got his foot caught in it.'

'Is he alright?'

'Yes, he's fine now. Dosed up on painkillers. I'm exhausted. Took us two hours to get a taxi back because of the snow. We got here and you weren't in. Where are you?'

'I'm with someone from school.'

'From Barton School? This line's awful.'

'No, my old school, Pennington.'

'Someone from Pennington? Who?'

'I'm afraid I'm going to have to stay the night here. We're snowed in.'

'Where are you? Who are you with?'

'As I said. Someone from school, a long time ago. David March.'

There was a silence on the other end, and Michael thought the line had cut out.

'Mum?

'That David March?' she said eventually.

'Yes, mum. He lives out on the beach.'

'You're out on the beach. In this weather? With *him*?'

'No, he's got a *house* on the beach. I can't get back tonight because of the snow.'

'Why are you with *him*? It sounds like you're ringing from the moon.'

'It's a mobile phone.'

'You're ringing from a phone booth?'

'No, it's a mobile...look it doesn't matter, I'm OK.'

'What are you doing with him of all people?'

'We just met kind of by accident and I came back with him to his house this afternoon. We got chatting about things and sort of lost track of time.'

'Are you drunk?'

'I've had a drink... but Im not drunk.'

'You're not taking drugs, are you?'

'Mum, please.'

'You know what he's like. What he did to you.'

'That was years ago. He's a successful person. Chairman of the Governors at Pennington.' Michael was grateful March was now distracted with Katya who had come down the stairs, the two lovers locked in an amorous embrace on the sofa, as if they were alone in the room, both of their dressing gowns open and their hands reaching and fumbling inside their robes. Michael turned his back on them as his mother's tone became more anxious.

'Have you eaten?' she asked.

'Yes, Katya made some food.'

'You've eaten cat-food?'

'No, scrambled eggs. Sandwiches.'

'Are you sure you've not taken any drugs?"

'No *Katya* made me something to eat'

He looked over at March who held his gaze and then kissed Katya.

'Who's Katya?' his mother asked, her voice's edge cutting through the bad signal.

'David's friend.'

'Are you alright? No after-effects?'

'From what?'

'The food. His food.'

'No.'

'Don't eat anything else he gives you. And don't have any more to drink.'

'Mum, I'm fine. I'm going to have to go.'

'When will you be coming home?'

'In the morning.'

'I'm worried about you. Hospital this evening and now this.' He could hear her muffled conversation and Joe's voice in the background.

'Hello, are you there?' she came back on.

'Yes, mum, but I need to get off David's phone.'

'I'm going to put Joe on.'

'What for?'

'See if he can talk some sense into you.'

Michael sighed, as she handed over the phone. David was now tuned in to Michael's conversation, whispering in Katya's ear and smirking with satisfaction at Michael's embarrassment.

'You OK, lad?' Joe said.

After his mother's fretting and David's intensity it was a surprisingly welcome relief to hear Joe's calm, friendly voice. 'Yes thanks, Joe.'

'Your mum says you're snowed in.'

'I'm OK, Joe. Are you alright? How's the foot?'

'Sore.'

'Don't tell me, mother made you take your shoes off at the door.'

'Yes, she'd been cleaning.'

'So, stocking feet in a mousetrap.'

'Serves me right eh? The mice thought it funny.' Michael winced at the thought of steel snapping on toenail and bone.

'Hope it's not too painful.'

'Your mum's been worried about you.'

'There's no need, Joe.'

'This line is awful.

'I know. It's the future, apparently.'

'That figures. The guy you're with. He's a drug dealer?'

'Joe, try to convince mum there's nothing to worry about.'

'I'll make sure she's OK. She's been in a bit of a state tonight.'

'Thanks, Joe. For looking after her.'

'Does your friend know anything about what's happened to that teacher?'

Michael was aware of David, no longer interested in Katya, but watching him and listening intently. 'Not really. I'm going to have to go. Goodnight, Joe. Take care of the foot. Have a whisky, or something.'

'Sounds a good idea. Goodnight, lad.'

When he put the phone down March unlocked his embrace with Katya. As he smacked her on the rear and sent her off to bed, she looked upset and annoyed.

'It's time we all turned in,' said March, draining his glass and then smiling over at Michael. 'Your mother seems to think I'm something of a legend. What on earth have you been saying about me?'

Michael shrugged. David, whose anger had now disappeared entirely, smiled and beckoned to follow him up the metallic spiral staircase to the upper deck. There were a series of steel doors leading off the long narrow landing, one of which David opened onto a modest functional space.

'It's not The Ritz, but any port in a storm. Katya's put some towels out for you. Help yourself to anything in there, have a shower, if you like,' he said, grabbing Michael's shoulder again. The smell of cigars clung to March's gown. 'Who was the guy you were talking to?' he said.

'Joe. He's my mum's plumber.'

'Does she require a plumber at midnight?'

Michael resented David's raised eyebrows and suggestive tone. 'He's just a friend,' he said.

'I see, and you were talking to this friend, a plumber, about Gilbert Soames?'

'His grandson is in Soames' class. The boy is worried about him.'

David shook his head and sneered, 'All this worry and concern for a man like that. But at least *you* know the truth now.'

CHAPTER FOURTEEN

As David promised, there were towels and pyjamas stored in the cupboards, the bed felt reasonably comfortable and the red-hot water from the shower pummelled his body and face, clearing his head from the wine, whisky and March's exhausting company. It was a relief just to be alone as he settled back on the bed, and leaving the light on for now, he closed his eyes and tried to relax. But he couldn't stop thinking about what March had told him. How could he make sense of it all? If what March claimed was true, if Soames had planted drugs in David's locker all those years ago and he truly thought Soames was not fit to be around young people, then why did March allow Gilbert to carry on teaching at Pennington? As Chairman of Governors he could easily have found a pretext to have Soames dismissed. However, David's view of Soames was not shared by everyone. According to Lawton, staff and pupils thought fondly of him, and he'd made a great impression on Joe's grandson. There were the great stage productions that Gilbert put on and the school would struggle to find someone as talented in that sphere. It might not be that easy for March to dismiss someone with such support and reputation. So, instead he had carried out a prolonged campaign of harassment and victimisation against Gilbert, if Joan and Lawton were to be believed. Was this a crueller, more satisfying form of revenge for David – to drive Soames slowly to the brink of breakdown and self-destruction? And then there was also Lawton's claim that Soames had some really damaging evidence on March, something involving Laura and Joan. Was this why David didn't have Soames dismissed – because Gilbert had damning revelations of his own about March that he was keeping in reserve? Whatever the truth was, the vendetta between Soames and March had endured and intensified over the years.

It was all so bewildering and at the centre of the mystery was the even more conflicting and confusing portrait of Soames that emerged. There was his mother's view of him as reckless and destructive teacher; Dillon's angry secret that had to be swept under the carpet; Lawton's eccentric old school colleague and fellow rebel; Joan's troubled but nevertheless still adored husband; March's corrupt, unstable burn-out. Finally, there was his own assessment that encapsulated all these ambiguities and more. Soames the charismatic role model, the lifelong inspiration, the only man who ever really understood him. And then also the man who, many years ago had an affair with one of his students who just happened, until Maddie, to be the love of Michael's life. And now the man who may have planted evidence to have one of his students expelled. The dark, disturbing enigma cast its shadow at every turn, feeding Michael's obsession. With each discovery about Soames, the more fascinated, the more compelled he was to find out more, these latest revelations only adding to the complex portrait, a deepening mystery that, perhaps, only he could finally unravel, because only he knew all the many manifestations of Soames' character.

Tired though he was, these contradictions held sleep at bay. The stink of sewage still pervaded and a low industrialised vibration hummed somewhere in the depths of the building. From the room down the corridor, sounds of lovemaking erupted, erotic moaning and groaning, culminating in a woman's cries of pleasure or was it something else, something more like pain and protest? Hard to tell in the muffled acoustics punctuated by the regular thunder of seawater and drainage cascading through the basement. March's house was a studio of unsettling sounds accompanied by the haunted whistling in the roof rigging and the distant surf roaring through the night.

He walked to the window where the blackness beyond stretched to infinity, the glass presenting his own reflection in the ceiling lights, the man before him a bemused phantom in a strange house, trapped inside a giant snow globe. Wild spiralling flakes, like swarms of grey thoughts and memories hurled themselves at the glass and melted. Maybe Soames was out there somewhere, freezing to death, could see this man at the window searching for him, looking out into the night. He shivered and blinked forlornly into the darkness and returned to the bed, switched off the lights and lay down.

The tightening around his temples increased and when he closed his eyes he saw the flakes still swirling before his eyes. The dream snow continued to tumble towards him, triggering other visions, a rolling camera of regret, unsparing, unstoppable, the scene unfolding once more of the boy, Carl Bridgford, moving under cover of darkness, making his way to the back of a classroom and a cardboard box which had held the brand-new TV with its plastic packaging. The sly handful of polystyrene flakes grabbed from the box. Sniggers building to laughter rippling through the room. Michael, oblivious, entranced as ever in the opening sequence of the film, the magic of that movie forever captivating. The camera stealing through the grounds of Xanadu, the nurse, the old man on the bed, Kane's dying words and the snow inside the globe filling the screen. But then other sounds, shouts and loud laughter from the back of the class – 'It's snowing in here as well' – and in the blue-dimmed light from the TV, the polystyrene flakes and squares floating down through the air, settling on the desks, on the chairs, in the girls' hair, the boys' collars and mouths. Michael trying to switch off the film, stabbing the remote with his fingers. Carl Bridgford in the shadows dancing in the plastic snow picking up and throwing handfuls from the box. The film running on but all eyes on the figure cavorting in the white flakes. Bridgford shouting and taking a handful of the plastic, scattering it in another boy's hair, small, bookish, timid, the only student still watching the film. The movie rolling relentlessly on, Bridgford dancing and laughing and the victim's tears now caught in the TV light. Michael, beyond shouting, beyond pleading, lost in panic and fury, grabbing the cardboard box in his hands, planting it squarely over that defiant, smirking face. Bridgford's hands resisting against the box as it came down hard, his legs collapsing under him as he sprawled on the floor, his muffled cries mingling with class laughter. Then the urge to escape, the frantic need to run away all consuming, to flee the mayhem, the daily stress and struggle to keep order, to be free of it all, the corridors, the staffroom, the heavy sky bearing each day the sadness of seeing but not being with Maddie. So out he goes through the double-door exit, and away, running, running until he is gone, back to his home town, back to his room, back finally to this night with the snow, still falling, turning to pink plastic floating in the air and sounds of arguing from the other room off the landing and a door slamming startling him fully awake, the grip on his temples bunching in ferocious waves of pain.

He needed water and when he looked out on the corridor all was silent in David's room again. He descended the stairs, the industrial vibration in the basement growing louder as he headed down to the light in the kitchen area and filled a glass from the tap. He took a long much-needed drink and then re-filled the glass, holding the cool surface to his brow. The smell of sewage was worse and there was another noise now, a man's voice, and muffled footsteps, somewhere below ground. The sounds grew louder as he approached a door which opened upon a dimly lit staircase leading to a small space that doubled back in darkness to a basement. Here the smell was at its strongest, as was the vibrating hum of machinery. The voice drifted up from out the depths.

'Time for bed, now, time for bed.'

Michael took two steps down the stairs when March called out loudly, 'Hello, who's there?'

'Sorry, it's just me.'

David, still in his dressing gown, appeared around the corner immediately at the bottom of the stairs. 'Stay there, it's not safe down here. I'll be up in a second.'

'Sorry, I came down for some water and heard voices,' Michael said, backing into the main lounge as March, carrying a flashlight, raced up the steps, closing the basement door quickly behind him.

'I wondered who the hell it was on the stairs,' March said as he walked him back to the kitchen area. 'I was looking for my cat. Somehow, he keeps finding a way in and out of the basement through the pipes running beneath this building. I wanted to go down before it floods in there again, to see if he's alright.'

'Is he OK?'

'I don't know. I thought I heard him crying in one of the pipes, but it was just the wind. I keep expecting him to be washed up drowned one morning.' Michael pushed away thoughts of a creature lost down there in that dark sewage-filled hole. March looked at him mischievously. 'I call him Harry.' He paused for effect. 'Harry Lime, in *The Third Man*? Come on. I thought you knew your films.'

'I know Harry Lime. The racketeer in Vienna. Hides and lives in the sewers.'

'Exactly. It would appeal to old Soames that, don't you think?' he said sarcastically. 'Seeing he was such a fan of Welles.'

Michael didn't want to start talking again at this late hour and badly wanted to go back to bed, but March was blocking his way as if waiting for him to say something.

'I hope Harry is OK. Sounds like you're having a lot of trouble down there.'

'I've told you we're running into all sorts of problems with tidal sewage. I've got a pumping system going day and night to extract the moisture, and hopefully the smell.'

'What's it going to be when it's finished? Your wine cellar?'

'Hardly. It's my survival cave, for when the world ends.'

'Sorry?'

March took a step back and leaned on one of the work surfaces. 'Us Cold War kids never forget there are plenty of madmen still around with their finger on the nuclear button. Global warming, population out of control, super-virus extinction, meteorite collision, who knows how or when the end will come. But come it will.' March looked Michael up and down. 'Am I depressing you, Michael? You look so down in the dumps.'

'I've got a headache. Feel a bit wasted.'

'Has what I've said about Soames earlier, upset you?'

'It's hard to believe. What he did to you. That he would do that to a student.'

March's eyes flared in anger. 'You think I'm lying? I'm making something like that up?'

'No, but it's a shock – to think Soames would do such a thing.'

'No, it *was* him. "Hank Quinlan always gets his man," – he said, after he planted the evidence and they turned out my locker, wrecked my life.'

March looked about to embark upon another tirade when Katya called from upstairs, 'Where are you? Dead, drowning in basement shit?'

'Another kitten calls,' said March, his smile returning as he turned to go up the stairs before finally looking down at Michael from above, his form silhouetted against the subdued landing light. 'Come along, Michael. You look washed out.'

Michael gulped down more water, returned to his room but sleep once more failed him. Raised voices down the corridor, another row building between March and Katya, rose to a crescendo with something crashing and then silence. Then the house began to vibrate and shudder, as the waste and water deep in the labyrinths thundered and blasted to the sea. What chance would a poor cat have trapped down one of those pipes? The sound of the waters subsided to give way to more muffled cries from the room down the corridor.

March was right, he did feel washed out, washed up, lonely with nothing for company but his own anxious thoughts through this longest night of winter. He longed for the oblivion of untroubled sleep, but instead the sounds from the nearby bedroom unsettled him, along with memories of when *he* was not alone, many weeks ago now, the last time he held Maddie in his arms. But all there was to recall was the deep sadness of that final night together, the inevitability of it, the school holidays almost over, the funeral that afternoon of Princess Diana at Westminster Abbey, Maddie in tears when Elton John sang 'Candle in the Wind'. The shadow of the young woman's death hanging over them into the evening, merging with their own silent burden. He held Maddie for a long time in the darkness that night, troubled by thoughts of his mother and her loneliness and depression, her claims she hadn't seen anything of him all summer.

He knew Maddie too wasn't really asleep and her

voice, when she spoke, sounded distant, as if she already had the answer she was seeking. 'I know we've talked and talked but I need to know,' she said. 'When you are going to move the rest of your stuff in here? When you are going to come and live with us, me and Tommy?' He didn't reply and it was a long wait before he heard the inevitable, 'You're not going to, are you? Michael,' followed several minutes that felt like hours later by her pronouncement, 'This isn't working, is it.' Soon after he heard her crying in the bathroom and when she came back he put his arms around her but said nothing. And now, months later, here he was awake listening to the sound of voices in the room beyond and once more wondering why he was silent that night back in early September. Why he said and did nothing then and all the hours after and all the week following, until Maddie, crying again, said it was over between them. And wide awake now, he wondered, as he did most nights, where Maddie was tonight. He thought of Rick Campbell and Maddie together in the Common Room, how Campbell had made her laugh, while he watched on, sad, confused, trying to look like he didn't care, the poison of regret stirring and settling deep in the pit of his stomach. He had run miles away to this town, this place of his birth, but could not escape the sound of her laughter, this night as any other, in the sound of the waves on the shore, in the wind, in the soundless snow falling, and her voice, her soft voice sighing, in the heart of the storm.

CHAPTER FIFTEEN

He collapsed into a dreamless, brief oblivion just before dawn and awoke suddenly in this unfamiliar room filled with white light. The morning sun shone through the blinds which he raised to reveal a scene of untouched calm and beauty. In a blizzard-transformed landscape, the long shadow of March's house stretched onto the snow-mountain dunes and beyond to the incoming tide fringed with ice at the shoreline. The early sun peering above the mounds beckoned him into the light, away from this room where he'd endured a night of such dark thoughts and memories. He needed to dress quickly and leave, hopefully avoiding any further encounter with March and his ill-tempered girlfriend. But after getting dressed, although there was no sign of David, he discovered Katya, still in her dressing gown, cooking breakfast.

'Good morning,' she said. 'Would you like something to eat?'

'Er, no, I'd better be going. Thank you for my tea last night. And will you thank David for his hospitality?'

'He says I haven't to let you leave. He wants to see you before you go. Says it's very important. Sit down, I will bring you breakfast.' This was the last thing he wanted to hear, but Katya was insistent. He returned to the same chair, the same table, where the same ten pound note still lay abandoned from the previous night.

'He'll be down in just a minute,' Katya said, bringing him coffee. As she bent over to hand him the drink, her gown fell forward and revealed her naked breasts. He recalled the sounds of sexual passion and pain that punctuated the night. His gaze lingered a little too long and she laughed and folded her gown.

'Sorry,' I didn't mean to....'

She was smiling at his sudden blushing. 'Sex and food, food and sex. That's all you men think about.'

'David says you're from Croatia,' he said, trying to change the subject.

She returned to the kitchen area, and with her back to him said, 'Dubrovnik. I don't talk about it.'

'Sorry. At least it's safer here.'

'Safe? What is safe? No such thing as safe.' She turned and looked over at him. 'David tells me you are single.'

'Er, yes.'

'You have no girlfriend?'

'Er, well, no. There was someone, but...'

'Was she pretty?'

'Yes.'

'You still in love with her?'

'Actually, it's over now between us.'

Katya shook her head. 'You are sad?' He wished March would appear quickly and he could be on his way.

'Well, we were friends for a long time.'

'Better to be friends than lovers, eh? You have heartbreak now though, all the same.'

Michael shrugged, paused and said finally, 'Maybe.'

'But maybe plenty more fishermen in the sea, eh?' she

said.

'It's fish'

'Sorry.'

'In the sea. Plenty more fish in the sea... Sorry.'

She laughed and she immediately looked much younger, probably in her mid-twenties. She had multiple piercings in one ear and her short-cropped hair, which the sun now caught as it slanted through the far windows had some hints of grey amidst the raven black.

'Plenty more fish in the sea,' she nodded. 'So, you go to catch them?'

'No, I'm...'

And she smiled at Michael again, a smile that quickly faded as March appeared on the landing, fully dressed in suit and tie.

'Morning, Michael,' he said, coming down the stairs. 'I hope Katya's been looking after you.'

'We've been talking about his love life,' said Katya, from the kitchen, mixing more eggs in a bowl.

'His love life?'

'Yes, he's been telling me all about his break with his girl, his heartbreak.' She looked at Michael and shrugged.

'Take no notice of her. She's a nosy little bitch. Aren't you, Katya?' March said.

'No, just being friendly,' she said stirring the eggs into the pan while shooting him a dirty look as smoke swirled briefly around her. Michael recalled the raised voices from their room throughout the night. There was obviously still tension simmering between her and David.

March turning to Michael said, 'You didn't mention a woman.'

'There isn't one. Is your cat OK?'

March stared out the window. 'Harry? Who knows? It was a big swell last night. Maybe it washed him out with the last tide.'

'I'm sorry. I hope not.'

'Don't worry about him. I'm away from here for weeks sometimes and he lives off wild life on the dunes. He's a survivor. What about you? Did you sleep OK, eventually?'

'Yes, thank you. I need to be getting on my way out of your hair. Katya said you wanted to see me before I left.'

The bright glare from the shore dazzled and he had to shade his eyes. March stood with his back to the light, his face cast in darkness as he spoke.

'Yes, actually, I've been wondering. What is all this really about, Michael?'

'What do you mean?'

'You know, you coming here.'

'I've told you, I found about Soames, bumped into Lawton and Joan and I was worried about him. Thought I'd have a word with you as well to see if you knew anything."

'But just turning up out of the blue like that. I've been thinking about it all night.'

'Sorry, I shouldn't have troubled you. I should be on my way.'

'Come on, Michael. Like you say you've been to see Joan, been to see Lawton, been back to the school. You've found me. What for?'

'I was just curious – about Soames.'

March shook his head in disbelief. 'I'm not sure that's all you're interested in?'

'Yes, I told you, after I read the newspaper article, I

was just upset hearing about him.'

'Quite a coincidence. All this bumping into folk. Bumping into Lawton. Bumping into Joan.'

'Well, actually, it's been good catching up with people.'

'All this detective work.'

'I'm not a detective.'

'You were acting like one last night – a lot of questions. Then mentioning that film.'

'What film?'

'You know, the one about the water trouble. I'm not stupid, Michael. We all know what that movie's really about.'

'You mean *Chinatown*?'

'Yes, were you trying to be funny, or what, exactly?'

'Sorry, it was just a flippant remark. It didn't mean anything.'

'A flippant remark about a film exposing deep-seated corruption. You're not thinking you're on some kind of *case* here, are you?'

'No, it was just you were having problems with the water in the basement.'

March was now facing the window so Michael could not read his expression. But when he turned and came out of the sunlight, he burst out laughing. 'Oh, Michael, Michael, I'm just kidding. Lighten up will you, man.'

Was March play-acting now, or did he sincerely think Michael was investigating him? Despite the night of wine, whisky, cocaine, and sex, David looked fresh, his eyes as full of mischief and malice as ever.

'I mean,' March was still smiling, 'I'm just as bad

with film references. Even named my cat after Harry Lime. Maybe that's what old Soames did to us, the old bastard. But seriously, I *really* wanted to talk to you about something else. I think the person you're actually investigating here, the one you really want to know about isn't your favourite teacher at all.'

'Sorry?'

'Come on, all of this smokescreen stuff about Soames. You're really after finding *her*, aren't you?'

'I'm not sure what you mean.'

'Yes, you do.'

'I'm sorry, David. I don't know what you're talking about.'

'Why didn't you say you wanted to see her in the first place?'

'I don't...'

'Of course, you do. You want to meet our darling Laura, that's it isn't it?'

He was blushing again, but there was nothing he could do to stop it. 'I didn't say that. I don't...'

'I can put you in touch if you want?'

'With Laura?'

'Yes, our paths cross from time to time.'

'Who's this Laura?' said Katya, scraping the eggs out of the pan. She clattered the plate onto the work surface looking furiously at March.

'Laura, the love of my life. The love of his life too,' he said, nodding at Michael. 'Am I right, Michael?'

'Not really. I haven't seen her since...' but he found himself lost for words, his attention divided between thoughts of Laura, and Katya glowering at David from the kitchen.

'Well, here's the love of your life!' she yelled and March dodged out of the way of the plate that came hurtling across the room towards him. It careered on its way to smash against the far wall.

March sneered, 'Well, that's one less for you to wash, Katya, isn't it?' he said, anger flaring and then fading.

'Go see the fucking love of your life. Let her do all the washing up, all the cleaning, all the cooking.'

'Katya, calm down will you. You've covered Michael in eggs.'

She stormed past him up the stairs, spitting a stream of Croatian invective as she disappeared behind one of the bedroom doors.

March called out sarcastically, 'Katya, Katya, come back, will you and calm the fuck down.' He then turned to Michael, the anger back in his eyes, but just about under control. 'Sorry about that. Are you alright, old chap?'

'I'm OK, thanks.'

'I like to wind her up,' he scoffed. 'She curses best in Croatian.' March picked at Michael's hair and small flakes of scrambled egg littered the armchair. Then he waved a hand dismissively at the stairs, at the bedroom beyond. 'Fuck her. No gratitude these people. Now, where were we? Talking about our old sweetheart.' March said, smiling once more. 'I met her only the other week, as a matter of fact. At the PM's get together.'

'The PM?'

'I've told you. Blair. He wants to get all the movers and shakers in the new economy on side.'

'Laura was there?'

'Oh, yes. Networking the hell out of everything and

everybody. I wanted her to do some work for me in St Vincent's. But she gave me some excuse. Said she couldn't face coming back here. I suppose your humble hometown is beneath you when you head up one of the top marketing agencies in London.'

'Are you and her still friends?' He regretted saying it immediately. It sounded curious when he didn't want to sound curious, but, despite himself, he just couldn't help being interested. Laura out there in the big wide world, making a success of her life, still connected with March.

'She's got three kids. A regular Superwoman. The eldest, the daughter, must be nearly eighteen by now. Other two are boys. All in private schools. Shame about the husband, though. Arrogant, entitled twat. He's in the City. That's how our paths kept crossing when I worked there.'

'You say she's doing, OK?' Michael asked.

'Terrific. I can get you in to see her if you want?'

'See her.... Er, No, it's fine, thanks.'

'Come on, Michael. I've got her details somewhere. Look her up for yourself.'

He took out his wallet and produced a business card, and handed it to Michael just as Katya was coming down the stairs, dressed, carrying a suitcase.

'Going somewhere, my princess?' said March.

'Yes, away. Rather die in Dubrovnik than stay here.' She stood there waiting for a response from March but he ignored her.

'That's it,' March said, handing Michael the card. 'Give old Laura a call, or pay her a visit. She'll be so glad to see *you*.'

'Look at you two,' Katya said. 'A couple of pathetic schoolboys with your old sweetheart.'

'Katya,' March said, still with his back to her, 'if you're going to remain in this country, you will have to acquire a sense of humour.'

'You are an asshole,' she said, 'and I'm done with you and your stinking house.' With that she stormed across the room and slammed the door on the way out.

March shook his head and then smiled. 'Don't worry about her. She'll be back by lunchtime. She hasn't got that many options. Actually, though, it might not be a bad idea if she doesn't come back. She's been a pain in the arse recently.'

'Sorry, will she be, OK?'

'She's a survivor. Stop worrying about everybody, Michael.'

'I feel I've caused her and you to...'

'Leave it. Katya will be home with my dinner ready when I get back tonight.' He pointed to the card in Michael's hands. 'What do you think. Fancy meeting up with her?'

Michael stared at Laura's card, turning it over in the sunlight.'

'It *is* real you know,' March said. 'That's her office address. All you have to do is turn up.'

'I don't think she'd be bothered about seeing me, after all these years.'

'Oops, sorry,' March said looking at his watch, 'I need to go. Obviously, breakfast is no longer an option and I've got to drive to London today.'

'How will you get your car out? After the snow?' Michael asked. But when March opened the front door his Mercedes stood on the drive, pristine, polished and shining in the bright sunlight. The road out of the dunes had been cleared and then gritted so that the surface now glistened as if merely a light rain had fallen.

'They came this morning while you were sleeping. It helps to have friends in high places. Especially here, in Chinatown,' March said, grinning. Michael managed a half-hearted smile in return. 'Come on, Michael, cheer up, you've got Laura's card there,' David said, picking up his briefcase. 'I thought it'd give you a bit of a boost, you've been looking so glum. Do you good to get out of this dump and down there to London, particularly as you've just broken up with someone. I'd offer you a lift back to your mum's now but have to be on my way. Important meeting, sorry.'

'That's OK, the walk home will clear my head.'

'Here,' he said, 'you've forgotten this.' He handed Michael the ten pound note.

'No thanks, it's OK.'

'Don't be silly.'

'No, I really don't want...'

March rifled through his wallet again. 'Here's a fresh one,' he said, handing him a fifty pound note.

'No, there's no need for that.'

'Of course, think nothing of it. It's not every man who will lend his last ten pounds so a friend can stick it up his nose. I won't take no for an answer. Buy yourself a train ticket to London. Maybe you can persuade Laura to come up here and do some work for me.'

Michael reluctantly pocketing the fifty pound note said, 'I really doubt she'd be interested. In me, I mean.'

'Don't underestimate yourself.' March paused and took a deep breath before saying, 'Look, just between you and me. For old time's sake, you ought to know, if you don't know already, that is. You always were the *one*, you know.'

'The one?'

'Yes, for her. She always says you were the one. The

one and only.'

'What do you mean?'

'I don't know – must have been something you two had going all those years ago. Maybe something to do with the way you were always there for her, and didn't come on too strong. Or maybe you did and... I just don't know. Who knows with women? Whatever it was, it worked its magic. You always had a bit of that man of mystery and all that. Anyway, you made a hell of an impression. She still talks about you. Like I say, you should look her up. Find out for yourself,' he said, ushering Michael through the door. 'What do you say?'

He was lost for words but finally said, as March waited by his Mercedes. 'Did she really say that? When did she say that... that one and only thing?'

'She always said it. Still says it. Even now, after all these years. Used to make me jealous as hell back in those days at Pennington. What more do you need to know? You really should see for yourself. You never know what might happen. Again, just between you and me, she's not that happily married, old Laura.'

Michael just looked at him dumbfounded.

'I've stunned you into silence. Just get your arse down there and see her. Now, if you don't mind, Michael, I really need to be getting along.'

Without more ado, March was in his car and, with a brief farewell nod, he drove away, leaving Michael standing outside the house, blinking and bewildered in the grey glare of the snow-filled morning. The sun disappeared behind a raft of grey cloud, but a mild thawing breeze was blowing off the land. He quickly made his way along the cleared road, past the white-crowned dunes, his mind spinning from this revelation. March's words, 'For her you were the one, the one and only,' filling him with wonder as he gently touched Laura's card in his pocket, stopping twice to look at it to make sure it really was still there:

Laura Travis
CEO
Travis, Parker & Manley
Soho Square
0207461234

He walked along the winding ocean road, contemplating this magical, incredible news. How had he so completely underestimated his effect on Laura? But then, when he was seventeen, he'd always struggled to believe he could ever be her boyfriend. But to think she had not only loved him then, but had continued to hold him in such affection in the many years that followed, was nothing short of a miracle. And now he knew this, what should, what could he do? He might ignore it, but then spend the rest of his life wondering. He knew his main joyous impulsive instinct was to make up for those lost years. To follow David's advice and seek a swift reunion with his first love. The woman on the card, the woman of whom March spoke, the wife, the mother, the highly successful executive, none of these people seemed real. The real Laura was still seventeen, was still at Pennington, waiting to go Cambridge. And with that same Laura from the long ago was also a great part of him still back there in her room, listening to Joni Mitchell or smoking cannabis in the park by the golf course, waiting for time to release him, for life to begin. Did she still feel the same way? Was it possible after all these years? Could he soon, as in the old days, be consoling her again as she confessed her unhappy marriage and then revealing how *he* was the only person she could ever really talk to, how she'd always secretly longed for him to find her again? Maybe he would listen and hold her hand like he did when they were children watching *Mary Poppins,* buy her another drink as they wiled away the afternoon in a London bar and relived the past and the years apart. Did she still drink Bacardi and Coke? Did she still love Captain Beefheart and fantasise over Robert Plant? Would she still think he looked like Dustin Hoffman? He headed away from the shore into the spiralling dry snow flurries all swirling and clearing the way ahead, firmly set on course, desperate now to discover the answers to these questions.

CHAPTER SIXTEEN

On arriving back at his mother's, the train ticket to London purchased on his way home, Grace was bent over, sleeves rolled up, clearing snow from the front path, her forehead covered in perspiration despite the freezing wind.

'Why couldn't you wait till I got back. I would've done that,' he said.

'I'd no idea how long you were going to be,' she replied without looking at him.

Snow banked up a foot high on both sides of the path leaving a skin of ice glazing the swept surface on which she now sprinkled generous fountains of salt. A shelf of melting snow fell from the roof onto the cleared area, just missing him by inches.

'Oh god, I'd just done that,' she said, hurrying over with the shovel.

'I'll finish off here, mum.' He wasn't even inside the house yet, and already back in his mother's world of confinement and guilt. But now with a rail ticket lodged confidently in his inside pocket.

'Mind you don't slip on the way in,' she said. 'And don't forget to take your shoes off.'

'Go and sit down. I'll just clear up and then I'll make us both a cup of tea.'

He swept the path, but more snow kept falling from the roof above so he gave up and went into the kitchen. Returning with the tea, he sat down in the living room opposite her. She looked tired.

'Hope you haven't overdone it out there,' he said.

'Bit late for you to be worried about that now.'

'How's Joe? Is he OK?'

'Dosed with painkillers but he'll live.'

'I told you not to bother with the mousetraps.'

'It's Joe's fault for not looking what he was doing.'

'Poor bloke. It must have hurt.'

'Serves him right for getting his feet too far under the table.'

'Joe's a nice guy, mum.'

She looked him in the eye and said, 'Why didn't you come home last night?'

'I told you, I couldn't get a cab in the storm.'

'We had no problem getting one to the hospital. And Joe got one OK, later, to get home.'

'I don't know. I rang a couple and couldn't get through.'

'How convenient. I suppose you stayed up all night, drinking, taking god knows what.'

'It wasn't like that. David kindly offered me a bed for the night. It was a blizzard out there.'

'So, it's "David" now, is it? Why are you bothering with these people? You really need to stop all this.'

'I'm sorry, mum, but there's no need to worry.'

'What's that in your hair?' she said peering at his scalp. 'Egg? You've got egg in your hair.'

'Katya threw some breakfast at David.'

'Who's Katya?'

'David's friend.'

'Throwing good food around. What are these people? Babies?'

'She's from Dubrovnik. She's had a terrible time.'

'What's she doing here, then?'

'She's David's friend. She made me supper last night.'

'You should be getting on with that research you're supposed to be doing. Instead of gallivanting around with these weird people. You'll be losing your job next.'

The room vibrated as another pile of snow slid off the roof above, scattering all along the garden path. She shook her head. 'So much for a morning's work.'

'I'll clear it up, mum, don't worry.'

'It's not snow on the path I'm worried about.'

He thought of the train ticket and Laura's business card. The journey to London tomorrow. Then, as if she read his mind, she said, 'You know what happened to you last time you got involved with that lot.'

'I was just a kid back then.'

'You're still a kid. Well, acting like one.'

'What's the harm in catching up with old friends?'

'Why would you ever want to see him again? Michael, I don't want you to be ill.'

He sighed and looked at her. 'I'll go and clear up the snow. You take it easy.'

'That March character. He's dangerous.'

He stopped by the door and drew a breath. He would need to tell her anyway where he was going tomorrow.

Maybe it would help them both if he explained what was on his mind, what had been on his mind ever since he read that newspaper article, and even before that. What had always been there as a stifling, hampering presence for the last twenty-six years.

'Mum, will you just listen for a minute? Remember Joan Turner from school.'

'Vaguely. She was with you in that awful man's class.'

'Well, she's Soames' wife now. She's worried sick about her husband.'

'She married that man? Well, I've no sympathy for her. Think about what happened to us all, and just stop seeing these people, will you?'

'That's just it. I think about it a lot. I've always thought about it. I don't think I can forget it.'

She raised her hands in exasperation. 'I don't know what to say to you. You think you're the only one who remembers what we went through. What that man Soames did.'

'Maybe if you'd told me sooner that Mr Soames had been here to see me, I could've gone and spoken to him. It might've helped.'

'Oh, not that again. How would that have helped anyone? I didn't tell you for that very reason. Because it would have made things even worse.'

'Well, I know you don't want to hear this, but something else has happened now as well.'

'I really just wish I'd kept my stupid mouth shut about him coming here.'

'Laura, you remember Laura?

She grimaced. 'Her! The one you were with that day?'

He took another deep breath. 'Apparently, she still

misses me.'

'You've been seeing that woman as well?'

'No but David got talking about her and...she's a successful businesswoman with three children.'

'What are you talking about? What do you mean she still misses you? What nonsense is this, Michael?'

'She wants to see me.'

'Who says she wants to see you?'

'David says so. David says I'm important to her, still.'

'David!' she spat out the name. '*David*? God, you'll believe any old poppycock won't you. It was the same with that Maddie woman from school with the little boy, trying to hook you in.'

'Maddie? She wasn't trying to hook me in. We were...'

'Never mind. Good god, Michael, you can be very naïve. You say you've just met up this David character?'

'Yes, he wanted to tell me about Laura. Said it was important for me to know. David knew what Laura meant to me back then.'

'You were children.'

'Yes, that's just it. That's how far we go back, Laura and me. All the way back to Tindall High, even back to primary school together, long before Pennington.'

'You've been reading that journal too much. It's all in the past.'

'It doesn't feel like the past. It feels like just... yesterday.'

'I'm really worried, Michael. Ever since Maddie you've been acting strange. Mooching about, up in your room, staring at that woman's photograph, reading that journal of yours, meeting strange people. Now you stay out all night.'

'Maddie's got nothing to do with this.'

'You keep disappearing somewhere. Never tell me anything anymore.'

'I'm trying to tell you now.'

'What you're telling me sounds frightening, Michael. Sounds like you're having that same trouble again.'

'I'm fine. There's just this thing I have to do. I want to find out more.'

'About what?'

'Mr Soames, Laura, what happened then, what's still happening now.'

'What does that mean?' she cried. She put her head in her hands and when she looked at him again there were tears in her eyes. 'If you really cared about anyone but yourself, you'd stop all this,' she said, shaking her head in anguish.

There was no going back now. He had to tell her the rest of it. 'It's fine, mum. If nothing else it'll just be a day away in London.'

'What do you mean, a day in London? Where are you off to next?'

'Tomorrow. I've got my ticket.'

'You're going there? To see her? This Laura.'

'Yes. Please don't worry, mum. It'll all be fine.'

'This will make me ill.'

He wanted to console her but knew if he did he might waver. Instead he said, 'I'll sweep up outside,' leaving her to stare at the frantic tree lights flickering silently on and off in the corner, the Santa in his sleigh suspended with the jaded white fairy perched above. Outside he breathed the sharp, clear air deep into his lungs. He shovelled and scraped the new snow away and swept it all to the side until half the path was clear. As he worked, he hoped she might come out and review the result of his labours, but she made no further appearance at the front of the house. It was pointless seeking her understanding for this trip to London. For her, March would always be the dangerous drug dealing youth who should've gone to prison, Laura, the siren luring him once more onto the rocks of breakdown and mental collapse. He understood her misgivings about David, but these were all bound up with the prejudices of the past. Meeting David had helped Michael see another side of the person he remembered from Pennington. Yes, there was still the insufferable arrogance and egotism of old, but David's disclosure of Laura's depth of feelings for him was perhaps evidence of a more generous nature than the monster his mother conjured. He'd even paid for his ticket to London. And for a man of David's standing and pride to admit to feelings of envy over Laura's affection for him somehow revealed another side of him, a capacity for humility and integrity. Maybe there was truth in the other things that March had also said about Soames, the way he had ruined March's prospects of Cambridge. If so, wasn't there some testimony here to March's continued tolerance, despite everything, in retaining Soames, as a member of staff at Pennington, a man who'd intervened so disastrously and immorally in his life? That he hadn't sacked Soames immediately on becoming Chairman of Governors in many ways showed great forbearance.

If only his mother could see it that way. As he cleared the last of the snow into the grey melting banks either side of the drive, he still worried about how all this stress might set her back with her depression. When he came back inside, he could hear her upstairs talking on the phone. Perhaps complaining to Joe who hopefully might calm her down. Her anxiety and low mood always seemed ready to overwhelm her and his ending the relationship with Maddie and coming back to live with her had done little good. Today he had tried to talk to her, to explain how he felt, but he was just making her worse. And although he felt guilty about it, he couldn't wait until the next chance to escape and his meeting with Laura. His mother said he kept disappearing and perhaps she was right, he *was* slowly disappearing – into a world of memories. But, more and more, that's where he wanted to be, where he might somehow rediscover the person he once was before that October afternoon in the pillbox many years ago.

When she left the house later that evening without speaking except to say she was visiting Joe, still laid up with his sore foot, it was a relief. He searched through her record collection until he found it. *Camelot*, the crumpled sleeve with Richard Harris and Vanessa Redgrave on the cover. As he lowered the stylus, 'How to Handle a Woman', the track he'd not heard since 1971, crackled into life. Back then he had missed all those real feelings Laura had for him, had been unable to see he was so much more to her than a stand-in replacement for David and Soames in her affections. But he must have been so much more, if his love for her had won such a lasting place in her heart. He played the song several times before he retired to his room to finish reading his journal. He felt strong enough now to put this final disturbing instalment behind him before he embarked tomorrow in search of his Guinevere of old.

CHAPTER SEVENTEEN

Friday November 8th 1971

Dear Mr Soames,

Why do I continue to write to you?

I don't know. I've asked myself this question many times in recent days. Maybe it's because, despite everything, you're the only person who ever understood me, understood that person I was before the world fell apart. And, the nurse, the doctor, they're both right. Although it's painful, it still helps in a way. To think of you. To write to you, although I know you will probably never see or hear from me again.

I don't want to see you. I don't want to see anyone from Pennington, but it helps just a little to remember you as you were, when everything briefly shone, before the shadows came.

I wonder now, did you make any attempt to catch up with me that day at Laura's house? Did you care about me running off into the darkness, out of my head with fright, running away from demons, but also from you and Laura and what you meant to each other? Did either of you care about leaving me out there? Lost in that awful afternoon, the terrifying street with the gaping trees and the melting, crying cars, with nowhere to go. Finally running back to dad at the factory. 'Bad comes back, bad comes back,' Laura's words following me all the way with the horrors chasing and closing. Then reaching the factory building glowing in the dark and the iron gates, avoiding puddles in the worn-down gravel, large pools of dark water that look like you could drown in them, sinking down into the core of the earth. Needing to see my dad, to tell him what's happened, tell him I'm in trouble, how sorry I am, for everything.

But he's nowhere around, and instead something dark and terrible follows me, something from that pillbox on the beach, waiting, along with the growling of The Creamer and its vibrations filling the warehouse, shaking the floor to the soles of my feet. Climbing up to the edge of the machine I stare into the deep revolving vat of plastic, water and steam. It's safer down there, a place to hide from the terror. I lean over further into the smoking mouth with my feet off the ground reaching deeper and deeper into the white fog below. Behind me something bad is creeping close, closer.... I clamber up on the rim, about to escape over the edge when the terrible thing grabs me from behind. I struggle and try to get away down into the vat – anything to shake off the hands that are holding me so tight, squeezing out my life. But there's no hope, the thing has a hold on my waist, then my shoulders, and it pulls me and lifts me away from the tank. Its arms fold around me and then turn me around to face the mask of horror and rage and I look straight into my father's eyes.

Monday November 18th 1971

Dear Mr Soames,

The purpose behind the medication is twofold to counter both anxiety and depression. Tranquilisers and anti-depressants. The tranquilisers have an effect of numbing everything. Beneath the numbness nothing is real. Beneath the surface of things, this bed, this room, the enforced meals, the unknown black terror still waits.

Mum visits today. She tells me it's impossible for me to see anyone from school. I need peace and quiet to recover. I don't want to see anyone from there anyway. The people there at Pennington, you Mr Soames, Laura, seem all part of the dream that became a nightmare.

Friday November 22nd 1971

Dear Mr Soames,

Dad visits today for the first time. He's just silent and angry.

I want to thank him for saving my life, for pulling me from The Creamer, but we don't say anything. I long for him to speak, even if it's just to be disgusted with me, to punish me for my stupidity, my disloyalty to him and everything he's done for me. But then part of me wishes he'd not been there, that he'd just let me fall right into the steam and plastic and roaring metal.

Don't get me wrong. I'm glad I'm not dead. Just not that interested in living.

I wish dad would say *something* though.

He looks tired and spends most of the time sitting on the end of my bed staring about the room at the other patients, particularly Mr Jones opposite who's having electric shocks for depression and can't remember anything now. He keeps asking the nurse what time it is, and then what day.

Dad looks at me and finally says, 'Michael, what're we doing here?'

Mum squeezes my hand and says, 'Let's not rush things.'

Friday December 6th 1971

Dear Mr Soames,

Dad hasn't come again after that one visit and mum hasn't been now for several days. I ask Nurse Sarah today if I can ring home but she says she will have to ask the doctor first. Then she doesn't come back.

Monday December 9th 1971

Dear Mr Soames,

I ask Nurse Sarah again if I can call home. She looks very upset and goes away without saying anything. When she comes back I follow her down the long corridor to Dr Carter's office.

'Michael, something has happened and we've been waiting for what might be the right moment to inform you,' the doctor says. He has a large folder in front of him like a teacher with some homework I've done. 'You've been making such good progress with your medication. And since you've made a request to call home,' the doctor says, 'it's only right you should be told the reason why you've had no visits from your family in the past few days.'

I expect him to say my parents have split up and that it's all my fault. So, when he says, 'The reason is bad news, I'm afraid,' I'm prepared. But I'm not prepared for this, for what he says next, as if he's reading from a script.

'Last Monday, your father was driving his car when he crashed into a tree. The post-mortem revealed the heart attack occurred before the impact.'

'Post mortem?' I say.

'Your father is dead, Michael, I'm afraid. He suffered

a massive heart attack at the wheel of his car. He was dead before the car hit the tree.'

I can't remember much after that.

I remember *Rumpole of the Bailey* being on TV that evening. Dad loved that programme. He imagined me a top barrister like Horace Rumpole and we would watch it together with mum in those evenings filled with hope for the future. Nurse Sarah found me late in the TV room staring at the test card, alone and long after all the programmes had shut down.

The doctor says it's important that I use this journal to be honest. That it might help with my feelings.

I have no feelings. I don't want to have feelings for anything or anyone again.

Tuesday December 10th 1971

Dear Mr Soames,

I think I have wished my father dead. My betrayal over Cambridge entrance, my drug-taking and then my illness and failure, my secrecy, my lies. Then my wishes he wasn't around anymore. I've brought this on. This is what I feel. I think I wanted him dead. I broke my father's heart and it killed him.

Wednesday December 11th 1971

Dear Mr Soames,

Nurse Sarah goes with me outside this afternoon and we walk around the grounds. She gives me one of her cigarettes and asks if I'm OK. I ask if she will leave me alone in the garden for a moment. My father's funeral today. Dr Carter advises I don't attend. I sit here by the dead roses crying.

Thursday December 12th 1971

Dear Mr Soames,

Mum visits for the first time since dad's death. She looks like she hasn't slept for weeks. Dad had gone to the factory Monday morning. Around midday a policeman came knocking on the door and she knew something was very wrong. Dad's car wrapped around a tree. Dad already dead inside, heart attack at forty-nine. I keep expecting he will come through the door any moment shouting at me for lying around in bed, being useless, letting him down again.

She says it was a lovely service, the church had been full and she wished I could've been there, but perhaps it was for the best. She'd discussed it with Dr Carter and he'd persuaded her to keep me away. I tell her I went out of the clinic into the garden that day. I don't tell her that I couldn't say goodbye, that I tried but it didn't work, that he is still here with me, all the time. That he knows I'm to blame for what's happened. That he follows me around, tells me he wishes he'd let me die. I think of The Creamer and its black vault waiting. At night he returns in dreams where he is ill, wounded, angry at what I've done to him.

Friday December 13th 1971

Dear Mr Soames,

Last night I manage to watch a film all the way through. Today I find a pack of cards in the TV room, Mr Potts the Painter, Mr Soot, the Sweep. When Sarah comes along, I ask if she wants to play Happy Families. It's not gin rummy but we would be like Jack Lemmon and Shirley MacLaine in the movie. She laughs and says she is far too busy.

Monday December 16th 1971

Dear Mr Soames,

Nurse Sarah and I walk in the grounds as usual in the morning and today she suggests we go down to the park to feed the ducks. I ask her if she's seen *The Apartment* and she says no. Her favourite film is *Love Story*. It's nice just sitting there for a while. I like looking at the bare trees against the sky.

Sarah's getting married in the spring to Darren who comes into the ward sometimes to pick her up. He looks annoyed when she isn't ready. He's a systems analyst and he doesn't like to be kept waiting. She tells me how busy he is when he gets home converting the spare bedroom into a nursery.

Sarah says I'm looking better and might be going home soon. It will be good for me to get back to normal life, she says. As long as I promise to stay with the medication for another six months. I think I'm just getting better at pretending, pretending to be someone who doesn't care about anyone or anything.

Down by the lake we sit on a bench where the boats are moored up for winter and smoke her untipped cigarettes. The wind whips up the leaves around us and ruffles the grey water. It's cold and I ask if we can go to the shelter although I don't tell her that's one of the places where I went with Laura. Through the trees we watch the golfers climb the hill and I look for my father amongst them.

But, he's not there, and never will be again.

Wednesday December 18th 1971

Dear Mr Soames,

I'm home now. This will be my last letter. After that the rest is silence, as Hamlet says. But here, life goes on, whatever that means. On the way home in the taxi, I see the Christmas lights decorating the streets but the colours are dull and the big lit-up tree in the square looks black in the rain.

Mum's selling dad's factory and business. She says we're comfortably off. But she understands we can't stay idle, and when she says 'we', she means me. She's contacted Pennington and told them I won't be returning. She holds the school responsible for what's happened. But I know it is all my fault really. The only thing I can do, the only thing that makes any sense is to make sure I look after her now.

I have no feelings about Pennington. It doesn't matter anymore. I can't concentrate to read anything and all that happened before the day in the pillbox feels like another world – Laura, Cambridge, you. None of it real. I hope you and Laura are happy together. Soon she'll be leaving Pennington, no longer your student, and you won't have to hide your secret. At least you'll keep her away from David March. I haven't told anyone what I know about you and Laura. What good would that do? I'm not angry anymore or bitter. You and Laura were the two people who meant the most to me back in a world where things once mattered.

One of dad's friends has found me a job. I start tomorrow on the Christmas Post. It's just seasonal work. Dr Carter says the fresh air, routine and exercise will be good for me. I can also get my job back at the bakery, mum says. After all, it's hell there and that's where I belong.

When the doctors said I should restart my journal, that it would help, they were right. It has helped, helped me understand that the person who started the journal all those months ago, the person who dreamed of being a writer, no longer exists.

I killed that person along with my father. I can never put that right. Writing won't put that right. It only brings back all the bad things that I have done.

He closed the volume on those final words. He always knew this extract would be the most difficult to read, had always avoided the whole journal because of this passage waiting for him at the end. But he was still unprepared for how vividly it transported him back to that isolated, stricken shame he could never share. He had *always* carried this burden through years that folllowed, had always felt unable to confide in anyone, not his mother, not the medical staff at the clinic. His private confession in these pages was an admission he shared with his dead father, something that kept them bound together and any thought of destroying that account felt like another betrayal. So, he'd kept it there on the shelf of his childhood bedroom, a reminder of his guilt and his debt to his mother. Except for the last few days, neither he nor she had ever mentioned its presence. Although she knew it concerned days at Pennington, days she would never discuss, he'd no idea if she'd read any of it.

He'd been true to his promise in the last entry, and, except for those few months under Maddie's inspiration, there had been no more writing. He could never summon again the courage he found for those final, bleak, entries. Afterwards, whenever he sat down to write, his father's stifling shadow gathered to remind him of that time and how he emerged from it as something else, something unformed, something unprepared for life, unable, at first to make it far beyond the garden path, until he took Dr Carter's advice and the job on the Christmas Post. Then after that another stint at the bakery which drifted from a few weeks into a year's sentence, with intermittent returns there over the next half a decade. And then other dead-end jobs for the local council – road sweeper, cleaner, gardener's labourer, and a brief disastrous posting at a bank.

Piece by piece he'd put himself back together over the years with books and films to compensate for the uncertain, unformed sense of who he really was. Eventually, there were the night school A Levels and a place as a mature student at university, followed by a degree while still living at home, still true to the pledge to his mother. The abortive relationships – Jenny, an alcoholic whom he matched drink for drink for several months, until he left her in a bar one night with her arms around the local piano player. And Louise, whose church-going decency gained even his mother's approval, until she dumped him when he lost his job at the bank. Then, the years of respectability, after graduating, with the teaching post at Barton and finally a house of his own, always dovetailing with weekends and school holidays back with his mother. An uncomplicated life confined to shadows and solitude. Until the bursting through of light as he and Maddie, his colleague and friend for many years, became lovers and he awoke to a world new, bright and blinding before the old impossible demands overwhelmed him.

What did it all amount to? The false starts, the bit parts in the lives of others, the failed career and hopeless relationships. Maybe, just maybe, finding Laura again now, the Laura who had always had such strong feelings for him offered a miracle, a lifeline, a way to reclaim the man who could have lived the life of a writer with her, who could have been the man Maddie wanted him to be. The man who could have been, and still might be, even after all these years, the one and only...

CHAPTER EIGHTEEN

The suit was always a big mistake. Chosen that morning at first light to impress, it now seemed far too formal. As he sat beneath the giant Christmas tree in Soho Square, staring at Laura's business card, trying to pluck up the courage to enter the large, stone-fronted building, he felt as if dressed for an interview. But that wasn't the main problem. It was the suit Maddie had picked for him for the Barton Summer Ball. That was the only other time he'd worn it, the night when he and Maddie, last to leave the dancefloor, walked barefoot through the summer-dew grass as dawn rose across the hotel lawn. And as he approached London on the train and all the way to Soho, he found himself thinking of that night more and more. The scent of Maddie's perfume still lingered on the collar and lapels, and the stain of red wine she spilled as they kissed on the balcony beneath the stars would not rub out from the sleeve. Far from providing a sense of confidence and assurance, and although the relationship with Maddie was over, wearing the suit still made him feel treacherous. It was as if Maddie was there with him now, reproaching him for this fool's mission, this leap into the dark false promise of the past. He no longer retained the optimism that March's words had given him. But then, in the square, it began to rain and with no immediate shelter, his heart beating, he entered the building, taking the lift to the second floor, where he was confronted by an officious-looking woman at Reception.

'Can I help you, sir? Have you an appointment?'

'I was wondering if I could have a word with Laura.'

'Is she expecting you?'

'Er, no, I'm an old friend.'

The receptionist looked at him as if he had some contagious disease.

'Laura Travis only sees people by appointment. Are you here to enquire about employment? Because we aren't recruiting at the moment.'

'Oh, no, I'm not in marketing. I'm just visiting.'

She shook her head in a patronising manner and sighed, eyeing him up and down.

'I'm sorry, I can't make an appointment for you. Laura has a full diary until the New Year. But if you give me your name, I'll tell her you called.'

'My name's Michael Freeman. I'm a friend of David March as well?'

The woman's eyes softened briefly in amusement. 'Does David March know you're here?' she said.

'Yes, he gave me Laura's card and said it would be OK to meet her here.'

March's name had an immediate effect. 'She will be at the Christmas party lunch. Bar Zero, on Tottenham Court Road. But it's a private event.'

He made his way out into the fading light and hordes of seasonal shoppers. The officious receptionist, the manic energy of the congested streets, and the irrational sense of betraying Maddie, all drained his spirit. It started to rain more heavily as he weaved in and out of the swarm. He thought of turning back, but March's words, Laura's words, 'you are the one, the one and only,' like a mantra, kept him moving forward. After asking a couple of directions from harried last-minute shoppers, he found 'Bar Zero'. The trendy, dark, glass-fronted establishment, with impenetrably smoke-tinted windows looked intimidating and he stepped aside as two men bustled past him into the bar. His suit was shining in the rain, the red wine stain absorbed into the damp saturated cloth. He felt his return ticket beginning to soften in his inside pocket, and he wiped his glasses on the sleeve.

He took some deep breaths and prepared to brave the party of strangers, when a slim angry-looking woman dressed in a black suit and coat slung over shoulders came out of the bar onto the street. She was holding a cigarette in one hand and a mobile phone, even larger and more brick-like than David March's, in the other. He took one step towards her, but as she began the phone call, he slid back into the adjoining doorway of an abandoned sandwich shop where he could overhear the conversation.

'Hi, Maurice can you just check those boys have finished the copy for the Commando Country account? They're both here now, half-pissed already, swearing blind they've completed, but Glen looks shifty and I don't believe him.' The woman took several intense drags on her cigarette as she awaited the reply on the other end. 'They haven't?' She turned and saw Michael standing in the doorway and looked straight through him. 'Fuck, Maurice. I told you to make sure they didn't leave the office before they'd finished it. You've a presentation to the client first thing in the morning.'

When he was seventeen Laura's looks were heart-stopping in their effect on him, but his love was not based on physical beauty. It was more to do with a glow of promise, a world of wild dreams beckoning. All that came back, suddenly, a jolt of memory like lightning in the grey afternoon. The red hair was cut much shorter in a bobbed fringe and, she was taller, and rather scarier than he ever remembered. But her overall effect on him had not changed in twenty-six years.

Then she began shouting again. 'No! No Maurice! You're going to stay there and finish the copy yourself. They're your team. You're responsible. And if it's not done well, and done today, it's Happy New Year and Happy New P45 for you. As for those two wasters who've just arrived, this was their last chance.' She hung up the call, took one final drag of her cigarette, ground the tab into the pavement with her toe, and turned to look at Michael once more. He nodded and half raised a hand, but she swivelled furiously and headed back up the steps to Bar Zero. He stood in the rain, unable to leave, paralysed to make that next move over the threshold into Laura's world. But he had to at least try before she reached the doors.

'Laura?' his voice sounded lost in the roar of traffic in the rain, but, somehow, she heard him and turned around once more, frustration still in her eyes.

'Laura, it's me, Michael Freeman.'

He moved towards her as she said, 'What the fuck...' She turned to go back into the bar, took two steps, then she looked around again, registering first irritation, then curiosity, and finally a dawning recognition.

'Do you remember, Laura, it's me, Michael?'

'Oh my god. As I live and breathe,' she said. He nodded and stopped as she stood in the entrance and then slowly walked towards him shaking her head. 'No shit. Michael. Michael Freeman? *You?*'

She looked up at the grey sky above and smiled. And there she was, standing before him: Laura, those green eyes, a little jaded around the edges, twenty-six summers' worth of life and longing later, but still the same face, a little slacker around the jaw, new lines from her nose to the corners of her mouth, but essentially the same magic, the same breath-taking effect. He remained rooted by the unreality of it all, afraid of any movement that might break the spell.

'What are *you* doing here, Michael?'

He could tell her the truth but it might sound scary, like he was tracking her down, which, in effect, he was. 'I was just in town for the day, passing by, and I noticed you come out of the bar, and I thought, wow, that looks like Laura,'

'Well, wow indeed, what can I say?'

'You haven't changed. I knew it was you straight away.'

'I don't know about that. I've aged about twenty years this afternoon.' She peered at Michael and smiled, not with the delight nor the adoration he had imagined, more with surprise and a hint of something, more like amusement. She shook her head and looked back at the bar.

'Say, I don't know about you but I need to get away. Have you time for a quick drink or something, somewhere?'

'Do you want to go back in there?'

'No, all they're interested in is my expense account.' She stopped for a moment. 'If I do go back in there, I'm probably going to sack someone on the spot.' Suddenly linking arms with him, she said, 'Come with me and let's get you out of the rain.'

Her arm in his was exhilaratingly surreal. Perhaps he should have brought a gift – flowers would have been too obvious. Maybe the journal. He imagined sitting down with her, the diary between them, reminiscing, rediscovering that those days might still mean as much to her as they did to him.

'I hope I haven't dragged you away from your party.'

'I hate Christmas parties,' she said as she ushered him across the road. 'Far too much goodwill for my liking. Come on, let's get in here.' She pushed through the revolving door of the pub, The Grapes, just across the street, and manoeuvred him into a booth. He sat down amidst the shadows of the dimly lit alcove, the late afternoon December darkness closing in on the mullioned stained-glass windows streaming with rain. He watched her entranced as she signalled her order to the barman from way back in the queue, returning promptly with a large glass of white wine and a pint of bitter. When she sat down, the soft light from the lamp above her head took away what small damage the years had done. She took a large gulp of her wine and stared at her glass.

'I've already had several of these, but so what. To tell the truth, now we're here, I actually won't be able to stay that long.' She looked at her watch. 'We've got a client breathing down our necks, presentation's due tomorrow.'

'What? On Christmas Eve?'

'Yes and I'm flying to the Maldives tomorrow. God do I need it. Just to get away from work, London, family.' She laughed bitterly. 'Have you got kids?'

He shook his head.

'Lucky you. Then again you're a bloke so it wouldn't make much difference for you if you *did.* Women are told they can have it all, but that's all bollocks.'

'How many children do you have?' He already knew the answer from March but thought it best to begin with safe small talk.

'Three. Girl and two boys. How've you managed to escape? Kids, I mean.'

Her tone was no softer but she obviously needed time to unwind from the stress of the office. She said she couldn't stay long, but once she'd settled down, she hopefully would soon relax and warm to their reunion. Maybe there was also a subtext to her question about kids – to discover if he was single or not.

'I don't think I'm parent material,' he said, and then added, 'I'm not married either.'

'Free and single then,' she said, casually, seemingly indifferent and still distracted by other concerns, looking at her watch, moving her large mobile phone from the seat to the table and back again. 'But none of us are really parent material when you come down to it,' she sighed, staring off somewhere, resentful and tense, taking another desperate draw on her cigarette. Then her mood lightened. 'Tomorrow I'm escaping from all of them and can pretend I'm seventeen again.'

In the Maldives? He'd only a vague idea where the Maldives were. Was she travelling alone? Obviously not with her husband and children. So with whom? He had a sudden image of him and her together like Bob Hope and Dorothy Lamar in *Road to Bali*, castaways together in tropical paradise. He needed some way to introduce their memories, to talk about the past, to bring back all the recollections of their time together when they were both seventeen. But, tongue-tied, lost in the suddenness of the encounter, and a waking dream of desert island romance, the immediate moment came and went. She lit another cigarette and scratched the surface of a beermat with her nail. Then she drained her glass and asked him if he wanted another, although he'd barely touched his pint. He shook his head and got up to go to the bar, but she was up before him and within moments, came back with a very large white wine refill. Her eyes, spidery with red veins, refocused, as if looking at him from a long distance. Maybe quite soon now she'd be ready to relax and talk of the past.

'I wonder how that wanker Maurice is doing,' she said, her nicotine grapy breath floating across the table. He had no idea how to take her mind away from Maurice, from the office and the presentation tomorrow. Should he drink his pint quickly, down another so he could catch up with her alcohol intake and mood?

'Happy days,' she said raising her glass and then she suddenly took hold of his hand and his heart juddered in his chest. The last time she had held his hand – it seemed like only yesterday – his life was before him, his life with her and the world that was snatched away so drastically.

He responded spontaneously with, 'It's so great to see you, Laura.' She smiled and patted his hand as the ringtone sounded.

'Fuck!' she said, pulling her hand away, her jawline tensing as she snapped open the mobile phone. She frowned, her eyes squinting with irritation at what she was hearing, the vein on her temple growing more prominent with every second.

'Look, Maurice,' she hissed, 'the client just won't wear that. They're called Commando Country for fuck's sake! They don't want grey haired wrinklies dancing to Joe Loss on some geriatric cruise in the Caribbean!' The tinny echoing voice on the other end spoke briefly until she interrupted once more. 'No, I don't have any ideas, Maurice. This is meant to be your copy, your account. But how about, fuck knows – "Throw away the Zimmer-frame and ski down the mountains, climb the stair-lift to the stars, fish for marlin not memories," – all total shit, I know, but at least it's the semblance of something.' There was more from Maurice before he was slapped down again – 'What I don't understand is why it's me having to do this now? You've to pitch tomorrow morning. You, Maurice. Not me. Do not fuck this up. If I've to come back to the office tonight to write this up then you're going to regret it, seriously regret it. Now, be a good boy and get it done.'

She flicked off the phone, muttering, 'Fucking useless,' before remembering Michael was there. 'Sorry,' she said, begrudgingly, 'work.'

'Commando Country?'

'Yes, you weren't meant to hear that. Client confidentiality and all that.' Most of the people in the pub had heard her shouting down the phone at poor Maurice.

'I couldn't help but hear, Laura. You're sitting right next to me.'

'Oh, what the fuck, yes, Commando Country. They're a holiday group specialising in adventure tours for single male seniors.'

'Climb the stair-lift to the stars?'

'Did I actually say that?'

'I thought it was rather good.'

'It's not, but it's not as lame as what Maurice has come up with so far.'

How could he relieve her from this state of stress, her furrowed brow, twitching jaw-line and ever tightening lip? She was looking agitatedly all around the room at anyone and anything and eventually her roaming gaze caught his eye again briefly.

'Any ideas?' she said, staring at him, and then laughing. 'I'm clutching at straws here. Think I'll put a memo out to everyone in the pub.' Then she began gathering her bag and coat. 'Sorry, Michael. I know we've just hooked up again after all this time, and it would be lovely to chat, but I really need to get back to the office, sort this out.'

It wasn't possible – he had to say something, anything, just so she wouldn't leave there and then. 'Er, how about – it's never too late for the great escape, fly where eagles dare, risk death with the dirty dozen,' he blurted out desperately.

She stood and looked at him, her coat halfway on her shoulders before she took it off again, and sat down. For the first time there was warmth, even admiration in her eyes.

'OK, wow, that's not bad. But it's meant to be a holiday, not a suicide mission.'

'Maybe we could exchange some ideas here. Save you going back to the office,' he suggested, hoping to build on this first hint of a rapport between them.

She then eyed him up and down, suspiciously. 'What exactly *were* you doing outside Bar Zero, Michael?'

'I don't know. I just happened to be there.'

'You looked so lost standing there in the rain.'

'I really was just passing by. At a loose end...you know how it is.'

'No, actually, I don't.'

'It's quite a familiar feeling for me.'

'Hang on,' she said, suddenly her eyes lighting up with an idea. 'Maybe *you* are just what I've been looking for.' She produced a pad from her bag and began jotting down some notes while looking up at him. His heart sank. Just when he thought he was making progress, she was preoccupied again. He'd come two hundred miles and twenty-six years for this meeting and, so far, it was like talking to an angry distant stranger. If he could just get her on to Pennington and the past, then maybe there would be a spark to reignite those feelings March had alluded to. Maybe if he finally just came clean, if she knew he had come all this way especially to see her, that it wasn't just a random encounter on the street – anything to change the dynamic between them.

'Actually, to be honest, I didn't meet you by chance. I went to your office first.'

She glanced up for a second, returned briefly to her notebook, jotted down a few more lines, before closing the pad and looking straight back at him.

'When?' she said, chewing the corner of her mouth.

'This lunchtime. I wanted to see you.'

'Why? How did you find out where I worked?'

'David March told me.'

'Dave? You've seen David? Why would he tell you that?'

'He said you might want to come down and do some work in St Vincent's with him. He asked me to try to talk you into it.'

He recognised the same brief hint of amusement in her eyes that he saw in the receptionist when he mentioned David March.

'Why didn't you tell me that at first?' she said.

'I was going to, later on. David said you wouldn't be keen on the idea, of working back in St Vincent's, so I didn't want to put you off straight away.'

Laura smiled openly now and shook her head. 'David said that, did he? How well do you know, David?' There he was, after all these years, once more discussing David March with her.

'I've just met him again. For the first time since school.'

'When did you meet him?'

'A couple of days ago. I went to see him about Mr Soames. Do you know about Gilbert Soames? How he's gone missing?'

Her eyes rolled in exasperation. 'Oh, him. Has something happened to that guy? I'm not surprised. He's a burn-out from what I heard.'

'He's disappeared. Everyone's really worried.'

'Probably holed up with some mistress somewhere.'

'His wife's devastated.' Laura just shrugged. 'Joan?

You remember Joan? Joan Turner? Joan Soames now, she's married to Soames.'

'I know they're married, Michael. You've been speaking to Joan as well? And she's been filling your head with nonsense, no doubt.'

'I thought you were both friends.'

'It's all a long time ago.'

'Joan says Dave March's got it in for Soames. Trying to push him out of his job, and the man's not well. It doesn't seem fair, and now he's disappeared.'

'OK. Why are *you* bothered about any of this?'

'Mr Soames meant a lot to me once.'

'You were just a kid then.'

'Laura, I know, as you say, it's a long, long time ago, but he mattered a lot to us both, didn't he?'

She took up her pad and perused her notes once more. 'I don't know. I can't really remember,' she said, draining her glass and holding it up for a refill.

'I'll get you another, Laura. And when I get back, I'll tell you some more about Soames, and what's happened to him.' he said. 'I know you'll be interested.'

She just shrugged and went back to writing in her book. He didn't want to risk leaving her at that moment, afraid that she might receive another call summoning her back to the office, notepad in hand. But she seemed fully occupied writing for the moment, and he welcomed the opportunity to take a step away, to think about this situation. He'd finally managed to start her talking about the past, although her response to Soames' plight seemed heartless. And any feelings she had for himself, her supposedly 'one and only', seemed shrouded in indifference. Had she been drunk or joking when she told March that Michael was her one true love? There was little sign at the moment that she ever had much affection for him at all.

But one more drink might loosen her tongue, and finally lead her back to their brief time together, the shelter by the golf course, Beefheart and cannabis in her bedroom, Bacardi and Coke at The Kings Arms, memories of Dustin Hoffman, *Straw Dogs* and pints of Double Diamond. But all this seemed, at the moment, an increasingly remote prospect. Never the most opportunistic at the bar, he moved crab-like through the clusters of determined young men jostling to be served. The pub rang with early evening festive promise as the executives and shop-workers chased down their drinks. A group of revellers sang along to 'A Fairy Tale of New York' on the juke box, the melody a poignant counterpoint to this strange reunion. Had his mother been right all along – that he was stupid to believe anything David March told him? While preoccupied with this, two more suited punters muscled in ahead and the gap to the bar he'd patiently been guarding once more closed.

'Where have you been for these? Back to St Vincent's?' she said caustically when he finally returned. At least she was still there, once more writing intently in her notepad. He decided not to waste any more time and to go straight back to talking about Pennington, the past and Soames.

'I don't understand, Laura, why you are so dismissive of Gilbert Soames. Someone who meant so much to you back then.'

'Yes, he meant something to me alright. He nearly got me expelled from school.'

'How? How could he have got you expelled?'

'It doesn't matter.'

'I'd like to know, Laura. I know it's a long time ago, but I'm still interested in all this.'

'Don't you know what happened to me and David back then?'

'I wasn't there.'

'Yes, I remember. Of course you disappeared off the face of the earth.'

There was no point in pretending about this anymore. 'Yes, I was ill for a long time.'

'Poor Michael,' she said. But the voice was devoid of feeling.

'Did Soames, or you, know what had really happened to me?'

Laura shrugged. 'Not really. It was all very hush hush. I think David made some stories up about how you'd done a bunk to India or something, whenever anyone asked.'

'Why? Why would he say that?'

'I don't know. Maybe he wanted to take the heat off himself. Make out there were others in the school dealing in drugs.'

'Like me, for instance? But that just wasn't true. You knew it wasn't true.'

'If I recall, I was mainly interested in keeping my own head down and my mouth shut around that time.' Michael had a sudden flashback to two nights ago – his attempt to convince David of his hippy trail to Benares. The embarrassment of trying to present March with a lie that David himself had invented.

'Besides, I think David thought it was funny,' Laura continued. 'The idea of you dropping out and heading for some hippy commune.'

'Well, that obviously wasn't what happened either'

'No, we gathered that.' And she threw her head back.

It was the first time that afternoon, that she had laughed. A cruel hollow chortling sound, empty of mirth or warmth in memory of a joke that had been shared, no doubt, many times over the years. And in that moment he just knew. He knew he'd been had. He knew with a sudden awful clarity, more demeaning and demoralising than any teenage jest. He couldn't immediately process it fully but there it was – the sickening realisation of David's latest prank, now as obvious as the council cleared path outside his house – the cynical cruelty of his claim that Laura still loved Michael, had always loved him, always considered him the one and only – all a monstrous lie, merely uttered as a ploy to send him away on an old fool's errand to nowhere. Was Laura in on this one with David as well? What kind of an idiot had he been to believe a single word David March had said? This was beyond humiliation, particularly if she already knew how he'd been enticed to seek her out. What was he doing here attempting to rekindle an affair that never really happened, except perhaps in his own imagination, twenty six years ago?

It was a hopeless situation and he wanted to get up and leave but that would look even more pathetic. He could dwell on the full horror of it all later, but, for now, he had to salvage some vestige of meaning and dignity, from this disaster, had to keep his emotions concealed if he could. There was nothing left for him here, except he still cared about Soames. Soames, who was still missing, the mystery of his whereabouts and the reason he came to see Michael all those years ago still unsolved. Maybe, despite his humiliation, he could still try to find as much information about Gilbert as possible. If nothing else it would keep his mind off what a fool he'd been until Laura eventually became completely bored and headed off back to the office.

'You say, Soames nearly got you expelled? How come?' he said, trying very hard to steady his voice.

She avoided the question. 'It seems strange, Michael.'

'What?'

'Why you've suddenly turned up out the blue to talk

about all this?' It was the same question March had asked him, loaded with the same suspicion.

'I never caught up properly with people afterwards. It would be good to know what really happened.'

'It's over twenty years ago.'

'David was more than happy to talk about it. Well, not happy. Not happy at all. More like he's still furious about it.'

She looked concerned. 'He *is* still furious about those days. And why shouldn't he be? The school framed him. He'll never let that rest.'

'Do *you* believe Gilbert Soames stitched him up?'

'We were all taking drugs. Including you, if I remember. David took the rap for us all.'

'Not for me.'

'No, you were, what I suppose you might call, collateral damage.'

There it was again. The dismissal of his existence, the absence of any meaning or value he might have once had for her. Only David mattered then, and still mattered now. Whereas he, Michael, meant nothing.

'But David says it was Soames who planted the evidence in his locker.'

'That's about how I remember it.'

'And Joan says Soames is now being victimised by David.'

'Oh, I wouldn't pay too much attention to what she says.'

'Joan? David said the same. What have you and David got against her?'

Laura took a mouthful of wine and banged the glass back down on the table. 'OK, seeing as people are obviously still talking about this...If you must know.... After you left, after you disappeared, sick or whatever it was, things got really heavy.'

'David thinks it's because of what happened to me with the LSD.'

'The Head was convinced there was a drug ring working in the school.'

'Yes. He was right. It was David March dealing drugs. Not me. David March. And some of those drugs were bad.'

She dismissed this accusation and its implications airily with a brief wave of her hand. 'A bit of weed, a few tabs. Hardly a drug ring, for Christ's sake. But Soames thought David was the rotten apple in the barrel, and he blamed him for everything.'

'Including what happened to me?'

'Probably. Soames also tried to warn David off seeing me,' Laura said flicking the ash off her cigarette. 'Accused him of ruining my chances of a place at Cambridge. That didn't work so Joan decided to have a word with David instead. Old Joan would have done anything for Soames. She was always obsessed with the guy and would've jumped off the end of St Vincent's pier to impress him.'

'Did Soames ask her to do that? Talk to David'

'Not sure but she went to David's house one night after school and there was no one there apart from her and David.' She paused and looked puzzled with an expression exaggerated by drink. 'Michael, are you sure you've never heard *any* of this?'

'No, you know, I was on the hippy trail,' he said sarcastically.

She laughed. 'Yeah, of course, the beach hut in Goa'

How did she think this could still be amusing? Dampening down his anger, he pressed on with more questions.

'What happened with Joan and David?'

'Well, don't you know? Joan came onto David. They had sex. That was her sad attempt to split me and him up.'

'Joan came on to March? That seems unlikely. She was always...'

'So sweet? So innocent?'

'No, she hated David.'

'Well, she obviously didn't. He told me about it straight away that evening. He felt really bad. He said she was all over him, trying to tear off his clothes.'

'And did that split you and David up?'

'No, but then it got even more fucked up. When I confronted her about it, she told me this ridiculous story that David had raped her. Raped her? Can you believe it? But then she told Soames as well, but she didn't want to press charges and she didn't want anyone else to know. Not even her parents. As you wouldn't if you were making the whole thing up.'

This was incredible. Of all the people at Pennington, Joan was the one Michael always trusted.

'How can you be sure she was making it up?' he said. He recalled the journal – how David had been turned on by the rape scene in *Straw Dogs*.

'She was a virgin and she'd thrown herself at David, and all for nothing. She took her anger out on him. She was never raped and I don't believe she was ever pregnant, either.'

'What do you mean? She was pregnant? With David's baby?'

'Yes, so she claimed, and then said she'd had an abortion and blamed all that on David as well. Hell hath no fury eh? But Soames was just as furious. He swallowed Joan's line completely. That's why he set David up. Planted the drugs in his locker and got him thrown out of the school. When David got expelled, that's when we split. He disappeared, stopped answering my calls.'

Shocked into momentary silence by these revelations, he took a drink of his warm beer. Laura looked at him as if waiting his response. He didn't know what to say. It was too much to take in, but there still was more he wanted to know

'But Soames looked after *you*, didn't he? Kept *you* out of harm's way. You got to finish your A Levels, got your place at Cambridge.'

'Soames tried to destroy David's life.' Again, it was all about David, just as it had been all those years ago.

'You've no feelings for Soames at all?'

'Why should I?'

'As I say, you were once so close.'

'What do you mean, Michael, "close"? He was a teacher. He got paid to do a job. Not act as judge and jury on some poor kid trying to get into university.'

Was her cold dismissal of Soames a way of concealing their intimacy, or had she convinced herself over the years that Soames also never meant anything to her? But if nothing else she needed to acknowledge what had really happened.

'You told me back then, you had a thing for him. That you...'

'OK, yes, well, maybe. Through the eyes of a seventeen-year-old he was pretty impressive. We met up a couple of times when I was upset about my parents separating.'

The journal still fresh in his mind, she had to

confront the truth, the truth that might no longer be important to her, but was, after all, still important, had always been important to him.

'But, Laura, you know I was there, that day, remember? That last day when we took the LSD?'

'Of course, I remember it. I had to account for the whole thing chapter and verse afterwards with the Headmaster. Soames spoke up for me or else I'd have been booted out as well.'

'You see, he was watching your back even then. And I know why. Because he loved you.'

She looked at him and laughed. 'What the fuck are you talking about, Michael?'

'OK, I was totally freaked out on acid, but I wasn't that far gone. You told me that day that you'd taken Soames to the pillbox during the summer. And then when we were back at your house that afternoon someone came to the door. You left me and went with him into the next room. It was Soames. I could hear you in the other room with him, with Soames. He was there, with you. He even had a key, a key to your parent's house.'

She looked at him curiously, a little concerned as if he was someone deranged, and then a dawning sense flared in her eyes and softened into pity.

'Michael,' she held up her hand, as if about to make an announcement. 'I'm a little drunk, now, so forgive me if what I say sounds blunt. But all this dwelling on stuff that happened a hundred years ago. It's a bit fucking sad.'

Why, if it all was meaningless and distant to her, would she not own up to what happened? She'd been found out, even if it *was* twenty-six years ago. Why not just admit it?

'But I heard you, Laura. I heard you telling Soames you'd missed him so much, and he said he'd never leave you again. I was there, I heard it all.'

She was suddenly bored. 'This is ridiculous. Forget it, Michael. Forget the whole thing. Soames, Joan, David. I need to get back to my work and get this presentation finished for tomorrow.'

'Why won't you just admit this is what happened?'

'OK, OK – god this is not what I should be doing right now – but you're dead right, you were tripping out of your head. But it wasn't him.'

'What? Course it was.'

'That afternoon. When you freaked out?'

'Yes, you remember now, Laura? We were in your living room with the cheese plant and everything driving me crazy and then you heard someone come through the front door and it scared us both. But you went to see who it was and it was Soames.'

'It wasn't Soames that day, at the house.'

'I don't understand.'

'No, you don't and you didn't. You were off your head and you ran away. I tried to call you back but you'd gone. It wasn't Soames and if you'd stayed you'd have seen who it really was. It was my father. He'd come back, out of the blue, that afternoon, after leaving mum, after going to the States, after splitting us up. He'd come back.'

He wanted to tell her she was lying again, just covering up the truth for whatever reason.

'What do you mean it wasn't Soames?'

'Listen to me. Daddy came back, that afternoon while you were at the house. It was the happiest day.' Then with barely stifled laughter she said, 'You thought me and Soames...?'

'Sorry, Laura. I need to just...'

It was all too much to take in. He shook his head and stood up, felt suddenly breathless and, had to get away from her. He headed for the toilets, found a cubicle and sat down. His mind reeling, he took some deep breaths and his heart rate settled as he tried to process everything. David setting him up for this ridiculous reunion, Laura possibly in on it too. The absurdity of this meeting and the illusion that this woman cared for him when, for many years, she'd hardly thought about him for one moment.

But along with the slow poisonous anger brewing, came even more serious reflections. Joan's claim that March raped her. Of all the people at Pennington, she was the one he recalled as being the most honest and decent. And she always despised David's arrogance and egotism. He was the last person on earth she would have come on to. Why would she ever invent something like that? Poor Joan. What effect would such a scandal, and such trauma have on a girl at eighteen? No wonder March had never mentioned any of this to Michael two nights ago when they were discussing those days. Surely a false accusation of rape would be more damning to his reputation, more cause for self-righteous indignation than being wrongfully accused of possessing cannabis in school. But he'd selectively chosen to remain silent about it. As you would if the accusation were true.

Michael also realised how he'd always condemned Soames for having an affair with his student. Laura's father was the unexpected visitor that afternoon. He'd thought it was Soames, whereas if he'd been allowed to see Gilbert, while he was in hospital, or if his mother had allowed Soames to talk to him when he came round to the house, all this might have been cleared up years ago. Instead, he'd retreated into his little world with his mother and their private fantasies and recriminations.

Out of the cubicle he stared at the mirror, took some more deep breaths, splashed some cold water on his face, but it couldn't wash away the sad, puzzled demeanour reflecting back at him. He recalled the frightening words from the journal – 'Bad comes back, bad comes back,' Laura's call to him that echoed all the way to his father's factory. And yes, after all these years bad had come back – this farcical reunion with Laura was undeniably bad, a very bad idea, a very bad experience. But how did those words he recalled so clearly from that day, make any sense? And then it came to him, a sudden realisation, that what he'd heard that afternoon wasn't some eternal curse chiming across the years, but actually just more LSD induced paranoia. That what she said wasn't 'Bad comes back' but, having just been greeted by her father returning from America, she'd actually called out 'Dad's come back, dad's come back,' as she ran, overjoyed into the street, to shout out loud that her father was home for good. While he ran on in terror to the factory where his own father plucked him from the mouth of the Creamer. There were no cursed incantations, except those conjured by the nightmare of that afternoon, echoes of which had followed him ever since.

In the toilet mirror he looked ghastly white and he was still struggling with the palpitations in his chest. He was nearing the age his father was when he died. Was he about to have a similar heart attack? He took some more slow deep breaths until his pulse gradually settled down and his colour slowly returned.

Back at the booth Laura was once more on her phone but she raised her eyebrows and smiled at him weirdly, as if she had been telling another joke at his expense, before launching into her phone conversation with Maurice once more.

'Look, I've got an idea for Commando Country. I'm a bit pissed, but I'm going to run it by you while it's still fresh in my head. OK, here goes. It's a TV ad.' She looked across at Michael, before continuing. 'He's an old guy standing in the rain outside a bar staring in at people all having a great time. Makes eye contact with a beautiful woman having dinner with friends and then she quickly looks away. The guy then walks off, sad and alone into the night. Maybe Elaine Paige, *Cats* – "Memories" – background music playing...some shit like that...I know it sounds depressing, Maurice, it's meant to be, just bear with me. Then, music shifts to M People, "Search for the Hero", and we see the same guy on a Harley in the sunshine, same guy bungee-jumping, wing-walking, I don't know what the fuck else – crocodile wrestling – any old shit that's cool and dangerous – and finally maybe dressed up like James Bond – meeting the same beautiful woman from the opening scene at a bar for cocktails....'

She was looking at Michael and her face, twisted with triumph and alcohol, resembled another Laura, one even more terrifying, one that had also haunted him down the years – the unnerving witch-mask of his drug crazed delirium that October afternoon many years ago.

'Maurice,' she continued, leering at Michael, 'we need a strap-line, and how about we go a bit L.P. Hartley on this one ...What?... No that's J.R. Hartley, fly fishing in the Yellow Pages, you moron, I'm talking about L.P. Hartley. *The Go-Between*?... No idea? Never heard of him? Jesus Christ. What do they teach at university these days? Anyway, how about, "The future is a new country. Discover that country, Commando Country."'

She put the call on hold, looked at Michael as if expecting a round of applause. 'At least we've got something for tomorrow, Maurice. Finesse this now and fax me a copy at home. I don't care how late it might be.' She looked up at Michael and smiled. 'Anyway, he's back now. I'll have to go.' She switched off her phone and held her glass aloft, 'Cheers, Michael. Let me get *you* another drink.'

'No, I'm fine thanks.'

'No, please, I insist. I'm so glad you dropped by this afternoon. These deadlines come at you thick and fast, and, as you know, the team I've got on this are clueless. And then, like Father Christmas himself, the answer turns up out of the blue. You... my Santa Claus.'

'I think I need to go now, Laura.'

She punched the air with her fist as she announced: 'The man at the window waiting for memories. And then there *you* were standing outside Bar Zero in the rain. Please let me get you another pint. Maybe a whisky. It's the least I can do.'

'No seriously, Laura, I really need to get the train.'

She looked over his shoulder and waved at the crowd behind.

'They're all here from the agency now,' she said, smiling. Then she got up and held his hands for a second and looked him in the eye. 'It's been good to see you. Merry Christmas, Michael,' she said, while her eyes drifted to the crowd waiting behind him. 'Have a good one. Don't mess too much with the ghosts of Christmas past.'

'Merry Christmas, Laura,' he said mechanically.

And with that she reached out to him for a fumbled embrace which he manage to avoid. She shrugged and stumbled over him as someone cried out, 'Hey Laura!' followed by drunken cheers. It was a blessing the door to the pub was on the opposite side otherwise he'd have had to walk past them, only to be acclaimed as Michael, the one and only fool, the man looking for Laura, the man looking for memories, the saviour of the Commando Country account. He stole across the room, to sounds of her laughing and joking in celebration with her team, and hurried for the door where he slipped through into the street and made his way back to the station in the never-ending rain.

CHAPTER NINETEEN

By the time he sat down on the train, he was shaking with the cold, the humiliation, the anger, Maddie's rain-soaked suit a fitting souvenir for this disaster. As the train made its melancholy slow retreat from the city into the darkness of the night, Michael became more and more lost in the revelations of that afternoon. It was so degrading – he meant nothing to Laura, nothing but cheap material for a last minute ad campaign. Laura with her mean drunkenness, her ruthless treatment of colleagues, her dismissiveness of husband and family life. And her cruel indictment of Soames who had only tried to help her. How had Michael's girl, the girl who'd held his hand in the cinema, who filled his heart with wonder, become this deeply unpleasant woman? She obviously had no feelings for him, and never had since those days at Pennington. Did she even care for him then, or had he invented the whole affair? Was the friendship he believed in from primary through secondary to sixth form, the love that blossomed into the most wondrous two weeks of his life, nothing more than an illusion? His whole life had been measured against the magic of that time and now he realised it meant little or nothing to her. The Laura he once knew no longer, or never even, existed at all. The dream of what his life could have been with her, if he'd not had a breakdown, also a fantasy. And amidst the anger, he also felt a deep sadness for something so precious, irretrievably tarnished and lost forever. When he got home, he would rip the journal into pieces. He could no longer bear its reproachful, mocking presence on the shelf above his bed.

And yet, despite everything, he couldn't hate this Laura, the one he had just met. He wasn't even sure who she was. No, he couldn't hate this stranger. But there was one person who served as a clear focus for all of his rising venom and rage – the man who deliberately set the whole meeting up, the man who had once more shaken his life to the core. David March, who enticed him into believing that Laura still had strong feelings for him. March who teased out his weakness and used it to mock and humiliate him. 'She says you are the one and only.' Those words were all it had taken to send him on this siren song of adolescent longing and yearning. But even David couldn't have foreseen the full extent of Michael's indignity, his reduction to comic material for some eleventh-hour marketing pitch. What had he ever done to March, to warrant this treatment? Was it because Michael once had feelings for Laura and March still felt a residual jealousy about that? That was hardly a reason, especially as it was clear now that Michael had never meant all that much to Laura anyway. Probably March did it just to amuse himself, so he might share the joke later when he met Laura again. Because he enjoyed playing with people's emotions, liked to play games with someone's dreams. Who knew what went on in such a man's mind?

It was beyond understanding. He wasn't sure of anything anymore. Had David tipped Laura off that Michael might be coming, expecting to be reunited with his long lost love? He recalled the barely concealed amusement in both the receptionist's and Laura's expression when he mentioned David. Was Laura's surprise at seeing him all an act, because she was expecting him all along? Were they always in league together, her and David, making up stories about people for their malicious entertainment? It was even possible she had lured him to the pillbox all those years ago in the same way she enticed Soames whom she tried, under David's instigation, to entrap with cannabis? Was she also under orders from David to cut the LSD tab the way she did and manipulate Michael into taking the larger dose, just to see what would happen to him?

Tired as he was with all these questions, he couldn't stop them like waves crashing relentlessly on St Vincent's shore, flooding his mind with anxiety, recriminations and fear, the horror of true understanding slowly revealing itself. Know your enemy, was the familiar maxim, and, now after this disastrous afternoon, he certainly knew Laura for what she was and probably always had been. But, more importantly, he knew March even better. There was no limit to what this man would do to get his own way, to avenge his grievances. With such a man as March, so devious, so vindictive and grudge-bearing, might there be something even more sinister than just callous manipulative amusement behind his actions?

Michael had witnessed the anger at first hand that March felt for Soames over the planting of drugs in his locker. If he enjoyed making fun of Michael with such spiteful pleasure what might David be capable of doing to someone with whom he had a real vendetta? Someone like Soames for instance. After all, March did have something dark and dreadful he needed to hide. He had raped a girl and maybe if he'd done it once then Joan might not be the only victim. Maybe March arranged Michael's charade with Laura because he was getting close to the truth and needed to be warned off, or humiliated so badly he would give up his search for information. Hadn't David taunted him with the reference to *Chinatown*, the movie about corruption and crime in high places, an indication that he suspected Michael was onto something, was getting close to the secrets in March's past? Those same secrets Soames knew and still harboured – that March had raped Joan Turner, made her pregnant and caused her to have an abortion. And now, twenty-six years later, March was bent on revenge, destroying a sick man, ruining his career, and driving him, ultimately, to emotional collapse and possible death. He wasn't joking when he claimed he could be Prime Minister by now, if only he'd got into Cambridge. Soames had got in his way, and Soames was married to the woman who was living testimony to his crime.

The further Michael pursued these speculations, the darker were his conclusions. March might have wanted to humiliate him, to deter him from investigating Soames. But he wasn't going to be put off so easily. He now remembered more of the night at David's house. March's barely disguised threat to Soames' life – 'We all know what happened to Hank Quinlan in the end, don't we? Dead and face down in sewage and shit.' Then there was the running argument in the early hours between March and Katya. He remembered Katya's cries of pain from March's bedroom, cries that Michael mistook for passion but which may have been something much more sinister. And then she had been so distressed the next day, walking out of the house in a desperate and helpless rage. Was David coercing and abusing Katya in the same way he had violated Joan? Did he now want to get rid of her because she was becoming a nuisance, asking too many questions? Had she suspected there was something more sinister in the basement and the sewers than just the water passing through the pipes below?

He remembered how quickly March had raced up the stairs from his cellar, before Michael could venture any further down there. How he'd covered his tracks with his smokescreen about building a refuge for a future apocalypse. There was the supposed night-time search for a cat named Harry Lime who lived in the sewers leading from the cellar. Was this just to tease Michael with yet another character from an Orson Welles movie? This time *The Third Man*, with the fugitive hiding in the town sewers, a chilling rejoinder to Soames' reference to *Touch of Evil* in his entrapment of March in the past. Was 'Harry Lime' actually code for Soames, bound and gagged in the cellar, or worse, 'dead and face down in shit'? Considering how he treated Katya, the woman in his bed and the way he talked about Soames, not forgetting the manner in which he had humiliated Michael, would David really be the kind of man to care about his cat, a stray animal who wandered in and out of the pipes that led to the sea? Would he really have got up in the middle of the night to see if the creature was safe? No, but he would have gone down to the basement to check on a kidnap victim, or to dump a corpse into the sewer pipes and let it drift away on the outgoing tide.

If he was right – and it made sense of all March had said to him that night at his house, his rages, his fluctuating moods, his implacable hatred of Soames – then at least meeting Laura had revealed to Michael more than his own naivety. It had also opened his eyes finally to March's evil, the full extent of his dangerous psychotic character. But knowing all this, what could he, alone, do with this theory, this information? Call the police armed only with mere speculation? March was a powerful figure in St Vincent's and it would be pointless to make such accusations. Neither could he just turn up at the man's door and confront him head on. March would have him charged with harassment and labelled as delusional. What could a man like him do against someone with such power and influence as March? Yet if what he believed was true, then if Soames was still alive, he remained in captivity and time was running out.

As the train made its way through the darkness, he stared at his lonely reflection in the rain-streaked windows with the backdrop of the black invisible country stretching beyond. It was so quiet and he realised he was the only passenger on this carriage. The heating seemed to have failed and he wrapped his wet suit jacket around him as the train sped north and the night grew colder. He tried to sleep but the falling temperature, the experiences of that afternoon and increased anxiety over Soames made him restless. He felt like the last man left on earth hurtling through the void with no friend to turn to. He closed his eyes but his own image reflected in the carriage window reminded him of his father, and he wondered what he would think of him on this train, angry, confused, and, yes, frightened by what he'd discovered.

Shivering, he managed to doze off for a moment and when he woke, the carriage was even colder, his breath visible in the yellow light. Someone was sitting beside him, a wraith in shadows, someone he knew who had come a long way to see him.

'Well,' the figure said, 'was it all worth it?'

'I found out the truth,' Michael replied.

'About what?'

'Those people. Laura, David March.'

'You knew all there was to know when you were seventeen. You found out then the hard way. Why put yourself through all that again?'

'For Soames.'

'You can't help him.'

'But I have to try. To put things right. This time it might be different.'

'Like it was with Laura this afternoon? Was that girl ever really worth all the heartache?'

'No, she wasn't. I know that now.'

'All that pain and suffering. You, your mother, me. All for nothing. What a waste.' The stranger's familiarity, his judgement, his sadness, filled the space between them.

'I'm trying to make it right.'

'You will only make it worse. You always do.' The stranger, his father and yet not his father, leaned over close to him but flickered in and out of view like a bad TV reception.

'What *should* I do then?'

'It's too late for all that,' the stranger said, fading into a darkness that engulfed the carriage.

Michael called out and he felt someone's hands on his shoulder shaking him.

'Wake up mate,' the guard said. 'You need to get off here. Journey's end.'

CHAPTER TWENTY

When he arrived back at his mother's it was after midnight but she was still up, in the lounge, fiddling with the tree lights. His heart sank. She was the last person he wanted to see at that moment.

'Well, lover boy returns,' she said

'And did you have a good trip and nice to see you too, Michael,' he replied.

'Well, *did* you? she said sarcastically.

'He sighed. 'Did I what?'

'Have a good trip?'

'Not really.'

'I take it from that, you won't be seeing her again?'

'Probably not.'

He was so tired and didn't want any more questions. He kissed her goodnight and made his way up to his room, his eyes automatically glancing up at the shelf above his bed where the journal lay in wait to rebuke him for his folly. He would take it down tomorrow and burn it somewhere. But there on the shelf the books were all in disarray, *Treasure Island* and *Beau Geste* both upended and a gap where the journal should have been and had been every day for the last twenty-six years. Maddie's photo and letter also gone.

His mother was still unscrewing a bulb on the set of lights when he re-entered the sitting room.

'Where is it?' he asked.

She didn't look at him, her attention focused on the tree. 'These damn lights are still not working,' she said.

'Where is it?' he said again.

'Where's what?'

'You know very well what. My journal.'

'*I* don't know.'

'Yes, you do. I left it on the shelf. And it's not there now.'

'What would I want with it?'

'I don't know but unless it's grown legs and walked off on its own, someone's moved it.'

She registered delight as the lights flickered back on. 'There! At last.'

'Mum, will you leave the damn lights alone for a minute and talk to me.'

She continued to arrange the tree, moving the decorations around. 'Well, if you must know, you're right. It's gone and good riddance,' she said.

'What do you mean "gone"?'

'Should have dumped the damned thing years ago.'

'What are you talking about? Tell me what you've done with it.' The wave of anger he had ridden all the way home on the train now returned with mounting force. His mother turned from the tree her own frustration clearly showing.

'You're not seventeen anymore. You're forty-three. And the way you're carrying on isn't doing you any good, or me either for that matter.'

'Where have you put it?'

'You're chasing around after people who made you so unhappy all those years ago, made us all so unhappy. And that horrible journal's making things worse.'

'Where is it?' he said again, trying but failing to calm the rising tide within.

'I just don't want any more of this.'

'For the last time, where is it?'

'If you must know, I gave it to Joe.' She suddenly looked tired, every day of her seventy-five years and more.

'Joe…Joe? What? …why?'

'I wanted it out of the house. I can't stand you reading it. What it's doing to you. I asked him to look after it for a bit. Just till you've calmed down again.'

'I am calm.'

'No, you're not. You're anything but.'

'That's because personal stuff's personal.'

'I just wanted things back to normal. To how they were before.'

His barely suppressed rage flashed to the surface.

'It's got other things in there as well. A letter.'

'I only want what's best for you. For you to be well. I worry about you when you're like this.'

'And a photograph. You've no right to give that to someone.'

'You mean the photo of that woman who led you a merry dance. The photo that you waste every day staring at. You're better off without that as well.'

'What do you mean "merry dance"?'

'That woman with her feminine wiles. You running around looking after another man's son.'

'Why do you think that about Maddie? Why do you hate her so much?'

'She broke up her marriage when she had a young child. But, as usual, you were blind to it all.'

'How many times do I have to tell you, her husband left *her*?'

'So, she says. You'd believe anything a piece of skirt tells you.'

She still had her back to him and he edged towards her as she continued to work on the lights. He wanted to go to bed but he couldn't let this rest. It had been a long, miserable day and this bottled up destructive anger made him sour and more than ready for a fight.

'Maddie was honest and kind. She wanted me to move in with her.'

'That's exactly what I mean. Once you were in there, she'd have had her hooks into you. You always looked worn out when you came back here. I always hoped you would see it for what it was. But you didn't, and you still can't see it or you wouldn't be up there moping in your room every day.'

'She didn't want anything from me other than someone to rely on. I was the one who let *her* down, mum.'

'Rubbish! She dumped you when you wouldn't move in with her. It's the truth, and you know it.'

'I was the one who led Maddie on. Making her think I could make a go of it when all along I knew it wouldn't work.'

'You saw sense thankfully before it was too late.'

'No, mum, I was constantly coming back here to take care of you. And she knew it was hopeless. That you'd never let me be.'

She shook her head and pointed her finger at him, the

wires dangling from her hand.

'Oh, so it was all my fault then. Maybe you wish I wasn't around anymore. Then you could go off with whoever you liked.'

'It's too late for all that now,' he said, echoing the words from the dream on the train.

'You just need to knuckle down, forget Maddie, forget that woman you went chasing after this afternoon, and stop all this Soames nonsense. Get on with your research.'

'I haven't been doing any research.'

'I can see that.'

He was angry and wanted to hurt her, but he also wanted now, suddenly and so badly, to end all this pretence.

'I'm not on sabbatical. There's no research project. I'm suspended from teaching.'

'What are you talking about?'

'I assaulted a student.'

She turned around from the tree. 'Oh my god. I knew it. I knew something was really wrong. Assault? What happened, for god's sake?'

'I stuffed a cardboard box over a boy's head.'

'You did what? What on earth were you thinking?'

'I wasn't thinking. I wasn't thinking at all.'

She sat down looking at her hands where she cradled the plastic Santa she'd taken from the branch, while he remained standing.

'I walked out of the school. Walked away from the place and didn't go back the next day either.'

'My god. You're lucky they haven't sacked you already.'

'I wish they had.'

'Listen to you. I can't believe what you're saying. What will you do?'

'Who knows?'

'This is awful. I don't know what we're going to do with you.'

She returned to the tree and was quiet for a while as she put the Santa back in his rightful place. He wanted to wipe away all the falsehood, all the silence, but it hadn't done any good this clearing of the air, only made the room feel poisoned with failure and bitterness.

She sighed. 'You need to forget all this nonsense about the past and those people at Pennington. Sort yourself out. It's a damn good job I got rid of that awful journal,' she said, muttering furiously at to the tree.'

'The photograph. What gave you the right to give that away?'

She turned her attention back to the lights as they went out again and she threw the wires to the ground in exasperation.

'Look,' she said, her eyes flashing with anger, 'I'm sick of you and that photograph. And just sick of that horrid little book from a horrid time. I know all the vile things written in there about you and your poor dad.' The tree lights coiled at her feet suddenly flickered on, a signal from the past, or maybe the dead.

Her lips tightened and she spat out the following words. 'What would he think, your dad, what would he think of you now, for Christ's sake? Losing your job.'

'Oh, yes, I know, dad would have had a field day with all of this.'

It was surprising how suddenly very tired he felt. The humiliation of the afternoon with Laura, the burden of

Soames' fate, the haunting dread lingering from the strange dream on the train, and now the theft of his journal, had all left him drained of life. And there it was, his father, his judgement, and the dream again, with its message telling him it was all too late, too late for so many things that had been lost and could never come again, but most of all too late to keep hiding from the truth.

'So you *have* read it, haven't you?' he said.

'The bits I could stand to read. Your poor dad never knew you felt that way about him.'

'Is this what it's all about? Why you've got rid of the journal. Some way to get back at me.'

'What are you talking about now?'

'For killing dad. You've always known that I killed him, haven't you? That it was my fault what happened. That it killed him what I did.'

She shook her head. 'Why are you talking like this? What's wrong with you?'

'Why don't you say it, mum? Face it. It wasn't Soames or Laura who destroyed us. Why don't you just finally go on and say it, say it was me who killed dad, destroyed this family! Don't tell me you haven't thought it! I know that's what you've felt all these years. Our guilty secret we shared in the shadows, behind the walls, lurking in corners.'

'Stop this madness, Michael.'

'I've carried it around with me all my life. What I did to him. What I knew you believed as well.'

'I really don't want to talk about this anymore!' she shouted back.

She stood there looking at him, shaking her head. They stood in silence and then she just waved him away and went back to picking up the wire on the tree lights.

'We could have talked about it. We could still. But instead, look at you, you just carry on messing around with...with those stupid lights, with the stupid Santa on his sleigh, and the same damn tree year after year, pretending none of it ever happened.'

She continued to arrange the decorations, as if he was no longer there. He waited, on the verge of another outburst, but was too exhausted. It was useless trying to say anything else. He left the room and halfway upstairs stopped to hear if she was crying. He thought about going back, to see if she was alright, but then the TV went on and he couldn't go back in there and pretend, once again, that nothing had been said, that nothing had been revealed.

Unable to sleep, he pulled back the curtain and in the streetlight outside his house the white diamonds of frost sparkled on the rooftops. He remembered the anticipation of nights like this as a child, the night before Christmas Eve, when he would look out onto the ice-filled sky and imagine an early sleigh drifting across the moon. This was home, always had been, this room, this neighbourhood, this familiar landscape of ordinary houses, the gardens dressed with twinkling seasonal arrays of silver, red and gold. He could see the empty space on the shelf where the journal had stood unopened for years, until now, its secrets spilling into the house and beyond, turning their lives upside down once more. Had this confrontation with his mother changed anything? There was no acknowledgment from her, no further condemnation or absolution either, just more silence and he knew that's all there ever would be. And because she gave him nothing he too felt nothing, no relief, no catharsis, no purging of years of remorse. It was as if he'd confessed to the haunted walls from where the ghostly scratchings came. Only for his words to be buried like the poor creature now outside in the cold hard garden.

After a while he heard her climb the stairs and make her way to the bathroom, then from there along the landing to her bed where she slept alone as she had done every night for the past twenty-six years. The light from her bedroom lamp leaked beneath his door. He got up and stood outside her room and knocked. He poked his head around the threshold.

'Are you OK?' he said.

She was sitting up reading and did not look up from her book.

'Fine,' but I'm really tired now, Michael. Goodnight.' She leaned over and turned out the light and left him standing in the doorway. It was as if he'd never said anything. All he had was her silence that now spread throughout the house in the cold and darkness. He opened the door to his room where the yellow streetlight shone through the thin curtains on the small cell-shaped space, so often his refuge.

But even here there was nothing for him now, not even Maddie's photograph to help him through the night.

CHAPTER TWENTY-ONE

The following morning, he rose early to find his mother already up with her coat on and about to go out. She looked tired and muttered a rather begrudging good morning. He couldn't find the right words to say to her and she refused to look at him as she rummaged through her handbag.

'I'm going to pick up the turkey,' she said.

It was easier just to fall in with the everyday exchange, as if nothing had happened. 'Do we need a whole turkey, mum? We'll be eating it for days.'

She ignored him. 'Can't fine that order slip. Where is it? Ah, there it is!' she said, before clipping her bag together and heading for the door. 'The tree lights have gone again,' she said, 'and need sorting out. Be careful though, the tree's not that steady. I don't want to come back to a mess.' Then she paused and said as she stood in the doorway, 'Seeing as you're not working anymore, you might as well make yourself useful.' And with that she hurried out to the waiting taxi.

He set about trying to fix the lights, trying to ignore her comment about no longer working, a jibe to mask her deep-rooted refusal to discuss anything, tried to ignore the realisation that this would always be the nature of their relationship. And he turned instead to the wave of questions that had plagued him through the journey home and had also robbed him of sleep. What to do next about Soames and the danger he was in. A restless night alone with his thoughts had only reinforced his belief that March had abducted Gilbert. But, despite hours spent in constant anguished deliberation, he wasn't any further in formulating a plan. He didn't want another dead man on his conscience, but how to save Gilbert, how to orchestrate a return to March's house and a search there? Despite fantasies of reenacting final scenes from *Die Hard, Die Hard 2 and Die Hard with a Vengeance*, he couldn't envisage a physical confrontation he would have any hope of winning. What if, when he arrived, March just laughed at him for his folly in seeking out Laura, or listened attentively before attacking him, locking him in the cellar too, or worse? Things could go wrong very quickly and if they went badly wrong, he needed to cover his back. Maybe he should inform Joan he was going to see March, whether she believed his story or not. If he ended up locked in the basement with Soames, or his body washed up on the beach, they all would believe him then. But if he didn't come back at least he would have warned Joan of the danger she might be in as well. That once March had got rid of Soames and Michael then she might be the next on David's list.

He found her number and phoned but it went straight to answering machine. He left a message telling her he had vital information about Gilbert and would she phone him back. While he was waiting for her return call he tried to alleviate his anxiety occupying himself with the ancient tree lights. Each year they presented the same problem. If one bulb failed it shorted the whole circuit, so he had to test each one systematically. He pulled and tugged at them through the plastic branches, whilst trying not to topple the tree over at the same time. It was tedious work and the longer he waited for Joan's call the more frustrated he became. Every moment that passed could be Soames' last. He could, of course, be wrong about all this, but he knew instinctively this was not the case. After spending such a prolonged time at his house, after what had happened yesterday with Laura, he knew March completely now, knew exactly what he was capable of. Steadying the tree again, just as it began to fall off its stand, he imagined Soames bound and tied and fighting for breath in that basement as the sewage rose around him. Then, mercifully, the phone rang and holding onto the lights flex with one hand he reached for the receiver with the other.

'Hello.'

'Hello, Michael? It's Maddie.'

'Maddie?' A moment's shocked silence then he gathered himself. 'Are you OK?'

'So, so, Michael. How are you?'

Her voice sounded strained and distant. So good to hear it though. But all he could say was, 'Yes, Maddie, I'm fine....' Followed by another uneasy silence, then, feeling he had to say something. 'Apart from having to fix the damned Christmas trees lights, that is and...' He moved across to keep hold of the flex as Maddie interrupted.

'I'm ringing about Derek.'

'Oh, yes, I got your letter and you said he was....'

'He died on Monday.'

'Oh, Maddie, Maddie...I'm so sorry.'

'I just thought you ought to know.' Her voice was business-like with a dragging undertone of grief.

'I'm sorry,' he said again, for the sake of filling the gap between them, his heart beating at the sound of her voice, the nearness of it, the distance. Derek was dead. Derek. The name heavily freighted with guilt implicit in Maddie's icy formality.

'The funeral will be at the Trinity Church, no day fixed yet, but it will be some time the first week in January.'

'How are you? Are you OK?' he said. How lame, how

hollow this sounded.

'Yes, I'm fine,' she answered abruptly, before continuing, 'and so, if you want to go you can ring the church after Christmas. They'll be able to tell you when it is.'

'OK, thank you.'

A long, awkward, bereavement-filled pause followed. Derek, his friend, dead. The injustice of it, a good man who deserved a long retirement. And a better fate and better friends than him. The silence from Maddie was almost physical, crushing his urge to say something, to keep her talking just to hear her voice, even if filled with reproach.

'You there, Maddie?'

'Yes, Michael.'

'It's all so sudden. Did you get my card? The one I sent.'

'Yes, I got your card this morning,' she said flatly. 'That's why I'm ringing you now. You said to let you know if things got worse.' Pause again before she continued, 'Well, yes, now you know…things have got very much worse.'

'I'm sorry, Maddie.' It didn't sound any more meaningful the second or third time he said it.

'It happened quite quickly, the end.' There was a pause and he remained silent. It was better to say nothing than keep saying sorry. 'But, as you know, it wasn't that sudden,' she continued.

'I kept meaning to visit.' He let go of the flex, and then the tree, as if in response, immediately fell to the floor, sending decorations crashing and splintering around his feet.

'Shit!' he cried.

'What?'

'It's nothing.'

'Sounds like something's fallen.'

'Christmas tree.'

'Well, I just wanted you to know. About Derek. I'll let you get on then, sorting your tree out.'

'Maddie, don't go. I'm sorry... about not going to see him,' he said stepping through the debris at his feet. The plastic Santa on his sleigh and the tree fairy both stared at him reproachfully.

'It doesn't matter now, Michael.'

'I know. It's just that when I came back here everything felt...different.'

'As I say, it doesn't matter.'

His brain clouded with remorse, couldn't fashion the words. 'It's been a difficult time.'

'I know, Michael. You were treated badly by the school.' Her voice sounded dead, drained of feeling.

'That's not the problem, Maddie.'

'I know, it's your mum. She still not well?'

'Mum, she's fine. Well, not really, but you know how it is.'

'Yes, Michael, I know how it is.'

'It's something else though.'

'What?'

Could he risk telling her, trying to explain how worried he was, in the midst of her own grief? Despite everything, she was still the person he felt closest to, the person he trusted most. He took a deep breath.

'There's this friend of mine, I've been worried about. He's disappeared.' There was more silence. Was she considering hanging up? 'He's not been seen for days and no one knows where he is. I'm really concerned about him.'

Her response signalled a softening, a moment of concern. 'Who is he?'

'He was my teacher at school.'

She sighed, but she was still speaking. 'That's a long time ago.'

'Yes, I know but I've been talking to people, asking some questions. Maddie, I think something bad has happened to him.' He had to keep trying to find things to say, to make her understand, to keep her on the phone, no matter how he strange it sounded. He could always confide in her, and so, he blundered on. 'There's this other guy, David March, he runs my old school, the town, in charge of everything and I know this sounds crazy, but I think he may have kidnapped him.'

There was another silence before she said, 'Really, Michael? I'm going to have to go now. I need to see to Tommy.'

'Maddie!' he blurted. 'How is he? Tommy?'

'Tommy? It's Christmas Eve. He's six. He's excited.' Then after another pause. 'Why?'

The question felt like a blow. But he couldn't leave it there. 'I don't know. I just wondered if…if Buzz Lightyear made it back to him for Christmas.'

'Yes, you also said that in your card. I haven't told him about Derek. I don't want to upset him. It's Christmas. I have to be happy for him.'

'Christmas – it's an awful time for this to happen.'

'Not easy being a single mum at the best of times, Michael. I just wish it was all over. Christmas, I mean.'

She was going to hang up whatever he said, and he knew this might be the last time they would speak together, so it wouldn't make any difference now, so he said it anyway.

'*Are* you still single then?'

'What do you mean?' her voice bristled.

'I don't know, you just said you were a single mum.'

'Well, I think even you should have cottoned on to that by now.'

'I just wondered if...'

'If what?'

'If, you know, you'd found anyone. Someone you could ...you know...be...' his voice trailed off hopelessly.

'No... why?' she responded curtly.

'So, you're not...?'

'Oh, for god's sake, Michael!'

He had no right, no right to say anything. But he was having trouble thinking, his mind way beyond any normal conversation, overwhelmed as he was with weeks of silent sadness, and now engulfed in this one last moment with her. He just had to keep talking, somehow make one last effort, before it was too late, to tell her how he felt.

'Maddie,' he said. 'Maddie, I know how much Derek meant to you, how close you were. I'm sorry I didn't go to see him. Maddie.... I'm sorry about everything, about every single thing. Everything I did was wrong...'

He paced up and down, wading through the mess of decorations at his feet, trying to transform the wild torrent of feeling into words. Encouraged by the fact she'd not hung up, he ploughed on.

'Maddie, I know it's a terrible time, but I just want you to know I'm sorry, I'm sorry, Maddie, for everything, how I messed everything up so badly. How I let you down...'

'OK, Michael, that's enough.'

'I know you don't care one way or the other what I

think, and why should you and I know it's all too late, but I need you to know how sorry I am, how I threw away…what we had…what I had… it was the…'

'Michael, stop,'

'…most wonderful thing that had ever happened to me and ….'

'Michael.'

'There I was, just selfish, cowardly…'

'Stop!' she exclaimed. 'Just stop it! I can't hear this now. Please.'

'Sorry.'

'Stop saying sorry.'

'I just want you to know.'

He silenced himself, exhausted by the desperate effort to express the magnitude of regret, the loss, the waste of it all.

After what seemed like an age he heard her sigh and then take another breath, before replying, 'Michael, I've just lost a true friend who was very dear to me. And to you, once. All I wanted was to tell you that.'

'Yes, thank you, Maddie. It was good of you but please listen…'

'No, *you* listen.' There was frustration in her voice, but also a deep and weary sadness. 'I can't hear these things you're saying right now.'

'I really don't want to make things worse for you.'

'Oh, Michael, you haven't made it worse. What you said isn't going to make me miss Derek any more. You talk about *your* friend, this teacher you're concerned about, going around asking questions about him, worried about him.'

'I *am* worried, Maddie. I think he's in danger. You don't know what this man March is capable of.'

'Michael, you might be worried but, to be honest, it sounds to me like some more of your typical make-believe. Living out some fantasy from adventure books and old films. Derek was your colleague.' She paused, her voice faltering with emotion. '*He* was a real friend who supported you and helped you at Barton. And...' she stopped, overcome with grief.

He was walking up and down around the fallen tree and through its scattered baubles, hearing this, her heartbroken reproach. In a last desperate attempt to make amends he cried, 'Maddie, is there anything I can do?'

'I don't know. I know, you've had a bad time, but, Michael, to be totally up front with you, what you really need to do is just grow up.'

Something crunched beneath his feet. 'Shit!' he exclaimed.

'I'm sorry, Michael. It's just such a sad day...and I need to go and see to Tommy.' She sounded like she was about to cry or was crying already.

'No, Maddie, you're right...I've let you down...it's ...'

'Michael, I have to go.' He could hear it in her voice now, the tears. He had made her cry. She had called out of kindness and respect and he had made her cry. He was lost for words and all that was left was the truth of his every day and night since they'd been apart.

'I am so sorry, Maddie. It's just...it's just...I miss you so much. I miss you so much, Maddie. I love you, Maddie, Maddie, I love you.'

Her silence lasted several seconds before it was followed by the dialling tone. She had hung up. He looked at the carpet beneath his foot, the long-cherished Father Christmas on his sleigh lay broken in several pieces. The

Christmas tree, the stupid decorations, the debris, the crushed Santa, all testified to this disaster. He called her back twice, although he wasn't sure what he was going to say even if she answered. Tell her he'd be there at the funeral, he'd go back to his job at Barton, try to win her back, prove to her he wasn't afraid of commitment? But she didn't pick up the phone. He knew it was all too late for any of that now anyway. All he'd done was convince her further what a pathetic mess he was, how much he deserved to be alone. He'd abandoned Derek in his final weeks of life. What kind of a person did that? Betrayed a good friend, just as he'd betrayed his father. Dad had been right about him. He always let people down in the end. Just as he'd let Maddie down with his fear of...what? Love? Life itself?

He kneeled amongst the shattered silver balls and scattered fake pine needles, picking shards out of the carpet. More humiliation, more failure, more mistakes. Even the fragments of glass from the broken baubles lay scattered beyond retrieval. He cut his finger on a piece embedded in the carpet and it began to bleed into the fabric. On his knees he remembered the factory floor those years ago, afraid to tell anyone of his wound, trying to do the right thing and making things worse. Look where it had got him again, trying to put things right – crawling on his hands and knees, bleeding amidst the wreckage of his life.

But amidst this catastrophe, as he scrambled along the floor, he also thought of Soames, on all fours in that cellar, being fed scraps and leftovers, like an animal, with the evil, gloating, presence of David March, kidnapper and rapist, standing over him. March, who supplied the drugs that began the ruin of Michael's life. March, goading him with the hope of a reunion with Laura, teasing him with references to Harry Lime in the sewers while he had Soames imprisoned down there lying in foul stagnant water. March laughing at everyone, sneering at Michael. What fun he'd have if he could see him right this moment, abject and bleeding all over his mother's carpet.

He just couldn't stay here forever pawing around, trying to clear up the mess. It was true he'd done nothing for Derek, could do nothing for him now. Could do nothing for his father, his mother, or even Maddie. He couldn't even save himself, but he still could save Soames. Soames, who had not, in fact betrayed him with Laura, who was the one person who really believed in him. Soames, who came to see him years ago to tell him something, something important, something that might have changed his life or given him hope when there was none. Soames, who needed Michael now because no one else, not even Joan understood the true extent of March's evil. He wasn't there to support Maddie through Derek's illness, or man enough to stay with her as her partner and help bring up Tommy. But maybe he could still be a man capable of saving Soames and bringing David March to justice.

He stood up, rested the tree upright on its rickety plastic stand and surveyed the bloodstains and debris littering the floor. He turned away from it all, put on his coat and then, stepping into the clear bright morning air, heard a momentous crash as the tree toppled to the ground once more, finally broken beyond repair amidst the chaos left behind.

CHAPTER TWENTY-TWO

The nearer he got to Joan's the more urgent his story seemed, the more obsessive his need to make her believe him, to make sure someone else knew what he knew, and then get to March's house as soon as possible. All the way there, Maddie's stinging condemnation rang in his ears. The humiliating episode with Laura, the horror that March raped Joan, the knowledge that Soames was now in real danger, all drove him frantically and urgently forward on his mission. By the time he arrived at Joan's house, he wanted to spend as little as time as possible explaining things. He had so much to say, had so little time to say it, and needed to say it all at once. So when she opened the door, there were no pleasantries, no time for tea or home-baked biscuits, and even before they were seated in the lounge, he was already talking.

'Joan, thank god you're at home. I think I know where your husband is.'

'Michael, hello, I've just picked up your message. I don't understand.'

'I think March's got him locked in his basement.'

'What?'

'Yes, I've heard David talking to him. He pretended he was looking for his cat.'

'You've been to see David March? You said you heard Gilbert? Did you see him?'

'No, March's keeping Gilbert prisoner, out of sight.'

Joan guided him swiftly out of the hallway to the lounge. He didn't want to sit down and stood his ground in the doorway. He needed to make a quick exit once he'd explained everything. But he was finding it hard to think clearly again. What he had to say all tumbled together and re-emerged in random, frantic order.

'He's got a cat called Harry. March's sick joke.'

'What cat, Michael?'

'It's all to do with that grudge he holds.'

'I don't understand...? You say you've heard Gilbert talking to David.'

'No, not exactly. But I know he's down there because of this cat of his called Harry Lime.'

She looked puzzled, afraid even.

'Down where?'

He didn't have time for long-winded details. And his mind kept closing down when he tried to think of a quick way to explain things.

'The film, *The Third Man*?'

'Sorry, Michael, I don't follow. Will you please sit down, get your breath?'

She had to understand. No time for sitting down, for taking a breath. He tried again – to go back to the beginning.

'Joan, listen, I've found out about Gilbert planting the drugs in David's locker at Pennington. Gilbert taunted him with that movie *Touch of Evil*. Remember, Hank Quinlan, the corrupt detective...'

'What's all this about, Michael. All these movies. Slow down, will you?'

'Well, when they found the drugs in David's locker,

Gilbert said to him, "Hank Quinlan always gets his man."'

'Where've you been getting all this, Michael?'

'March...he then tells me – told me to my face just the other night at his house, "We all know what happened to Hank Quinlan in the end, don't we. Dead, face down in sewage and shit." March's basement's full of sewage most of the time. March then tells me his cat Harry is locked down in the basement somewhere. The sewers run under March's house and he says his *cat* hides down there.'

'Sorry, Michael. You say you went to see David March?'

'And that's why I know who he's got down there. It's not his cat in the basement. It's Mr Soames.'

'You're not making any sense, Michael. It was a bad idea to go to that man's house.'

He sighed. Why couldn't he explain more clearly? She wasn't helping with her expression, her puzzled, anxious, thinly veiled annoyance. He pointed to the wall and the photograph of Soames imitating Welles in the Harry Lime scene from *The Third Man*.

'Don't you see, it's a clear reference to that picture? March says he's named the cat 'Harry' after Harry Lime, the black marketeer Welles plays, who hides in the sewers. David threatens Gilbert with the same fate as Hank Quinlan, dead and floating in sewage at the end of *Touch of Evil*. It's all connected. It's March's way of taunting us. But I've worked it all out. It's actually Gilbert down there. He thinks there's nothing we can do about it. That's how he operates. He likes to play games with people.'

'Got Gilbert? Down in his cellar?'

'Yes.'

'You've seen him?'

'No. I just know. Believe me, it's definitely him down there.'

'How? How do you know?'

He had to try another angle to make her believe him. She had to believe him

'I know what March is capable of. He set me up with Laura.'

'You've seen Laura?'

'Yes, I went to see her, because he told me to.'

'Who?'

'March. He told me Laura wanted to see me. But it was just a wind-up. It's just another example of how he enjoys pulling strings. That's the kind of man he is.'

'I know only too well what kind of a man David March is. You've seen Laura as well?'

'Yes, David persuaded me to go. But it was just a way of making a fool of me.'

'I told you to be careful with David.'

'I know. You were right. But that's why we have to get over there before it's too late. For Gilbert.'

'But how do you know he's got Gilbert. Have you any proof?'

'Isn't what I've said enough?'

'Michael, you're making very serious accusations here.'

'You have to believe me, Joan. I want you to know before I go over there. In case I don't come back. Will you come with me? Create a diversion, while I investigate the cellar.'

'Michael, you've got blood on your hands.' This took him aback. What did she mean? Did she somehow know what he did to his father? 'Your finger,' she said.

'Oh, that!' he said with relief. 'I cut myself on a tree

decoration. It's OK, it's stopped bleeding.'

'Let me get you a bandage and a plaster.'

'No really, there's no time. We need to get over to March's house.'

'Michael, I'm having a lot of trouble with this...'

'He's got him locked in the basement. With sewage.'

'You're insisting he's kidnapped Gilbert?'

'Yes, because he has to shut Gilbert up, has to keep him quiet because of what he knows.'

'What Gilbert knows?'

'I know the truth, Joan. I know what happened with you and March. Back then. What he did to you.'

They were both still standing in the doorway to the lounge and she took two steps back into the room. She looked stricken.

'Who told you?' she said.

'You, of all people, know what he's capable of.'

'Who told you? About that....'

'Laura. She told me other things as well.'

'What things?'

'About the pregnancy and then...after....'

Joan looked pale, like she was going to faint. She staggered against the fireplace and reached across to steady herself. Her eyes began to brim with tears. He regretted bringing this ordeal back from the past, being so direct, but he had no time for sadness or discretion.

'Joan, I'm sorry, but can't you see what we're dealing with here? We need to move quickly. Get over there to March's.'

'Laura told you. Why would she tell you all that?'

'She wants to defend March. As she always does.'

'Defend him?'

'With his version of things.'

'Oh god, this is awful. They're still talking about this?'

'David hates Gilbert and he hates you. You've both got something on him. Man of the people, pillar of the community and all that. Can't have nasty skeletons in the cupboard. That's why he has to get Gilbert out the way. Even you might be in danger.'

She rose and walked to the window facing the morning fog as it rolled in over the garden. She spoke to the glass, her voice sounding suddenly very serious and firm.

'Sorry, I know you mean well, Michael, but this really isn't helping. This isn't helping at all. I've tried, tried so hard to forget what happened, what he did.... I only ever told Laura back then to try to get her to see David for what he really was. But she wouldn't listen to me.'

'I'm listening, Joan. I'm here. I want to make him pay for what he did to you.'

'You need to let this whole thing drop.'

'Laura says you made it all up. That you were the one to blame. That's what they do these people. They twist the truth and lie and manipulate and...'

'I can't do this, Michael.'

'But why...Gilbert's in danger. He needs our help. Right now. Please....'

'Why are you involved in all this, Michael? Seeing David, seeing Laura?'

He was exasperated but kept calm, was willing to keep explaining if only she would eventually see how urgent all this was.

'Like I said, March told me Laura wanted to see me.

But it was all a lie, a trick to humiliate me. Laura's changed. Changed a lot. You wouldn't recognise her. Lives the London life. Big career. Family, husband, kids.'

'Michael, like I said, I'm so sorry you've got yourself mixed up in this. Please go home. Forget the whole thing. Try to get some rest.'

He shook his head. 'I can't do that, Joan. Will you come with me, or not?'

'Michael, I don't know what you want from me.'

'To help to save your husband, before it's too late!'

'Laura's got kids. Family, you say.'

'Yes, three kids.'

'Three children,' she said, sadly.

'But she doesn't seem to care for them. Or her husband, for that matter.'

'Maybe it all came too easy for her.'

'Yes, exactly,' he said. 'March's the same. He's got a maid who he uses for sex. Probably abuses her. She's a refugee. She suspects what's going on as well and he's trying to get rid of her now.'

She turned from the window to face him, her expression a mask shut off from horror and loss. 'I've tried,' she said, 'to forget, even tried to forgive, and now all this coming back, along with Gilbert missing. It's too much. Please, Michael. Just go back to your mother's.'

'But think of what March has done to you, to Mr Soames, to us all.'

'Three children she has, you say.'

'Yes, she's off to the Maldives on her own. Can't even spend Christmas with her kids.'

Joan stared into space, her voice hollow and vacant.

'Gilbert and I could never have children...you know...not after what happened.'

She and Soames had no children. Behind the mask her broken face and sadness said it all. No children. After what happened. The rape. The pregnancy and then the abortion. Back in the early seventies, an abortion fraught with danger and damage. He moved to the window, to comfort her.

'We need to get even with the man responsible.'

She waved his hand away. 'Thanks, Michael, but there's nothing you can do. Nothing anyone can do.'

'I want to help. Can't you see, Gilbert was the only one ever believed in me? Even after I left Pennington, he tried to see me. Came around to our house.'

'Yes, Gilbert always worried about you, Michael.'

'I think maybe he came to tell me all this, to tell me exactly what kind of a person March was. What he'd done to me, supplied those drugs, what he'd done to you, what he was still doing until Gilbert put a stop to him. My mother sent Gilbert away and I never knew he came to see me.'

She suddenly shook off her sadness and looked at him so warmly, with such affection, and kindness it made him feel like a lost child. She seemed calm again, as if the horror of the past could, once more, be endured silently, without complaint.

'Michael, I know you might mean well, but you really need to stop all this. Let it go.'

He was bewildered. How could she be so accepting, how could she say this after all she'd been through? After everything March had done to her, raped her, ruined her reputation, destroyed her chances of having children. Her resilience was admirable but how could she just give up on her husband in this way, when he was in so much peril, when he'd told her Gilbert was imprisoned in that evil man's basement? He didn't want to be complicit in such compassion and fortitude when a man's life was at stake.

'I can't. I have to face him!' he cried. 'Gilbert's there at March's house. I know it, seriously, know it.'

'No, seriously, you don't. Look, if you're so sure about this, Michael, then call the police.'

'And tell them what? I suspect the honourable David March of kidnapping his old teacher. The guy even gets his drive cleared of snow by special treatment from the council. The police will probably be in his pocket as well.'

'But of course, all that will change when you tell them about the cat.'

'Well, you know how all that will sound to them.'

'Exactly, Michael. It will sound exactly like it sounds to me, to be totally honest. That's why it's best for you to leave it all alone.'

Her scepticism, her sweet reason were exhausting. 'But you're not *them.* You're not the police. You know the truth about March. I can't leave it alone! He has to pay for everything he's done!'

'Michael, please sit down.'

'I'm going to find out, one way or another, right now, with or without your help.'

'Michael, please.'

'Joan, you're the only person I can rely on. If I'm not back later today, then you can call the police. I'll be down in that cellar with your husband, or worse. Then you'll have your proof.'

'Sit down, Michael.'

'No! I need to go.'

'Michael, calm down.'

'I *am* calm!' he shouted.

She looked at him patiently and gestured to the couch. 'Please sit down, Michael. I do have something you want to hear, something important.'

'What? About March? Has he done the same to other women?'

'It's not about David.'

'I haven't got time for this.'

'Yes, you have. You need to hear what I have to say.'

He reluctantly sat down, mainly because she was blocking the doorway and he would have to push her over to escape.

'Joan, please...' he protested.

'You want to know why Gilbert went round to see you at your mother's years ago?'

'It's been driving me mad thinking about it.'

'Well, he didn't go round to tell you anything about March. You were ill, weren't you? Back then. You had a breakdown, didn't you?'

'Joan, sorry, not this now, I need to go right away, to save Gilbert.'

'No, you need to listen. When you were ill...'

'I don't understand. What has that to do with March and your husband?'

'It's about your father.'

'My dad?'

'Why Gilbert came to see you.'

'I know, and my mother sent him away. But stop trying to stall me, Joan. I have to...'

'Your father told Gilbert what had happened to you.'

'When?'

'Your father saw Gilbert.' Her voice, like the journal now lost, summoned once again that time distant and yet so close at hand.

'He came to see Gilbert that morning as he left for school, waited for him outside this house. He came around to challenge him. He was ranting at Gilbert about your university choices, accusing him of destroying you and your future, how you'd had a complete nervous breakdown and it was all Gilbert's fault, how he'd poisoned your mind to your family.'

'Yes, but it wasn't Gilbert's fault, it was March who...` he was about to go on to tell her how David had supplied him with the LSD, but Joan interrupted him.

'Listen, Michael. Your father then drove off and shortly after he had the heart attack in the car. It was awful. Gilbert was probably the last person to see him alive.'

'My dad was here the day he died?'

'Gilbert always felt guilty about it. That he'd been responsible for arguing with him, that the stress might have brought on his attack. He also felt guilty about what happened to you. Your dad made a good job of convincing Gilbert that he'd somehow led you astray and put you under too much strain. Caused your breakdown.'

'Gilbert came to see me. To tell me this?'

'He wanted to make a clean breast of it to you. To tell you the truth. To see how you were. To try to talk you to coming back to school. But your mother sent him away before he could explain anything.'

'She never even told me Mr Soames had been round to see me. Until a few days ago.'

'Maybe she wanted to protect you. Your dad had the heart attack pretty much immediately after he drove away.

Gilbert always felt bad about keeping it all quiet. He was a young teacher in his second year in the job. There was already a lot of scandal in the school about drugs. He was afraid people were connecting him to all sorts of trouble. He wanted to keep his head down. In the end he never mentioned the argument with your father to anyone but me, years later, after we were married.'

Here it was, revealed at last, yet another episode breaking the silence of the past, a secret Soames would have shared but for the walls his mother had built around them both. Could he have helped Soames with his guilt had he known? And Soames too might have helped him, put his life back on track. Instead he'd remained isolated behind those walls, walls within walls that had buried him and his mother from truth, from life.

'You and Gilbert were the only ones who knew about this?'

'He just couldn't forget it. He felt bad about abandoning you. But he could never get to see you.'

'We could've...made him pay, put March in prison for what he did to you.'

She shook her head and the protective mask came down again.

'We still can,' he pleaded. 'Together we still can.'

'Michael, if Gilbert could've done that he would have done it years ago.' She explained slowly, as if dragging the words from somewhere far away, remote and rarely visited. 'Always blamed himself for what happened to me. Although it wasn't his fault. I went round to David's that night on my own accord. I wanted to protect Laura, to try and get David to stay away from her. But...after it happened...Gilbert wanted to go to the police, wanted to go to the Head, wanted to tell my parents about what David did to me. But I stopped him from doing any of that. March wouldn't even have been charged, Michael. It was my word against his. The police would never have been interested. And back then, if I'd said anything to anyone, even my parents, David would've just called me a slut who came on to him. Which is what he said anyway.' She looked wistfully out of the window and he followed her eyes into the mist where the robins had returned and were feeding on the patio. 'Gilbert was the only one I could ever turn to. I couldn't have got through those days without him.'

All this startling news – his father's visit to this house, Gilbert's guilt over Joan and his father's death, in turn mirroring his own guilt, all this slowing him down, dragging him back to the past, to those days of his own isolation and illness when he needed a friend. He could dwell on it forever. But there would be time to think about all this and his father's final hours later. He'd already had a lifetime to think about it. Meanwhile Soames' life still hung in the balance.

'Joan, believe me, please, I know you mean well telling me all this, but no matter what you say, March has still got Gilbert locked in the basement. I know it. He could be starving him to death down there as we speak.'

He stood up from the sofa and she stood in his way. She seemed to return from that distant painful place, her mask discarded with the pressing issue of what to do next. He still hoped she would see sense and accompany him to the beach house. But instead she said, 'Michael, does your mother know you're here?'

'No, why?'

'Sit down again, while I make you a cup of tea and then maybe we can discuss this plan of yours in more detail.' She smiled at him and insisted on guiding him back to the sofa. 'We'll talk it all over a cup of tea. And biscuits. You liked those biscuits, didn't you? I baked some more for Christmas. Chocolate chip?' She wouldn't leave until he was seated once more. 'OK, Michael,' she said. 'Just take it easy for a few minutes, and I'll be right back.'

The morning fog had settled, the world outside dissolved in a soup of lost shapes, damping down all vision and sound, cutting him off, shrouding him from his mission to save the man who cared enough to come to his house, to share with him all those feelings of guilt over his father's death. He needed to get over there now, make his getaway while Joan was in the kitchen. The house was quiet, except for the distant sound of the kettle warming up, and he crept into the hallway. Joan's voice filtered through, trying to speak quietly but still forcing to make herself heard. She was on the phone. He crept to the kitchen door where he could hear her voice more clearly, her sentences broken in dialogue with the other person on the line.

'...intent on confronting David March with this ridiculous idea he has, he seems obsessed with the man...yes, Mrs Freeman, he's here now.... You're right he's been talking about the past a lot...seems agitated...You say he's suspended from work...he came here a few days ago as well claiming to be doing research...that's all nonsense you say and he's wrecked the house, you say, smashed up the Christmas tree and decorations...blood all over the carpet... he has a nasty cut on his finger, that's all...I'm getting some plasters and a bandage for him...I know, it's all very worrying... you think he's having another breakdown... you're worried he could harm himself...Yes, he's in the lounge...I'm making him tea and biscuits....I'll keep him here until you and your friend, Joe, get here...

He took his coat from the hallway stand and, quietly closing the front door behind him, disappeared into the fog. He could trust absolutely no one and had to do this alone now, without Joan, without backup, ready, finally, to face March and whatever was to be found there down in his basement. He would prove to them all, Joan, his mother, Maddie, that he should be taken seriously, that he wasn't living in a world of make believe, a fantasist with a fragile mind. He was about to bring an evil man down and when Soames was saved and March was behind bars – oh yes, then they would have to believe him.

CHAPTER TWENTY-THREE

The fog came down in dense impenetrable layers, concealing his progress, even dampening down the sound of his footsteps up the private road. He couldn't see the surrounding dunes that lined alongside the route, couldn't even see his feet beneath him, as he pulled his overcoat collar around his chin for protection from the chill and felt the cold misty droplets gathering and soaking his hair and face. The distant waves on the shore sounded muffled and uneven as he drew closer to his destination. He had no plan, no coherent strategy, his mind as fog-bound as the December afternoon. He could attempt a direct physical attack on March, but that wasn't really an option. Maybe he could engage him dialogue, disarm him with pretending to laugh at his stupidity going to see Laura, while he waited for an opportune moment to strike. But none of this seemed convincing or even real, until there it was, the fake mast in the shape of a cross looming above the outline of a large oblong shell, floating wraith-like in the grey dissolving sky.

As he approached the porthole-shaped entrance, the fog momentarily cleared, and he slowed down. He was now visible from the tinted windows and the front door of March's house had been left slightly open. Had David noticed his approach through the mist and set a trap? Was the open door an invitation? If so, an invitation to what? A confrontation with a rapist and possible murderer? A man who would stop at nothing to protect his reputation and further his revenge. But there was no turning back now.

He took the giant ship's bell knocker and wrapped three times. Summoning an encounter face-on was better than stumbling into the building only to be felled by a blow to the head. He would have to confront March sooner or later. But no one answered and the he pushed the door open and went straight through into the large downstairs area.

'Hello.'

His voice echoed in that warehouse space and he called out again. No reply. Two suitcases were packed and ready in the entrance area but nobody was around. Was March planning to make his escape? If so, he'd got here just in time and would have to work quickly to rescue Soames, if it wasn't too late already. There was the smell of stale cigars, and beneath that the same rank odour of sewage that grew stronger as he made his way, heart beating rapidly, to the basement stairs. He called out once more and then turned the handle on the cellar door. It opened and a cavernous black rectangle gaped ahead.

The smell of effluent was even more pronounced as he fumbled along the inside wall for a light switch. One bare bulb came on above his head and revealed the set of wooden steps leading down to the wall with indications of a larger space around the corner. He closed the door behind him and crept down, listening intently for sounds above and below, but there was silence except for the soft trickle of water somewhere beyond in the darkness. As he reached the lower steps the wall at the bottom ran along the side of the building and the basement space doubled back on the staircase. The electric light from the top of the stairs only reached so far into the cellar and then the bare room opened out into the dark. March had said the basement, his nuclear fallout shelter, was a work in progress, but progress seemed to be in short supply down here. The area had been carved out of the earth beneath the house, but there was little else other than blackness and damp. Reaching the bottom, he looked around on the wall for another switch, but there was no sign of any wiring or makeshift lighting into the main basement. The dark cave reeked of sewage seasoned with trapped brine and it felt like he was walking across the bed of a poisoned ocean.

'Mr Soames!' he called out into the black spaces without corners. 'Mr Soames, are you there?' His voice sounded flat and dead swallowed by the depths before him. He'd been so hasty to leave he hadn't even brought a torch with him. Above him there was movement – a door slamming and footfall in the main house. 'Mr Soames,' he whispered. 'Mr Soames. I'm here to help you.' Was Gilbert tied up somewhere in the recesses of the cavern and left to die? The air was rank, of course, but maybe it was also the smell of death, a corpse left to rot. March looked like he was planning a trip, maybe closing down the house for winter, or forever, while leaving the body to sink and dissolve into the mud. Would he lock the basement door before he departed, leaving Michael also trapped like an animal that stumbled down a well?

Which way to go? Forward to find Soames into the far reaches or head back up the stairs and confront March? The dense blackness gathered, as if the fog outside had descended, thickening the air, sealing him off from any safe return. He took one or two more steps into the unknown and a distant rumble grew to a thundering, cascading roar and water flooded around his feet. He was moving quickly backwards into the electric light until his shoes were clear, when something attacked him from the stairs behind, scratching and digging into his neck and shoulders. He struggled to be free as the thing screeched and gouged into his back with claws and teeth. It bit his injured hand and scoured at his ears and then sunk teeth into his thumb and wrist until he was able to grab it by the back of the neck with his other hand. He tried to throw it off and down on the ground but it scratched him across the face. Frantically grasping a handful of fur, he hurled the spitting shrieking creature as far away from him as he could, and in the light from the stairwell Harry the cat landed, turned and arched his grey and white back. The creature hissed venomously and then padded away on the soft sand into the dark corners of the cave, back to the sewers, leaving Michael utterly and irretrievably alone. Scum lapped at his shoes and the sound of rushing water gave way to the grinding of an engine pumping fluid out of the basement to the sea.

Shaken by the attack, he sat down on the cellar stairs. His face, neck and ears were scratched, the bite on his hand bled onto his coat and he tried to stem the flow. But the physical pain was negligible compared to the anguish he felt, now trapped down here in this rank hole by his own deluded, futile endeavour, an unwavering certainty that had all amounted to nothing but a clawed face and bleeeding hand. March had been talking to his cat, that night, all along. He sat there, immobilised by the ridiculousness of his actions, the dead end uselessness of it all. But he didn't have time to dwell on his momentous folly as another noise above stirred him and amidst his despair he knew he had to get out of the basement before March locked the door. What would he say to David? Unless he wanted to be buried here and starve to death over Christmas, he would have to confront him and explain what he was doing clambering around in his sewage infested cellar. He stealthily made his way back up the stairs, but when he opened the door back onto the main floor the area was still deserted. He decided to make a quick shameful dash for it and, taking off his shoes so as not to make any noise across the laminated surface, he ran for the main entrance. He made it past March's suitcases to the large porthole-shaped door when a woman cried out from the upstairs balcony.

'I'm going, mister, don't worry!'

Katya emerged, hurrying downstairs looking flustered. 'I'm packed and ready!' she cried and then, on recognising Michael her expression changed. 'Mr

Fisherman!' she called. 'Mr Fisherman, you're here. You've come with a message from David?' She was dressed in her coat ready to leave, but looked pale, and her eyes were red as if she'd been crying.

He stood there frozen by the front door. 'No,' he said, holding his thumb up in the air to stem the bleeding, his sewage-soaked shoes in his other hand. 'I've not seen, David. I've...'

'I have to leave soon,' she said, closing the door. 'He took my key.' She looked about to cry again. 'You've not come from him and that bitch?'

'No, I've just come to...' what could he say to explain this ludicrous venture.

'You been in fight?' she said, taking a closer look at his blood-covered coat and his thumb held aloft.

'Cat, attacked me. Outside...in the fog.'

'Horrible creature. Bites everybody but David. Him every night down there in the shithole calling, "Time for Bed, time for bed." Big monster looking after his little monster. Come with me,' she said, summoning him to the sofa, taking his hand gently. 'Sit down, I will see to that for you. You are trembling.'

'It was a shock, the cat,' he said. He wanted to get away, but he suddenly felt sick and couldn't muster the energy to rise from the sofa where she sat with him still holding his hand and shaking her head.

'There is First Aid in the kitchen. Wait here.'

He sat back and stared at the windows and tried to breathe. David might appear any moment, but he hadn't the will to escape or resist what might happen next. He just sat there, shaking, his heart missing beats, like an engine misfiring.

Katya returned from the kitchen with bandages and

plasters and sat down next to him. She treated his thumb with antiseptic, and tendered to the wound, and bathed his ears, neck and face. He remembered briefly another girl bandaging his hand, a long time ago. And he sat there in silence and wondered who Katya meant by 'that bitch', while she nursed his wounds, and he listened, trying to breathe more regularly, as she slowly related her distressing account of events.

David had told her the previous evening he was not spending Christmas with her. He'd heard from an old friend and was on an early flight today to join her for the holiday. Katya thought at first it was one of his cruel jokes. But when she saw his suitcase this morning she realised that he was really going away. He then told her she would have to leave for good. But he ordered her to clean the house first and warned he would inform the police she was in the country illegally if she wasn't gone when he came back. When he left he took her key with him. He would be sending someone round this afternoon to check that she really *had* left and to make sure she'd done a good job of tidying up the place beforehand. Any problems, anything missing, or broken and this person would track her down. That is who she thought Michael was at first.

'Why did you think I would be that person, that I would do that for him?' he asked as she finished bandaging his thumb.

'You know them both? David and that bitch he's with. It's her. The one he says is love of his life.'

'Laura?'

Laura, of course. The Maldives, the Maldives and March. The morning flight, the place where she could be seventeen again. With David. The final punchline in the joke.

'You in love with her too.' she said.

'No. I was, once. A long time ago.'

'But you went to see her? No longer the girl of your dreams?'

'No, Katya. Let's just say, David and Laura....They deserve each other.'

'I have to go soon,' she said, 'before this man comes back to check on me.'

He sat back on the couch. He felt himself unravelling, disappearing into the late afternoon winter light beckoning from the windows to the sands and sea beyond, where he could fade into nothing, with just these absurd fragments of fantasy left to mock him. He was so very tired of this life, could fall asleep out there by the incoming sea, and dream he had never come here, never read the newspaper article, never left Barton and Maddie, that none of it had ever happened. Perhaps none of it had. Perhaps it had all been a figment of his imagination. But then the ten pound note from the night with March was still on the glass top table and Katya was crying silent, real tears.

'What are going to do, Katya?' he said.

'I go back home to Dubrovnik.'

'Will you be OK?'

'I will be fine. I go back to daughter there. She's six years old and with her grandma. I come to England to find better life for her. But no good here. I go back now.'

'What's she called – your daughter?'

'Anna, I miss her very much.'

'Do you have money?' he said, fumbling with his good hand in his pocket for what few pounds he had.

'I have some money. Enough. I save while I'm here.'

'Do you want to come back, stay at my mother's tonight? Just until you can sort yourself out. You're welcome to Christmas dinner tomorrow.'

Her face softened and she smiled and turned her head to one side and looked at him carefully. 'You inviting me to meet your mother? Before you propose marriage? Have yourself a nice Bosnian wife. Do all the cleaning. All the cooking?'

In another universe, yes, he could propose to this strange beautiful woman, fly away with her to Dubrovnik and a new life. He imagined himself in a flak jacket and helmet distributing food parcels in some war-torn city. It made as much sense as anything else that had happened.

She laughed. 'Mr Fisherman, I'm just kidding you. You all the time so serious.'

He smiled back and shook his head. The trouble was, he wasn't serious, he just wasn't a serious grown up person at all. No wonder Maddie thought he was a hopeless dreamer who didn't live in the real world. He'd been so wrong, so spectacularly wrong every step of the way. March had done many bad things, but he hadn't kidnapped Soames. Joan was right, he should have left all this well alone, should even have listened to his mother. He wasn't some avenging angel, a lone man pitted against evil and corruption in Chinatown – just a fool in a ghost town of his own imagination, chasing phantoms from the past. And here he was now, a man beached on the shore of his own false clues and made up conspiracy, scarred and scratched by a wild cat, his shoes and trouser bottoms covered in sewage.

'Why *are* you here?' Katya said. 'Why have you come back to this man's shithole?'

'I came looking for a ghost.'

She held his bandaged hand in hers. 'You're a mess, Mr Fisherman.'

'You're right. A complete mess.'

'And I think you're a bit crazy.' Yes, he was more than a bit crazy. Everyone knew it, except him, but, too late as always, he now knew it too. 'And you smell,' she said.

'It's my shoes. You want to know why my shoes smell like they do. Where Harry the cat really attacked me?' He pointed to the cellar door still half open.

'You really are crazy if you went down there. But at least you wash. Not like the other crazy man. At least it's just your shoes that stink and you don't smell like rotten fish.'

'No, I don't' he said. 'That's one thing you can say for me, I don't smell like a rotten fish,' he said putting his shoes on. 'Do you want to know what I was doing down there in the cellar, Katya?'

'No, what?'

'I was looking for a man I once knew.'

'What man?

'He's gone missing. He's probably crazy too.'

'Another crazy one?'

'Yes, another crazy one.'

'The other crazy one who was here earlier?'

'Who's that?' he asked, his heart missing another beat.

'The one who really stinks like a dead fish,' she replied, pointing to the window, to the outside, the shoreline beyond.

'The other one?'

'The one who came. Just before you arrived. The one who wouldn't leave. Kept on and on about David.'

'What crazy man? Who do you mean?'

'The one with the rotten smell and dirty beard.'

'The guy March sent to check on you?'

'No, not him. The crazy one. Really crazy one.'

'Crazy one, you say?' His heart racing now, he stood up. 'Crazy, how crazy?' He was already at the door.

'Not crazy angry or crazy mean. Just crazy. Wanting David. Wanting him right now. Kept calling him Caliban or something. Talking crazy. Acting crazy. I threatened to hit him with the paddle to make him go away,' she said pointing to the plastic oar from the balcony, now standing propped against the door.

'Where did the crazy man go?'

'I followed him along the path, down to the beach, in the fog. Then the fog goes away and I see him running. Then I come back and find you bleeding and a mess and I think you're from David, but no.'

'Show me. Show me where this crazy man went.' He looked outside at the fading light, the day narrowing down to darkness on the horizon. He was so anxious he couldn't tie his shoes, especially with the bandaged hand.

'Let me,' she said.

'Thank you, Katya. We haven't much time.'

He hurried out into the fading grey afternoon light and she followed, indicating the pathway between the dunes.

'Here,' she said. 'This was where he went away.'

'Show me exactly,' he said.

She shook her head in exasperation and led him to the opening in the sand hills that stretched out onto the muddy plain beyond. The clearing fog had left one last hour of muted daylight to reveal the incoming tide advancing on the shoreline, a man walking his dogs, a horse and rider at the water's edge, bulldozers far away excavating another section of sand. But no sign of a crazy man.

'Go back, Katya,' he said. 'It's OK, now.'

'Why you care about this tramp of a man?

'He's someone who tried to help me. A long time ago.'

'You want me to go back and get paddle? For weapon?'

'No, no need for that.'

'You can't go out there. It will be dark soon.'

'You need to go, Katya. Back home to Dubrovnik, to your daughter. I'll be fine.'

'You need dressing, injection. For the thumb.'

'It's OK, Katya.' He held her hand in his. 'I'm so sorry, Katya, for what's happened to you.'

'I'm OK. I'll see my family again soon.'

'And thank you.'

'What for?'

'For this,' he said, holding up his bandaged thumb. Then he pointed to the vast expanse of beach. 'And for helping me find my friend.'

'There's no one out there,' she said. Then she kissed him gently on the cheek and stepped away. He watched her slender figure walk away from the water's edge and finally she turned to look at him and called, 'You should go home too, Mr Fisherman. Leave crazy man to the sea.'

She waved before vanishing into the dunes and then he was alone with the deserted, vast stretches of sand and the incoming tide.

CHAPTER TWENTY-FOUR

From the week's high water, the lines of seaweed and debris had pushed higher up the beach, almost into the dunes in places. The afternoon swell was running rapidly along channels and inlets, the low-lying sun suddenly emerging from a bank of cloud like a lidless eye, flooding the beach with eerie red light. The dog-walker and horse-rider had gone and there was no sign of life except for the seabirds that scattered from their feeding, and a helicopter scanning the dunes and shore. He searched the horizon for a lone figure, but there was no one. 'Mr Soames! Mr Soames!' he shouted to the empty sky. And there was Harry the cat, suddenly staring at him from the long grass in the dunes. He felt the abrasions on his neck and then waved. 'Where is he, Harry?' he shouted in desperation. The cat stared at him and then set off back and he followed until he reached another opening in the dunes further on from where Katya had departed. And there before him was a single set of footprints, leading out to the strange stone building squatting in the sand, taunting him, as it always had in flashbacks and bad dreams. And deep down he knew all along where Soames had to be – across the wet expanse of sand to the pillbox and the rapidly approaching sea.

The tide was circling around the back of him cutting him off if he didn't make it there and back quickly. The pillbox set on a raised sandbank would not submerge as rapidly as the lower land behind him, but the waves were close at hand, foaming red and grey all around beneath the setting sun as he waded through water ankle-deep to reach the bank. Driftwood floated by his feet, making its way safely back to shore, as he ploughed ahead to the building hunkered down in the sand, its slit windows staring back with blank eyes. Water gathered in a steadily widening, swirling channel pulling at his feet, the soft sand clinging at his shoes in an attempt to hold him back. If he returned now, he would be safe, but another five or ten minutes and the tide would fully surround and soon after flood the bank and the rest of the beach. He pressed on through the wind and water until he reached the sandbank and the pillbox.

'Mr Soames,' he called through the dark opening of the bunker. 'Mr Soames, are you there?'

Silence reigned inside. It felt like the end of the world out here, amidst the wind, the waves and the dying sun. But this building would never be deserted. It would always contain ghosts that would forever haunt him. Walk away and he would get back before the tide engulfed the beach, but he would have run away again, not only from the sea, but from that afternoon out here long ago and its shadow that followed him everywhere. He ducked his head inside the aperture and was greeted by a loud voice from within, a voice so close, almost at his ear, so resonant it could have sounded from the deep.

'Be not afeard the isle is full of noises!'

That voice so recognisable even after all these years.

'Mr Soames,' he called out into the darkness of the pillbox within. 'Gilbert, are you OK?'

'Are you Sycorax?' the voice within replied. 'The blear-eyed hag, the foul witch. The one with the oar?'

'No,' I'm a friend,' he replied, lowering himself into the pillbox. His vision struggled to adjust to the darkness and his foot sank immediately into a stagnant pool of seawater. Light from the dying sun slanted through one of the lookout holes to reveal a large man, grey-bearded and unwashed, his hair matted and his poor man's coat covered in stains wrapped around him. Through the dimness of the light, through the grey-white beard and long greasy hair, through the dirt around his forehead and side-whiskers, through the frantic glare of his eyes and the sorrow etched deeply in his features, there were the remnants of that face.

'Mr Soames, Mr Soames, we need to get out of here, now. The tide is coming.'

'Keep your cabins. You do assist the storm.' Soames pointed at the water gathering quickly within. He looked distraught, frightened, cornered.

'Mr Soames, Gilbert. Please come with me.'

Soames shook his head. 'My staff is broken. My book is drowned.'

'Gilbert, I don't know if you remember me. I'm here to help you.'

'Sea nymphs hourly ring his knell,' he said, looking beyond Michael at the concrete wall behind and beyond to some distant space. The sound of the sea flooding in like the approaching roar of an engine, like the grinding of The Creamer, vibrated in the confined walls of the pillbox.

'Hark! Now I hear them – ding-dong dell.' Soames shouted.

'Joan is waiting for you, Gilbert. She's outside and wants you to come home.'

'Prospero awaits her here, in his cave.' said Soames, backing up against the far wall.

'No, she won't come in here. We have to go out there to see her. And we have to do it now.'

Gilbert backed against the wall cried, 'Summoned by the memory of a sea-girl long ago.'

Michael felt the channel rising around his knees, the freezing waters surging in. The thunder of waves outside sounded like the bunker was already half submerged. At best, they had little more than minutes left. He moved towards Soames and held out his hand to him.

'Come Gilbert, please.'

'Good boatswain, have care!' Soames stood up defiantly holding out the palm of his hand to stop Michael in his tracks. The sea was now flooding the bunker, lapping at Gilbert's knees, but he couldn't leave him to drown alone and mad in this concrete coffin.

'Mr Soames, Gilbert. Steve Lawton wants you to come home. Your students need you.'

The interior darkened as the last sunlight vanished. Soames voice softened and he smiled the wreckage of a smile. 'Do I know you?' he said.

'Gilbert, Mr Soames, please! It's Michael. I want to help you. Joan is waiting outside, but we haven't got much time. Please come with me.'

Gilbert's stare fixed on Michael. 'Yes, I know you,' he said.

'Yes, it's me, Michael, your student, remember?'

'Freeman!' Soames said, his eyes glaring in growing terror. 'Thou canst not say I did it! Avaunt and quit my sight!'

'No...I'm not...I'm Michael Freeman, remember?'

'Imposter!' Soames waded through the water and lunged at Michael wrapping his arms around him. 'I know you now!' Gilbert cried, his face a mask of rage and fear, his breath foul in Michael's face, his hold around his ribs forcing the life from Michael's body.

'It's me, Michael,' he choked out the words and tried, hampered by his wounded thumb, to wrestle himself free from the crushing hold Soames had on him. But the grip was far too tight as the waters deepened around them both.

'All sink with the king!' Soames yelled, squeezing harder and tighter. Michael felt his ribs crack and his lungs folding as he tried to fight for breath that would not come. There was no release and with his last sensations he heard the rotor blades of The Creamer, roaring in a terrible duet with the waters beneath. And then all was darkness as he fell beneath the waves.

FULL FATHOM FIVE

Deep and dark he fell and as the black cloud gathered he searched for Soames down there with him. But there was no one, just the dead grey waters tasting of kelp and brine. He tried to call out but his lungs were full of ocean. Deeper and deeper he sank until he finally came to rest on the sea bed.

And there it stood, The Creamer, black, rusting, waiting for him, as it always had, covered in green lichen and mould, roaring away in the darkness of water. It had never stopped for a moment all these long years of churning and grinding. He knelt down and began to cut up the plastic on the sandy floor with a knife that was very sharp, slicing through the shreds and strips, trying to be precise, to make an excellent job of it this time. But then his hand was bleeding again and the strips ran red in the water. His father would be angry when he returned. Just the two of them, forever, down here with the machine.

If he could speak, if his lungs were not waterlogged and broken, he would cry out for her.

Maddie, Maddie where are you now?

But she didn't come, nobody came down here in the darkness where he scrambled in the wet sand, and the blood from his thumb mixed with the water and the plastic sheets. It was so hard to breathe now but he carried on kneeling and cutting with no rest. He tried to cry out for her again but no one heard him except The Creamer, waiting for him to tire of all the slicing of the sheets and make an end of it, to climb its sheer grey cylinder walls and descend into the blackness. Where he could rest and hide forever from the bloodstained failure on the ruined strips.

And so for what seems like years The Creamer waits, blades rotating, and he waits too, still trying to call, above the grinding gears, through the blood grey waters, through to the lost and forgiving sky, calling, his voice clear from the depths, so even the stars could hear, hoping somewhere, somehow the cry will reach beyond the chambered roar of ocean and machine, hoping that she will come and a hand will close over his, taking the knife, letting it sink into the darkness below, and with it The Creamer will slowly fade from sound and view, a wreck sunken on the ocean bed, and the one who comes will carry him up and up, to the rippling surface of the sea where the blood dark waters turn blue with the light of day finally returning.

NOVEMBER 11TH 2018

Morning

First thing after the two-hour journey he texted her to say he was there safely. He knew she would worry about him – said he daydreamed too much at the wheel. Sometimes she wished he'd never passed his test, almost ten years ago now. Wished she'd never got him to overcome his fears of driving after what had happened to his father. Anyway, he was here safely. The notice on the door at St Mary's Church announced the Remembrance Service at the memorial in the square. The one hundred and seventeen red flags in and around the churchyard to commemorate soldiers from the parish who perished in the Great War drooped in the still wet air of morning. Most of these men were lost forever or buried in a Flanders field, so the red markers stood alongside the graves of the nearest relative. There they hung, scattered, lifeless, limp and damp – the colour an odd choice given that red flags warned ramblers on military land of artillery fire. But this morning all was quiet in the churchyard.

Holding the carrier bag, he wandered to the memorial in the square, putting off, for the moment, the trip into the cemetery. He stood beneath the monument in the damp, grey light. At the top of the plinth the bronze head with a soldier's helmet shone grey in the rain. Then came the long line of one hundred and seventeen fallen, a list etched across three columns of stone. Only half as many names listed for World War Two. On the last column were just five names of those killed since 1945: one for the Falklands; two in Iraq; two in Afghanistan. That left a blank space below these names for those that would follow.

Beneath it all was the inscription:

To commemorate the brave men of St Vincent's on Sea who sacrificed their lives in the Great War 1914-18 and the Second World War 1939-45 and those conflicts thereafter. This Memorial was designed and erected by the March Foundation and unveiled by LORD MARCH: OBE, on 13th September 2018

This was a shock but there it was, the name of his old adversary, David March, now Lord March, Conservative party fundraiser and life peer. David March, Lord March OBE, who only last week had made that infuriating speech. Michael's eyes roamed from March's name back to those of the dead, before he set off back to the churchyard.

He dreaded what awaited him – he'd only been a few times since his mother's death ten years ago to the day. When he reached the grave, it was worse than he expected. The surrounds were barely visible beneath the grass. Weeds and brambles clambered around the dirty weather-stained headstone. 'Sorry, I've left it so long,' he said. He took the two red winter roses out of the carrier bag, along with the rubber gloves, the bottle of water, the cloths and pruning shears. He then set about clipping and clearing away the debris, cleaning the headstone with the water, replacing the artificial flowers in the vase at its foot with the roses alongside, until the inscription before him was clear once more:

A Beloved Husband and Devoted Father

William George Freeman

Died December 2nd 1971 Aged 49 Years

His Loving Wife

Grace

Died November 11ᵗʰ 2008 Aged 85 Years

He searched for the right words, but struggled to find any beyond the same questions that would never be answered. What would his father, Bill, make of this country now, stumbling, bewildered towards Brexit? Great Britain, a nation he fought for, going it alone again, but somehow diminished in the process. What would his father make of a world where Tommy, not yet thirty, had already amassed a fortune from designing algorithms on smartphones? He couldn't imagine his father into this modern world, this divided, angry nation. And yet had the country been any more united back in his day? His father never thought so. He'd fought for his country but the victory in war never afforded him any peace of his own. He was always fighting some battle or other. At odds with the world, the culture, the workforce, even his wife now buried alongside him. And what of her – did she ever wish things might have been different, that she had tried to be more of a grandmother to Tommy? Or Emma when she came along? There was nothing Michael could ever say to answer the troubled mystery of their love for him, or his for them, nothing they would say to him now from beyond the grave. But the headstone was clear and clean again, the two roses embracing in the jar. He turned and headed towards the memorial where he would pay his respects and then go home to Maddie, to Tommy's Skype that afternoon and Emma's phone call.

In the square the congregation gathered and the service began with the bearers of wreaths to the plinth. He quickly checked his phone and read a message from Maddie: 'Hope all OK at cemetery. Have a safe journey back. Love xxx' He switched his phone to silent as the ceremony began. The rain on his hood and in the surrounding trees dripped and ticked like countless clocks, measuring the passing of time. He bowed his head for a few moments, thought of his father battling through the jungles of Burma, the leeches, the malaria, the dysentery, the awful sacrifice of those lives. And when he raised his head, the last wreath was being placed by an old man, possibly a veteran of World War Two. However, as the man rose from the ground Michael realised it was no war veteran at all. He watched him rejoin the congregation welcomed by two small boys and a man Michael's age. Although Maddie worried about him driving, hadn't wanted him to come at all, insisted he came home straight after the service while there was still light, he realised the journey home would have to wait. There was now something he had to do first, someone he had to see.

Afternoon

Michael handed Joe the coffee and sat down next to him in the discharge unit. A frog croaked in the old man's pocket.

'Sorry, damn nuisance,' Joe said, handing the coffee back while taking out his phone. 'These damn things. The ringtone – it's my great grandson's idea of a joke. Text from John. He's on his way now.'

'I hate those things as well. That's a nice photo, Joe. Your family?'

Joe's screensaver sat in his lap with a large gathering on view – three or four generations with Joe there at the centre.

'My ninetieth birthday last March.'

'You must be very proud.'

'I'm just very lucky.'

'You did well this morning, Joe, the wreath, the ceremony. And you're looking a lot better now.'

The old man put his phone back in his pocket and Michael passed him his coffee. Finally, after the fainting in the church, the ambulance, the paramedics, the tests, the all clear, he now had Joe here alongside him. And a chance to properly catch up, but more than that, the right moment, to say what he wanted to say.

Joe blew on his coffee. 'I was already feeling wobbly there at the cenotaph. Nerves, probably. Wanted to do it right for my dad.'

'I remember you saying, he was at the Somme.'

Joe shook his head and sipped his drink. 'Doesn't bear thinking about. We never realised as kids what he went through.'

'I never really understood my dad either – what he experienced in Burma.'

'How could we?' said Joe. 'It worries me now, you know. What we all take for granted. All this Brexit stuff. We've had seventy years of peace. Don't folk realise what that means?'

'There's a guy whose name's on that memorial.'

'Too many names there.'

'No, I don't mean those names – David March. I knew him from school.'

'That Lord March? I know he's from round here. The one who made the speech. Saying he should lead the country.'

'Yes, calling for Parliament to appoint someone from the Lords to finally get us out of Europe. When I met years ago, he wanted to be Prime Minister then.'

'Was he always such a chancer?'

Michael looked at Joe and said, 'More than that.'

Joe shrugged and they both fell silent until the old man said, 'Did you ever hear again from that other one? The one you saved.' Joe's eyes were as bright as they were over twenty years ago. Did this old man remember things clearly from that day, remember just how much he changed Michael's life?

'I didn't save him,' Michael said.

'Yes, you did. You saved him. You were a hero.'

Even now he needed to explain, put the old man straight. Joan, turning up at March's house, meeting Katya, the phone calls to the police. 'I'm no hero, Joe. The guys who picked us out the water were the real heroes.'

'If you hadn't been there, he would have drowned and no one would have known. But, have it your way.'

'I'll have it my way. No hero stuff.'

'What happened to him afterwards?'

'Soames. He's fine. He lives on a houseboat near Stratford. We visit him and Joan a couple of times a year.' Michael thought for a minute of saying more about March. How Michael had tried to persuade Joan and Gilbert to press for a historic rape charge. But once Soames had recovered and left Pennington both he and his wife had no appetite for this. The rich and powerful would always find a way to fight back, to destroy you, Gilbert said. And Joan and Gilbert had had enough of fighting.

'A houseboat? You'd think he'd want to stay clear of water,' Joe said.

Michael smiled. He decided to let the subject of March drop. Today was not a day for recriminations and old scores. That wasn't what he was here for.

'They perform Shakespeare. Bard on the Barge it's called.'

'To the manner born, eh?'

Michael smiled again. The old man's memory and sense of humour were still razor sharp.

'Is it still going? The plumbing business?'

'Still going strong. My son's ready for retirement, but he's passing it on to his lad.'

'The one who went to Pennington?'

'No. He's a lawyer. He always remembers Mr Soames. We always remember them, don't we? Those teachers. The good ones and the bad.'

'Soames adopted a young lad, Matt – he's a teacher too, like his dad.'

'And you, Michael, any kids?'

'There's Tommy from Maddie's first marriage – you know about him. He's in Dublin doing something digital... don't ask. It's beyond me. Then there's Emma. She's just started at Cambridge. English Lit. Here...I'll show you...' he said, padding his pockets. 'Damn...must have left my phone in the car.'

'Your daughter take after her dad then?'

'She's a lot brighter than me. And she's got a lot more about her than me at that age.'

'Youngsters do these days. But I try to keep up.' He held up his phone. 'And then they take the mickey with these flaming ringtones.'

'I can't wait to tell Maddie we've met up. She'll be thrilled.'

Joe smiled and said, 'Give her my best regards.'

Michael still hadn't said what he wanted to say and he

knew Joe's son would soon be here to pick him up.

'What happened to you, Joe? Back then. Mum said you'd gone away. Sorry, I know it's a long time ago...'

Joe sighed and then shook his head. 'She never forgave me, your mum, for ringing that lass of yours. She said it was none of my business. Didn't want to see me anymore.'

'She never really told me what happened. But then again she never did talk about things.'

'It was all a bit odd. Your mum just cut me off completely. Soon after that I went to my sister in Australia. Her husband had just died. The guy who flew over Dresden in the war. Poor man. Cirrhosis of the liver. Well, I'd just lost Sally, and Betty had just lost Rich. We were a comfort to each other. I stayed there five years.'

He looked at Joe. The old man probably didn't really care but it still mattered, still needed saying. He just wished he could have said it many years ago.

'I'm sorry for the way my mum treated you.'

Joe looked at him and smiled. 'Oh, your mum. I only knew her a very short while. Didn't know her that well. I remember I used to make her laugh though...until she fell out with me, that is. It was strange why she reacted that way.'

'I'm so sorry it's taken all these years to find you at last.'

'There's nothing to be sorry about. All water under the bridge.' He looked again at his phone to see if there were any other messages, before turning back to Michael. 'What you doing with yourself?' he said. 'You retired now?'

'I do some writing for radio. Comedy mainly.'

'Radio? Like Hancock? Round the Horne?'

'I try, but probably not in that league.'

'Then before that, Tommy Handley and ITMA. I remember my dad listening to that all through the war. It was about the only thing that used to make him laugh. Until he heard old Adolf had topped himself, that is.'

Through the window Michael saw a car pull into a parking space and a man he recognised from the ceremony that morning and two boys got out. He had only a few moments left to say what he needed to say.

'I think your son and grandchildren are here Joe. Before they get here, let me say something else. Something I never got chance to back then. To thank you.'

'What for, lad?'

'It's just that, you know...I don't think I'd be here doing any of this if it wasn't for you.'

'Doing what?

'Any of it. Maddie, my family, the life I've had.'

'Don't be silly, Michael.'

'I'm not. Maddie would never have known what happened. If you hadn't called her. You calling her that day. It changed my life.'

Joe laughed. 'Yes, I remember, that journal with the letter and her number. The little lad picked up the phone. He thought I was Father Christmas. I said I wanted to speak to his mum, to find out if he'd been a good boy.'

'Maddie said she thought you were a crank at first.'

'Once she knew what had happened to you she came straight away to the hospital. Christmas Eve, brought the little lad with her. I remember I was there at the hospital that night. We didn't know if you were going to be OK. But then your mum...'

'I still can't believe she stopped you coming.'

'Well, who knows why people do what they do. She wasn't happy when she saw Maddie there.'

'I wanted to find you to say thank you. When I got out of hospital you'd gone away.'

'I needed a change. When Sally died,' he looked at Michael sadly, and shrugged. 'I was lost. She was my best pal. I was lucky I had all those years with her.'

Two small boys, the ones with Joe at the service, burst into the unit and ran up to the old man who held out his arms and hugged them both close. The man from the car park and the ceremony, around Michael's age, followed the boys into the room. 'What you been doing to yourself, dad?' he said. 'You should've come home with us straight after the service.'

'I'm fine, John. Stop worrying. Fit as a fiddle. Been well looked after by this young man here.'

John grabbed Michael's hand. 'Thanks, mate, for hanging around,' he said. 'We would've got here sooner but I put my phone on silent during the service and forgot to switch it back on.'

'These damn things,' Michael said. 'How did we ever cope without them?'

Michael turned to Joe and hugged him. The old man's body felt frail in his arms. 'Thank you again,' he said. 'So glad I got the chance to say it after all these years.'

'It was nothing, son. I'm glad things turned out alright for you. Give my love to your Maddie and your family. Have a safe journey.'

He watched as Joe climbed into the passenger seat of the Range Rover and waved at the car as it drove past, although he could no longer see the old man clearly through the darkened windscreen.

When Michael arrived back at his car, he found his

phone and three missed calls from Maddie.

Late Afternoon

He clung to the slow lane as the heavy vehicles roared past. The rain continued and settled into a low visibility mist that stretched across the motorway. He wanted to drive faster, to speed up his return home, but the string of cars in front and the stream of wagons in the next lane hemmed him in. He phoned Maddie twice before setting off but she didn't pick up and he was anxious he'd missed her attempts to reach him. He sat forward in his seat as another car cut in and the vehicles ahead hurled into the darkness. How could they all drive so fast in this patchy swirling fog?

He thought of Joe at the memorial, his dignified honouring of his father, the sixty thousand casualties on the first day at the Somme. He recalled the red pennants in the churchyard so many miles from those lost in a foreign land. The gravestones with the names engraved but no body buried beneath. What place did they have now in the nation's memory? Who would remember them at all in another hundred, another fifty, or even twenty years? He thought of his father in Burma – who would honour the sacrifice of the Forgotten Army in the decades to come? Just two minutes in November each year wasn't enough. But at least he'd paid his respects. To the dead and the past.

To brush aside thoughts of death and melancholy, he switched on Radio Two and Johnny Walker's Sound of the Seventies, the veteran presenter introducing the next song as an early Christmas number. Michael immediately recognised the opening piano chords, how they took him back to those long, lost days at Pennington with Laura and how the very same song had beckoned him into Vic and Steve's café all those years ago, the day he started his journey to find Soames, the journey that nearly ended but then saved his life. Joni Mitchell's 'River'. The song, full of regret, full of yearning, fitted the mood of the day. But homage had been duly paid to the past and now the present resumed and the future lay ahead. Maddie waiting for him at the end of his drive home, and then Christmas in a few weeks with his family – Tommy with his partner Denise back from Dublin, Emma home from Cambridge.

Not a day went by when he didn't pause at some stage to give thanks for the life he had, the second chance he was granted by fate, fortune, and most of all Maddie. Seeing Joe today had sharpened his astonishment and gratitude all the more at how his life had turned out. Now he needed to get back to hear Emma's Sunday afternoon call from the college, to hear the voice of his talented, beautiful daughter who carried all his hopes and dreams for the future. He indicated to merge into the central lane, when the radio cut off with his phone ringing. At the same time a vehicle pulled up very close behind with headlights flashing, as he took the call on speaker.

'Hi, Maddie.'

'Michael, are you alright?'

'Yes, I'm fine. On my way home now.'

'Where've you been?'

'I'm sorry, love, for missing Tommy's Skype.'

'Oh, yes, that. We cancelled it. Why are you so late?'

'You cancelled Tommy? Why?'

'It doesn't matter. I'll tell you later. How far are you away now?'

'I'm getting there. Sorry for not telling you I'd be back late. I left my phone in the car. But you never guess who I saw…Jesus.'

'Are you alright?'

'Sorry, it's this idiot behind. It's OK, he's got past now.' The white van hurtled by in a torrent of sound and spray. 'As I was saying you never guess who I saw?'

Silence on the other end, so he continued anyway. She needed to know the amazing news about Joe, about being able to tell him, after all these years, how grateful he was.

'Joe, you remember, Joe?'

Still no answer and he could hear another voice in the room with her.

'Joe, you know, Joe the plumber?' Again silence. 'Anyway, I saw him at the ceremony laying a wreath and I went to speak to him, and you'll never believe it but he passed out as soon as I went over. I thought he'd had a heart attack.' He was still speaking into a soundless void, but carried on. 'Anyway, I went with him to the hospital and thank God he was alright. And we had a great chat. Talked about old times when he found your letter in my journal and then he called you and told you I was in hospital, and…Maddie, are you listening? He's ninety years old. He's incredible – it was so wonderful to see him again.'

It was a woman's voice in the room with Maddie. There was now a lorry behind – the same blaring horn and angry flashing lights.

'Michael, you just need to get home,' she said sharply.

'What is it? What's wrong?'

'Nothing. I just phoned to make sure you're alright. Thought there was something wrong when you didn't call.'

It was annoying that she was so unappreciative of this meeting with Joe. Surely, she understood how important the old man had been in both their lives. They'd talked about it often. But now she seemed so cold. It was just not like Maddie.

'I'm fine, Maddie. Are you, OK? You sound a bit stressed.'

'I'm fine,' she said.

And there was the other woman's voice again in the background.

'Who's that there with you?' he said.

'Just a friend.'

'I was telling you about Joe.'

'I know, I'll talk to you later. As long as you're OK, I'll let you go.'

Something was clearly not right here. Maddie cancellingTommy, her manner distant, irritable, distracted by this other voice, coming through clearer, this time unmistakable.

'Maddie, is that Emma there with you?'

'No, I've told you it's a friend.'

'Don't lie to me, I know it's her,' There was another silence. 'Maddie?'

'Yes, she's here, don't worry she's OK.'

'She's not due home for another month.'

'Well, she's here.'

Something must have happened, something urgent to bring his daughter home from Cambridge in the middle of her first term.

'Tell me what's going on will you,' he said, as reasonably as he could, while trying to maintain his position in the heavy fast-moving convoy of vehicles ploughing down the motorway in the thickening fog.

'It's no good getting worried, Michael. Everything's fine.'

'Really? Put her on. Let me speak to her.'

'Not now.'

'Why not?'

'She doesn't want to talk right now.'

'There's a services coming up, I'll try to pull in there.' The lane to his left was blocked but he indicated to move over, hoping someone would let him in.

'This is really odd, Maddie. What's she doing there with you?'

'I've told you she's just come back home.'

'But why? Just tell me for god's sake.'

The lorry close up behind flashed him along with another prolonged blast on the horn. He had to get across onto the exit lane somehow.

'She just wanted to be back here a while. No big deal.'

'She's only been at college a few weeks. It'll be fine when she settles in. She can have a couple of days back home and I'll take her back next week. Wednesday or Thursday.'

'Yes, we'll discuss it later.'

'Maddie, I know there's something wrong. Tell me what's going on, will you.'

'Just get home safely. That's the main thing.'

The lorry behind, the traffic that would not allow him in, Maddie's evasiveness, Emma's baffling behaviour, all fuelled his growing frustration. He could not understand any of this. It was less than a couple of months ago he and Emma had travelled across the country, taken three trains, and spent the first two days at the college together for the induction week. They'd walked the cobbled lanes, the cloistered college grounds, joining the footsteps of the privileged, the entitled, the chosen. It wasn't possible she was having difficulties there. Emma took everything in her stride.

'Is Emma back to do some work at home?' he said, hopefully.

'Honestly, all these questions can wait until you get back. I'm going now.'

In the rear-view mirror, the lorry looked almost touching his bumper and there was still no way of getting over to the exit. He heard Emma's voice again followed by her crying.

'No, don't go. There's something wrong, Maddie. Let me talk to her.'

'Not now, Michael.'

'Why? Why has she left college? Why is she crying?'

'She's fine. Everything's fine.'

'I can tell by your voice, everything isn't fine.'

'Honestly, it's all OK.'

'Then why do you sound so stressed out. Look you need to tell me. I want to know. Really, this can't wait until I'm home.'

'Don't get upset. That's not going to help.'

'What do you mean "help"? Help with what?'

'She's just...I wish you'd got back here earlier. I really do.'

'Oh, for crying out loud, Maddie, just tell me what's going on! Tell me! For god's sake tell me! Is she sick? Is she on drugs? What is it? Has someone given her some bad drugs? That's it isn't it? I warned her...I knew there'd be bad drugs...it's always the same...'

'Calm down, Michael.'

'It is drugs isn't it?'

'No, Michael, it's not drugs.'

'Then what?'

'It's...nothing.'

'You can't just say that and not tell me.'

'Just get home.'

He couldn't manoeuvre to the exit lane, the traffic behind and to the side forcing him onwards.

'I need to know. Not knowing is more distracting than anything. I can't concentrate on the road. Tell me, just tell me!'

'Oh, Michael. Please...'

'Tell me, for Christ's sake Maddie, tell me!'

Oh, for god's sake!' she cried in exasperation.' She's...pregnant.'

'She's what? She can't be.'

'Well, she is. I wanted to wait until you got back. But you just....'

'Oh Jesus.'

'It's OK, just get home.'

'How's she got pregnant?'

'She's fine. That's the main thing.'

'How can this be OK, eh? How can it?'

'Just please calm down will you.'

'How far gone is it?' There was another silence on the other end. 'Maddie speak to me for crying out loud. Who's the father?'

'I don't know – it doesn't matter right now.' The services were just ahead. He needed to get off this road, to absorb the sudden sickening horror of this news.

'Are you alright? Michael?' she cried as he put his foot down on the accelerator in reply and drove right up to the car in front and flashed his own headlights.

'How can anyone be alright about this, Maddie?'

'She's upset.'

'So she bloody well should be. How could she be so...stupid. Let me speak to her.'

'She's not stupid, Michael....please...you know that.'

'She can't be pregnant. She's at Cambridge. She's got her whole future ahead of her.'

'We can't talk about this now. Sorry, I'm going to have to go.'

'Maddie, just get her on the phone now, will you!'

'Emma's crying again. I need to go to her. Look, Michael this is making things worse. Try and get parked up and safe at the services. I'll talk to you when you're off the road. Right now I need to see to her.' And then the phone went dead.

The lorry behind was pushing him on past the service lane, and he needed to get over so he could talk to Emma, talk some sense into her, right now. This could not wait until he got home. He veered across into a narrow gap – not seeing the Mercedes Sprinter in the blind spot to his left until the last second, just enough time to break and, without checking his mirror again, he swerved in behind. He braced himself for impact and time froze and unlocked again as the lorry's brakes hissed in anger and then something thundered on past him with horn booming. Light and sound flooded the lanes ahead as the car in front veered away and out into the middle lane and all around him the wild swerving dance of brake lights, hysterical horns and frantic indicators lost and reclaimed balance and passed by as he snatched the wheel over and away to the hard shoulder. And by the time he made it to the service exit lane he could no longer say what was on his mind to Emma, could not, in fact, speak at all.

He pulled into the car park, switched off the engine and collapsed his head on the wheel. Half an hour later he was still in the driver's seat, still shaking, not with the news from home, not with the sheer awfulness of what had happened to his darling Emma, but with the terrifying realisation of how close his blind, selfish rage had brought him to never seeing her ever again.

Evening

The baby girl played with her mother's hands, the endless fascination of the child for those fingers and thumbs. He sipped his coffee and stared at his phone. He messaged Maddie to say that he was OK, he was safe and taking a break from the journey and would call back soon. She texted back saying that she was would speak to him before he set off again, that Emma was fine and they were just going for a walk.

The young mother looked across at him and when he smiled at her, she smiled back and then nuzzled her forehead close down to her child's face. In a moment he would call Maddie again to say sorry. He would speak to Emma if possible and tell her that everything would work out and it didn't matter about Cambridge or anything else. The only important thing was that she was safe and well. He would tell her how much he loved her no matter what had happened or what she decided to do, no matter how difficult things were. He would tell her this, not because it was the right thing to do, but because she was his daughter, not some projection of a lost dream he'd once had of his own, but a real person whom he loved more dearly than anyone else in the world, and who right now, needed her dad to love her and tell her everything was going to be alright. Which it would be.

The baby started to cry and the mother unbuttoned the top of her blouse. He picked up his phone and left. By the car he tapped in Maddie's number, breathing in the night air slowly. The rain had stopped and the fog had cleared. The ringtone cut off and Maddie answered and the welcome relief in her voice was the most important thing in the world. That and the fact he was still alive and could drive slowly towards the twin stars of his blessed life, shining low and bright in the southern sky to guide him home.

THE END

ACKNOWLEDGEMENTS

Many thanks to the writing community at South Manchester Writers' Workshop whose advice and feedback were invaluable. Particular thanks to Tricia Cunningham, Rosie Cullen, David Beckler, Peter Barnes and David Qualter for their insightful close reading of the novel which made such a significant contribution to the final version. And to Julian Edge for his advice and encouragement with the publication process.

I want most of all to thank my wife Lorraine for her inspiration, guidance and support throughout the years it took me to complete this novel. She was there at the very beginning and kept me going through all the ups and downs of writing. Without her *Disappearing Acts* would never have appeared at all.

ABOUT THE AUTHOR

Tony Harrison

Tony Harrison is a writer, teacher, lecturer and examiner. He has a PhD in American Literature from the University of Manchester and has worked for many years in secondary education and in higher education at MMU, Salford University and Manchester University. Tony has an MA in Scriptwriting from Salford University, was a member of the Royal Exchange Theatre Writers' Workshop, and has written several plays. His short stories and poems have appeared in online publications and have been broadcast on local radio. He lives in Manchester with his wife, Lorraine, and their three dogs. Disappearing Acts is his first novel.

Printed in Great Britain
by Amazon